I0714884

YOU MUST BE THIS TALL

N.K. REINERT

This book is a work of fiction. Names, characters, businesses, places, events, locales, and incidents are either the products of the author's imagination or used in a fictitious manner. Any resemblance to actual persons, living or dead, or actual events is purely coincidental.

ISBN: 978-1-956575-24-8
Cover Artwork: Marish/depositphotos
Cover Design: N.K. Reinert

Dedication

To the people running the rides, making the burgers, stocking the t-shirts, sweeping the floors, and dancing in the parades…
You're the heroes of this fairy tale.

CHAPTER ONE

Tabby

Tabby rubbed between her eyes with her fingers and wished the day would end.

The bells in the clock-tower above Liberty Hall had scarcely finished bonging their way through the noon hour, but Tabby was already sweating right through her so-called "calico" dress. Hah! Calico. More like hot, sticky polyester. The actual pioneers would never have survived in this outfit.

There were dark patches showing up in embarrassing places across the flowered green bodice, like under her boobs and across her back. Her cotton camisole, worn specifically to sop up all that excess moisture, couldn't keep up with today's perspiration levels. She wanted to tear off her costume and plunge right into the murky brown waters of the Mighty Missouri.

Tabby had to smile to herself, thinking of the

commotion, both online and in real life, this would create. She'd go so viral, her brief Internet fame would almost make the certain job termination worthwhile. *Almost.* If she had anything else in the world she thought she could do.

Of course, sweating profusely was nothing new for a Patriot of America the Beautiful. Heavy-duty deodorant was recommended in training and sold in the company store. Southeast Georgia was half-swamp and half humidity; the occasional field or pine tree forest was all an elaborate ruse. The new interns came each summer, gasped at the heat, and promptly lost five pounds of water weight, which they put right back on via an endless consumption of theme park snacks, usually for likes and clout.

Tabby squinted up at the sky. The sun was already a livid late-July yellow, even though the calendar claimed they were still in early June. Mugginess had crept up from the swamps and spread across the pastures, suburbs, and city streets surrounding their little manufactured city, and it wouldn't abate until September. She sighed.

This would be Tabby's third summer working at America the Beautiful Theme Park and Resort, and she knew what to expect.

Bad tan-lines, sweat-stained bras, and frizzy hair were just the beginning.

"How much for these sunglasses?"

She glanced over at the park guest, a red-faced man waving a pair of plain, black, faux Ray-Bans from the front display. Everything on the front display was the same price —the most expensive glasses on the Conestoga wagon, to drive up the price per transaction. "Twenty-four ninety-five," she answered him automatically. "Plus tax."

The man shook his head at her and slapped the

sunglasses back on the rack, stomping away. The midday crowds swelling the promenade quickly swallowed him up and he was gone. Mornings could be deceptively slow in Old Dodge City, since it was so deep into the park, but by lunchtime, the walkway was hard for Patriots to cross without tripping over strollers and squalling toddlers.

Tabby watched him vanish and then promptly forgot he had ever existed. There were so many red-faced dads who didn't want to pay theme park prices for sunglasses, their complaints and frustrations didn't register with her anymore. Park guests floated in and out of her vision, occasionally requiring her to say something, but mostly she just listened to the banjos and fiddles of the Old Dodge City music loop, watched children run away from their parents, and tried not to jump out of her skin every time that damn side-wheeler went steaming past on the Mighty Missouri.

Behind her, the ten-minute timer pinged, reminding Tabby it was time to walk around the wagon and check inventory. She reluctantly left her tiny patch of shade and started a slow, bored perusal of her shop. It wouldn't take long. The wagon was only about four feet long and two feet wide, with racks of sunglasses on both sides and a cash register station around the back, on the riverside. This was the shadiest, nicest place to stand (except for the wailing shriek of the side-wheeler's steam-whistle every thirty minutes) but of course Patriots couldn't stand in comfort, in the shade. They had to be available, close to the promenade through the center of Old Dodge City, adding atmosphere and reeling in prospective customers.

Conestoga wagons didn't provide the best shade at midday, so a lot of Patriots just ignored this rule and hid back by the register until a lead or a manager came and dragged them out again. Tabby had some vague idea of "moving up," though, and while she didn't know what this would look like, she knew she would not get promoted to an air-conditioned role without standing by the promenade the way she was supposed to.

"These are just gorgeous," a voice said, and she came back to the front of the wagon, reaching out to reset the timer as she did so. A middle-aged man wearing a vintage America the Beautiful cap was admiring the wagon, running his finger along its gleaming lanterns and realistic iron rings. "The workmanship is stunning." He looked at Tabby and gestured at the nearest wagon-wheel. "They made these in a genuine wagon-maker's shop in Missouri, you know!"

Tabby hadn't known this. "That's really cool," she replied, genuinely impressed.

"I bet you didn't know you were working with such history!" He stepped back and lifted a sizable camera to take a picture. The camera strap had left a sweaty mark across his shirt. Tabby didn't know how he could bear to have all that weight on him in this heat. "I don't suppose— how about you get in the shot? Gaze off into the distance like you're about to cross the prairie in this schooner?"

Tabby took a quick breath. "Oh, I don't know—"

"It would be so atmospheric. With your little costume and all. Come on, please?"

He sounded like a little boy. So many of the real enthusiasts here did, though. They had boyish faces, shy smiles, childish clothing. Occasionally a reporter would do a story about them, something like *Super-Fans of America's Best Theme Parks,* and they'd always say the theme parks kept them young, but Tabby had to wonder if they all expected to just stay young forever.

Herself included.

"Fine," she said, because it went against all of her training to say no to a guest request. She placed her hand on one corner of her miniature Conestoga wagon, tried to pretend it wasn't a merchandise rack covered with sunglasses, and looked out across the sea of park guests before her as if it was truly the rippling ocean of the prairie.

"That's it!" the photographer enthused, his camera beeping obediently. "Oh, these are fantastic." He glanced at her name-tag. "Thank you, Tabby from Kentucky."

"Are those going on social?" As if she didn't know the answer.

"They sure are." He was tapping away at his camera, looking at the photos he'd taken. "You want me to tag you?"

She thought about it. "Sure," she said finally, as if admitting a weakness, and she let the guy add her on Instagram. "Thanks," she told him as he turned to leave, as if he'd done her a favor, instead of the other way around.

The Conestoga Wagons lined the riverbank of the Mighty Missouri, just across the wide promenade from the storefronts and raised boardwalk that comprised the frontier town of Old Dodge City. There was a hat wagon, a leather-goods wagon, and the sunglass wagon. Tabby had worked at one of these wagons nearly every day for the past two months, and she was heartily sick of the sight of them.

Which was too bad, because someone had beautifully crafted these kiosks. They'd clearly been built with love in the theme park shops by master craftspeople with a passion for their work. Tabby had loved these wagons once, studying the hand-hewn beams, the authentic wooden pegging, the real canvas canopies shrouding the tops. The overpriced merchandise on their shelves and pegs could have been anything, and it would still draw people to look at it, enchanted by the perfectly nostalgic character of those imitation prairie schooners.

These days, Tabby ignored the wagon altogether. That was probably why the photographer had caught her off-guard, wanting to take her photo like that—he'd reminded her she'd once thought this wagon precious. She should have told him no; if one of her managers spotted her on Instagram, she'd get taken to task for participating in unauthorized photo-shoots. She shook her head at her own foolishness as she completed another slow circle around the wagon, completely missing the *Missouri Queen* as she came steaming around the bend in the river. When the side-wheeler sounded her whistle, Tabby nearly jumped out of her plain black loafers.

"Dammit," Tabby muttered, putting a palm to her racing heart. That stupid steamship came around the bend in the Mighty Missouri twice an hour and she *still* had to be looking right at it or the whistle would scare her half to death. "Stupid *boat.*"

Tabby found her way back to the patch of shade in the wagon's lee and waited for the next guest to come wandering up. They passed back and forth in front of her, a blur of families in flip flops and tank tops, wearing fanny-packs and camel-backs, arguing and laughing and dropping popcorn and looking at their phones as if a day at one of America's most popular theme parks was just another walk around the dead mall in their hometown.

Across the promenade, May Johnson wandered out onto the porch of Professor Cloud's Curious Artifacts and looked out at the crush of people. She was wearing the same costume as Tabby, but with a little green jacket which set her apart: May was a lead. Not a very good one, but sometimes seniority could get a person into a position of semi-authority whether or not they deserved it. One good thing about May, though: she was always up for a conversation and since she was a lead, it could look to managers like she was providing a little feedback session instead of a gossip catch-up.

Tabby could have been a lead in Ride Ops, if she'd been willing to stay in that department. But she had been working in Ops for two years, including her internship, and she'd worked at too many outdoor ride queues and loading stations. Tabby had been thinking only of climate control when she put in her request for Retail. Most stores were fully enclosed and had both working air conditioning *and* heat, a necessity in Georgia's yo-yo winter season. She had once spent the coldest February of her life slamming down safety bars on the Sequoia Expedition ride vehicles while a few dozen feet away, the sheltered Retail Patriots of Sequoia Suppliers shed their coats and laughed together in bare-armed contentment. As for summer? That didn't even bear talking about.

Tabby's true passion, she had discovered since coming to Georgia, was air conditioning. Ice-cold, goosebump-raising, finger-numbing air conditioning. The coldest place in all of America the Beautiful was Patriot's Place, where the so-called Double Patriots worked in a warren of cool, dark shops, selling freshly dipped candles, pewter mugs, and jars of preserves. The lady Double Patriots wore a ridiculous colonial-era costume: a massive jumper with a lace-up bodice and a full-length slip, covered with a heavy overskirt of blue floral "calico" (it was polyester, everything was polyester) which came to the ankles. Under the bodice, they wore a frilly sleeved blouse and topped it all off with a ridiculous mobcap.

If it wasn't for the arctic conditions of Patriot's Place, the costume's designer could have been prosecuted as a mass murderer. No one could wear that dress outside in the Georgia heat and survive. But the area was the only one in the park which had no outdoor retail kiosks. The Double Patriots rejoiced in total climate control.

Tabby would have worn it all, mobcap and all, if only to be indoors during the summer. She loved the dim ambiance of the Patriot's Place shops anyway: she could spend hours inhaling the honey-scented confines of the Colonial Market, where jars of preserves lined eighteenth-century cabinet shelves, and soaking up the ice-cold air in the candle-dipping shop, which was kept frosty to prevent the handmade candles from melting back into wax puddles. She had marked Patriot's Place top on her preference list, although of course she would have been happy to accept a transfer to retail in The Forgotten Forests, Smuggler's Bayou, or The Big Apple; hell, even Liberty Plaza, the bustling theme park entrance and exit, would be fine! All of them had plenty of air conditioning!

So of course, when the transfer out of Ops came and Tabby was scheduled for her very last week of loading and unloading park guests from the longboats of Pirate Bayou Adventure, a form letter declared she was heading to Old Dodge City. A western frontier town of little shade and long, scorching afternoons, with those Conestoga wagons notorious as black holes for transfers with low seniority, it was the worst possible place for a person searching for a break from the weather.

She'd just nodded resignedly when she'd gotten the news.

The trade unions had strict rules around accepting and declining transfers, and if Tabby turned down Old Dodge City, she'd be stuck slapping the STOP/GO button and yelling *"six to a row, please, six to a row!"* on the Bayou Pirate Adventure boats for another six months or the rest of her life, whichever came first. So Tabby buttoned her new flower-sprigged blouse right up to her chin, looked at herself in the Wardrobe department mirrors, and told herself this was just another stepping stone on a long, uncertain path to greatness.

Plus, even dressing up like Laura Ingalls to hawk sunglasses was better than being back in her mama's trailer in Kentucky, surrounded by barking dogs and Bibles.

Tabby waved at May, who waved back, then put a finger to her earpiece and arranged her face into a serious expression. *Typical.* If you wanted a lead or a manager and they didn't want to bother with you, they just pretended they'd received an urgent call.

"Hey, hey you, how much for these sunglasses?"

Tabby trained her gaze on the sweating man who had addressed her with such grace and respect. He was bald and cherry-cheeked and looked as if he came from a long line of men who yelled at waitresses after a bad golf game. When had "excuse me, miss," dissolved into "hey you" anyway? Was she totally undeserving of respect since she was dressed up in a polyester prairie girl get-up? Tabby's thoughts were repetitive on this line; she had a lot of time to think them in a job which required very little brainpower.

The man waved a pair of plastic-armed sunglasses at her. "How much are *these?* There's no tag."

Tabby held out her hand. The glasses weren't a very popular style, and she didn't know the price off-hand. "I'm not sure. Can I see them?"

"You're not sure?" The man squinted at her. He seemed to be looking down at her in her polyester costume, which Tabby found extremely ironic, as he was wearing a t-shirt from a Fun Run, which she doubted he had successfully completed. This particular 5K had been sponsored by half a dozen community banks, car lots, and chicken restaurants, all of which he seemed happy to advertise from his back throughout his theme park day.

Tabby noticed this phenomenon a lot: dads showing up for expensive family vacations, during which they would be photographed dozens, if not hundreds of times, for photos the families would treasure for decades, all the while wearing t-shirts they'd gotten for free from some sponsored event or another. Fun runs, fishing tournaments, hot rod festivals: the sweet spot in their wardrobe was anything which had a cartoonish logo, a date at least three years in the past, and a listing of six to ten corporate sponsors. They would preen in these shirts before plate-glass windows, complain about children spilling ice cream on them, and pose for photos in front of Promise Mountain surrounded by their adoring families, all of whom were wearing much nicer shirts.

The wives were usually wearing a custom t-shirt they'd bought off Etsy with an America the Beautiful-specific phrase like *Living the Beautiful Life!* or *Lavender Lemonade Anyone?* The kids got matching Patriot Pals shirts or something with cutesy sayings about ice cream cones and liberty. The photos were extremely staged—except, of course, for Dad.

Tabby watched these matching-shirt families walk by and wondered what had happened to just wearing a shirt in a color you liked.

Fun Run Dad was clutching the sunglasses protectively. "Is this your shop or what? You should know the price!"

Tabby had tried explaining that prices changed often and seemingly randomly, but park guests rarely cared how things worked, so she went with a memorized Themed Reply. As usual, she used her best Kentucky drawl when she deployed Themed Replies in Old Dodge City.

"I'm sorry for the confusion, sir. This is Shopkeeper Sam's store, but he's down at the train station picking up a new shipment from Back East. I'd be happy to check the price for you if you just let me check this here ledger." Tabby smiled as winningly as her sweaty cheeks would allow.

Fun Run Dad wrinkled his gleaming red forehead at her, his black eyebrows coming together like two fat caterpillars, and Tabby knew that, as usual, the Themed Reply had been a mistake. *"Shopkeeper Sam?"* he repeated in an incredulous voice. "Do you think I'm some kind of idiot?"

There was no Themed Reply for this, which was ironic because of how often this was the response, and because most of the time, yes, Tabby did think the person was an idiot. Instead, she had to retreat to the Standard Patriot Reply, which was not written down but instead passed from old Patriots to new Patriots at America the Beautiful Theme Park and Resort, in a grand verbal tradition of cop-outs, poor training, lack of reliable management, and rude customers. This reply did not require an accent.

"No, sir, I'm just saying what they tell me to. I'm sorry."

It was the equivalent of: "I don't know, I just work here," but the reply usually elicited a complicit grin and de-escalated the situation. Tabby waited, puppy-dog eyes in full effect, as the man considered, and then relented. He handed over the cheap sunglasses, the arms rattling against the frame, and Tabby scanned the bar code. The register beeped obediently.

"Twenty-four ninety-five," she announced, not particularly surprised. Every year there was a golden price which the number-crunchers liked to assign to everything they could.

"Twenty-four-"

"Plus tax," she finished.

She handed back the glasses.

"Are you kidding me?"

And it was back on. Tabby was prepared to wait this one out, but then escape came in the form of a tiny computer print-out, the size of a receipt, handed to her by a fellow Patriot. It read: *Winslow, please take over Sunglass Wagon. Tabby, please go to break until 12:54.*

She smiled at her rescuer. "I reckon this fine gentleman will be purchasing those sunglasses," she told Winslow in the heaviest Themed Reply she could muster, her voice one hundred percent Appalachian Holler.

Winslow grinned appreciatively. He loved some good Theming. Winslow was a goofy-looking guy with long jowls, long ears, a long nose, and, somehow, long eyes, but he was nice, as most goofy-looking guys are, and he had a thing for Tabby, which also seemed to be a common trait of goofy-looking guys. He had crumbs down his faux-leather vest and on his red-and-black plaid shirt, so he'd clearly just come from break himself.

"Enjoy your time at the Chuckwagon," he told her, and whisked his hand through the air like a maitre'd pointing to her table.

Tabby sighed and made her escape without a second glance at Fun Run Dad, dodging park guests coming at her from left and right as she skipped across the hot brown pavement of Old Dodge City. A collection of Old West storefronts lined the wide walkway across from the riverfront, their elaborately carved signs advertising the Old Dodge City Shootin' Arcade, Sam Sweet's Candy Emporium, Professor Cloud's Curious Artifacts, and Tumbleweed Treasures.

All but the Shootin' Arcade were retail stores, all were blissfully air-conditioned, and all were out of Tabby's reach, staffed by long-time Patriots who used their seniority to keep themselves in shady comfort all year long. It was a pioneer's life for her, and would be for a long time. America the Beautiful had been around for thirty-four years, and a startlingly large number of people had been content to run registers and stock shelves for all of them.

Tabby's roommate, Molly, had gotten so sick of the seniority backlog at America the Beautiful that she'd transferred right out of the park and into the much younger sister park across the street. By all accounts, it was much easier working next door at Legacy of Heroes Adventure Park, where the roller coasters were themed to great American conflicts (and, to a lesser extent, the movies that celebrated them. The Escape From Atlanta had won several industry awards for a particular animatronic figure right before the final lift hill: a dark-haired damsel who looked remarkably like Vivien Leigh, slapping the reins of an emaciated animatronic horse. Riders were granted enough time for a quick but amazed glance at not-Scarlett before they were cranked up the last lift hill into the munitions warehouse, after which an explosion blew them straight out of Atlanta and into the bucolic country night of a plantation that looked suspiciously Tara-like.)

At Legacy of Heroes everything seemed to be less strict than at tradition-bound America the Beautiful—you could occasionally walk through a themed area in the wrong costume, for example. America the Beautiful had been built on the site of a much older theme park, which had closed back in the 1970s, a victim of the energy crisis which had slowed American family vacations.

That first park had been built by a millionaire real estate king with Walt Disney-like ambitions, and the park layout was an earnest copy of everything the Disney theme parks did best: a hub-and-spoke design with broad central avenues above ground, and a network of corridors beneath where employees could work at the dirty business of running a theme park…from getting to their lockers to throwing away the day's garbage. Blue Lake Gardens didn't last out the 1970s, but when Lawrence Taylor of Taylor American Studios decided he wanted his own theme park, the property was just what the tycoon doctor ordered.

Taylor American's prize IP, *The Patriot Pals,* wasn't exactly on par with *The Mickey Mouse Club,* but the puppet show about American ideals had been especially popular in the South, and the cartoon spin-offs were part of the collective memory for enough children that America the Beautiful quickly became a national attraction, with annual attendance measured in the tens of millions. Lawrence Taylor kept the

Disneyland aesthetic in mind as he re-crafted the park into a tribute to America's key tropes: big cities, Manifest Destiny, and purple mountains' majesty. Plus pirates, because everyone loved pirates.

While Taylor had crafted America the Beautiful as an ultra-Patriotic ode to Disneyland, no one could deny that little sister Legacy of Heroes was more like a fancy Six Flags. It lacked the tremendous infrastructure which kept the original park's themed areas so meticulously in-period. But it also lacked the thirty-year Patriots who used their seniority to scoop up all the good shifts and training, leaving the new staff out in the cold (or the heat). Legacy's staff were almost uniformly young, irresponsible, and thoroughly relieved to have escaped the stuffy atmosphere on the other side of the parking lot. They called Legacy "the real world" with an air of weary knowledge, as if all the Patriots at AtB were just fooling themselves at their aging theme park with its false walls, hidden passages, and subterranean stock rooms.

Well, there were some days, Tabby thought, when America the Beautiful's principle conceit—keeping the modern world so far outside the gates that even admitting the employees there were actual, modern humans would break every rule—provided a welcome escape for the Patriots as well as the park guests. The Wild West stayed outside where it belonged while Tabby went on break. If she'd *really* had to eat her lunch at a chuck wagon, she would have been pissed.

She slipped gratefully through an inconspicuous door in a faux-log cabin wall, marked with a small sign reading "Shopkeepers Only Please."

On the other side of the door, everything changed as if

she'd stepped through a portal. The plucky banjo music ceased, the walls went from unfinished pine logs to drywall painted battleship-gray, and cold air rushed up an industrial staircase to replace the hot, humid climate outside.

Thank goodness for subterranean passageways cut through Georgia clay, Tabby thought, and then congratulated herself on her lyricism. Maybe she hadn't lost her touch when she quit on her English degree after all.

Two flights down and a world away, the AtB Underground waited. Tabby walked close to the right-hand wall as indicated by the directional signs hanging from the pipe-lined ceiling: pargo drivers in the middle, pedestrians to the sides. Now and then she had to detour around a puddle of something unnamed; it was probably water, but all the Patriots avoided drips from above with shrieks of *"Ugh, tunnel water!"*

The service tunnels running beneath America the Beautiful's principal promenades were about twenty feet wide and lit with a wan shimmer of blue-gray fluorescent light panels, sort of like a subway passage crossing under a city park. It would have been bleak if it hadn't come as such a relief to over-stimulated employees from above-ground. In contrast to the bright colors and lush landscaping and cheerful music of the park, the tunnels were a place of semi-industrial work, earnest conversation, and the hum of Lite 97.3, South Georgia's At-Work Station. The walls were lined with stockroom doors, warrens of low-ceilinged offices, pallets and flats of everything from Christmas ornaments to individual portion cups of cheese dip, and the electric cargo vehicles, called pargos, that Patriots used for supply runs and occasionally just zipping around, honking the horn vigorously, when they were supposed to be somewhere else.

After passing a beverage cage, a Dumpster, a half-dozen pallets of boxed toys, and two female interns having a hushed and intense discussion by the Bayou Pirate Adventure stairwell ("He doesn't deserve you," one whispered to the other as she passed), Tabby passed the open door of a stockroom and paused to peek in at the young woman working inside. "Hey, Antonia!"

Antonia was pulling tiny geodes out of a box of packing peanuts and dropping them unceremoniously into a plastic shelving bin. Tall, slim, and incalculably beautiful even in the plain black pants and gray shirt of a floor-stocker, Antonia had just a few extra years on Tabby's twenty-two, but somehow seemed a decade older. At least, that was how she seemed to Tabby, who envied Antonia's cool, rational response to every disaster AtB could throw at them.

She pulled an earbud out of one ear when she saw Tabby. "Hey girl, what's up? You look like a total mess. Those damn pink cheeks of yours! You look like vanilla ice cream when someone's eaten the cherry off the top."

"Thanks." Tabby pushed a limp lock of dirty-blonde hair, damp with sweat, behind her ear. "You look cool and comfortable. So I hate you."

"Hey, I don't know how I keep getting these early morning stocking shifts. But I ain't complainin' either."

"Someone in scheduling loves you. Because I'm pretty sure Juanita has higher seniority than you."

"Why're you thinking that?"

"That's what she was telling everyone." Juanita had been complaining about working evening floor-stocking shifts since the long summer hours went into effect at the beginning of June.

"I bet she messed up her bid. You got to choose whether you care more about time of day or where you work. I chose time of day just to see what would happen, and I put mornings on top. She probably chose stocking over time of day. Now she's mad about it because they need more people at night in summer."

"I chose time of day and preferenced mid-shifts, so I wouldn't get stuck closing one day and opening the next." Tabby leaned her head against the wall, ready to get into the weeds with this topic. The mystifying rules of schedule bids and seniority dominated tunnel conversations. Talking about it in guest areas was strictly prohibited. But everyone was constantly scrutinizing the posted schedules and taking offense to any seniority infraction, real or supposed, even if they didn't really want the shift that supposedly should have been theirs.

Winslow, sitting across from her in the Chuckwagon every time their breaks coincided, liked to say all the schedule bid drama was how management kept them distracted from the actual problems facing the park's employees. He never would say what those problems were, though. Just shrugged and went back to his sandwich. Typical Winslow.

Antonia was also happy to discuss scheduling all day and night. "Yeah, I hear that. Close/opens are the *worst*. They still get me with those sometimes. Tomorrow, I don't come in until four o'clock. And today I started at five thirty and I'm done at two. How's that for no sleep schedule?" Antonia poked a loose curl into her updo. Her black hair gleamed under the stock room lights. Tabby loved Antonia's hair, so lush and shiny, so different from her own lank braids. "Gotta take a nap after work so I can stay up late and get ready for tomorrow night. It's been weeks since I had a closing shift." She reached back into the box and dug out another handful of cheap geodes, shaking the packing peanuts onto the floor in a styrofoam snowfall. "Nick was down here earlier."

Tabby's stomach made a slow, nervous back-flip. "Oh yeah?" She hoped her voice had stayed steady.

Antonia grinned at her sideways. Maybe it hadn't. "Mmhmm. He was here. He says, 'Didn't Tabby get any morning shifts this week?' I says, 'She's opening up the wagon all week, that's like her new home.' He was like, 'Oh, I meant five a.m. shifts,' and I told him, 'Nah man, I got all those.'"

"That's a good story," Tabby said. "Thanks for sharing."

Antonia cackled. "Girl, he's looking for you! Go see if he's in the Chuckwagon."

The two women eyed each other for a charged moment. A pargo went whining past, its cargo bed rattling with ladders and toolboxes. A crowd of college interns went strolling past, wearing the flowery skirts and ruffled aprons of Cowboy Cal's Good Grub. They were loud, their conversation echoing off the low ceiling of the tunnel, and all their noise masked Tabby's half-apologetic goodbye when she turned away from Antonia and headed for the Chuckwagon.

Antonia doesn't care, she's over it. She told me we could still be friends, nothing has to change. All of Tabby's self-reassurances couldn't stop her from glancing back over her shoulder as she trudged down the concrete aisle, and when she did, she saw Antonia duck back into the stock room. Perhaps, not wanting to admit she'd been watching Tabby go.

* * *

Nick was sitting in a corner booth of the noisy break room, underneath a TV blaring Headline News. It was past one o'clock and the early lunches had gone to the older Patriots; now there was hardly anyone left of an age to care what was on cable news. Still, one lone custodian sat a few booths away, eating rice and beans from a microwavable container, his eyes trained on the screen. Everyone else was under twenty-five and couldn't have cared less. They were too busy making their own content.

Nick's thing was videos; he made hilarious videos and shared them on every social media channel available: anything he could do to semi-anonymously share the strange life of a Patriot at America the Beautiful. He had more than twelve thousand followers on Instagram and he'd tell this to anyone who asked if he had an account, or why he was making a video, or what he did for fun. He was talking to his phone now, nearly shouting to be heard over the curvy TV reporter announcing the latest death toll of America's freshest tragedy. As Tabby paused in the break room doorway, watching him work, she could picture the way he had the camera positioned, so only his mouth and chin showed as he spoke. It was a half-hearted attempt at anonymity, to get around AtB's strict no-social media policy.

She wanted to sit across from him and make faces until he burst out laughing and screwed up his video, but she was hungry, too. Too bad her lunch was sitting on the counter back at her apartment, slowly spoiling, and she'd been too late to stop for anything at Spirit of '76 Cafe, the main cafeteria under AtB's main entrance.

The Chuckwagon had nothing as fancy as a cafeteria, just a tiny shop built into a former custodial supply closet, where a small elderly woman of Korean heritage sat on a stool and watched the college students and younger generation of Patriots nose around the bags of chips and the slow-rolling hot dogs with the same intense concentration as a 7-Eleven shopkeeper. She smiled hugely at each purchase, however, which made up a little for the bleak feel of the space where the Patriots bought their pre-made Subway sandwiches and their five-dollar Lean Cuisines.

Tabby considered a snack pack of hummus and pretzels —too small—and a wilted ham-and-cheese sub—too depressing—before settling on an overpriced fruit and yogurt parfait, which at least gave some suggestion of freshness and health. You had to break up the ramen routine sometimes. She handed over a five-dollar bill she'd kept squirreled away in her company lanyard for a few days, an illicit tip a rare happy guest had given her when she'd found his kid's missing autograph book after it had fallen off a fence and into the bushes behind the covered wagon, and basked in the glow of Miss Annie's approving smile for a moment before returning to the doomsday news patter of the break room.

Nick spotted her instantly, which could only mean he'd known she was in the room and had been watching the commissary door, waiting for her to reappear. She felt her stomach do another leisurely backflip. There was something about Nick—short golden hair with a flyaway bang that slipped over his left eye, slim nose and pointed jaw, thin lips and sky-blue eyes—that was just so All-American, 50s sitcom, Pleasantville perfect Tabby almost didn't know what to do with herself when he was in the room. He made her crazy, plain and simple. He made her forget her own name. He actually had when she'd first met him. He'd had to look at her name-tag as she'd stared at him, tongue-tied, instead of taking the assignment slip he'd held out to her. "You are Tabby, right? You're supposed to go out to the Candy Wagon and send Joanna on her break. I'm not food-safety trained yet."

He'd certainly knocked whatever ideas she'd had about Antonia straight out of her head. And it had upset her a little, on a philosophical level, that she could drop a sexy Black female like yesterday's park schedule when a blonde white boy with a Dennis the Menace sprinkle of freckles appeared on the scene. It just didn't seem very feminist, or progressive, or twenty-first century, to give up a promising multicultural same-sex relationship for something as basic, something as unapologetically normal, as Nick's Mayflower genetics.

She slid into the booth across from him, and he flipped his phone around. "Check this out. I did a vlog on the social injustice of the break room hierarchy."

Tabby obediently watched the video, which seemed concentrated on the fact that old people came into work at five a.m., set all the TVs on Headline News, and then expected them to stay that way all day. "One man in this room is happy right now," video-Nick intoned passionately. "And it's that man right there." Cut to the Ecuadorian custodian gazing at the television, mechanically bringing forkfuls of rice and beans to his mouth. He certainly seemed enraptured by the news. In the background, she could hear the Headline News reporter describing stab wounds.

Tabby wasn't one hundred percent sure if the video successfully showed how difficult life as a Patriot with no seniority was, but she nodded anyway, sliding the phone back across the yellow Formica. "Riveting," she said. "You're going to change the world someday."

Nick smiled down at his face on the phone. "I think so, too," he said happily. "Start small. Think locally. All that."

Tabby dug into her yogurt, finding, with little surprise, that the fruit was frozen and tasted mainly of ice. "Maybe you could do a report on our corporate overlords choosing to selling overpriced lunch items to desperate, poor Patriots."

He waved a plastic bag at her. "Or you could bring your own lunch."

"I don't have any food at home," she explained patiently, as if to a toddler. "I've been working every day this week. I had leftover Chinese to bring and forgot it because I was running late."

"Mandatory OT?"

"Just voluntary. Gotta get that overtime while they offer it."

"I try not to work more than four days," Nick said, tapping at his phone as he posted his video. "I give away the fifth day whenever I can."

Tabby wished they weren't talking about scheduling. Surely, they were capable of something less mundane. But she couldn't think of anything else, so she said, "I'm thinking of taking some time off in August."

Then she filled her mouth with icy blueberries and a single, anemic strawberry. Was she really going to take time off in August? She couldn't afford to.

"What are you going to do?" Nick's pale blue eyes flicked up. He was interested at last.

"Maybe I'll go to Palmetto Beach," Tabby suggested serenely. Internally, she was screaming. She absolutely didn't have the money to go to the beach. But she needed Nick to believe she was more interesting than just the usual empty break room talk about locations and schedules and bids.

"Who's going with you?" Nick was thumbing rapidly on his phone, tweeting out his vlog link.

"I haven't asked anyone," Tabby hinted. "It's still very up in the air. Did you think maybe…"

"I was going to go to New York in August," Nick said, still typing.

Tabby sat back, deflated.

"But the beach sounds really nice," he went on, and then: "Maybe I could come with you?" and he put down his phone and smiled at her, and Tabby felt herself lift up out of her body and hover, if not to the heavens above, then at least up near the water-stained drop ceiling above them.

CHAPTER TWO

Antonia

Antonia had fifty-two boxes left to unpack and less than an hour left on her shift, so she was trying to hustle. She threw rocks into boxes like a miner who just struck it lucky. Geodes here, fool's gold there, flat agates over along that wall. The stock-room shelves rose seven feet to the concrete ceiling and were labeled with Antonia's own even hand-writing, black Sharpie marker on masking tape, easy to rip off and move when unpredictable shipments changed storage needs and hasty rearrangements had to be made. The fluorescent lights overhead hummed steadily, a friendly buzz to Antonia, who was tired of discordant clamor and only really enjoyed working in the theme park during the slow season.

The balance of organization was her zen, a calming antidote to the constant calamity of working with the guests in the park. In theory, Antonia loved working in the park as much as anyone who had done this work full-time for nearly five years still could, but there was a lot to be said for sitting downstairs in a quiet stockroom while the endless chaos and non-stop demands went unheard high above her head.

She, too, was a victim of the long-time Patriots of Old Dodge City Retail, but her seniority at least got her back-up positions now. She couldn't get work in the stockroom full-time, but whenever an old-timer was out on medical leave or on one of their constant vacations, she got scheduled in their place. She'd spent the past three weeks in charge of the Professor Cloud's stockroom while Leeann was out for surgery on her elbow, and she'd loved every moment. Tomorrow Leeann would be back, presumably working this physically demanding job with just one good hand rather than cede her position of power for one more day than absolutely necessary, and Antonia was privately grieving for the state she'd find her perfect stockroom in the next time she was scheduled for the morning shift. Leeann did not have Antonia's innate sense of order, and having one arm in a sling would not improve matters.

Sometimes she thought about changing work locations, looking for an area with some potential openings for a Patriot with five years of seniority. The churn of Liberty Plaza offered some possibility, since the park entrance's extra-long hours and constant chaos ground through Patriots like a wood-chipper. But Antonia wasn't sure she was that desperate. Not yet. Old Dodge City was a comfortable place. Once you rose above the constant drag of working the Conestoga wagons, of course. The shops were interesting and pleasant; the area was deep enough into the park to have slow mornings and quiet late nights, and the costume was relatively inoffensive. Antonia would have quit before she'd wear that ridiculous floor-duster in Patriot's Place. She thought the lace-up bodice made everyone there look like tavern wenches, and she wasn't about to go out on show like that.

The closest she'd come to actually putting in a transfer request hadn't been work-related at all. It had been back in April, when Nick had shown up and it became painfully apparent that Tabby wasn't into her, after all. There'd been a brief period when Tabby, although clearly apprehensive about entering her first female relationship, had allowed Antonia to squire her around a little, take her out to dinner, visit the park as a guest with her, buy her ice cream, hold her hand, kiss her lips gently, squeeze her tit just enough to get a little moan out of her reluctant throat. She'd known Tabby wasn't mentally prepared, despite her two years of liberal arts education and her impressive reputation as a Patriot on the prowl, to actually involve herself romantically with a woman. But Tabby had tried, she'd given it a really solid try actually, and her dogged determination to keep at it had given Antonia hope that maybe she'd snagged this slim little blonde-haired puppy-dog when no one else could tie her down.

Then Nick, golden-haired boy-next-door Nick. Even Antonia could see that theirs would be a perfect union, a silver screen duo worthy of Nora Ephron. He was a straight-C student with a skateboard and a dream. She couldn't boil water for spaghetti but had the heart of a poet. Together they'd…what? Make blonde babies, probably. Nick's genes looked pretty solid from Antonia's point of view. You didn't stay that white down through the ages without a steadfast refusal to intermarry with other skin and hair-shades.

Antonia didn't see the attraction to Nick personally. But she knew why Tabby did. The boy was pretty. And unobjectionable. Antonia doubted even Tabby's Bible-thumping mama could find a reason to hate floppy-haired and friendly Nick.

"Antonia? Antonia, helloooo…"

Roseann was in the doorway. Antonia stifled a sigh and plucked out one earbud.

"Yeah boss," she said to Roseann, using her grandmother's best Caribbean accent because she knew it made her youngest manager uncomfortable.

Roseann, only weeks out of college and dressed like a cocktail waitress, stepped over the metal sill of the stockroom's double doors on dangerously high heels.

"You're not supposed to have both earbuds in," she began.

Antonia, lofty from the respectable old age of twenty-six, was gregarious towards Roseann and her many shortcomings as a manager. Roseann did not have Antonia's obvious advantages of being raised by Haitian-Americans, for one thing. Roseann was just another privileged white girl who had to learn how to treat people with respect, and Antonia was happy to assist her on that journey. "Roseann how may I help you," she said, her voice patient but without the comfort of commas and question marks. "I still have fifty boxes and I'm off in as many minutes."

"Well, that's what I came to ask you about…" Roseann paused and waited to be asked to continue. She put a hand to her tightly curled auburn hair, pinned in an elaborately messy up-do that Antonia did not think met AtB's rigorously traditional appearance standards.

Antonia, rather than encouraging Roseann's reticence, went back to opening boxes, ruthlessly efficient as she demonstrated safe box-cutting technique, per the safety video all Patriots were required to watch before touching one of the dangerous instruments.

"Can you stay today and help on register?" Roseann asked plaintively. "We've had some call-ins…"

"Which shop?" This was important.

"Well…the Wagons…"

"Sorry, can't do that." Antonia dug a handful of polished agates from the box and dropped them, with a rattle like a hailstorm on a tin roof, into their plastic storage bin. "Cloud's, I could do."

"The call-in was for Wagons," Roseann explained, as if Antonia did not understand how scheduling worked.

"You could move someone to Wagons from Cloud's, and I could cover Cloud's." Antonia was not working outdoors after an entire morning in the chilly Underground, and she was definitely not working Wagons alongside Tabby. She'd already given Tabby a hint about Nick, and that was the limit of her generosity today. Antonia, unbeknownst to many—including Roseann—*did* have feelings.

"I can't do that because Roger is in Cloud's tonight, and he has seniority. He'd never go for it."

"Well." Antonia opened another box. "I am sorry. I hope you find someone."

Roseann hung on for another few moments, hoping Antonia would take pity on her, but if there was one thing Antonia did not pity in this world, it was the green-as-grass managers who were promoted from the ranks of interns who arrived each January and June with their eyes wide, and their need to prove themselves making them inherently annoying to the experienced Patriots who knew their jobs and just wanted to be left alone to do them. Antonia had been a Patriot for five years. She could run Old Dodge City through fire and flood. She did not need to please Roseann to feel confident in her ability to do a good job. And Roseann did not have enough pull in the manager's office to do Antonia any favors.

Roseann was learning this. "Thanks anyway, Antonia. Great job today." She departed, clicking through the tunnel in her inappropriate shoes.

Antonia put her other earbud back in. " 'Great job today'," she muttered, in a rare moment of complaint. "Like I need her approval." She looked at her tidy shelves, which tomorrow would go back to a state of disarray. "I *know* I do a great job."

Someday, maybe, she'd be a manager. And then she'd do more than just show up, say foolish things, and drop a lame, "Great job" on the way out the door.

Good leadership made the difference. Antonia was sure of that.

Antonia's next visitor was Nick himself, who came into the stockroom and settled down on the floor at the end of the central row of shelves, where he couldn't be seen from the passersby in the tunnel. Antonia recognized this visit was not about her excellent company; it was just one of his many hiding places. Nick wasn't exactly a dedicated worker. She knew for a fact he had a napping spot upstairs, in a weird nook above Professor Cloud's where you could hear the soothing harpsichord music of the White House Gallery on the other side of the wall, wafting in from neighboring Patriot's Place. What she *didn't* know was why he wasn't up there now, fast asleep, instead of bothering her. He kicked out his feet and tapped an annoying rhythm against the metal shelving unit.

"What you want now, Nick?" she asked once she couldn't take the beat anymore. "Don't you have to do some work?"

He looked up from his phone. "Is that any way to thank me for my wonderful company as you work alone in this subterranean basement, Antonia?"

"Subterranean and basement mean the same thing," she informed him. "Pick one word."

"The Grammar Police. Send help." Nick flung his arm over his forehead in mock despair.

Antonia threw an empty box at him, fed up. "Get out your cutter and flatten these for me. You can do that sitting down."

He pulled out his box cutter and obliged, so she took the rest of the pile, at least a dozen big cardboard boxes, and threw them his way. "There," she said. "Keep yourself busy if you're going to bother me. I was listening to something."

"Listen to *me*. I have problems," Nick sighed.

"Your problems are boring," Antonia suggested. "Your struggle bores me."

"It's about Tabby, though."

Antonia didn't say anything. She opened another box, ran her hands through the peanuts. Fool's gold winked at her through the styrofoam. She sighed. She would need another shelf for all these damn rocks. Time for new labels. "Hand me that masking tape, would ya?"

Nick passed her the roll of tape, along with the Sharpie. "So Tabby," he began. "I think she's into me."

Everyone in Old Dodge City knew Tabby was into Nick, and had been since April. They were now well into June.

Antonia was starting to think this boy had the brain capacity of a radish. "You know that about Tabby? You're a clairvoyant. You should tell fortunes up in Liberty Village."

"Come on. Be nice. You went out with her, right?"

"I did." Antonia measured out the tape against the shelf, and wrote *"Fool's Gold, Bulk Rock,"* on it with the Sharpie. She emptied a few containers of assorted gems into one mixed box, placed it on the shelf. Methodical. Calm. Organized. The way she liked everything in life. "A lot of guys have gone out with her, though."

"Not a lot of girls."

"No." Antonia was proud of this, although maybe it wasn't really an accomplishment, being some college-age girl's one-and-done lesbian experience.

"Is she um…does she have…is she really…"

"I don't know."

"You gotta know!"

"I was taking it slow."

"Damn." Nick leaned his head back against the shelving unit. He looked like a Disney Channel star, Antonia thought, annoyed. He was wasted in this tunnel somewhere in Georgia. Maybe he was a bad actor,gh. "She has a weird reputation," he said finally. "Like she's very experienced on paper, but she acts very innocent. She blushes a lot. I didn't know if there was something I'd missed, or if she just puts on a good show, or what. Then I heard maybe she wasn't what they said she was."

"What did they say she was," Antonia said calmly, knowing full well.

"They said she was the wildest intern in years."

"And you believed that?"

"At first. Yeah. Was that dumb of me?"

Antonia wished she was anywhere but here, answering questions about her ex-girlfriend for this stupid, pretty boy. "She wasn't wild. She just went out on a lot of dates. She didn't know how to say no. Hopefully, she learns it before you ask her out."

Nick made a pouting face. "I didn't say I was going to."

"Then why are you bothering me about her?"

"I want to understand what's going on with her. She's so quiet."

"She was pretty sheltered as a child. Her parents are very religious, but she isn't anymore," Antonia added, relenting somewhat. For the good of Tabby. "This is the first time she's been on her own. She was living at home when she went to college. When she quit school to stay here after her internship, her parents freaked out. They actually came and tried to drive her back home. It was a hell of a scene at the dorms. This was summer before last."

"Were you there? You weren't an intern too, were you?"

"Hell no." Antonia took a moment to lift her eyebrows meaningfully and remind him of her lofty status as a five-year Patriot, not a spring break hire who had stuck around for summer, like he was. "But it was pretty common knowledge. Anyone who knew Tabby knew it happened. And then she transferred out of Operations and into Retail, so the story followed her through two departments. You know what this place is like. Everybody's up in each other's business."

"That's for sure." Nick pulled over some more boxes to flatten. Trying to please her, she thought. Butter her up. "Well…what do you think I should do?"

"You're asking me? Her ex-girlfriend? That's some shady shit, Nick."

"I thought you two were still friends."

"That don't mean I want to play matchmaker. You're on your own. Don't break her heart, either, or I'll come after you." Antonia turned the full weight of her frown, a serious and frightening thing she had inherited from her serious and frightening Haitian father, upon Nick. She was gratified to see him quail, edging backwards from her and unconsciously wiggling free of his hiding spot behind the stockroom shelves.

She was still frowning at him, earbud dangling over her collar, when Roseann came back down the tunnel and saw Nick's golden head at the end of the stockroom's narrow aisle. "Nick!" Roseann exclaimed. "I've been looking for you."

Antonia rearranged her face into a smile and turned it on Roseann. "Nick's helping me with all these boxes, so I can finish on time. Otherwise, there'll be a mess for Leeann in the morning, and you know how she gets about a messy stockroom."

Roseann's face crinkled into an involuntary wince; she was the opening manager on Wednesdays, so any of Leeann's unholy outrage would be vented at her should there be boxes left behind. "Thank goodness, Nick. Thanks for being so helpful. Listen, I know you're on floor-stock tonight, but can you do register? Because we have call-ins."

Nick looked at Roseann, and then Antonia, as if asking for her to bail him out a second time. Antonia smiled at him. "It's Wagons, Nick. Better do it. You can get to know Tabby better."

CHAPTER THREE

Sonia

Sonia tried to think of another moment in her life as frustrating at this one was, just to take her mind off what was happening, but unfortunately it only took about a second's thought to come up with the answer: this exact same situation, yesterday.

She rubbed at the sweat that dribbled in endless waterfalls down the back of her neck, from beneath the black ponytail snugly tied up in her felt cowboy hat, and wondered if she should ask management for tuition reimbursement on a Spanish-language course.

A slow realization of a fallen silence broke into her thoughts and she realized the guest was done shouting at her. "I can call the language assistance number for you," Sonia said slowly, carefully enunciating her words. Sometimes that helped. "Or you can let me find someone else to help you?"

The woman narrowed her eyes, spat out something else in Spanish, and turned her back on Sonia. She promptly began shouting at her husband, who was all too happy to shout back.

Sonia looked around in hopes of back-up, but there was no one else to palm off the bickering couple on. Her current post, Greeter at Gold Rush Rapids, was pretty isolated. The closest other Patriots were stationed around a little bend and behind a wooden frontier train station, where a steam train periodically pulled up, tooted its whistle with deafening strength, and took on a straggling army of guests who sat down on its metal benches with a look of abject relief, while the guests who had alighted at Gold Rush Station staggered off in a state of exhaustion and shock, dismayed to find themselves on their sore feet again. Just past the train station, the sunny entrance plaza to the Gold Rush Rapids ride was filled with sweating guests in the overflow queue.

There were job positions at AtB that were full of fun. Sonia had personally been paid for eight hours shifts in which she had overseen long games of hop-scotch and Pin the Tail on the Prospector's Donkey with park guests of all ages. (They used a magnet, not a pin, obviously.) She loved the challenge of grouping, directing the different-size parties to ride vehicles so that each one went out fully loaded while keeping everyone happy with their companions. She absolutely adored picking up extra shifts on the afternoon parade route, where she could lead cheers and ham it up with the crowds waiting for the parade.

But Greeter was not one of the positions which gave Sonia, or really anyone else, a lot of joy.

Because of its proximity to the train station, the roller

coaster rattling behind her with its minor but still frustrating (to parents of toddlers) height requirement, and very little else, Gold Rush Greeter was a prime position for verbal abuse. Telling parents over and over again their toddlers weren't tall enough to ride, or explaining to confused and exhausted guests that no, they had to wait for another train and *keep riding* if they wanted to get to the park exit, or explaining the ride was down due to unexpected mining activity on the mountain (code for shit's broke, come back later) really took the spark out of everyone's day.

So, they usually moved Patriots out of it every thirty minutes to make up for the misery.

Sonia had been standing here for two hours.

The shouting couple's little daughter blinked up at Sonia from her large, plastic rental stroller. She was wearing a pink princess gown and a glittering tiara. Her black curls twirled around her ears in beguiling shapes, defying the summer humidity. Sonia wondered what products could possibly power through the boiling south Georgia heat of late June. "You're a beautiful princess," Sonia told her, just to break the silence. She figured the kid couldn't speak English anymore than her parents could.

"My mother says you are a traitor to your country," the little princess replied carefully, as if she had rehearsed the words.

Sonia nearly choked on the chewing gum she'd been hiding behind her back molars. "Excuse me? I was born in New Jersey. How old are you, anyway? Six? Seven?"

The princess, having said her piece, was now finished. She produced a lollipop from a pink backpack and began to lick it with great solemnity. She blinked slowly at Sonia as her mother, exhausted with shouting, grabbed the stroller handle and wheeled the girl away. The father followed, still yelling with enough energy for both of them.

Sonia was still trying to recover from the scene, and taking a few restorative chews of illicit gum, when a lone older man walked up to her. He looked ready to chat. She stuck her gum behind her teeth again, then considered his attire: Gold Rush Rapids t-shirt, America the Beautiful 30th Anniversary Spectacular ball-cap, souvenir America the Beautiful Patriot Name Tag.

Sonia gave up on the gum, swallowing it whole. He looked like the type who took America the Beautiful heritage *way* too seriously; in other words, he'd complain at Guest Services that she'd been chewing gum on the job, and he'd have written down her name to be sure he got it right, too. Sonia wasn't sure what AtB founder and theme park legend Lawrence Taylor had had against chewing gum, but the rule was iron clad.

"Howdy," the guy said, stopping in front of her.

"Howdy, partner," she replied, adopting the cartoon cowboy accent she saved for the guests she thought would appreciate the theatrics. Anyone who put this much AtB merch on his body would insist on at least an *attempt* at spaghetti western dialect. "And how are you on this *fine* summer's day?"

"Real good, real good," he twanged happily, and she knew she'd cased her audience correctly. "Just been out for a stroll through Old Dodge City, and it sure is fine to see the Mighty Missouri sparkling in the sunlight."

Sonia glanced past his shoulder and towards the shallow brown waters of the Mighty Missouri, which looped lazily through Old Dodge City on its way to join the equally tranquil Hudson River in The Big Apple. A few kids leaned against the railing of a side-wheel steamship puffing its way around Wilderness Isle, looking into the trees in hopes of spotting something computerized. The river was pretty, and under-appreciated, Sonia often thought. The side-wheeler and Wilderness Isle were both so sparsely visited, they closed early on weekdays.

This guy would probably make a point of enjoying both several times today, and Sonia respected him for it. Like most of the Patriots, the long-time park fans knew the value of the place was in the atmosphere, not in the thrill rides.

"Yessir," he said. "Sure is a fine river."

Her turn.

"I reckon it's a fine day to take a sail on the side-wheeler," Sonia offered, hoping he'd agree and amble off to the dock rather than continue making 19th-century conversation with her. She didn't have a huge repertoire of Themed Replies; Gold Rush Rapids conversations were mostly about height requirements and just how scary the ride really was. (The height requirement is thirty-eight inches. No, you can't let him stand on his tiptoes to ride. Sorry. Is it really really scary? Not really really, just kind of scary. No, not really scary at all. Honestly, it depends on what you think is scary. No, *I* don't think it's scary.)

"Mighty fine," the old-timer agreed, and Sonia realized he was pretty light on Themed Replies, too. "Can I ask you a question?"

"Of course." This would be about her job. It was always about the job: working conditions, where she lived, where her uniforms came from.

"Is it true they're going to take out the side-wheeler and

the ride here, and make it all into a rapids ride in the river?"

At first, Sonia just thought he was confused. He was getting older, after all, just like the park. The early fans of America the Beautiful were senior citizens now. "Well, sir, Gold Rush Rapids is right over here," she said, indicating the entrance plaza behind her. "It's not really a rapids ride, though, it's a family coaster that goes through some mountain caves and past some waterfalls—"

"I *know* what Gold Rush Rapids is," he interrupted, looking a little peeved. "Heaven's sake, I rode it the day it opened. You weren't even born yet." This was indisputable. Sonia let him continue. "But the actual river, they're saying that it's going to be a white-water rapids ride, really wild, like a thrill ride…now, that *can't* be true, can it?"

"I never heard that. Where did you get it?" Sonia knew the answer, but she asked anyway. To receive confirmation that everything terrible came from the same place.

"It was online," the man admitted. "But, it was on AtBLive. That's a good website! There's a guy that posts on there, Nate, and he has all the dirt. He was right about The Big Apple expansion last year, and look—" he waved his arm at the crane that rose above Old Dodge City's false fronts and towered over the forced-perspective spire of the Empire State Building. "Here comes the Grand Central Ghosts ride, just like he said. And everyone denied it was coming, too." He emphasized the *too,* as if Sonia had disavowed the impending change to the Mighty Missouri's tranquil waters with the casual nihilism of the typical corporate shill. Instead of the reality: a front-line worker wearing a faux prospector's outfit simply had no idea what the suits were doing in the office complex a couple miles away.

"Well, sir, they don't tell us about new rides until there's a press release." Sonia shrugged. "And I think AtBLive has gotten a few things wrong. That guy said there was going to be a dinner show added to Old Dodge City, too, and that didn't happen."

"Budgets," the man said knowingly. "Whatever gets the turnstile clicking, that's what they green-light. Rides, not shows. They're too cheap for shows. Not enough *capacity*, y'understand."

"Okay," Sonia agreed. "I honestly have no idea how they decided these things."

"Well, fine," he said. "But it will be a travesty if they destroy the Mighty Missouri. A crying shame. Lawrence Taylor would be spinning in his grave."

"That might be true," Sonia said. "He sure did love this place."

They gazed at the river together and considered the potential athletics of America the Beautiful's passed founder. A few moments of respectful silence followed, during which time Sonia wondered what it would be like to care about anything so deeply as some of these AtB fans cared about the park where she worked for twelve dollars an hour. She loved it here, but some of these people literally lived for the place.

"Another question," he said eventually, as a crowd disembarked from the steam train and went rowdily down the hill towards Gold Rush Rapids, thankfully without noting her, the Greeter who was supposed to welcome and direct them. "What was that woman yelling at you about?"

"Which woman?" For a moment, Sonia was genuinely confused. She got yelled at a lot. "Oh—the last one?"

"There's that many?" The man looked concerned.

"Haha, well." She didn't actually answer, and he noticed. His face grew concerned, and she hurried to reassure him. "It's nothing, honestly. She thought I spoke Spanish, and I don't, and that upset her. It happens a lot, weirdly. Something about my name and my face."

"I would never assume you spoke Spanish," he said valiantly. "You don't have a Spanish flag on your name tag."

"No, I don't," Sonia agreed, glancing down at her name tag as if to confirm that it was bare of ornamentation. "But, you know…I look it."

"*Are* you Spanish?" he asked, genuinely curious now.

"My parents are from Puerto Rico. I'm from New Jersey. A lot of my friends in school spoke both languages, but I didn't. I guess some people think I'm a Latina, and some people think I'm just a Jersey girl, and either way," Sonia laughed self-deprecatingly, "with the wrong person, I lose!"

"Folks can be so racist," he agreed. "Do you pick and choose what you tell people?"

"Honestly?" Sonia said, smiling. "A lot of times, I just tell them I'm from Florida. People love that answer. It's like you can make any mistake in the book and they just say, 'Well, she's from Florida.'"

The old-timer laughed hard at that, and Sonia had to join in.

Sonia's break was late, and she knew it was because Kenisha was the one clocking in next, but Kenisha was definitely by the clock-in computer talking to Richie. He was the new lead who had just transferred over from Legacy, and as such had an unknown policy on dating the Patriots he supervised. Kenisha had a thing for power.

When she finally took her leave of charming Richie,

Kenisha shuffled up to the Greeter position with her hiking boot untied and her hat flopped back on her neck, exposing her forehead to the midday sun. Sonia didn't think that looking unkempt and getting a sunburn on her face were good ways to get the new lead to break the dating rules, but whatever, she was hungry and hot, and hoarse from shouting, "Gold Rush Rapids is that way! Straight down the hill for Gold Rush Rapids! Gold Rush Rapids, please turn to your left!" as confused people wandered the wrong way from the train station and ended up staring, perplexed, at the Mighty Missouri rippling away in their path.

"How is it today?" Kenisha asked, leaning over to tie up her boot. Her hat flopped over face and landed on the ground, and she swore at it despite being in a guest area.

"Pretty slow, actually. No one knows where they're going, but that's normal. Just a couple of rudes, so I would say it's…not the worst."

"Good," Kenisha muttered. "I got no energy for this today. People better just lay off me."

This was unlikely, but not Sonia's problem. "Good luck," she said, in a tone which indicated she didn't like Kenisha's chances, and headed for Old Dodge City and the closest stairwell to the Underground.

"Have a yippie-ki-yi day," Kenisha monotoned after her. "Bitch."

Whatever, Sonia thought. She was going on break.

Sonia sighed as the cool Underground air hit her face, and she hustled on the long walk to the break room. Gold Rush Rapids was at the very end of the western Underground, and before they'd added the Chuckwagon break room, it had been impossible to make it to the main cafeteria, eat, and get back to work on time. They'd all had to eat lunch in a little break area behind the Gold Rush exit shop, Gold Rush Gem Exchange & Outfitters, and if you forgot to pack a lunch, your choices were Vending Machine Number One and Vending Machine Number Two. It was still a challenge to clock back in on time even after getting the Chuckwagon, but at least now she had a chance.

Once inside, she darted past a table full of Patriots from Patriot's Place (Patriot Patriots, or Double Patriots, they called themselves, to differentiate from the rest of AtB's Patriots) wearing their mobcaps and long dresses and knee stockings and knickerbockers, before sliding gratefully into a booth containing a lone Dodge City Patriot with damp blonde braids and red cheeks. Tabby looked up from her yogurt parfait and smiled. "Hey girl," she said. "You look hot."

"Hot sexy or hot sweaty?" Sonia asked, ripping open the lunch-box she'd snatched from the shelf on her way in. There was pudding in there. Cool, smooth pudding. Sonia wanted nothing else right now. Dessert first.

"Hot sweaty," Tabby said. "Sorry. But I am too. And I only have ten more minutes of break."

"Sorry for you. How late are you here today?"

"Five."

"Not bad."

"Not the worst."

They were quiet for a few moments. Sonia slurped down her chocolate pudding. The sugar hit her veins and made her feel like she could cope with the world again, even if there were yelling guests in it.

"Got yelled at for not speaking Spanish again," she offered after a few minutes of dedicated eating.

"By a guest?"

"By a guest, thank God! Can you imagine if a Patriot did it?" Sonia laughed. "But the weird part was her kid. This kid is like six years old and she looks up at me and says, 'You're a disgrace to your country.' Like a little evil robot. It was *creepy.*"

"Holy shit." Tabby winced as her teeth met a frozen strawberry. "That's *super*-creepy. Do you think she even knew what the words meant?"

"That's a good question. She might have been reciting something they taught her."

"Who would even do that, though?"

"Around here? Who wouldn't?"

They nodded, considering the people they encountered every day. You really got to see what people were like, working in a theme park. And it wasn't always pretty.

"Nick was here," Tabby said eventually. She pushed aside her empty yogurt cup.

"Anything good happen?"

"He asked if he could come to the beach with me in August."

Sonia looked up from her pudding. "Seriously? That's awesome!" She knew Tabby had been obsessed with Nick for a solid two months, ever since he showed up in a big Spring Break hiring rush. There'd been a sea of new people flooding the Underground, and for a while it had seemed like every face was unfamiliar, but now they were all a family, assimilated into the long-time AtB group.

"I know! Except—"

"Hmm?" Sonia dug deeper into her lunch-box. Baby carrots. Also cool and refreshing. Perfect. A+ job on packing your lunch this morning, Sonia.

"He hasn't asked me out or anything. Or given any

indication that he'd like to. So it's June and in six weeks we go to Palmetto Beach and…what? I don't even know what he wants. So now I have to figure out what happens *in between* now and then. I feel like I didn't get anywhere, you know?"

Sonia snapped open a pack of ranch dressing she'd liberated from Cowboy Cal's Good Grub when she'd come to the park as a guest last week. There were many ways to make a penny stretch when you were a Patriot on near-minimum wage, and condiment hoarding was one of the basics. "Girl. Didn't your mama teach you anything? Boys only want one thing, remember?"

Tabby smiled weakly. Sonia considered her, the dusting of brown freckles on her slightly upturned nose, her creamy skin which turned first pink and then tomato-red when she was hot, her big brown eyes, her fine blonde hair falling from its braid. Even without the prairie-girl costume, Tabby would be a straight-up Laura Ingalls Wilder lookalike. Or maybe just Laura Ingalls. Before she was old enough to be married. Because Tabby also had a beguiling fifteen-year-old never-been-kissed aesthetic going on, too. Sonia didn't find it attractive personally, but she knew it had driven Antonia absolutely wild. And before she'd come to Old Dodge City and met Antonia, it had spurred a succession of young, male Patriots to ask out the shy girl as well. Tabby had never lacked for partners, even if she'd never known what to do with them.

Too bad that now she had to moon over this pretty-boy, clueless skater kid Nick, while Antonia was just down the corridor outside the Chuckwagon, beautiful and clever and completely in love with her. Typical, though. Just typical. Sonia was highly skeptical of the dating game in general.

She preferred to keep herself to herself.

Tabby sighed tragically. "What should I *do?*"

"I think you're playing the right game with Nick," Sonia said finally. "You can't ask him out. He's too much of a guy. You're going to have to push him into it. Maybe flirt with someone else."

Tabby sighed. "With who? Winslow?"

"God no, not Winslow. You'll break his stupid heart." Sonia waved her carrot in the air. How was this her responsibility, exactly? "Tabby, do you realize you have two people completely into you and you're choosing to fixate on the one who's playing hard to get? This could be a bad tendency. Maybe it's best to get over it right now."

"I can't help it," Tabby shrugged. "It's just the way I am. I'll probably just end up hating him, anyway. That's the usual for me, right? I never get a second date. But I'm not usually into the guy like *this*, Sonia."

"You should be like me," Sonia suggested. "Nobody's into me, and I'm not into nobody. So much easier."

"That sounds ideal," Tabby agreed. "Maybe you're the lucky one."

Tabby's break was several minutes over, so she hopped up to clock in at the computer in the corner of the Chuckwagon, the one they officially weren't allowed to clock in on. She waved as she darted out the door, and Sonia sighed at her carrots. "Sure," she said. "I'm the lucky one. Only if I don't get Greeter again."

She had her fingers crossed for an air-conditioned position when she got back to work.

Nate

Nate couldn't control his excitement, and he didn't want to.

So he showed off to the crowds. Not that anyone was looking at him. The crush of people shoving through the turnstiles at America the Beautiful weren't looking at each other. They were stepping on each other, in fact, shoving each other in their rush to get into the park. There was no enmity as faceless as the family next to yours who might get into line for Gold Rush Rapids or Pirate's Bayou Adventure right before you; there was no peril as real as the group of tall strangers who might snag the last curbside seating along the afternoon parade route.

But Nate wasn't at AtB for the first time, or on his single cherished trip of the year. Finally, *finally*, he was here to *stay*.

So he let the crazed families carry him through the main entrance and past the steam engine guarding the front gates and into the neglected center of Independence Plaza's town square, with the miniature cannon and its miniature cannon balls stacked in a neat pyramid on the grassy lawn to his right, and the Victorian bandstand with its swags of Stars-and-Stripes bunting on the grassy lawn to his left. Directly ahead of him, past the bright Victorian promise of Independence Plaza, was the rocky peak of Promise Mountain. The waterfall plunging down its side to feed the curving Mighty Missouri off to its left was catching sunlight in its droplets; Nate knew there would be a mist hanging over the rocky grotto at the waterfall's base, with a rainbow dancing over the wispy branches of a weeping willow planted there when the park opened decades earlier. He couldn't wait to go seek it out.

He wanted to skip; he wanted to sing; he wanted to waltz along with the tinny ragtime piano playing from invisible speakers somewhere in the bricks arching over his head. He was here, this was happening, he had made it!

Nate pulled out his phone and began to live-stream video. The Independence Plaza Marching Band was due out any minute, and he had a job to do.

By the time the band had finished playing their brassy rendition of *Yankee Doodle*, he had about two hundred users on his live-stream, which was pretty good for mid-afternoon on a Tuesday. Not exactly star metrics, but he had just started this full-time theme park blogger gig, and he knew the numbers would come, as long as he kept pushing the content the fans all wanted.

And the theme park fans wanted all America the Beautiful, all the time. They all wanted to be *here*, not sitting at their desks, pushing paper and filling in spreadsheets. They all wanted to be *him*. The man who gave up the real world and returned to AtB for a life fulfilling his childhood dreams—to never grow up and never go home. The vacation that never ended, the check-out morning that never came, the wistful looks backward through a car's rear window that were never cast—this was Nate Potter's life now. He was literally living the dream.

And now he was going to sell it.

Nathan slowly turned his phone in a gentle roundabout, taking in a three-hundred and sixty-degree view of Independence Square which would give his viewers a thrilling view without making them feel a little green around the gills from motion sickness, then walked slowly towards Independence Street, Independence Plaza's central street. This shop-lined funnel led visitors into the park each morning and then gently booted them out, laden down with souvenirs, at the end of the night.

Nate's plan was to showcase a few of the beautifully decorated shop windows, maybe stop for a glazed doughnut at Betsy Ross's Bake Shop, and then take his viewers all the way to the shining rainbow grottoes beneath Promise Mountain. By then, he figured, he would need to pause and plug his phone in for a quick recharge.

Also, his feet would be tired and there was a cafe behind Promise Mountain where he could sit for a while.

But first, the glory of bustling Independence Plaza. He positioned his phone to give viewers the best view and started his stroll, avoiding the hustle of morning park-goers with some fancy footwork. Around him, the music swelled into a jaunty rag-time tune, a horse trolley squeaked past with the familiar clip-clop of hooves Nate only associated with this place, and the sugary scent of sweets came billowing out of Lady Liberty Treats and Notions.

"Good afternoon!" the fire chief called as he chugged by

on a shiny antique fire engine, waving a gloved hand in Nate's general vicinity.

Nate suppressed a wave of tears threatening to spill from his prickling eyes and gingerly waved back with his free hand, careful not to shake his phone too much as he pointed it at the grinning fire chief. "Good afternoon!" he called, his heart full.

The fire chief directed his engine on down the street, occasionally reaching down to squeeze the horn, honking it at laughing children, wary teens, overly excited parents. Nate turned the phone back towards the view down Independence Street. It was perfect, he thought. Completely perfect, with a few long-skirted young women waving from street corners, a young man in circusy stripes selling bright balloons, and the scent of cotton candy filling the air. Too bad he couldn't film that last part. He was contemplating saying something about the scene, perhaps describing the sugar-scent filling his nostrils, although he hadn't decided if personal narration was going be part of his brand, when the prairie girl entered the scene.

Nate stopped in his tracks and promptly had his ankle clipped by a tail-gating stroller. He howled and swore—so much for the debate about personal audio—and took a second to glare over his shoulder at the father pushing the stroller, who didn't so much as glance back at him, intent on getting his offspring to the carousels and flumes and coasters awaiting as quickly as possible. Then he focused back in on the prairie girl.

She had come out of a hidden door next to the sign for Madame deBussy's Piano Lessons and was hustling across Independence Street as if she thought speed was going to camouflage her.

Not so fast, Patriot, Nate thought, his mood somewhere between glee and outrage, and lifted his phone to capture the intruder.

Her green calico skirt swirled around her ankles and her fair cheeks were pink (with embarrassment? With exertion in the early morning heat?) above the frills of her coffee-colored blouse. Despite her skirt length and old-fashioned blouse, Nate could easily say she looked *nothing* like the refined Victorian Patriots of Independence Plaza, and she was ruining the perfect scene around her. Not quite an anachronism, but bad enough. What was next? Pirates wandering the street?

He decided it was time to go verbal to his live-stream audience. Forget his misgivings of before; he was going to be a narrator. After all, this was part of his brand at AtBLive: showing off the perfection of America the Beautiful *and* pointing out the careless and destructive people who marred that perfection!

He kept the phone trained on the prairie girl Patriot as she hustled up Independence Street, his commentary low-pitched so he wouldn't upset nearby park guests who might not understand the importance of his work. Casuals never did. "So here we have a Patriot blatantly flaunting park rules about character and land integrity, folks. Have you ever seen anything like this? A Patriot from Old Dodge City right here in the middle of Independence Plaza, totally ruining the magic. And oh look, she's got a shopping bag under one arm, so maybe she thought she would teleport from 1860s Old Dodge City and arrive here in 1910 Independence Plaza just to do a little shopping fifty years in the future! This is just unbelievable, folks. Lawrence Taylor must be spinning in his grave right now—"

"Sir, can I help you?" A hand on his arm. He had the foresight to end the live-stream before he turned. Across the Square, the Dodge City Patriot scurried through an arched doorway next to Town Hall and disappeared from view. Nate looked right and found the grave eyes of a park manager boring into his.

"No, I'm fine," Nate said automatically.

The manager, a small woman in her fifties who would have looked at home wielding a ruler in a one-room schoolhouse, brought her eyebrows together for a moment and regarded him. Sized him up. Nate began to sweat.

"Video recording for profit requires a permit from the press office," she said finally.

"That's not—I wasn't—it's just for personal use—" Nathan stammered. He'd heard about bloggers getting in trouble. Getting trespassed. Losing their right to visit the park at all! He'd have to be more careful. He watched her eyebrows slowly part.

"I'm sure it is," she agreed in a voice which told him she was not at all sure it was. "Just a friendly reminder. Enjoy your day at America the Beautiful."

And she strode away, a majestic figure in low black pumps, her litter-picker outreached to snag an ice-cream wrapper already cast to the ground.

Nate made sure he was safely hidden behind a willow tree near the foot of Promise Mountain before he was bold enough to take his phone out again. He opened up his streaming app and saw that he had three hundred and fifty-two new followers.

And they were commenting on the Old Dodge City Patriot footage, which meant he'd created controversy. On his *very first day*. Controversy was the currency of the internet, and Nate had bills to pay.

He made an involuntary squeak of joy, which the thundering waterfall thankfully drowned out.

Buoyed with the knowledge that on the very first day of his new life as an AtB blogger, he'd created a bona fide AtB fan scandal, and thrilled by the way his follower numbers were clicking skyward, Nate pushed his floppy brown bangs out of his eyes and decided to head deeper into the park, to ride some attractions and attempt more daring documentary exploits. Time to boost his engagement numbers!

He opened Twitter and posted: "Quick pick: Gold Rush Rapids or Bayou Pirate Adventure?"

Then, while he was waiting for his Twitter audience to provide him with his next adventure, a recorded announcement voiced by AtB's breathy female announcer stepped into fill the gap.

"In just five minutes, Petals and all of her friends will invite you on a wonder-filled journey through the spirit of America!"

"Perfect," Nathan murmured, checking his phone's charge. Almost full. He could stream the Promise Mountain stage-show before his next ride.

In front of the fiberglass peaks of Promise Mountain, a dozen or so families were gathering for the mid-afternoon performance of *America: Still Dreaming!* This preschooler-friendly (kind reviewers called it "vapid") seventeen-minute show featured characters which had been popular on Lawrence Taylor's old cartoon show, *Patriot Pals.* One show or another featuring the Patriot Pals had been in place at Promise Mountain Stage since the nineties.

In this adventure, Petals the Goose falls asleep the night before Independence Day and has a nightmare that the United States of America never fought the Revolutionary War. So she and her animal friends (including Lucky the Indian Pony, Maracas the Parrot and the real star, Edgar Eagle) have to work together to get the colonies to rise up against the British, staging everything from the Boston Tea Party to the ride of Paul Revere—this was Lucky the Indian Pony's big moment.

The whole thing wound up with Petals waking up to a huge Fourth of July party with all her friends and a fireworks finale shot from the peaks of Promise Mountain.

Although widely criticized in fan circles, the show always hit Nathan in all the feels. And his engagement on his blog, AtBLive, told him he wasn't alone in his affection. So now, he crept out of the misty grotto beneath Promise Mountain and into the hot sun of the plaza, finding himself a comfortable spot leaning against some iron railings, and as the show kicked off with a blaze of pyro and patriotism, he contentedly began to live-stream.

About midway through a bouncy musical number during the tossing of tea-chests, Nathan felt a pair of eyes on him. He looked to his left, through a cornfield of children on shoulders, and spotted the manager from Independence Plaza standing to one side of the crowd, picker in hands, expression grim, gaze trained on him. She'd followed him all this way?

Rattled, his hands started to shake and the appreciative comments on his stream immediately turned to complaints about the wobbling feed. He flipped the stream off and slipped the phone into his pocket where it burned against his leg, dangerously hot with the strain he was putting on it.

He'd have to upgrade, he thought, if he could just manage not to get thrown out of the park.

The very idea made a wave of nausea wash over him, and he suddenly had to sit down or risk fainting. His knees buckled and he slid down the iron railings, shoving several kids and parents on the way down. There was a buzz of "watch it buddy!" and "hey!" which turned to concerned questions as he leaned his head back against the bars and closed his eyes, his hands in fists at his sides. Then that sound, as well as the music from *America: Still Dreaming!* was drowned out by a rushing roaring in his ears that seemed to take over his entire being.

Nate strolled out of First Aid an hour later with a new lease on life, a free bottle of water in his hand, and a mandate from his Twitter followers to ride Gold Rush Rapids—which he fully intended on living up to, despite the nurse's stern command he take it easy the rest of the day and try to stay out of the sun.

"Heat stress can turn into heat stroke in no time," she'd informed him, placing another cold compress on his forehead. "It's going to be ninety-five degrees today. You'd be best off going back to the hotel, maybe taking a swim later."

"I'll do that," he promised, not bothering to tell her he lived here, a proud resident of American Gardens, the closest (although not the newest and certainly not the most luxurious) apartment complex to America the Beautiful's front gates. "Thank you. I'm not sure why the heat hit me so hard, it's never happened before."

"Heat and humidity can be harder on certain body types," she said morosely, eyeing his waistline. "It's a wonder more people don't drop out there. If you ask me, we ought to be running misting fans over the whole place."

Rejuvenated and wholly uninterested in the nurse's opinion, Nate swaggered over the wooden bridge into Old Dodge City and admired the view: Conestoga wagons and the waterfront to the right; a line of false-front frontier buildings bearing whimsical shop names to the left. A raised wooden boardwalk in front of the shops beckoned, where he could pretend he was keeping his gleaming white sneakers from growing dusty and begrimed in the manure of the streets; he clumped up the stairs and walked along it with heavy, clumping steps, enjoying the air conditioning gushing from each storefront. At Professor Cloud's, he paused and wandered inside; this was always one of his favorite shops. The decorations of fanciful ironwork, and all of Professor Cloud's wily inventions hanging from ceilings or draping from shelves, made him feel like he was walking through an old western movie every time he entered the store.

He was taking pictures of Professor Cloud's One & Only Rainmaking Device, Patented, when a door in the back wall opened and out walked the prairie girl.

Well, she was one of many in identical clothing. Green skirt, coffee-colored blouse, black flats: one of dozens in Old Dodge City. But she was definitely the girl he'd seen earlier crossing the Square, breaking all kinds of protocol by being in the wrong costume in the wrong area. She left the shop without looking left or right, heading outside, a grim expression on her face.

Nate followed her without thinking, leaving the cool confines of Professor Cloud's for the hot walkway outside. The girl crossed the flow of traffic with the artless way

Patriots had, dodging strollers and power-walking families on their way to and from Gold Rush Rapids without breaking stride. He watched her hasten to a Conestoga wagon bristling with sunglasses, where she had just handed a white slip of paper to another Patriot, who left here there with a sigh of relief and a twitch of calico skirts.

As soon as she was alone, Nate picked his way across the walkway and strolled up to the Conestoga wagon.

"I saw you earlier," he began, before the girl had even finished signing into the register.

She looked up from the screen, thin eyebrows raised, and Nate felt a quivering in his gut that wasn't unlike the heat stress/fear of being trespassed which had sent him to First Aid just an hour earlier. But it *was* something different. He gazed into her upturned eyes, pools of brown like a forest floor in autumn, looking back at him with wide-eyed worry like a startled deer, and then let his eyes slip down to her nose, to her cheeks, with four freckles—he counted them! —on either side. Eight perfect freckles and a slim pink mouth—she was like a cartoon princess lost in the woods, and he was a prince, and he would rescue her.

"Howdy, pardner," the princess in calico said, and her voice was a monotone with the slightest attempt at a spaghetti western drawl, as if she'd never heard anyone from Texas in real life and definitely didn't care to. "Did you need some sunglasses?"

Nate felt unreasonably angry, and he knew it was unreasonable, but that didn't stop the sudden, unexpected emotion from bubbling up. He saw everything good about her—the best she could do was give him a Themed Greeting, same as she would anyone else? He *wasn't* just anyone else, dammit. She should know that! A princess always knew her prince. He'd seen all the movies; he'd met most of the princesses, lounging in their air conditioned halls back in Fairytale Courtyard, their bow lips simpering as they treated him with the same deference they would a four-year-old girl in a gauzy costume gown.

"I saw you in Independence Plaza earlier," he pressed on, returning to his original intent, before thirty seconds ago, before he fell in love. "You were in the wrong costume. You broke the theme."

Her thin eyebrows flew up to her hairline—her adorable, wispy, flyaway brown-golden hair escaping the confines of her tight braid. "I broke—I'm sorry, what can I *do* for you, sir?"

"Admit you shouldn't have been there," Nate said desperately, because he had just realized he had no end-game for accosting her. He'd simply wanted to call out her wrongdoing. He'd done it; mission accomplished. But what was he supposed to do with his sudden new vision of her, a beautiful and wild creature who longed for him to save her? Nate was out of his depth. He backed away and nearly fell into a passing stroller.

"Watch it, buddy," the mother pushing it sneered. "You're not the only one here, you know."

He stumbled forward again, and the Patriot took a step back. His gaze fell on her name tag. *Tabby.* "Look, Tabby, we started off on the wrong foot here…"

"I'm just doing my job," Tabby interrupted. "My manager says to cross the Square in costume, so I cross the Square in costume. The parade floats were blocking the backstage entrance. I don't have a say, okay? I come to work, I do as I'm told, I go home. Now, do you want some sunglasses or not?"

"I have sunglasses," Nate explained, fishing them from his shirt's front pocket and holding them up for her to admire. They had a little etching of Edgar Eagle in one corner, because he'd bought them here, two years ago, on a summer vacation.

She didn't look at them. "So you just came over here to tell me you saw me in the Square?"

He put on the sunglasses to escape her glare. Those limpid brown eyes. Where had they gone? She had eyes like an eagle's. She had eyes like a wicked queen's. She had eyes like she wanted to murder him and dump his body in the Mighty Missouri. "I—what I meant was—"

Lost, confused, frightened: not words Nate expected to associate with his first day of his new life. Too flustered to speak to the girl, he pivoted and walked away, leaving her behind, pacing quickly towards Gold Rush Rapids. But he could feel her gaze on his back as surely as he'd felt the manager's pitiless eyes back in the plaza, promising him a world of hurt if he got caught acting out again.

CHAPTER FIVE

Sonia

The Gateway Pub was more like a TGI Friday's or an Applebee's than an actual pub, but it would've been a thriving dinner and late-night scene no matter what it was named, based solely on its prime real estate amidst the apartment complexes and subdivisions that housed the many Patriots of America the Beautiful. With an operation hungry for people to man everything from water slides to hotel desks to five-star restaurants to marketing professionals to sanitation workers, America the Beautiful's growth over the decades had resulted in an impromptu company town that grew up in the shadow of its rear gates, the "employee entrances" which were really just service roads leading to the property's jumble of theme parks and hotels.

Through the boom years and the bust decades, the Gateway Pub reigned serenely as a source of cheap beer and a place to blow off steam after a hard day's work in a theme park. All around it, housing developments rose and fell with the fortunes of Patriots dependent on the American leisure dollar. Townhouses and cheap old apartment houses clustered around the warehouses and employee recreation areas where Thursday night softball leagues still played each spring. Farther away, square footage and front lawns grew in size alongside the ambitions of Patriots moving up into management and corporate positions during expansion years. Luxury apartments crowded their way into vacant lots during the good years, and were promptly overrun with far more roommates than their leasing agents had ever expected.

And through it all, Gateway Pub remained a constant source of cheap beer and late-night appetizers, secure in its status as a hang-out for all ages, for all colors, for all creeds, for all departments. During their intern programs running rides and flipping burgers, the college students would discover Gateway's astonishing quarter wing nights; after their internships ended and they stayed on, slipping slowly into full-time gigs as leads and ride operators and front desk agents, the specials remained part of their lives.

They came for weekday specials on their hospitality industry "weekends" of Monday/Tuesday, or Wednesday/Thursday. Then they came on real-world weekends after they finally broke into management or a professional job at the big office building complex built near Legacy's back gate; as they got married and became fruitful and multiplied, they brought their children to the pub for chicken fingers and shared plates of nachos. Their lives changed, but their employer didn't, and neither did their devotion to the Gateway.

At Gateway Pub, unlike many other businesses in town, there was no Patriot discount, because it would have been issued to ninety percent of the patrons, and Gateway management was nice, but not stupid.

This evening, Sonia sat on Gateway's sunny back patio, which overlooked a rather uninspiring manmade lake with a single fountain shooting a pointless stream of water into the air, and drank a Long Island Iced Tea. It was well, not shelf, because she'd only gotten thirty-five hours last week and none of them had fallen into overtime, and she technically didn't have enough money to pay her share of rent unless she got at least twelve hours of overtime per month.

She was drinking a Long Island Iced Tea, not because she enjoyed it, but because it had more liquor in it than other mixed drinks, and when you weren't making overtime, you learned to stretch the few dollars you had. In the far distance, the hills of western Georgia loomed against the yellowy summer sky. She wished their dark ridges would swell and condense into storm clouds, and blow this way. Now that she wasn't at the park and at the mercy of thousands of angry tourists, none of them willing to shell out ten dollars for a cheap poncho and all of them furious that Rapids was closed because of lightning, she could afford to wish for a nice exciting thunderstorm.

Her roommate Elena was inside at the bar, picking up an order of Gateway's famous buffalo fries, the ones topped with hot sauce and melted cheese and sour cream. A large order. With extra cheese. Elena hadn't been able to wait another second for the bartender to bring them over, and Sonia hadn't slowed her down when Elena had decided she was taking matters into her own hands.

It had been that kind of day.

"That bartender is so slow. I'm standing there, and I see the fries sitting in the window, and I can't get him to bring them for like, five minutes." Elena returned, dropping the plate with a clatter on the table between them. "And then when I say, hey bring me those, he wants to look at me like I don't know, like I'm stealing them or something. He got a lot of nerve."

She threw herself down in the chair and applied the straw of her own Long Island Iced Tea to her face for a long, soothing pull. She smacked her lips and sighed. "Sorry. Long day," she mumbled around the straw, apparently unwilling to give up her conduit to alcohol just yet.

"You and me both," Sonia said with a grimace. "Everyone today was bitching about something. The regulars bitched about new rides. The new people bitched about old rides. Don't you start too."

"Ai, no," Elena said, waving a hand in apology. "I won't, I won't."

They picked at the fries, slowly at first, and then without reserve, plowing through the plate, licking their fingers clean of sauce between bites. It was the way close friends binged, a judgment-free zone of dripping hot sauce and slowly congealing nacho cheese. Elena and Sonia had been roommates since their college internships, more than a year ago, and after their sessions had ended, they'd gotten a shabby one-bedroom apartment together and stayed on at AtB as full-time Patriots. Elena worked in retail in Independence Plaza, which meant her hours were all over the place—the Plaza, as the entrance and exit of the park, was open first and closed last, the Patriot on door duty trailing the very last park guests to the store exit and locking it behind them. It was a notoriously exhausting place to work.

"I'mma transfer to Legacy," Elena remarked after they'd been chewing in silence for a few minutes. She wiped her fingers and pulled her ponytail back tighter. Her cheekbones, always flawless, seemed to grow in prominence, as if she'd given herself a mini-facelift. "In Ride Operations. Maybe the Betsy Bombers ride. I like the costumes there."

"You'd look good in the Betsy costume," Sonia agreed. The female Bombers Patriots wore a bright blue 1950s style dress, with a high waist and a full skirt. There was a wide red belt. It was the kind of thing that looked great in concept art, but with results that varied wildly in the real world. Elena's sultry curves would be perfect for it, but she looked great in most things. She even made the Plaza's Victorian garb look hot. "They'll call you Betsy Bombshell. I heard that's what the best-looking girl is called over there. There's a bulletin board of past winners in the break room, like a pin-up girl type thing."

"That's good," Elena said contentedly. "I'd be a good bombshell." She waved to a waitress and held up two fingers: a second round. "You should go too. Rapids is making you crazy."

"What's crazy about me? I'm sitting here quietly, enjoying an adult beverage. You're the one who went off on the poor bartender."

"That bartender, he has no problems. He should try being a Patriot sometime. We're like saints after the people we deal with all day. We should go straight to heaven when we die. I do all my purgatory at work all day."

This was probably true, Sonia reflected. She wasn't terribly religious, but there was no doubt her soul was being forged by fire on a daily basis. Just looking at her credit card bills was surely penance enough for any wrong she'd done to others in life. "Well, still. Anyway, I should stay in one place. I think I'll apply for Ops Lead. It's time to think about moving up. That extra dollar an hour would help a lot, as sad as it is to say that."

"*Everyone* wants to move up at AtB." Elena rolled her eyes. "You got too much competition. At Legacy, you actually have a shot. There's not a thousand old people in your way who never want to do anything but be a lead so they can sit at a desk half their shift."

"But I don't want to leave America," Sonia said. "I like it there. And it's busier than Legacy. There's like no overtime at Legacy, so I go from not being able to pay my bills to actually going bankrupt. Also, I get pushed harder. It's better experience for management. If I'm a lead at Legacy, they're not going to make me a manager at AtB. I'll have to wait for a position to come up at Legacy. Why take the risk and wait longer?"

"Says your manager, who doesn't have any spots open for Ops Leads, so what difference does it make?" Elena accepted her fresh glass from the server with exemplary manners. She did everything but kiss the waitress's hand. Show-off, Sonia thought. Typical Elena. "You gotta make your own opportunities, my dear Sonia. Push and shove a little. Show off your New Jersey, if you refuse to show off your P.R."

"What does that mean?" Today was apparently Pick on Sonia's Heritage Day. "Why is everything a contest to see how Latina I can be?"

"Everything? Girl, sounds like you've been thinking about this on your own time. Don't look at me that way."

Sonia realized she hadn't told Elena about the woman who'd shouted at her for not speaking Spanish, or the weird little girl who told her she was a disgrace to her people. Except for the kid, the incident was too common to have really stood out. Or it should have been. But the fact that she was still thinking about it troubled her a little. Usually she laughed this stuff off. *You're just getting tired,* she told herself. *You need a vacation. You need a few days at the beach.*

June was not the time to need a vacation when you worked in a theme park, though. That ship had sailed for the summer.

"Hey Sonia! Hey Elena!" A chirpy little voice came from the parking lot. Sonia looked over and saw Tabby waving her skinny arm.

"Oh, here we go," Elena muttered.

Sonia narrowed her eyes at her roommate. "You be nice." She turned back to Tabby. "Hey girl! Come sit with us!"

Tabby's face lit up with an embarrassing level of happiness. At least, it embarrassed Sonia. She wasn't sure what she'd ever done to garner this level of affection from the willowy little Tabby, besides being thoughtful and listening when they'd first come to AtB in the same internship session.

It had been a long six months—all the program veterans said the summer-fall session, from August to January, was the hardest one, because it took the students away from their families during the holidays, often for the first time in their lives. There were no breaks for Thanksgiving or Christmas, just mandatory overtime and crowds. No one got through their session without their share of tears and breakdowns, but Sonia seemed to remember Tabby falling apart more than most. Many nights, Tabby ended up in Sonia's living room, the one she shared with two other girls besides Elena, even though she lived three doors down, with a group of presumably less-understanding girls.

Then, once she'd decided to stay at AtB and not go back to college, she'd turned that frown upside-down and started a series of brief and ostentatious flings with departing Patriot interns and sundry hot guys visiting on vacation. They'd ended when Tabby had, briefly and startlingly, begun seeing Antonia, a cool and collected Patriot who liked the early shifts and didn't speak unless she had something worth saying.

Too bad that didn't last, Sonia often thought. Too bad about Nick.

"Be nice," Sonia hissed to Elena. "She's having boy problems."

"Ai, Jesus Christ," Elena sighed. "What else?"

CHAPTER SIX

Tabby

Tabby slipped into the patio chair across from Sonia and Elena and smiled excitedly at them both. So nice to be included! It was one thing to eat with Sonia at the Chuckwagon; it was another to be part of the gang outside of work. Tabby wasn't sure she'd ever stop feeling like an outsider. Her isolated childhood, her evenings filled with silent prayer, hadn't exactly set her up for a successful social life. It had been tough enough trying to figure out how to behave out in the world, and she knew she'd made a lot of mistakes—even given herself a reputation for a sex life she was pretty sure she wasn't capable of living up to. So, after those first rebellious months after she'd quit college, Tabby hit the brakes on trying to fit in. It just wasn't going to happen for her.

But she was happy to be on the periphery of things.

Reassured of her place with Elena and Sonia, who

sometimes felt a bit like the couple of their trio, Tabby settled against the back of the chair with pleasure and ordered a margarita from the approaching waitress before she could even come to a halt at the table. She knew from commercials and movies that margaritas were what a girl drank in summertime. Tabby never ordered anything else when the temperature was over seventy degrees. In the winter, she drank wine, mostly chardonnay. She'd never figured out what else was okay to order, what looked normal for a twenty-two-year-old girl, and she wasn't willing to ask. If she asked, she'd have to explain.

Of course, her friends didn't know she needed the coaching. It would have been too embarrassing to share that she came from a dry house, a staunchly religious house without a TV or a cable modem, and had never tasted alcohol before she'd come to America the Beautiful. It was bad enough that her roommates had seen the tearful altercation when her mother had come to collect her from the AtB dorms at the end of their internship, refusing to accept that Tabby wasn't coming home, wasn't going back to the Bible school thinly veiled as a private university, and was staying at a godless theme park instead of returning to her mother and her duty and her Gospel. The prayers, the wailing, the hymns flung at her like bullets!

Sonia had seen all that, and some others had shared it around; AtB knew that Tabby Wilkerson came from a very disturbing background, as much as AtB knew about or cared about Tabby Wilkerson. But that didn't mean she cared to discuss it.

There were too many other things to think about to worry about what a girl could drink besides margaritas and white wine, anyway. Every single day at AtB was an eye-opener in some way or another. Every shift, Tabby heard or saw something that hadn't been part of her world back in the hills of Kentucky.

Antonia, of course, had been the strangest thing of all.

She still wasn't sure exactly what had happened.

"You'll be exposed to worldly people," her mother had said sadly when Tabby started driving to town for college classes, and again when she announced she'd been accepted to the America the Beautiful internship program.

"Of course I won't," Tabby lied boldly, because being exposed to worldly people was all she wanted, all she'd ever wanted since she was a little girl and had realized her family wasn't just different. They were insanely different. TV-movie different.

But just being exposed to worldly people wasn't enough to make Tabby feel like she was one of them, even after three years out here on the other side. So instead she pretended, hard, to be normal. She pretended, hard, that she wasn't disappointed with the mundane reality of the real world. The truth was, her parents seemed to have oversold the wickedness of the worldly. Tabby found that when you took away the veneer of enchantment which America the Beautiful painted across everything from hotel rooms to stairwells, the world wasn't a tempting and delicious place Satan had built to trip her up after all. It just had fewer rules than the world she'd already lived in.

Maybe Antonia had been what they'd been afraid of.

She still wasn't sure exactly what had happened there. Had she been in love with a girl? Was that what that had been? She still lay awake in bed some nights, wondering how to name what she'd felt with Antonia. The excitement she'd felt when Antonia had touched her like a favorite possession, stroking her hair or the sensitive skin of her neck, when she'd laid her lips on Tabby's with the most gentle, delicate of kisses, when Antonia's fingers had strayed beneath her shirt and cupped her breasts—or rather breast, only one at a time, never both, lest Tabby run away like a frightened hare—had been the most thrilling sensations her body had ever shown her. Nothing about it had felt wrong. And since her sole knowledge of homosexuality, before heading off to college, was that the word meant two men were in love with one another and that her parents said it was wrong, she hadn't been afflicted with the immediate repulsion of the idea that a similarly religious girl should have felt. She'd just felt wonder.

In fact, that was the main thing Tabby had felt from the day she'd arrived at America the Beautiful. She'd felt *wonder*.

The elaborate set-pieces that were her living stage, where she dressed up in costume and performed for guests every day, were a complete departure from the real world. Tabby wandered the theme park on her days off with a constant sense of wonder, living a half-dozen new lives with every visit.

In Patriot's Place, she was part of the colonial era, part of the American Revolution, as surely as if she'd traveled back in time, but without the really dirty parts, the manure and the sewage in the streets and the body odor. It was similar whether she was in Liberty Village, or Old Dodge City, or The Big Apple, or Pirate Bayou, or the Forgotten Forests—she was transported completely, to a place that was better than real life.

Coming to AtB on that internship had been a genuine revelation to Tabby, and that was why she decided she would not leave. On the hardest days, the hottest and coldest and wettest and the most frustrating of shifts, she still clocked out and thought, "Today was wonderful."

She still felt so lucky to be here.

She'd never felt such perfect happiness in her life, and she understood why families came from all over the world to vacation for just a few days inside this joyful bubble, reveling in the perfect interpretation of yesteryear, of the best of America.

Sure, it wore thin some days. And when she was around some of her coworkers, especially the older long-time Patriots, her spirit of wonder just seemed to annoy them. If you went too long without taking some time to visit as a guest, to "play" in the park, as they called it, you got bitter and miserable and mean. One of the lemon-faced old Patriots, who worked the morning shift Monday through Friday in Professor Cloud's, hadn't visited the park to play in more than twenty-five years. You could tell. She hated the place.

But once, she must have loved it.

That kind of thing made Tabby nervous. Her mother, and some of her college friends who came for one session before going back to their studies, told her she'd end up the same way, that she'd ruin the wonder for herself. But Tabby couldn't imagine herself anywhere else. She couldn't picture herself back in the real world, where life was just classes and the trailer where she'd always lived and stopping at the grocery store and bringing home McDonald's for supper because it was too late to cook anything she'd bought, anyway.

Life out there was a series of chores and nothing else. Where was the show? Where was the wonder? Where were the fireworks and the parades and the happy, perfect, always-in-tune background music playing her through her day?

A life without everything she had at AtB didn't even compute for her anymore.

She knew the others found her naïve, but she hoped they also found her charming. She hoped they also found her worth protecting. Because she was giving America the Beautiful all she had, and when real things happened—things like missing a rent payment, or needing new tires for her battered old car, or Antonia, or Nick—she really did need help processing them.

She sipped at her margarita, the salt tingling against her sunburned lips, and smiled at her friends. "Thanks again for letting me join you. I hope I didn't interrupt anything."Elena dabbed a hand in the air: please. "Tell us what's new, girl."

Tabby glanced at Sonia: should she talk about Nick? Did Elena know Nick? Everyone knew everyone, but Independence Plaza people kept their own hours and their own secrets. They should have seemed like outsiders, but instead they just made everyone else feel like they were the outsiders, like the Plaza was where it was at, and all those outlying territories were just waiting rooms for the Patriots who couldn't hack it with the toughies at the front of the park.

Elena might know something about Nick she didn't; or she might think Nick wasn't worth talking about, and then Tabby would have ruined their conversation. She gave Sonia a pleading look: *please start this for me.*

Sonia sighed. "Anything good happen with you and Nick after your break?"

Okay, Sonia was opening with Nick. That meant it was

okay for Tabby to talk about Nick. Tabby took a deep breath. "He actually came out to help at Wagons, so we got to talk some this afternoon. It was nice. But he seemed really like—shy? I don't know. Like he didn't know what to say to me. And I didn't know what to say to him. So, that was a problem. And then there were guests. So, um, I don't know."

"Oh well," Elena said vaguely. She put a finger on the empty plate on the table, swirled the tip around in the leftover sauce, brought it to her mouth, and sucked it off. Tabby watched attentively, as she watched everything the others did, ready to learn what was acceptable and what wasn't, how far she could go, what responses their actions would elicit. She was a human sponge, soaking up behaviors and reactions.

"Stop that," Sonia told Elena, sliding the plate out of her reach. She held up a hand to the passing waitress. "Another buffalo fry, please."

Interesting. Had Elena's intention been to get Sonia to order more food? "I got this one," Tabby offered, because she knew people loved free food. "I got an hour of OT today. Nick got three. Elsa Barrett called sick, and so did Renata Forsyth, but I think they just went up to Atlanta for the night."

"Nice," Sonia said appreciatively. "And thank you."

"So, Nick," Tabby began. "He said he doesn't want to stay in Retail."

"No one wants to stay in Retail," Elena said. "Retail is awful."

Tabby shrugged. "I like Retail."

"You've been in Retail like, two months? Just wait."

"I was in Operations for an entire year," Tabby reminded

her. "You want to talk about awful. I wore that scratchy Patriot's Place dress until I thought I was going to tear my own skin off and run naked out of the White House Gallery. All the animatronic first ladies would have seen me and clawed their robot eyeballs out. The Liberty Bell would have cracked again, from the horror of it all. I was lucky to get to Pirate Bayou when I went full time. But really, we were all lucky."

There was a moment of silence while Elena and Sonia soaked up this impressive imagery. Tabby congratulated herself, for the second time that day, on her ongoing mastery of the English language. She totally could've gotten that degree with honors.

"On the other hand," Elena shrugged finally. "The guests would have loved it."

"They'd probably write letters of appreciation," Sonia added.

"Well, either way. Have you ever spieled an attraction? It's the most boring job imaginable. You are basically a robot." Tabby shifted her voice into an amplified version of itself, like the woman who read the TSA announcements at the airport. " 'Welcome, ladies and gentlemen, to the White House Gallery, where we recognize the great symbols of the United States of America. In 1776, our great nation's forefathers came together to create a more perfect union, where freedom of expression and thought would reign, instead of kings and queens. Throughout the next two hundred and fifty years, our country has weathered many challenges and seen many changes, but our crowning principles still shine as a beacon to the world. Now, America the Beautiful invites you to take a seat, relax, and witness some of the America's most spectacular shining moments. Please stand clear of the doors until they are fully open, then move all the way down the row before sitting to make room for everyone. Oh, (chuckle) and no flash photography, please. And now, the White House Gallery!' "

A few people around the patio applauded, including the waitress, who had just set down their second plate of fries. "You Patriots are so cute," she said condescendingly, and departed.

"And you say that three times an hour," Tabby concluded. "And in between, you tell people where the restrooms are."

"How is that unlike what you do now?" Elena countered. "Except you say, 'That will be twenty-one dollars and forty-three cents,' and then 'Have a beautiful day!' fifty times an hour, *and* you tell everyone where the restrooms are. At least with the spiel you have a lot more down-time."

Sonia, who did not work at a spieling attraction but found herself repeating the same boring lines over and over, had the grace to keep quiet.

Tabby took a gulp of her margarita, letting the tequila shiver its way down her spine and into her legs, tickling happily along the way. It was nearly impossible for her to explain to people that she didn't *want* the down-time. She wanted to talk to people, to everyone, to make sure they understood and loved America the Beautiful as much as she did.

Some days, like today, sure, she got tired, she got hot, she didn't put enough energy into her Themed Replies and the guests just didn't get it. And yeah, sometimes weird people bothered her, like that guy who came up to her after her fifteen-minute break this afternoon, talking about when she'd gone across the Square earlier. Like it was any of his business that she had to run a dropped stuffed animal up to Lost and Found and the parade floats were backed up in front of Town Hall's back entrance! Such a weirdo. He was probably a character-chaser, Tabby reflected. Lining up to talk to college girls dressed like cartoon characters, as if he was still a little kid. Some of them ended up getting obsessed, having to get trespassed. He seemed like that type. She hoped she would not end up with a stalker before he did.

But, ultimately, he was not a big deal. Not the norm. Today was just a bad day. Everyone had them. Most days, she woke up and raced to work because she couldn't wait to be there, being part of the wonder.

Most days.

"I think Tabby should stay in Retail," Sonia said seriously. "She likes a lot of guest contact. She wants to talk to everyone."

Tabby looked up, surprised. "I do! I actually do, even though I don't really feel like that on the outside. How did you know that?"

"Because you haven't changed," Sonia explained. "You're the same Tabby that came here from college and had her mind blown by America the Beautiful. You haven't burned out. And I wish we all could be like you."

Tabby excused herself to visit the restroom while the others were slowly and determinedly plowing through the second plate of fries, and gave herself a quick once-over in the mirror. The Gateway restrooms were decorated with vintage AtB photos, lots of black-and-white pictures of bobby-soxers dancing in front of The Big Apple's own Empire State Building on the old Big City Stage (since replaced, rather anticlimactically, with a pretzel cart, although at least it had an authentic green-and-white umbrella just like the ones in real New York City parks) and smiling children with shaggy haircuts and striped shirts holding up Technicolor balloons shaped like Edgar Eagle, the park's quietly moldering cartoon icon.

Old Edgar got little love in the wider world these days—he was no Mickey Mouse—but there was still a significant subset of America who grew up with, and loved, the half-fierce, half-goofy bald eagle. Tabby knew, because she sold them t-shirts and sunglasses and caps with his image emblazoned on them all day, every day, for $29.95 and up.

She pushed her wispy hair behind her ears and made a face at herself, blowing out her cheeks, then pouting her lips. She had an idea that if she made clowning, kiddie faces at herself, it might make the resulting image more adult. It never seemed to work; it just left her with an image of herself that stayed put for hours; Tabby as a blowfish. But she kept trying, because nothing else was working. Nothing made Tabby look her age.

Not her amateurish hand with makeup, which frightened her so much she kept things to a strict max of a swipe of lip gloss and a dusting of powder to keep her nose from getting too shiny on hot days. Not her thin head of hair, which never seemed to do anything but rest limply on her shoulders and fall into her eyes when she was trying to count back change to guests. Not her limpid brown eyes, which looked to her, now and always, like the eyes of a frightened animal who just wanted to find its den and hide there, safe from hunters. Certainly not those eight damned freckles, four on each side of her nose, settled in a contented dapple across her thin cheeks, making her look like an over-conceptualized animation, before the artist realized some things had to be left to chance if it was going to look real, and deleted a couple.

That was the problem, Tabby often thought. She was half-done, a maquette who had never gone to production, like one of those prototype Ophelia Owl sculptures on display in the Independence Plaza House of Wonders. Everything was just almost there, realized in part, and then abandoned before it was completed. No Ophelia Owl cartoons, no Ophelia Owl movies—just a display of what might have been, if the artists had been motivated to finish what they'd started.

And she wasn't just talking about her face. She couldn't imagine doing anything more than the handful of one-night stands she'd invented her racy sex life out of. There was no one out there who could have a relationship with a half-finished girl. They'd find her out immediately.

The door opened and Molly, Tabby's roommate, came in. She jumped as if Tabby had pointed a taser at her. "Tabby! Holy shit, you scared me."

This was a weird greeting considering the fact that Tabby had not moved, but Molly was very dramatic. "I thought you were working a double today."

Molly sighed. "We ended up over-scheduled and I offered to leave early. There was a huge group checking in but most of them are on late flights, so it's going to be the graveyard crew's problem after all."

"It must be weird to know exactly when your guests are going to arrive," Tabby said. She gathered up her purse to go back to the patio.

"You know when they're going to arrive at the parks," Molly said with a grin. "All the time, from nine a.m to ten p.m., seven days a week until September."

"You know what I mean. The hotel just seems like a completely different life."

"Oh it is," Molly agreed, disappearing into a stall. "Thank God."

And what was that supposed to mean? Tabby mulled it over as she made her way back to the table on the patio. What exactly was wrong with working in her beautiful, magical theme park? She was still feeling a little miffed when Sonia and Elena beamed at her.

"We've decided on something," Elena said. "We're going to set you up with Nick."

Tabby sat down with a thump. "What? Why?"

"Someone has to do it," Sonia said, shrugging. "You two would be cute together."

"It's community service," Elena told her. "You need an actual boyfriend. Not whatever that was last year."

"Oh." Tabby blushed. "You mean all the dates I went on…"

"And the rumor that you put out on every single one, yes," Elena finished mercilessly. "That's what I mean. What were you thinking? Don't answer that. I know you weren't thinking at all."

"It's complicated," Tabby said miserably. How to explain the need to drown twenty-two years of indoctrination all at once, like stuffing a struggling donkey into a rain barrel? Freed of her mother and her suffocating brand of Christianity, Tabby embarked on her own personal rumspringa, but the vamping she'd picked up from TV and movies hadn't exactly matched what she was actually willing to offer the lifeguards and ride operators who had taken her out for wings and nachos at the Gateway. It had only taken one night rebuffing a particularly vindictive guy's octopus-like embrace in the Gateway parking lot for Tabby's reputation at AtB to go from nonexistent to slutty. Naturally, her perceived status got her a lot of new inquiries, and for a while, she accepted them all.

Then she quit dating.

Then, Antonia.

And now?

Tabby drank more of her margarita than was wise and choked. When she finished spluttering, Sonia and Elena were engrossed on something on Sonia's phone.

"What are you watching?" Tabby recognized the background music from Liberty Plaza. "Is that a park video? Did something happen?"

Sonia flicked her gaze at Tabby. "Uh, Tabby? Did you go up to Liberty Plaza today? In your Dodge City costume?"

Tabby felt her fingers go numb. "What? What are you watching?" She snatched at the phone, and Elena spun it around. Tabby saw herself crossing the Square, looking conspicuous in her out-of-place costume. "That's so weird," she said. "Who would video me like that?"

Then she remembered the guy at the wagons. The weird one who had said he'd seen her at the Square. She'd been so creeped out she'd given him an angry glare that ordinarily would never make it onto her face at work, and he'd left her alone. But this—she looked at the video title. BIG COSTUME NO-NO BREAKS CHARACTER AT AtB!!

"What the hell? Who sent you this?" Tabby looked around the Gateway patio, and her heart sank. One by one, heads were lifting from phones and looking in her direction.

"It was Tawny, from Pirate Operations," Sonia admitted.

"You used to work with her, right?"

"I did, yeah, but why would she be spreading this around? We got along just fine."

"Someone else sent it to her, and she said she didn't have your info, so…" Sonia realized it was a flimsy excuse. They all had each other's info. It was the magic of a place called Facebook.

Tabby shook her head. "My manager sent me. It's not like I chose this."

She leaned back in her chair, hurt and shaken beyond measure. And when she noticed a group of people headed her way, she seriously considered climbing under the table. Thinking only of escape, Tabby looked around the patio, meeting all those eyes without meaning to.

And then she realized something: no one was laughing.

"Hey." A lanky guy with a pirate flag tattoo on his forearm stopped next to their table. "You're the Tabby from the video, right?"

"She is," Sonia said, "and if you bother her—"

"That blogger guy is bullshit," the pirate said. "What, we don't work hard enough, all hours of the fucking day and night, for these people? They gotta come in and fucking document us?"

"I'm sick of it." The young woman just behind him was wearing an Ophelia Owl t-shirt. Tabby thought she'd seen her working the turkey leg stand at the crossing between Patriot's Place and Old Dodge City. "It shouldn't even be legal for him to do that to you. If we see him in the parks again, we're gonna make sure he knows how we feel."

Tabby's heart was pounding so hard against her ribs, she couldn't draw enough breath to speak. She just stared, with glistening eyes, as her fellow Patriots drew around her table, promising dire consequences for the next time Nate of AtBLive patronized their park. Empty threats, maybe, but it sure felt good to know she was part of the pack.

CHAPTER SEVEN

Antonia

Fireworks were popping outside Antonia's living room window, but she couldn't be bothered to watch tonight, and her sheer apathy made her a little sad.

After all, when she'd first moved to Gateway Club, the fireworks view from every room in the tiny apartment had been a major selling point. Talk about a launch-pad for dreams! Antonia shed her old, crowded self, the person who had grown up with two other siblings in her bedroom, the person who had just spent six months living with three giggling, apparently insomniac college girls while trying to work impossibly varied theme park hours, at the front door of her own personal five hundred and twenty-five square feet. She'd paid extra for the third-floor apartment with the fireworks view, which had meant cutting back from a large one-bedroom with a den to the small base model—a bedroom, a bathroom, a kitchen that peered into the living room over a short counter.

Well, what did she need a lot of room for? She was just one person. For the first time in her life, Antonia *felt* like just one person.

What she hadn't banked on was loneliness, and to be fair, she wasn't lonely, very often. Just on nights like this, after a disappointing day at work. It just seemed like now, three years into this career, there were more disappointing days now than ever before.

And after coming home feeling defeated by the very park shooting off pyrotechnics a few miles away, who could feel like getting up from the couch to watch them?

Antonia shifted, slipping the fleece blanket with a grinning Edgar Eagle on it from her shoulders. She was always under a blanket; the apartment was usually so cold in the summer that flannel pajamas were not out of the question. This was intentional. Antonia reveled in her central air; she'd never been in control of her own thermostat before, and her childhood summers had rumbled with the struggles of insufficient, battered window units. She adored coming home and turning her thermostat down to sixty-nine or sixty-eight, watching condensation gather on the sliding glass doors, letting the heat of the day melt from her bones. Southeast Georgia was hot and muggy in summer, and this year she'd turned the AC on in early May and hadn't looked back.

The electric bill was becoming a problem, though.

Everything was becoming a problem.

So she'd turned the air conditioning up to a steamy seventy-eight and she hated it.

She flicked her thumb up her phone, watching the lives of old friends and current coworkers go sliding by.

Cocktails in Manhattan, coffee in Seattle. Social media was a series of cliches, everyone vying to complete as many hackneyed movie-star versions of themselves as possible before they got old, before they slowed down, before they started posting pictures of their children holding up vaguely threatening signs that said things like "I'm starting pre-K today!" These grinning preschoolers looked like they were holding up newspapers with the day's date on it, like tiny well-dressed kidnapping victims, but Antonia had found that sharing this information with the handful of cousins and friends who had already begun breeding did not go over well. No one wanted their cliches ruined with cynicism.

And she, Antonia, was not supposed to be cynical anyway! She was supposed to be the *least* cynical of all of them. Her business was wonder, her business was suspending reality, so that stressed humanity could flock to the gates of her theme park and let their cares drift away. The cynical Patriots ruined it for everyone. Working at America the Beautiful required an almost unearthly level of enthusiasm and cheer if you were going to do it right. Let the working hours, near-impossible standards of behavior and dress, brutal extremes in weather, demanding guests, and slippery promotion opportunities get to you, and you were lost for good.

Antonia told herself things weren't that bad. She wasn't where she wanted to be—a lead, on her way to management, the first big stepping-stone in a prospective thirty-year-career working for the cartoon eagle—but she had time. It took time. She wasn't the only one with big dreams. And tomorrow was another opportunity to shine.

Or melt, she thought morosely, kicking off her socks in

another concession to the rising warmth of the room. It didn't seem fair that if she had to be baking hot at work all summer, she had to deal with it at home, too.

Oswald, Antonia's cat, stalked into the living room and glared up at her from the bland beige carpet. His black-and-white fur bristled with his obvious disappointment in her. He wanted to be in the bedroom, curled up on her pillow, with his feet on her face.

"Meow," he demanded. *"Meeeeeeooooooow!"*

"It's not bedtime yet," Antonia told him. "You hush."

Oswald jumped onto the coffee table, a place where he was not supposed to sit but where he spent most of his waking hours and a decent chunk of his sleeping ones, and fixed his green, unblinking eyes upon Antonia. The effect was unnerving. She sat upright again, the blanket now falling to the floor to join her abandoned socks. "You can't tell me what to do, cat," she announced, but even she could tell it sounded more like she was trying to convince herself. "Go eat some supper." She pointed at the untouched dish a few feet away in the galley kitchen. "You'll feel better after you eat."

The cat blinked at her, slowly, insolently. He didn't like the food in the dish. It wasn't his usual food. It was the store brand. *The store brand?* his insolent gaze said. *I should fucking kill you for this.*

"Well, that's what there is," Antonia said stoutly. "I eat food I don't like all the time. That's part of being poor. You learn to deal with it."

She reached out a tentative hand—you never knew how Oswald was going to react—and was relieved when he leaned into her touch, letting her rub his luxurious fur coat. She loved him despite his constantly shifting moods.

Oswald was the first pet she'd ever had; there were no pets in the seven-child household of the Johnsons, back in Baltimore. Who had room or money for animals when there were children underfoot everywhere: children sleeping on couches, children sleeping on the floor, children dozing on the stoop on hot nights because the street was cooler than the stuffy, crowded rooms behind them?

"A *cat!*" Mrs. Johnson had rumbled in horror on the family's one and only road trip down to visit Antonia in her new life. "What you want with a *cat* in your house?"

"I wanted a dog," Antonia explained patiently, "but the deposit was too much and they only charge fifty dollars to add a cat to the lease. Plus, I don't need to walk it. I don't want to work late and then come home to wander around waiting for a dog to poop."

Her mother seemed to physically stagger backwards, but it really was only a gesture, one of her signature moves that made social workers leap up to make tea and door-to-door salesmen apologize for knocking on her door. "Poop, she says! *Poop!* And what about the money, huh? You gotta pay to feed that thing."

"I make enough money to feed a cat," Antonia told her firmly. "I make enough money for this whole apartment, and to take care of myself and one little cat. And in a year or two, I'll get promoted and I'll make even more."

This had been two years ago. Her fingers curled in Oswald's fur.

At the time, she'd really believed that. Who could have predicted that two years later, she'd still be in the same position, still just a Retail Patriot, with the only advantage that her five years' seniority gave her the chance to pick up the stockroom shifts and avoid constant guest contact?

Patriots got content stocking shelves and spent years doing it. They spent careers doing it. Antonia had to guard against complacency; she had to be ambitious every single day, even if that simple act of resistance was enough to induce an exhaustion and depression she hadn't previously thought was in her nature.

Oswald grew tired of her touch and jumped to the floor, where he stalked, stiff-legged with a show of resistance, over to the plastic cat-food dish. After a moment, she heard him crunching, slowly, as if every bite was a torture to him. But at least he was eating.

"I'm sorry, buddy," she said out loud. "I'll try to get some OT next week." Of course, she needed the OT money to pay the electric bill, and to buy herself a new pair of black work shoes—the ones she had were ripping apart at the heel, and if she ended up with all guest-facing shifts once old-timer Leeann was back on the schedule, her managers would not appreciate her shoes looking so rough. But she figured she'd have to spare an extra five dollars to get the more expensive food Oswald preferred. Who knew what was in that cheap stuff? It wasn't fair to him. He hadn't asked to be a poor Patriot's cat. He could probably eat better in the Dumpster behind the Gateway Pub.

Antonia shifted uncomfortably again and then decided: to hell with the electric bill. It was June—there would be overtime—she could pay it. She got up and knocked the thermostat down with slow, deliberate taps. *Tap*—75 degrees. *Tap*—74 degrees. *Tap*—73 degrees. *Tap*—72 degrees. The motor was running outside, hidden somewhere three stories down and in the bushes; the cold air was pouring down from the vent above her; the goosebumps were rising on her flesh. She put out her bare arms and sighed with pleasure. This was what it felt like to drown your miserable childhood: to put on your air conditioning as cold as you liked and pretend you were the ice goddess of your own tiny land.

Antonia was nodding off over the overtime shifts on the AtB PatriotPortal app, her thumb loose on the screen of her phone, when the damn thing began buzzing all over the place. She jumped and dropped it with a clatter, which sent Oswald into a panic. The cat went racing around the room, knocking over Antonia's tiny collection of AtB bric-à-brac she'd picked up from the company store, adding further damage to the already shopworn display items.

"Stop it, Oswald! My God, cat, get it together!" Ophelia shouted, racing to save her precious Ophelia Owl porcelain figurine from tipping off the little bookshelf next to the television. Oswald shoved off from the top shelf, leaving Ophelia rocking in her hands, and made a beeline for the bedroom. Antonia raced after him and slammed the door shut, leaving him to rattle around in there until he was over himself. The little bedroom was bare of decoration; there was nothing in there for the brat to destroy.

"Sorry, Ophelia," Antonia muttered, returning the bird to her place of honor and making sure nothing had happened to the jaunty flower in her red cloche hat, the cartoon character's signature look but a particularly destructible aspect of any piece of Ophelia fine art. This piece had only a slight chip in her little brown-and-white tail, enough to knock her down to the 70% off shelf in Patriot's Mercantile, the company store in Legacy of Heroes' expansive office campus, but not enough to detract from her adorable good looks. "I guess it's always cats against birds," she added, chuckling. Antonia talked to Ophelia Owl a lot, probably more than she should, she thought, but Ophelia was her favorite character—a never-finished deep cut from the Lawrence Taylor film library, a favorite of genuine fans only.

Meanwhile, the phone had stopped buzzing. Antonia picked it up with a sigh and waited to see if a voicemail was forthcoming. The number was unknown…which, at this late hour, usually meant a manager from Old Dodge City was calling to see if she'd work a different shift the next day. The company mobile phones all had blocked numbers, to keep Patriots from getting hold of the numbers and trying to work around the centralized scheduling and call-out operators. Of course, all it took was one desperate manager leaving a message with the magic words, "Please call me if you can take this shift, here's my work cell number" and the forbidden digits were on the market, to be shared or withheld according to the lucky Patriot's personal whims and alliances.

Antonia glanced at the time: nine fifty. Technically, she could still be asked to work the early shift, rather than her scheduled three p.m. Professor Cloud's shift. Maybe Leeann wasn't coming back tomorrow after all, and she could go back to her stock room…but that would mean a four a.m. alarm.

She shifted impatiently, waiting for the voicemail icon to light up. "Come on, come on," she muttered. "If I need to get to bed right now, I'd like to know."

The red number one blinked into existence and Antonia jammed her thumb down. She set the phone down expectantly. "Let's go."

"Antonia? This is Marcia. From Old Dodge City. It's

uh…it's almost ten on Tuesday night…uh…listen, this is kind of last-minute, but we accepted you into the lead program, and we'd like you to start your training…um, tomorrow. At twelve. Can you do that? Is that okay? Call me back if you get this. Or just show up at twelve instead of three tomorrow. Either is fine. Here's my number…I'll be here until midnight. We could really use you tomorrow. There's um…we'll talk about it tomorrow. Thanks. Bye. Call me. Bye."

Antonia stared at the phone. It stared back at her until the screen timed out. Then she stared at her own reflection for a few minutes more. "Lead?" she asked her face, ghostly in the black mirror of the screen. "Just like that…I'm a lead?"

It didn't make any sense.

Not that Antonia didn't deserve the job. Not that Antonia wasn't qualified for the job. It was just that this wasn't how promotions worked at AtB. Especially not at the hourly level where union contracts had to be honored. There were rules and timelines and training schedules written weeks in advance. There were papers to sign and rules to acknowledge. There was, at every single stage in the promotion process, enough bureaucracy and red tape to choke a government official.

A phone call at ten o'clock offering a promotion that began the next day?

This wasn't how things were done at all.

Antonia picked up her phone again, her face disappearing as the background image of Oswald wearing an Ophelia Owl hat reclaimed its rightful place on the screen, and played the message back so she could write down Marcia's phone number.

After tomorrow, she thought gleefully, she'd have all the manager's phone numbers.

She accepted the promotion and the schedule change, assured Marcia the late phone call was no problem at all, and then let Oswald out of the bedroom for a celebratory kitty treat. Then Antonia settled back onto the couch and flipped on the TV. The air conditioner blew cold, cold air over her hair, and she smiled, letting the expensive breeze tickle her neck.

CHAPTER EIGHT

Martin

In the living room next door, Martin heard Antonia's TV come to life and wondered why she'd turned it back on.

He knew Antonia's schedule pretty well. They'd been next-door neighbors for two years or more, ever since she'd moved to Gateway Apartments. He couldn't quite remember when that was; Martin wasn't good with dates. He summed up life into two categories—Before Amy, and After Amy. The best part of his life, the part in the middle, didn't need a title. Because that was the only part he ever really thought about.

Before Amy, of course, didn't bear much thinking about —he'd just been Martin O'Keefe, a regular guy who did regular guy things like watch Dr. Who in his underwear and play a little more on his computer than maybe his mother would have hoped and take complicated assessments on computer programming languages in hopes of getting promotions at his increasingly regular, boring office jobs.

After Amy didn't bear much thinking about, either, but unfortunately that was the present day, and the past three years, and just like Before Amy, each day was much like the last, unpromising and unexciting and underachieving. The difference was that Before Amy, he'd had some expectations things might get better, and After Amy, he knew they *had* gotten better, but then they'd gotten much worse, and things weren't going up again anytime soon.

Another difference was that sometimes he simply couldn't take being alone anymore. That hadn't happened Before Amy, because he hadn't ever realized he'd been alone back then.

He got up and made a quick decision, always a very big deal for Martin.

Antonia opened the door a few minutes after his timid knock and stood back to let him in. He filed past her with a shy, embarrassed smile and put the six-pack of beer he'd brought as an offering on the kitchen counter, where Oswald was crouched in black-and-white splendor. The cat fluffed up, either in pride or irritation; Martin could never tell what a cat was thinking.

"Thanks for letting me in, Antonia," he said, pushing his owlish, tortoiseshell glasses up his short nose. The eyeglass arms touched his round cheeks when he spoke and shifted on his round-lobed ears when he smiled sheepishly, as he was doing now. "You're up later than usual. I heard your TV on or else I wouldn't have knocked."

"I'm off the early morning shift," she sighed, but she was smiling as she opened a flimsy kitchen drawer and pulled out her bottle opener. "I don't have to work until noon tomorrow."

Martin peered at her grinning face. "You have good news," he chided her. "Tell me!"

Antonia handed him a beer, its insides hissing and spitting from the open top like a djinn escaping its gilded lamp. "I got promoted to lead, Martin," she admitted. "They want me to start tomorrow! I just found out."

Martin was excited for her, but he knew enough about Patriot life and its discontents to know a next-day promotion was not a thing. Not for front-line Patriots, anyway. So his pleasure for Antonia was instantly tempered with worry. What were their motives? Why break protocol? "What do you think happened to make it an overnight thing like this?"

She shook her head, mouth full of beer, and swallowed. "I couldn't possibly say, Martin, but I am up to handle whatever trouble they've gotten themselves into."

Martin pulled out his phone and thumbed through Twitter for a moment. Speaking of trouble, he'd seen something earlier…here it was. He held out the tweet from @AtBNate. "Call me crazy, but…isn't this your friend Tabby?"

Antonia shook her head at him, refusing the phone. "You and your fandom. Can't you stay away from these crazies online? I'm telling you, Martin, you need more interests. You need a real hobby. Following theme park people around a theme park when you are also at the same theme park? That's not a hobby."

"What is it, then?" He persisted in holding the phone out to her. "It's a pastime I pursue in my spare time for pleasure. It's the definition of a hobby."

Antonia took the phone, hissing an exasperated sigh. "What is this, a video? I don't watch these idiots vlog."

"Just watch it," Martin insisted. "I'm sure it's Tabby and if you're going to be a lead, maybe this is the kind of thing to watch out for."

She looked at him now, really looked at him, and Martin experienced a disquieting feeling of triumph. Not that he *wanted* Antonia's attention any more than the next person, even so, he felt gratified when she looked at him that way. As if he could surprise her, when she'd long ago made it clear that nothing Martin did in his sad, boring, After Amy life could ever surprise her.

"Watch it," he insisted again, and she finally accepted the phone, mashed the play button on the video, and watched it.

He took a slow pull of his beer while he watched her expression change from skeptical and annoyed to *shocked* and annoyed. The annoyed part, he reflected, was a permanent part of Antonia. She had a just a touch of a permanent scowl etched into her face after three years at America the Beautiful. Amy had acquired that look, too. He supposed there were only so many times you could answer the same idiotic questions before it affected you at a cellular level.

When she finished watching, she brought her slim arched eyebrows together and then pressed play again. She frowned at the phone, then up at Martin. "Who is this guy?" she asked, her voice tense, but level.

"His name's Nathan and he runs AtBLive. He moved here to blog every day. A super-fan."

"If he thinks he's going to bother my Patriots and put up videos of them, he is dead wrong," Antonia declared. "I will murder this bastard and dump his body into the Mighty Missouri. No—I will dump it into the emergency overflow pool up at Gold Rush Rapids and then I will hit the red button and stop the whole damn ride and dump the water and let the chemicals and trash filling the bottom of those flumes crush his bones and dissolve his skin."

Martin took a step back. "Wow, Antonia."

She handed back his phone with a sly smile. "It's important to have ideals and stand up for them, Martin. Let me tell you something. When *I'm* a manager, my Patriots will be protected one hundred percent against pricks like this guy. I'm not going to have anybody worried they're going to lose their job because some idiot thinks he is making a living out of making phone videos of them just trying to get through a day. This dick has *no idea* what it's like being a Patriot. He has *no clue* what we go through. We're out there dealing with their stupid-ass questions, we're out there in the hot sun while they complain about the heat, we're out there risking life and limb for them because they're too dumb to come in from a storm and too foolish to pull down their lap-bars when they're told and too—" Antonia stopped. "I'm sorry. I got carried away."

Martin saw the look on her face and his free hand traveled to his own, to feel the deep grooves which had appeared between his eyes and above his eyebrows and next to his nose and along his lips. They were the folds his face made when he was making one of his ferociously awful frowns. He tried to force his muscles back into more friendly territory. "It's fine, really. I understand."

"It's not fine," Antonia insisted, guiding him to the sofa and sitting down next to him. "I was being insensitive. I'm always being insensitive to you and I'm sorry. I don't know why you even put up with me."

He wasn't a man who had real friends. Well, he had

online friends. People with avatars and handles. He was happy enough with them, left alone to chatter on Twitter about AtB and other theme parks.

And he had…other…friends.

The costumed and kind residents of America the Beautiful.

Martin was willing to concede that he might be a little crazy, and he was willing to accept a few looks from other regulars at AtB, and he understood these residents were paid to be nice to him (and thousands of other park guests), but he enjoyed their company and he was never creepy or disrespectful to them, and that was something very few of the character-chasers could say about themselves. So he didn't let the outside world's prevailing opinions bother him on that count.

But anyway, Antonia was his real, human, uncostumed friend.

She was frowning at him. "You made a real face at me."

"I promise it's fine. I was…I had a stomach cramp. From the beer."

Antonia shook her head at him. "You been okay? I haven't seen you in a few days. Not even at the park."

Martin considered the question. Was he doing okay? Not in the usual sense of the word, no. In the Martin sense, in the After Amy sense, maybe. But he hadn't felt like leaving the apartment in a week, which wasn't exactly normal for him, either.

He usually went to America the Beautiful on Mondays and Tuesdays, to see his favorite Susie Q. on Independence Street, and his favorite Miss Sallie Mae in Old Dodge City.

Monday-Tuesday's Susie Q. always made time for a little chat with him in between the skits she put on with the

Plaza Mayor and Mrs. Debussy, the piano teacher. And Monday-Tuesday's Miss Sallie Mae had a spray of real freckles on her heavily made-up face he just couldn't get enough of.

He tried not to miss seeing them regularly, because he knew beneath their costumes, they were really college students or young adults in their first acting jobs. In a year or two, maybe less, they'd be gone, replaced by other aspiring actresses or penniless liberal arts majors. And when they were gone, so would his handful of fake friendships, until he found new characters in the new recruits to fall in one-sided love with.

"I'm doing okay," he decided eventually. "Maybe I had a cold for a couple of days."

She frowned. "I feel like you would know for sure if you had a cold."

He shrugged. Sometimes he desperately wanted Antonia to take care of him, because she was so sure of herself, so in charge of her own destiny—she was like an empress, a formidable force to be reckoned with. It was funny because Amy hadn't taken care of him—that had been his role in their relationship, to be the mother hen who made sure she had everything she needed to shine, everything she needed to be a star.

And what a star she had been, shining up there, at the top of Promise Mountain, with the whole park watching her.

In the end, Martin went back to his own apartment with what he wanted, an assurance Antonia was okay, and a lecture from her on how he should take better care of himself. Martin always felt stimulated after one of Antonia's brusque talking-tos. He thought she liked them, too; when she hit her stride, he thought he could see her truly terrifying Haitian grandmother shining through her stern eyes and taut jaw and slanting cheekbones. Martin could imagine Antonia dressing him down in silken French with a serrated edge cutting through the purring vowels, and it was a fantasy he liked to recharge every few months. Maybe it was odd to daydream about being in trouble, but at this point in his life, he couldn't imagine much for himself besides being told off.

Back on his sagging brown couch, the leather crisscrossed with claw marks from a rescue cat who had rejected his efforts at civilizing him and run away, Martin opened his laptop and flicked through AtBLive, that guy Nate's blog. He'd uploaded the footage of Tabby earlier, but now it was gone. The whole post was deleted. Martin furrowed his brow, curious about the lack of evidence, and clicked around a few other forums and group pages where there was sure to be chatter about the situation.

Sure enough, on the popular AtBExpress message boards, he found a thread titled *Vacation ruined!!! Bitchy N strikes again*. Well, with a title like that, who could resist? Eager for a little Internet drama to distract him from another empty late night, Martin clicked through and glanced through the thread.

Edgar8mychldhd: Did u see the latest from Bitchy N? A Patriot was breaking theme in the wrong costume on Plaza and he flipped his lid. That guy won't last two months at the parks. Either he gets trespassed or committed, who wants to give odds on which happens first?

GoldRushJen: he's an asshole

Taylor1968: they're not supposed to break theme tho so I

hate to side with bitchy n but uh yeah this is just more evidence the parks are going downhill

Edgar8mychldhd: you can't berate college students for breaking theme tho

Taylor1968: this is true

GoldRushJen: also he totally took it down, dude is probably so scared of getting trespassed. He is so not up to this. Can't wait to watch it all explode.

OpheliasGhost: but rlly how many moms screamed vacation ruined thats the vid I want to see

He was pleasantly surprised to see so many commenters taking Tabby's side. Even though the hard-core AtB fans had a serious antipathy towards the bloggers who tried to monetize their love of the parks, and disliked the AtBLive site with particular vitriol, they were also quick to leap upon Patriots who they didn't feel were doing a good enough job of maintaining the parks. Sometimes, AtB fans had to make a decision about which perceived enemy they hated most on a given day. Would it be the Patriots, the bloggers, or the guests? Today, Tabby won the lottery and everyone else was the enemy.

Well-deserved, Martin thought. Tabby was a sweet girl. When she was out there on the Old Dodge City pavement, she fit the character theming perfectly. He loved to watch her in rare moments of downtime, pacing along her wagon with her skirt swishing around her ankles, looking like a pioneer maiden in search of adventure on the Great Plains. He rarely spoke to her without the buffering presence of Antonia, but he knew she had a kind nature and a trusting demeanor. She was the sort of woman that noble hearts wanted to protect. Antonia had felt it; Martin felt it, too, from afar.

Following his usual evening routine, Martin left the AtBExpress forums in favor of Instagram. He skimmed through some character accounts, admiring his favorite character actors for a few minutes, before he typed #OldDodgeCity into the search bar and thumbed through a montage of images, many weirdly similar. Guests in the same poses in front of Conestoga wagons and the rainmaking machine in Professor Cloud's, performed by hundreds of unfamiliar faces and bodies. Martin didn't see their grins and their peace signs and their proudly displayed churros, held up like trophies for the camera. He was looking at the backgrounds of each picture, pausing and searching.

There she was, looking hot and tired, staring into space from next to the cash register on the sunglass wagon. There she was, face lit into a huge smile, fitting a cowboy hat on a small boy's tipped-back head. There she was, lost in thought, gazing at the passing side-wheeler out on the Mighty Missouri.

Martin used to look at Amy's pictures like this, and he could feel that old hunger inside. It was guilty, as if he was eating a pint of ice cream against doctor's orders. It was weird to look at her like this. It was wrong, it was creepy. But he didn't search out her actual profile, and he reasoned this was a positive sign. He wasn't so far gone that he couldn't recognize the symptoms of an internet stalker. He'd stay here on thin ice, close to the shore, where things couldn't get too complicated.

The *opposite* of what he'd done with Amy.

CHAPTER NINE

Tabby

Tabby smiled at her reflection in the mirror and tugged at both pigtails, pulling them out to the sides of her head like she was Pippi Longstocking. When she went all out with the theming, going beyond just pulling on her wardrobe-issued costume, the results were always fantastic. The tight grip of the braids made her thin face almost ethereal, with hollow cheeks and dramatic cheekbones, a pointed chin and big deep-set eyes. Her silly symmetrical freckles worked with this look and no other, so she didn't even have to hate them.

She thought for a moment, looked at the time on her phone, and then pulled out two green lengths of ribbon from the bathroom drawer. She tied them neatly around the rubber bands holding the pigtails taut.

"Ma, Pa, I'm goin' to the general store!" she called, turning away from the mirror with a giggle.

Molly looked up from their worn, plaid couch as Tabby passed through the living room. "Oh God, you're doing the Laura Ingalls thing again today."

"It's called theming," Tabby corrected her loftily. "I am engaging with my character in order to surprise and delight my guests."

"Did you just have a refresher course or something? You're talking like they spiked your Kool-Aid with first-day good vibes."

"I just woke up and decided to have a good day," Tabby said. She opened the fridge and pulled out a yogurt. She bit her lip, thinking, then pulled out another one. It was a long shift today. "This week was kind of rough to start, but I think it's going better now."

She smiled to herself. Things were definitely going to be better today. Last night? At the Gateway Pub? That had been unreal. People had stood up for her. They were on her side. Tabby felt herself on the winning side of some kind of righteous war against the public, with their live-streams and their weird forums where they discussed people like her all night long. What had started as a miserable moment had turned into a definite win.

Yes, everything was coming up Tabby. She decided carbs were in order and pulled out the wheat bread. Toast and jam—her favorite breakfast. Let Molly fuss over egg-whites and spinach all she wanted; Tabby would give up bread when the sun rose in the west and AtB opened a park themed to Soviet Russia.

"Thank goodness," Molly replied, her voice disinterested. "You were being really lame the yesterday at the Gateway, looking at yourself and sighing like a sad princess. Honestly, that stupid video got you way more attention than you deserve."

"So nice of you," Tabby said, amused. "My dear friend, always so supportive!"

"I'm just trying to keep you humble," Molly said. "And I guess you think this is going to help you with Nick."

"What?" Tabby watched her bread turn orange in the toaster's glow. "What does Nick have to do with it?"

"Well, he's like a blogger on the other side, right? He's got to be on Team Tabby when this gets out at the parks. And he likes attention, so he'll probably appoint himself your official bodyguard or something."

Tabby grinned to herself. "No," she said dismissively. "That won't happen."

"Your ears move when you smile, Tabby! I can tell!"

"Okay, maybe this could help me out with Nick," Tabby allowed. "But we're really close already. I think it's going to happen." A real boyfriend, this time, instead of just another ride operator who heard she put out on the first date, then got mad when he found out the rumor wasn't true.

"Just make him take you on a real date, okay? Don't let him just kiss you in a stockroom. You're worth more than that." Molly laughed. "Jesus! It's about time this idiot figures out how into him you really are. I hope this does the trick."

"He's not an idiot." Tabby spread margarine across her toast, watching it dissolve into the brown dimples left by the knife. "He has a perfectly acceptable brain."

"And that's what you love," Molly agreed. "His acceptable brain turns you on."

Tabby slathered strawberry jam, quivering red, onto her toast, and said nothing. She knew Nick wasn't a genius. But it wasn't very nice of Molly to point it out. Was Molly a

MENSA candidate? No more than she, Tabby, was. They were all basically of average intelligence. That's why they'd gone to average colleges and then dropped out to work at a theme park as soon as the opportunity presented itself. This was not a genius move. They were not living enlightened lives.

"Don't be mad."

"I'm not mad." Tabby's mouth was full of toast. It dissolved on her tongue and she closed her eyes. Toast was divine. "I'm eating."

"I don't understand how you can eat bread every day and stay so skinny."

Tabby thought of her spherical mother, back home in Kentucky, surrounded by her Precious Moments figurines and her wood-paneled living room and her sorrowful, drowning, suffocating faith. "It'll catch up with me," she recited, hearing the twang in her voice as she repeated her mother's words, spoken so many times, with exasperation, with love, with envy, with malicious anticipation all rolled into one unfathomable tone.

Nick wasn't in until the afternoon, so Tabby had to spend the first three hours of her mid-shift thinking about him. Which was fine, as she picked up the sunglass Conestoga wagon the moment she clocked in, and the morning was cloudy, with a persistent mist rolling through the trees behind the Mighty Missouri and clinging to the Victorian curls and frills embellishing the false fronts of Old Dodge City's line of shops. The threat of rain hadn't kept any crowds at home—it never did, in summer, when people were locked into their annual vacations by school holidays and non-refundable flights from all over the country—but they certainly didn't need eye protection, so Tabby absently twirled her skirt to and fro, her pigtails bobbing at her shoulders, and smiled at the crowds without seeing them.

Antonia strolled onto the porch of Professor Cloud's around noon, Roseann at her side. Tabby noticed them immediately, more because of Roseann in her skimpy skirt and tight button-down blouse than because of Antonia's supervisory uniform of gray slacks and white shirt. Spotting managers, who wore professional attire as if they were going to work in an office, was easy even on gray summer days, when every guest was committed to their tank tops and shorts. Leads blended in a little better, but they were still not in period costume, to give them a little more authority to guests in shorts and tank tops.

Tabby did a quick presentability check over her shoulder: no guests were perusing the racks of sunglasses and baseball caps. She did a quick rundown of her behavior over the past few minutes—smiling, check; looking approachable, check; not leaning on the wagon, check. Roseann was not coming over here with discipline on her mind. Just an average manager check-in.

Antonia, though! A lead? This was news!

She tossed her smile to Antonia lightly, without concern for the feelings it might stir in her sort-of-ex-girlfriend, and resumed flicking her skirt from side to side, as if she was standing on the sidelines of a square dance, listening to a fiddle sing her friends round and round, doe see doe.

Well, Tabby couldn't say she was surprised Antonia had been promoted to lead. The coveted change from skirt to slacks meant Antonia was one step below a manager, with the all-important power to say "no" to a guest. She probably would, too, and enjoy it. Some managers wouldn't even do it; they'd send an upset guest to Guest Services at the park entrance and tell them a quick, easy lie: Guest Services could handle their disappointment, Guest Services would make it right. Here in Old Dodge City we just didn't have the ability, you see, to take back that scarf without a tag which you clearly bought at Walmart, or to replace that snow globe you purchased on your last summer trip which our Patriot apparently did not wrap well enough for you. Guest Services, that's who can help you. Could they help these scammers and sad cases? No one knew but Guest Services, and they ate lunches and hung out together in tight-knit groups, clustered in sober little covens of dark blue suits at their round tables, shutting out the rest of the Patriots and keeping their own secrets.

Antonia, though, she wouldn't send a complaining guest to Guest Services and those girls with their star-spangled scarves around their necks. Hah! She'd just say no, let the guest bluster, say no again, and then threaten to call security. Tabby just knew it. And she loved the idea. Imagine if Antonia had been here yesterday, when that psycho started in on her about being in the wrong costume on Independence Street! Antonia would have set him straight in a hurry.

"Hi, miss?"

Tabby whirled in surprise, her pigtails whipping around her face. While she'd been absently staring across the crowded walkway at Antonia, a guest had been nosing around the Conestoga wagon. He was holding up a baseball cap with Lucky the Indian Pony cavorting around the elaborately western letters of Old Dodge City on the front. Lucky's black spots were splashed around his white body as if the artist had been picturing a horse-Dalmatian. Tabby studied Lucky's toothy grin for a moment because she had recognized the guest as soon as she'd turned, and she didn't want to acknowledge him.

"You want this hat?" she mumbled eventually, without putting on her accent. "Should I cut the tag off?" She reached out to take it from him, but she wasn't standing close enough and came up short, fingers spread open in front of him.

Nate, the blogger of AtBLive, because of course now she knew who he was, stepped closer to her. But he pulled the hand holding the hat back to his chest, as if he had suddenly changed his mind about buying it. His round face flushed; Tabby remembered him turning red like this yesterday, but it had been because of the heat, she'd thought. Today, he had no such excuse. Today was just *weird.*

She considered backing away, waving to Antonia for back-up, but paused. Maybe he was going to apologize. She waited for him to say something, retracting her own hand and clasping her fingers behind her back in the classic Patriot pose, the one which kept them all from leaning against a wall or column even when their feet were screaming and their hips were swaying with fatigue, and which kept them from folding their arms or putting their hands in their pockets, all prime examples of looking unapproachable.

He responded to her professional manner by dropping the hat, swearing and bending down to pick it up…

…At the same time, Tabby leaned down to pick it up…

…Somehow causing his head, his round head capped with a fluffy mop of nut-brown hair which should have been cut two months ago, at least, to collide squarely with

Tabby's chest.

She gasped and jumped backwards as if his touch had scalded her. It wouldn't have been so bad if he had done the same thing, she thought later, but instead of looking horrified to have placed his forehead between Tabby's breasts like he was going to nuzzle her bosom and missed, he burst into nervous laughter, his face redder than ever.

"Did you see…oh, hahahaha!" the blogger gasped.

"What's *wrong* with you?" Tabby shrieked, her hands across her chest as if she was wearing something much more revealing than the ruffled, high-necked blouse. "Why would you do that? What were you *thinking?*"

People stopped now. Park-goers always stopped for a guest-Patriot altercation. They'd walk past a crying, lost child without a second thought, but they'd never pass up a fight that didn't concern them.

Angry tears were pricking at Tabby's eyes, and she swiped at them impatiently with her fists. This was always what happened when she was overwhelmed. She always cried and it was so embarrassing. And of course, the hot shame of crying like a child just made her eyes spill over even faster. She turned to face the register so her blushing, burning skin was hidden from the eyes all around her, but she knew they were there, pulling out their phones, nudging their friends, and he was still there, still laughing like he'd just pulled off the most awkward high school stunt of the decade. She longed for the mini-army of Patriots she'd been promised last night at the Gateway Pub. Where were they now?

"What did he do?"

The voice was low and angry, so fierce it was as if he'd been personally attacked. *Nick,* Tabby thought wildly, hearing the possessive note in his tone, and then she thought, *No, this is a man's voice,* and as crazy as she was about Nick, he was still just a boy in many ways, his high-pitched, laughing voice not least of them. She turned her head a bare inch to the left, away from the blogger, and saw a familiar face: blue eyes beneath shortish black hair, sharp cheekbones and a long nose with tired grooves beside it, leading to taut lips and a jutting chin. She couldn't think where she knew him from, but she trusted him anyway. Maybe because he looked ready to burn down America the Beautiful on her behalf.

And then he would get trespassed. She felt a sudden, urgent need to defuse the situation. Tabby had never caused trouble. It was against her very nature. "It's nothing," she whispered, and coughed when the lump in her throat said otherwise. "He just—it was a misunderstanding."

"That's all it was," Nate agreed. She slid her gaze to the right and saw him still standing there with that stupid hat, a hat for a child, clenched in his thick fingers. She narrowed her eyes, but he didn't see the warning this time. He continued, "I just dropped this hat and things got awkward for a minute. I laugh when I'm embarrassed. Didn't mean anything by it."

"Maybe you should look at hats somewhere else," the man at her back said, his voice like broken granite, rough-edged and heavy.

Nathan fully took in the height and breadth of the man behind her. She watched his eyes widen. "I don't mean it like that, buddy," he said, a whine creeping into his voice. "I didn't mean any disrespect."

He put the hat back on the rack and backed away, the crowd of interested guests parting to allow him clear passage. Behind him, the mud-colored water of the Mighty

Missouri lapped listlessly, and the side-wheeler emerged from the fog a few hundred feet away. Its whistle peeled out a long, shrill warning, or perhaps it was a greeting, depending on your mood and how many times it had interrupted your conversation on that particular day.

The whistle was loud, but it wasn't loud enough to drown out Nathan's parting comment: "Jeez, not like I *meant* to feel up your girlfriend."

The man jumped from behind her, his fists clenched, but Tabby grabbed his arm and dug her fingers in, feeling the rope of muscle there and pinching at it, pulling him back. "Please don't," she said urgently. "You'll end up getting trespassed."

He was tense for a long moment, and the waiting guests held their breath and their grins, even as Nathan beat a steady retreat, disappearing towards Promise Mountain's half-hidden bulk in the lowering fog, beyond the log cabins marking the entrance to Old Dodge City. Once it was clear the blogger was leaving, he relaxed his muscles and stepped back beside Tabby. She let her grip ease, but kept her hand on his arm. He was wearing a plaid shirt that was a touch too much for summer, unbuttoned over a white t-shirt. The cotton was soft beneath her fingers.

He turned to look at her, deep blue eyes studying her face with concern. "Are you okay?"

She nodded, parting her lips to tell him how much she appreciated his intervention. Then she saw Roseann and Antonia approaching. A spark of recognition ignited; this was Antonia's friend Martin. Her sad next-door neighbor, who lived for the parks. Tabby dropped her fingers from his arm. "You should go," she whispered. "My manager— they're going to ask questions. You don't want to get involved."

Antonia had told her Martin was here a few days a week, wandering around in between visits with his favorite characters. One of those everyday park guys, but not a creep. She wouldn't want to see him lose his happy place because he'd stood up for her.

But Martin didn't take off. He hovered nearby as Antonia and Roseann arrived at the wagon.

"What was that about?" Antonia demanded, while, Roseann addressed Martin and Tabby at large with a generic, chipper: "And how are we today?"

Antonia and Tabby both slid their eyes to Roseann for a beat before looking back at each other. "Things are fine," Tabby said carefully, hoping to answer them both. She shook her head slightly at Antonia: *please don't ask.*

Roseann intercepted the head shake and misinterpreted it. "Antonia is training as a lead today!" she announced brightly, as if the costume change wasn't enough of an indicator. "So she'll be around if you need anything, and also just to assess that we're meeting our goals and providing outstanding guest service."

"Congrats!" Tabby told Antonia. "You deserve it!"

"Thank you. Just know I'm here if you need anything," Antonia said meaningfully. "And I'll check up on you until your partner gets here. The second sunglass position picks up at one, before the parade."

The second position at the sunglass wagon was a back-up person, to make sure no one was stealing from the backside of the wagon during the busiest part of the day, while the first Patriot was theoretically working a nonstop line at the cash register. Usually on a cloudy day, the second position was removed from the schedule and that person was used somewhere else or sent home to save payroll. But apparently Antonia had made a decision—maybe her first decision as a lead—to give Tabby back-up.

She didn't have to say why. It was in case Nate came back, and they both knew it.

Roseann, oblivious, walked around to look at the far side of the wagon, and Antonia moved closer to Tabby. From this proximity, Tabby could smell her familiar Antonia scents: the coconut in her sunblock, a touch of baby powder, something spicy in her slicked-back hair. She felt a stirring of nostalgia, remembering resting her head on Antonia's strong shoulder, feeling protected. But it wasn't desire, just a longing for someone tougher than she was to take over, if only for a few minutes.

"Was that the blogger guy?" Antonia asked. "From yesterday?"

"You know about that?" Tabby felt a stab of terror. How viral had it gone? She could end up with a black mark on her permanent record if Roseann was called on the carpet and chose not to take responsibility for sending her to Independence Plaza in costume. A disciplinary note would put six months between her and the potential for transferring or promotions. If something better came up, like a new area or attraction opening, Tabby would be stuck here shilling sunglasses while Patriots with less seniority got to move on.

Antonia glanced at Martin, hovering nearby. "Martin showed it to me. Don't worry, I've been checking the numbers and it's not getting a lot of traction."

"The guy deleted the blog post," Martin offered. "But the video is still on his Twitter account."

"He probably thought it would go viral, but it's just not

that interesting to most normal humans." Antonia looked around at the passing crowds. "Our guests are normal humans, by the way. Nate and Martin are the weirdos."

"Martin's nice," Tabby said, looking at him with a plaintive expression. "Why would you say that?"

Antonia grinned at her. "Martin, tell this nice girl you're a weirdo."

"I'm a weirdo," he admitted. "But a nice one?"

"Yeah, I'll give you that."

Roseann came back around the wagon, waving a handful of sunglasses with no price-tags.

Tabby whispered: "I'm sorry you have to spend the day with her. But I'm glad you're going to be a lead."

Antonia smiled, and Tabby felt another surge of nostalgia, for all the times she'd felt the warmth and power in that smile as it was turned on her. "Thank you, Tabs. I am too."

The day took on a more normal cadence after that. The sun came out, despite all indications to the contrary, and guests began realizing they'd forgotten their sunglasses at home, in hotel rooms, on the dashboards of cars, in the seat pockets of airplanes. Tabby had been blowing bubbles for a while, amusing kids who ran to pop them, but by the time Nick arrived and took his position along the side of the Conestoga wagon, flashing her a knowing grin and waggling his golden eyebrows at her on the way, Tabby already had a line at her register six people deep.

So the afternoon passed, in a haze of sweat and sunlight, parades and patriotic programs. The side-wheeler huffed past, its whistle interrupting all conversation, every twenty minutes. People screamed on the splashing final descent of

Gold Rush Rapids, every forty-five seconds. The plastic rifles made popping sounds from the shaded porch of the Shootin' Arcade, non-stop. "That will be eighteen oh six," Tabby said, over and over again as guests bought $16.95 sunglasses, the most annoying dollar amount in the world when tax was added, because most guests paid with twenties and she had to give them change from every single cup in the till, right down to four freaking pennies.

"And eighty-four cents is your change," she would trill, dropping a heavy load of coins in their waiting hands.

"I don't need these pennies," one out of four guests would say, pushing them back at her.

"I'm sorry, but you have to take them," she would reply. "Because if my till is off at the end of the day, I'll get in trouble."

"But I'm making you money," the ones who had never worked retail would say.

"If a drawer is always off at the end of the day," she explained to an indignant mother with a may-I-see-your-manager haircut, "then it's considered a warning sign that I'm stealing by giving back the wrong amount of change. And that can cause a lot of trouble for me. So, I can't keep the pennies."

"Fine," the woman sighed, pocketing the offensive pennies.

She was the last in the line for a few minutes and Nick came over to talk to her, grinning. "I thought she was going to throw those pennies at your head."

Tabby smiled half-heartedly. Her cheeks hurt, as they often did after a long run of transactions, and she was drenched in sweat. She wasn't as excited to have Nick around now as she might have been in a more air-conditioned state. She hadn't felt confident about her deodorant since her last break had ended, more than an hour ago. The end of her shift was a bare hour away, and she was counting the minutes. The seconds, even.

But wasn't it better to have Nick hanging out with her now, at her worst, then to always look and smell like roses around him? There was a certain logic in that, right?

Either way, Nick stood companionably beside her and they watched a handful of children pressing their noses against the windows of Sam Sweet's Candy Shop while their mothers took carefully composed pictures on their phones.

"There are pictures of *everything* now, because of phones," she said. "Too many, if you ask me." She was thinking of the video, still out there. It irked her to think about the many, many unauthorized images of herself floating around the internet.

"Well, I think we should stop saying 'phones,' " Nick replied thoughtfully. "Why don't we just call them cameras? I've literally never taken a phone call on my phone, but just today I've recorded three vlogs and taken at least sixteen pictures."

Tabby laughed. "You started work at one! When did you have the time?"

"I was over at Legacy before work."

She smiled at him. This was what she loved about life here: the playing. Mundane stuff like getting groceries happened late, after hours. Daytime was for the parks, for having as much fun as possible all the time. For indulging in the fantasy, nonstop. For living the dream, every single day. For having in their grasp at every waking hour, what so many had to save for years just so they could enjoy it for a few days. "What did you vlog about?"

"The new Sweet Magnolia cupcakes they've got at a cart outside Escape from Atlanta. Have you tried them? They're vanilla and peach on the inside, but they have this big flower on the top—look—" Nick slid his phone from his pocket and started flicking through his photo album.

Tabby was startled. "Nick, put that away," she hissed. "Roseann is still around and she'll go nuts if she sees your phone out." She didn't know what Antonia would do if she caught him…maybe nothing, because Tabby wanted Nick? Or *something*, because Tabby wanted Nick?

"Roseann's been here since noon and it's seven; by now she'll be in the office pretending to work on a project and counting down to eight o'clock." Nick waved his hand, dismissing the young manager's ambition with a single gesture. "I know how these managers work. It's the only way I survive without getting fired."

He laughed, but Tabby didn't. Was all this a joke to him? America the Beautiful, the park life, all of it? They had rules for a reason; taking out a phone while they were in Old Dodge City was every bit as against those rules as her crossing the Square in the wrong costume had been, but *she* ended up on a viral video while he just played with his phone, uncaring of the potential consequences. She frowned at him, but he was already holding up his phone, showing her the Sweet Magnolia cupcake, perfectly captured atop a table with an actual magnolia tree in the background, its glossy leaves the richest, darkest green imaginable.

"It's really nice," she agreed. "Now, put that thing away." She spotted a guest wandering around the sunglasses behind her and turned around to greet her. When she turned back around, Antonia was walking over, hands behind her back, chin jutting. Nick, she realized, still had his phone out.

"Let's go over there on your next day off," Nick said, not looking up from his phone. "I'll get you one. My treat." He finally took his eyes from his phone and realized it wasn't Tabby standing in front of him—it was Antonia, looking stern.

"Can we talk?" Antonia said. She had a phone in a holder clipped to her belt, Tabby noticed, and an earpiece. She was in full lead mode after just a few hours of training. Roseann was probably using her as cover while she hid in the office, like Nick said. "In the back, not in front of guests?"

Nick slipped the phone into his pocket with a wobbly grin. "Let's go," he agreed, and fell into step next to Antonia. He cast a rueful smile over his shoulder as he went, and Tabby felt her stomach lurch. She was off soon, and he'd been in the midst of asking her out—she *thought* he had been, anyway. A cupcake date at Legacy of Heroes —that was the perfect first date for them! How much trouble could having a phone out get you in, anyway? Probably a lot. It was one of the most strict rules they had.

The light suddenly changed; the sun had slipped behind Gold Rush Rapids' rocky peaks, and the gas lamps lining the walkway and lighting the boardwalk all flamed to life at once.

Tabby felt goosebumps rise on her exposed arms; the night blew in with a sudden chill that wasn't at all summer-like, but she wasn't just feeling the cool breeze. She was feeling *all* of it: the evening wonder of Old Dodge City sweeping over her. This place was truly enchanting. For a moment, she really was in a gaslit frontier town, with the cool waters of the meandering river lapping the shores beside her.

"Alone at last."

The voice cut through the swooping song of the fiddle playing from the hidden speakers scattered around them. The fiddle was singing from high birdhouses and from behind shop signs and from within cleverly hidden fiberglass rocks. *My Old Kentucky Home,* an oddly comforting tune with uncomfortably racist lyrics. A Kentucky girl herself, Tabby often hummed along, and then felt guilty for doing so. It was a beautiful tune for the gaslight and the ethereal deep blue of the evening sky—but, once again, Nate the blogger was ruining a moment for her.

She turned around unwillingly, her fingers clenching the smooth wood surrounding the cash register, brushing the canvas trim of the Conestoga cover arching over her head.

"What do you want now?" she asked, dropping all pretension of Themed Replies or even basic pleasantness. This guy wasn't a customer. He wasn't here to buy sunglasses. And there was no point in pretending she was the best little guest-service provider in Old Dodge City, either. Somehow, they already had a backstory of their own, one that went deeper than her printed-out responsibilities as a Patriot. "And why did you wait until Nick was gone?"

CHAPTER TEN

Antonia

Antonia was not leaning, not exactly, against the door-frame of Professor Cloud's. She had her hands fisted behind her, pressed into the aged-looking wood, and against them she was resting her full weight. It took the pressure off the balls of her feet, which were exhausted from a day pounding the concrete walkways of Old Dodge City, climbing up the hill to Gold Rush Rapids, and standing at attention during *Celebrate! America's Parade,* during which leads and managers watched both the parade Patriots and the crowd control Patriots for any potential run-over situations as the massive floats lumbered by, cheerful music blasting from their on-board speakers.

The not-leaning-but-leaning trick was an old Patriot hand-me-down, passed verbally from trainer to trainee on Day One of Park Training since time immemorial. Leaning, of course, was against the most basic "look approachable and happy" behaviors mandated by the 5 Patriot Virtues. Antonia imagined she'd be doing it still in a year when she was a manager-in-training.

Because yes, that was what she was going to do—spend her next year as a supervisor and then make it into the management program, itself a lengthy and annoying process of being assigned a mentor, entering a management internship, attending management classes and filling in a mysterious management binder. Today it all began. Her first day as a lead.

She *liked* being in charge.

Even tripping around after Roseann, which she'd assumed would be the most annoying possible way to spend a day at her favorite theme park, possibly her favorite place in the world, had been thoroughly enjoyable. Gone were the doldrums of the post-lunch slump, trying to stay awake and look cheerful as you stood next to a cash register disguised as a crate of oats or a barrel of XX, whatever that was. Gone was the stupefying silence of Gold Rush Gem Exchange when the Rapids ride was on a temporary downtime. Gone was the utter helplessness of logging into the Patriot Portal and waiting for a computer scheduling program to tell you how to spend your next hour or three, until someone else logged in and got your break, starting the cycle anew.

Antonia had always hated feeling like just one more cog in a vast machine, interchangeable with all the other Patriots who had taken successfully taken the Retail Revolution training course and been signed off on their cash handling test. And she'd hated the monotony of being stuck at one cash register for two hours or more, unable to move around the area without express permission from someone who was certainly no smarter or more able to run a theme park retail operation than she was.

Now, it seemed like even that might be behind her. Free to roam, to help Patriots, offer register swaps and bathroom breaks and extra hours, even free—and this was especially pleasant—to say *no* to the persistent guests who were making her Patriots crazy with unreasonable demands. That was one of her jobs, Roseann assured her—Antonia could now respond to Patriot calls for managers, and she could say that magic word which had been forbidden to her just one pay-grade ago.

No.

What a word! Talk about wonder!

So she'd done all of that the moment Roseann left her in charge. She was the manager she wished she'd had: she gave Alana permission to get out the coloring books and engage tired kids with crayons and coloring contests in Professor Cloud's; she asked Juan to hand out fudge samples from the boardwalk in front of Sam Sweet's; she stepped in when a guest was speaking a little too loudly to Marissa and suggested he take his complaints to Guest Services, where they would give him the same answer she was: *no.*

And, amidst all that support, it had been pleasant to deliver Nick to his fate just now, too. She was tired of seeing him do things like pull out his phone in front of guests, and she really didn't want him doing that with Tabby and getting her into bad habits…or simply suffer guilt by association. Tabby loved it here, but she was impressionable. She didn't have Antonia's force of will. She'd let Nick get her in trouble.

Antonia wasn't about to watch that happen, not when she actually could stop it. So Nick was off to sign a discipline card under Roseann's cold gaze, a union shop steward watching to make sure they handled everything according to the rules, and then he was going home to think about what he'd done. He could come back tomorrow and hopefully try a little harder not to break the most simple of rules. Antonia smiled to herself. She didn't like his chances. Three discipline cards, and he was out.

Roseann stepped into the doorway next to her. "That's done."

Antonia turned her head slightly, sharing her smile with Roseann. "We have another half-hour," she said. "Do I need to do any paperwork?" She knew leads had closing paperwork for their shifts which took the last thirty minutes —signing off on the balance in the safe if they'd made change for any cashiers, reporting on any Patriots worthy of praise, adding notes to the daily report the managers would turn in at the end of the night. But she had technically been on a job shadow with a manager today, even if half the time she'd been on her own, walking her own circuits of the area. The formal training process didn't seem to apply here.

Roseann laughed. "I wouldn't even know where to begin —I've never been a lead. Tomorrow you can shadow Mark and he'll give you more formal training. Today was just… well, headcount wasn't working out and we needed the extra person with keys and a radio. Ordinarily you'd be shadowing other the leads for the next week."

Antonia nodded as if she understood, but she knew something was seriously off. Protocol was revered at AtB, as much because of the inner workings of the union as because it was a company founded on the idea that if every department followed the exact same rules, then people could float between the different areas without disruption to the daily flow. When a park is open 365 days a year, having a flexible staff is a matter of some importance. Antonia herself had been shipped off to The Big Apple and Independence Plaza on more than one occasion when those areas were short-staffed and had no one to carry in the morning shipment or man all the registers before the park opened.

In short, there was no way her sudden promotion and off-book training had anything to do with a badly written management schedule.

"So it turns out, I'm also closing tonight," Roseann went on, sounding tired. "Luis is the closing lead, but he's busy on change runs. Can you hold the MOD radio while I grab some dinner? And then when I come back, you can head home."

"You're closing? But you came in at noon, too."

Roseann smiled. "I told you we were short-handed. Everything is on-the-fly today."

Antonia took the manager-on-duty radio and told Roseann to go get some dinner. She watched the young woman trot through Professor Cloud's on her teetering heels, smiling and nodding at shopping guests as she went. Then she was through the back door, the fluorescent lights of the nondescript hallway breaking the intense story of the old western town for just a few blazing seconds, and was gone. Antonia imagined her leaning on the elevator button, hoping the Mobile Merch Patriots hadn't clogged the elevator and its tunnel corridor with their light toy carts, which often caused a traffic jam at this time of night. For the first time ever, she felt a flicker of compassion for Roseann. The manager had just never seemed particularly human to her before. But a twelve-hour day on those heels! Well, at least Antonia knew how to dress herself. She looked down at her sensible black loafers and wiggled her toes.

A shout made her look up, one hand ready on the radio she'd just clipped to her skirt's sagging elastic waist. Through the teeming crowds on Old Dodge City's gaslit main thoroughfare, she could see a man looming over a skirted Patriot at the sunglass wagon. "Dammit," Antonia muttered. "If that's the same guy, I'm gonna lose my mind."

She shoved off from her comfortable spot against the wall and dove into the chaos on the street, where a few hundred families were in the cheerful process of going in a hundred directions all at once, some hampered by balloons they'd foolishly bought that morning, others by spilling popcorn buckets, large sloshing sodas, heavy strollers laden with every conceivable snack and emergency supply, squalling toddlers who would not walk and would not sit but had to be held, uncomfortably, on the hip-bone, blistered feet in poorly chosen sandals, phones plugged into portable chargers which were operating at much higher temperatures than mentioned in those Amazon reviews, and park maps which had been folded and unfolded a few hundred times as the hub-and-spoke layout of the park had managed to overcome the guests over and over again.

From the boardwalk, a bystander might have thought this crossing was unenviable, maybe even impossible, but Antonia was a professional and she wove through the mess just as quickly as any other person would have crossed a completely empty street.

But it was just enough time for the situation to change.

She emerged on the other side of the surging crowds to

find Nate. The blogger was looming over Tabby with a truly alarming look on his face. Not angry, though—was this—was he—hitting on her?

Antonia's generally kept her personal feelings tamped down carefully at work, but at this affront they reared up. She could handle Tabby's not being into her—really, she could. But she could not handle anyone frightening or attacking a person she still considered very much under her protection. And while Antonia was here to protect *all* of her Patriots, Tabby was special. So she dropped all pretense of being a professional and shoved between the two of them, her hands up, ready to take Nate by the shirt-collar and show the blogger what happened when her rich Creole blood was boiling.

Then there was someone else there, stepping between them. She fell back and Tabby caught her, while the other person grabbed Nathan's shirt in both hands, just as Antonia had been planning, and flung him away from the wagon with impressive force. Antonia gasped as she realized the newcomer was Martin.

Nate stumbled backwards, tumbling into the pathway of one of those huge park rental strollers, being pushed by a very disgruntled looking mother. She didn't slow down for the lurching blogger in her path. The big plastic wheel on the stroller's side rapped Nate's bare ankle and he yelped in pain.

Shoulda worn socks, Antonia thought derisively. Then—oh, God, *Martin.* What was he doing? Why had he just shoved Nathan?

She got between Martin and Nate before anything else could happen, her heart beating in her throat. This was physical enough to get them both hauled before the county sheriff's deputy. There was one sitting at the front gates of the park right now, waiting for situations just like this. He signed the trespass orders.

A trespass would kill Martin. AtB was all he had.

She put a hand back, resting it on Martin's chest, and felt his pounding heart inside his soft flannel shirt. Then she focused her most dangerous gaze on Nate, still standing in traffic, buffeted by passing guests like a lone tree in a mudslide. "Do you have a problem with my Patriot, sir?" she asked chillingly.

"No—I—this guy! He's been following me," Nate complained, a whine in his voice. "All day. I saw him in The Big Apple, when I was in Luigi's Pizzeria, and then I saw him in the Forgotten Forests, near Sequoia Suppliers—"

"I need you to stop coming back here and harassing my Patriot," Antonia commanded, refusing to acknowledge the complaint about Martin. "Twice in one day is two times too many. If you have a problem, you need to bring it to Guest Services and they will handle it." She paused. "I think you're well aware of that, sir," she added meaningfully, and watched his face slacken with worry. *That's right,* she thought. *I know you're a regular and I know nothing scares you more than getting trespassed.*

"What about him?" Nate said. "Following me, shoving me, that's assault."

"What did he get in the middle of?" Antonia challenged. "Why did I hear yelling over here between a guest and a Patriot, if everything was so innocent? Why were you in her face? I don't think you want this all brought up in front of the sheriff. I don't think you're going to look very good." She paused again, considering him. He was pale, all right, you could see it even in the dim gaslight; this was a man who knew he'd been caught behaving badly and was afraid someone was going to tell Mother. Or the Internet. Or Edgar Eagle. "Might be hard to write that blog from outside the turnstiles," she suggested coolly, delivering the final blow.

Nate held up his hands, a man who has given up. "Fine," he said. "Fine, you've got me. I'll go. I can go, right? I'll go. I apologize." He looked over Antonia's shoulder. "Tabby? I apologize."

"Don't say her name," Antonia snapped. "Don't let me hear your name come out of her mouth ever again. You stay far away from her or Security will be on top of you and you'll be escorted right out of this park and you'll never come back again. I don't ever want you anywhere near her and I don't care if she's working, if she's not working, if she's in a different region, if she's in a different *park*—if you see her, you just turn right around and walk the other way. You got that?"

Nate's eyes were wide; his thick eyebrows reached his shaggy hair. "I got that," he repeated. "Yes, I understand."

"Go," Antonia said coldly. "Go home. I better not come across you in this park again tonight."

Nate nodded, the picture of subservience, and disappeared into the flood of families frothing through Old Dodge City.

Antonia took a deep breath and focused for a moment on the bright lights inside Sam Sweet's Candy Shop across the street. Then, satisfied she'd cleared her mind and smoothed her face, she turned around.

Martin was there, his sharp profile cast into gold and ebony by the sconce on the wagon beside him. Tabby was there, small and sharp-chinned and tired, her pigtails wilting in the humidity, her eyes wide with shock. Antonia felt a flood of affection for her that she knew wasn't worth exploring. And behind her, half-hidden in the shadows, tall and skinny like an out-of-place flamingo, stood Roseann.

"That was really something," Roseann said. "Not the way I would have handled it, maybe, but effective."

"Everyone has their own management style," Antonia said weakly, wishing like hell Roseann had just gone to dinner like she'd said she was going to. Could you really not trust any single member of management? This place could be an elaborate game of Big Brother sometimes.

"You said it," Roseann chuckled, but there was a discordant note to her cheer. "I came back to see if you wanted a coffee. But maybe you're just going to go scare the food and beverage Patriots into giving you one."

Now, Antonia did not have to scare the food and beverage Patriots into giving her anything. If she wanted a three-course meal of chopped salad and roast beef sandwich with tater tots and a tiny strawberry shortcake in a plastic tub, all she had to do was mosey over to the back door of Cowboy Cal's Good Grub and wink at Laney or Maureen, two kitchen supervisors who liked her style.

But she didn't say that. A manager offering coffee to a Patriot was kind of a big deal. It meant she was going to be welcomed to go into the office to drink her coffee while still on the clock, learning manager-things over the shoulders of whoever might be typing away in there. Even if that someone was going to be Roseann, she could still feel her heart lifting, reaching far above the chaos of the night.

"I could really use a coffee, thanks," she told Roseann.

"When Luis gets back from his change run, he'll radio

you," Roseann said. "Meet me in the office, then." She teetered back through the fray on her ridiculous shoes and disappeared inside.

Antonia looked at Tabby, who had recovered herself at this point. "Good for you," Tabby said. The significance of the manager's coffee was not lost on her, either.

"Did I miss something?" Martin asked, looking at Antonia's uplifted face and Tabby's appreciative one.

"Patriot politics," Tabby said with a shrug. "Thanks for pushing him away from me," she added softly, and Antonia heard a little quiver in her voice. "He really had me cornered against the register and I didn't know what to do."

"What did he want?" Antonia asked, even though she already knew. "I'll put it in the report."

"An incident report?" Tabby looked concerned. "Those take forever and I get off soon."

"No, just adding it to the closing report. You only have to fill out an incident report if you call security or first aid."

"He just said some nasty stuff about…it was nothing." Tabby blushed and looked down. "I'd rather not say. You can imagine."

The rage that had simmered down came back to a boil. Antonia clutched the corner of the wagon for a moment to steady herself. "And, Martin?" she asked as soon as her voice could be trusted again.

"Yeah?" He looked at her warily.

"Were you following him?"

"Not really."

"Martin!"

"You know that thing where you see one family in the morning and then all day it's like they're everywhere—you get lunch at the same place, you decide to ride something at the same time as them, you end up right behind them when you're leaving? It was like that. It wasn't intentional. But I didn't look away when we made eye contact, either."

"That would give anyone a stalker vibe, Martin."

They were quiet for a minute, looking out over the dim walkway and the brightly lit interiors of the storefronts beyond. Over the hidden speakers, a harmonica squealed out the tune of *When Johnny Comes Marching Home*. Antonia thought: *"Down, and around, and out of the rain,"* as the chorus finished another cycle.

The closing Patriots had another two hours of this, as the crowds slowly thinned, as the fireworks popped overhead, lighting up the old west with flashes of unwestern magenta and yellow and green. Then the park would empty of guests, and only Patriots would remain in the wide thoroughfares, their shirts untucked, sweeping and gathering discarded strollers (and the occasional discarded wheelchair, always a source of hilarity and shouts of *Another one miraculously healed by America the Beautiful!*). Soon after, the work lights would switch on, the music would switch off, and the white trucks of third-shift maintenance crew would arrive for a night of painting and cement-pouring and sign-hanging and shingling and flower-planting and lightbulb-changing and all the thousand and one things done between close and open to keep the park beautiful. Antonia loved watching the night cycle over from theme park to busy construction site; she'd missed that when she'd switched to mornings. Now, as a lead, she'd see it a few nights a week. That was nice.

But not tonight. Tonight, she was going to have coffee with a manager and then take her leave.

"You two take care of yourselves," she told Tabby and

Martin, and they nodded obediently.

Her radio chattered into her earpiece. "Back at base, I can take over for the night—you copy Antonia?"

Antonia smiled into the gaslit world she'd been entrusted with for a few minutes and pressed down the button of her microphone. "Ten-four, Luis. Have a great close."

CHAPTER ELEVEN

Sonia

Sonia liked being sent on supply runs.

There was the obvious cheerful aspect of just getting backstage, away from guests, for a while. Some roles included behind-the-scenes work as part of the day, whether it was hanging t-shirts or making cotton candy or wrapping silverware or just counting the money for the hundreds of cash register tills located all over the theme parks and resorts. But others, like Sonia's day-shifts at Gold Rush Rapids, did not offer any such respite from the onslaught of crowds, questions, and outright abuse that came at her every day.

Working at a place like Gold Rush, with a height requirement—albeit a very modest height requirement— was what management called a "high-touch position" and what Patriots called a "high-transfer" position, because very few people lasted much beyond the six months required before they could request a transfer to a new location or position. The entire concept of "You Must Be This Tall to Ride" could induce eyeball-melting fury in previously normal-seeming adults who just wanted their little angels to experience a classic America the Beautiful attraction for the first time.

And of course, whoever worked Greeter was the person nearest the official height stick. Thirty-nine inches wasn't tall enough to ride Gold Rush Rapids. Neither was thirty-nine and a half. It had to be forty inches. The safety restraints were designed for forty inches and up. Anything shorter than that, and no one could guarantee the kid would stay in the ride vehicle.

This could be very hard to explain to a shouting parent. Especially when the kid started crying. People got very used to flexible rules and "just this once" in the outside world. Even in the Retail and F&B locations around the parks. The height restriction rules were just about the only hard and fast rules AtB had.

There was a box behind the height stick filled with adorable little certificates entitling "Junior Prospectors" to go straight to the front of the line when they came back and passed the height requirement for the first time, and Sonia loved handing these out...when they were accepted, and the parent didn't just shout, "What makes you think we can ever afford to come here again?"

That always made the kid cry more.

Sonia had been considering a transfer for the past thirty-two minutes, ever since she'd drawn Greeter again the second she clocked in, and then had to deny *triplets* the right to ride their parents' most beloved attraction. And so when Bobby, the bright-eyed young management intern who was dedicated to lowering the historically atmospheric transfer rate at Gold Rush Rapids, offered her relief in the form of a supply run, she nearly burst into tears of relief. How had Bobby known that today, of all days, she couldn't handle the abuse?

Maybe if she had checked her mail last night, instead of this morning, she'd be over it by now. But they'd gotten home from the Gateway Pub fairly late, and Elena had driven right past the mailboxes to park by their apartment building, and Sonia hadn't felt like walking back. So she'd stopped and checked on the way to work this morning, and when she'd seen the envelope from the collection agency, she'd gone cold all over, then very hot, then cold again.

She hadn't been brave enough to open the letter until she'd gotten to the Patriot parking lot behind AtB. Then, with the car turned off so she couldn't accidentally drive off a convenient cliff, she tore open the envelope. Her fingers shook as she read how much they were chasing her for; it had taken her three tries to focus on the numbers and realize how well and truly screwed she was. The since-cancelled credit card that had saved her ass a few too many times was now sending postcards from Hell.

Sonia was still shaking, an hour later, as she walked towards the closest Underground stairwell. So much money! And for what? To make ends meet while working a job that barely paid rent. Why had she even gone to college? If all she'd planned on doing with her degree was letting guests yell at her in from in front of a mountain made of fiberglass and chicken-wire, she'd have skipped the student loans that ate her paycheck, and maybe avoided the impending doom of insolvency.

To be fair, she wasn't alone. Plenty of other Patriots were

facing collections, or bankruptcy, or skipping just ahead of it. She could ask for help. She could find out what they were doing, if anything, or if it was just a warning, or just a good reason to get a new phone number, or what.

But she'd still found it almost impossible to smile at the guests, even the nice ones. So Bobby's reprieve had been incredibly timely.

Now she was driving an electric cargo cart through the tunnel under Old Dodge City, the cold damp air plucking at her sweaty arms, feeling like a million bucks.

She had to drive carefully; the mid-morning Underground corridors were a hive of activity. Stock-room workers, arriving mid-shift Patriots, and day-shift maintenance crews finishing their day behind the scenes were all using the corridors as their workshops. The walls of the corridors were always lined with pallets and parked cargo carts and unused merchandise displays and wobbly popcorn carts which needed wheels replaced. Patriots were emptying pallets, or refilling them with returned and damaged items for shipment back to distribution hubs; they were filling mister fans with water at spigots and loading water carts with ice cubes; they were doing beverage counts and processing damages out of inventory and changing batteries on shopworn display items.

Between these energetic work zones were occasional pallets bearing mysteriously shaped items wrapped in diaphanous white sheeting, which might be new props for attractions or just new menu-boards for restaurants, both of which would be closely guarded state secrets either way. These items were always positioned close to security cameras, which were monitored, along with the theme park cameras, in a miraculous room filled with monitors, lovingly called Mission Control. Security knew the temptation those white sheets represented for the camera phone generation, and they weren't above dismissing the youngsters who couldn't display enough self-control to keep the park's secrets off of Instagram.

Sonia had never taken a picture of anything in the Underground, not even the adorable painted sign of Edgar Eagle in his best top hat and tails, pointing one wing to the left to indicate the Underground's exit.

Sonia turned right at Edgar Eagle, headed up to the bustling corridors under Liberty Plaza, where the office supplies closet was located.

"Hey Sonia," someone called behind her, and she paused the cart briefly to wave hello to Nick, who was walking in from the Underground's main entrance.

"Nick," she said pleasantly. "Is today the day you make me a happy woman?"

His blonde good looks clouded into confusion.

"With *Tabby*," Sonia clarified, glancing around to make sure no one was around. It was a rare private moment in the corridor, with only the timeless, husky croon of Sade coming from the speakers to keep them company. "Not with me."

"Oh, thank God," Nick grinned. "I was so worried for a minute. I thought I'd completely misunderstood you."

"You and Tabby like each other," Sonia said, slowly, as if talking to a child. Which was worrisome, considering the subject matter at hand. "Go ask her out already."

"I'm going to," Nick said. "I'm glad you told me. She's hard to read sometimes, you know?"

Sonia pictured Tabby's winsome brown eyes and the way her gaze followed Nick around a room. "Yeah," Sonia lied.

"I know."

Nick looked at his phone. "Oh shit," he said. "I gotta go clock in like…ten minutes ago." He took off down the corridor.

Sonia sighed. "That boy is an idiot, Tabby." Then she took off down the tunnel again, weaving around some custodians who had just appeared around the curve ahead with their backpacks on and their daily supply of fucks long gone. They trudged down the center of the tunnel, deep in conversation, and let the cart traffic flow around them, regardless of the posted rules.

She found a parking spot along the corridor wall about twenty feet away from the office supply closet and wedged the cart into it with a little difficulty. Parallel parking was not her strong suit when she got her driver's license, and it definitely wasn't with a glorified golf cart boasting a cargo bed six feet long, which had a disconcerting habit of coasting despite pressure on the gas pedal until it suddenly, with a great whine, burst into speed. She wasn't alone with this problem; the walls of the corridors were scraped throughout with long yellow streaks from the abused noses and tails of the cargo carts.

The cargo carts were part of one interesting problem all Patriots faced when they came to work at America the Beautiful. Everyone expected to do the usual parts of working with the public: the counting cash registers, the hanging of t-shirts on hangers, the shouting of "please stay behind the yellow line, this attraction cannot operate if anyone is across the yellow safety line"—but the light industry that came along with it, like driving electric cargo carts, using a cardboard baler with all its dire graphic warnings about being crushed into goo, or running electronic pallet jacks—that was all a big surprise to them. Working at the Gap or McDonald's had never prepared them for this.

But Sonia liked the odd industrial skills she'd picked up during her time here. They made her feel accomplished.

A guest tour flooded around the far corner of a cross-park corridor as Sonia prepared to hop out of the driver's seat, so she sat tight for a moment and let them flood past. The guests had wide-eyed looks of amazement on their faces, and everything their gazes touched—the white-painted cement walls, the old signs with characters pointing out the direction of different areas, even Sonia herself, in her Gold Rush Rapids costume of khaki shorts, hiking boots and chambray shirt—as if they were the most wonderful things any of them had ever seen.

Sonia loved that look, even if she thought it was the strongest case of the emperor has no clothes she'd ever witnessed. Coming to America the Beautiful altered people's minds, made them willing to suspend disbelief not only over the magnificent themed environments out in the park itself, but below the stairs and behind the scenes, where the fluorescent lights were prone to flickering, the air was damp, the floors were occasionally smeared with the trails of sticky-oily-goopy garbage bags from food and beverage, the smell of trash was always drifting down from the park's garbage chutes, and that supply closet for custodial nearby was notorious for some sort of noxious chemical odor which Sonia could only describe as a combination of chlorine and celery.

The guests on the backstage tour didn't seem to smell or see or step in any of these things. They saw only the magic that made their favorite place tick, and they didn't even notice how often the ticking went out of time.

Once the herd of guests had been shepherded past, on their way to look at a display case of Patriot costumes—which their adoring eyes would surely transform from faded polyester to the brightest and most regal of silks—Sonia slipped from the cart and down to the supply closet. The door was really just a chain-link fence gate, locked shut with a chain and lock as if she was trying to get into a garbage dump after hours. She used the big brass key on the cart's key-ring (a vintage leather fob of Lucky the Indian Pony galloping, a huge horsey smile on his face) to pop open the lock, fed the heavy chain through the hole in the chain-link, and slipped into what she privately thought of as her own Aladdin's Cave.

The supply closet was actually a huge, low-ceilinged room with every kind of office supply, from rubber bands to tape dispensers to the never-sharpened pencils that Retail Patriots used backwards, punching their touch-screen cash register displays with the erasers to save their fingers, arranged on endless shelves under the wan overhead lights. You took what you needed, tallied it up on a clipboard hanging near the door with your area's cost center for charging, and dumped it into one of the empty boxes stacked there if you had too much to carry back to your cart.

Today Sonia only needed some basics for Gold Rush's back offices—printer paper, some filing cabinet dividers, a new calculator to replace one which had been dropped into the Fossil Pool near the second lift-hill under mysterious circumstances—but she diverted first to the back corner where the old binders were kept. If there was no one else in the supply closet, this was *always* her first stop. The old binders came from all areas of the resort and were free to be re-used for any area...but they weren't always emptied of the ideas and records which they'd been used for previously.

Here Sonia had found old menus from the 1970s, featuring disturbing-sounding dishes like cottage cheese and shrimp with pineapple surprise (she had no interest in knowing what this surprise might be), and unrealized plans for Retail stores like the Edgar Eagle Haberdashery, where guests could try on hats from every century represented at America the Beautiful and presumably buy them, although Sonia assumed once the design team consulted Retail and realized guests didn't buy novelty hats, they just tried them on, took their pictures with them, and then discarded them on the floor, they canned the idea as an expensive waste. The space where the unrealized haberdashery would have gone was now the Independence Plaza Photography Exhibition, where you could buy a souvenir picture frame for twenty dollars and up (way up, actually) and they did a much more brisk business than a novelty hat shop could have done, in Sonia's opinion.

She'd allow herself ten minutes, Sonia decided, and then she'd gather up the basic stuff and hustle back to Gold Rush before Bobby got antsy and didn't send her on any more supply runs. She settled down on the floor before the shelf of binders, smiled in anticipation, and pulled one out at random.

The first binder wasn't that old and was relatively boring —just a lot of old financials for the ice cream shop in The Big Apple. The next one was a fat one-inch thick monster, which held promise at first, thanks to colorful art on the cover with Petals the Goose and Maracas the Parrot dancing under a palm tree. But inside it was just pages and pages of inventory counts from all the Retail locations in Smuggler's Cove. While it was kind of interesting to know that last April, the Pirate Galley had held a dizzying two thousand, five hundred and thirty-seven Souvenir Doubloons in its stockroom, this wasn't exactly worth skipping off from work over.

The third binder was a thin quarter-incher, and its edges were a little frayed with age. Sonia pulled it out without any expectations at all, good or bad. She had time for a few more. Either it was something, or nothing…either was fine.

The cover of this binder didn't have any artwork or title slipped behind its plastic sheeting, and she flipped open to the first page, mildly disappointed there wasn't a cute character. The managers building these usually found the strangest, most non-canon clip-art available online to decorate their work with—showing scenes that the official onstage artwork could never have, like Edgar Eagle marrying Petals the Goose, with Maracas officiating. She'd once seen that gem on a binder filled with prospective wedding cake ideas. Since everyone knew Edgar was sweet on Penelope Lark (although perhaps their relationship was haunted by the ghost of the never-realized Ophelia Owl) the mere act of taking this binder out in front of brides-to-be could have gotten the creator in trouble. Sonia loved these dalliances with the forbidden. In a company where everyone walked on eggshells, it was nice to know there were still ways to flaunt the rules.

A blank cover on a binder didn't impress her much. Even so, she'd committed herself. The first page was a list of chapters. Her eyes flitted down the list.

Her eyes widened.

Sonia looked up and around her, scanning the aisles for security cameras. She'd never taken a binder with the pages still in it before—you were supposed to empty them into the recycling bin before you left the supply closet. She'd never even taken a picture—she'd heard too many break room stories of Patriots fired after security camera footage revealed they'd taken a quick pic, even if they never shared it, of park secrets backstage.

But this was big. Forgotten, perhaps never known to more than a few people, and abandoned here like it didn't exist.

And, if handled carefully, this binder could solve the problem of that letter she'd shoved into the glove compartment of her car.

That made it worth the risk.

Sonia dropped the binder into one of the spare boxes by the door, and when she left a few minutes later, she didn't log it into the order. Would anyone ever notice a missing secondhand binder?

She doubted it.

Elena was already picking at a plate of nachos when Sonia slipped into the chair beside her. The sun was setting in lurid shades of red and orange behind the distant hills, and everyone on the patio of the Gateway was glowing golden. The scene was beautiful, but Sonia wasn't in the mood for beautiful. She was still shaking, if not on the outside, then definitely on the inside—her very organs were trembling, her nerves were on overdrive. She took a sip of Elena's Long Island Iced Tea, then a longer one. Elena narrowed her eyes.

"You can't get your own?"

Sonia put the glass down. "You can have some of mine. Sorry. Long day."

"You're not kidding. We had all the registers in the plaza go down at the same time today. Right after lunch, so I go on break, I come back, everyone's screaming. Crash kits out. Stupid kids saying they don't know how to calculate sales tax. I'm like, we were never that dumb. Tell me we weren't, Sonia." Elena shook her head, frazzled all over again. "It took an hour to get the system back up."

"We were definitely not that dumb," Sonia said, but inside she was wondering if she'd just reached a new level of dumb. "You get stuff from the supply closet under the plaza, right?"

"Yeah, why?"

"Are there cameras in there?"

Elena looked up from the nachos and smiled wickedly. "What did you take?"

"Are there?"

"No. Plaza Patriots take shit all the time. Last week one girl took home a bronze Lucky paperweight that came off some bigwig's desk. I guess when he retired, they just emptied what he left in his office into a box and threw it on a shelf."

"No one said anything?"

"Not even the manager, and she saw the girl come up with it and stick it in her locker."

Sonia nodded. The waitress, swinging by the table, interpreted the nod to mean yes, Sonia would like a Long Island Iced Tea, and continued towards the bar without stopping.

"What did you take?"

"A binder," Sonia whispered. "With plans in it."

Elena's sculpted eyebrows went up another inch, higher than Sonia would have thought humanly possible. "Confidential?" Her tone matched Sonia's.

"It didn't say." Sonia had flipped through the entire binder in the parking lot, not having been ready to take it out of her backpack until she was off property and parked some place relatively remote, where no passing manager could somehow peek through her car's tinted windows and see the pilfered documents. "But it's definitely plans for…" she looked around, and leaned in conspiratorially, "a redo of the Mighty Missouri. Maybe the one that guy was asking me about yesterday. I told you about him, right? Thinks they're closing Gold Rush Rapids and putting in a full-size wild rapids ride instead of just the one little flume we've got now?"

"No way," Elena hissed. "Are you serious? You have *proof?*"

"Shhhh…" Sonia looked around the patio nervously, but the other customers all went on with their own conversations, drinking away their day's discontents and absently watching baseball on the screens over the bar. There was no one nearby in a suit and tie, or an AtB polo shirt—the preferred outfit of the park designers and artists, who would be very interested to know an entry-level Patriot had found out that every hard-core park fan's fears were about to become a reality. "I'm serious. And the date on it is only a month old. It's a presentation, like what they'd use to sell it to the bigwigs. Someone must have dumped their copy in the recycle bin by accident."

"What are you going to do with it?"

"Sell it," Sonia admitted.

"You can't sell it," Elena whispered, her glass at her lips

as if to mask her words from any potential spies in the Gateway. "You could get termed if anyone finds out. Maybe even prosecuted."

"No one will find out. Unless you're telling." Sonia's words were bolder than her emotions.

"You know I'm not."

Sonia felt marginally better at having told someone else about her crime. And for finding out there were no security cameras in the supply closet. If a Patriot could steal a bronze paperweight out of an executive suite, she could definitely make it out with a binder that from the outside was a perfectly innocent used office item. She took a particularly cheesy nacho from the plate, ignoring Elena's impatient huff of breath, and bit down. It was the first thing she'd managed to eat since the morning's supply run had set her nerves dancing, and the cheap array of molten cheese, thin sour cream, and sprinkle of diced tomato tasted like heaven. "We're going to need another plate of these."

"You can buy it, high-roller," Elena grumbled, looking back at her phone. Sonia supposed the excitement of her secret was over. Elena's ability to just move on was comforting. It wasn't a big deal. This really wasn't a big deal.

She worked her way through half a drink and the second plate of nachos. By the time the table was clear of everything but crumbs and a few lost drops of sour cream, the clock was ticking towards ten and the pub was an uproar. In another hour, when the park and resort closers started arriving, even the airy patio would be standing room only. Sonia rarely stayed this late, but Elena hadn't seemed to notice. Or maybe she attributed it to Sonia's nerves over the binder. She glanced at the time on her phone once more, and her heart thudded wildly.

"I'm going home," she said, standing. "You coming soon?"

Elena was poking her straw around a glass of water, her alcohol funds gone for the day, and flicking her eyes around the tables, letting them rest briefly on decent-looking guys. "I might stay and see if I can get another drink," she said. "I'm off tomorrow. There's no reason to rush home to bed."

"Well I'm not," Sonia said. "So please be quiet when you come in."

"I promise."

The corner parking spot where she'd parked earlier, hoping to remain unseen, was now surrounded by other cars; under the orange streetlights, their decals of assorted AtB characters and ride slogans (*Meet me at Promise Mountain, Smugglers Cove is for Lovers*) glinted dully, the mark of employees who lived, breathed, and slept their jobs. They were all so obsessed, Sonia thought, until the day they weren't. And then they turned on it all with ferocity. She'd seen it happen at least a dozen times in the past two years. People who couldn't take the endless cycle of broke and tired and abused one more time, for whom all the bubbles from the champagne of theme park life had finally popped.

Sonia just wanted to avoid that. She wanted to keep on loving AtB. She wanted to make enough money to pay her bills. She wanted to move up and become a manager. She wanted a desk and a little time away from the guests so she could take a deep breath once or twice a shift. Sure, she wanted to be somebody. But she wanted to be somebody *here*. She didn't want to leave this place, or lose the feelings it gave her, ever.

In that context, how could selling the binder truly be bad? She was doing it to keep herself going here, to keep doing her part. This was her contribution to the future of America the Beautiful, and if the binder was stolen, well, she would pay the theme park back tenfold over the course of her career to come.

She leaned against the hood of her car and checked her phone. He hadn't texted her yet. In his email, he'd said he'd be here around ten. Well, it was ten fifteen. *Come on, come on,* she thought. *I want to be done with this and in my bed.*

Her phone buzzed while she was looking at it. *It's Nate. I'm in the parking lot, like we agreed. Are you here?*

CHAPTER TWELVE

Nate

Nate's first day at America the Beautiful had not gone the way he'd expected.

He was limping, for one thing. Hot and tired was to be expected; limping from a blister felt like the rankest kind of theme park newbie complaint. Someone who didn't gear up before their trip with long walks, wore the wrong shoes, wore cheap socks; *those* people got blisters, but not him.

Well, evidently, he did.

And the walk to the parking garages was a long one with a limp. Nate longed, as he so often did, for the olden days. Before Legacy of Heroes was built over top of AtB's vast acreage of parking lot, hundreds of rows of spaces torn up and replaced with roller coasters and food vendors, there had been a parking lot tram. Its roar and the cloud of diesel smoke it left in its wake had counted as the first and last moments of countless America the Beautiful vacations for so many people, Nate's included.

Nate knew, from the ceaseless nostalgia of threads in the AtBLive forums and on AtB Twitter, that he wasn't the only one who missed the parking trams. Now, it was true, theme park fans could be nostalgic for anything: an old bathroom with outdated tiles; a background music loop that was just recycled movie tunes; a particular brand of corn dog batter that was changed out in the nineties.

But the parking trams had been special *and* saved everyone a walk. Granted, the Petals and Pals parking garage complex was just about a five-minute walk from either park's front gates. This did not change the fact that he'd already walked ten miles today, and every step on his blistered heel was torment. Also, he was really sweaty and hot.

Nate turned to his only refuge from physical discomforts: his phone.

"We should rise up and petition AtB to bring back parking trams!" he tweeted. "This forced march to the Petals garage is BS."

After a few seconds, his phone screen lit up with responses, the majority of which agreed with him, and Nate smiled, forgetting his blister for a blessed moment.

He was walking along a very pleasant promenade, which he'd acknowledge and even live-stream in a better frame of mind. Lit up with blue-white globe lanterns and lined with blossoming shrubs, led between two hulking parking garages. At the center, where the elevators and escalators hummed, he was greeted with the illuminated face of Petals the Goose, her wings outstretched around a flock of other cartoon birds who were equally interested in promoting space-saving car parking options.

As Nate approached, a group of teenagers were taking selfies with the sign. He ran his eyes over their faces to see if he recognized anyone from Twitter, but no. All strangers. He hoped he started meeting fans in the parks…maybe he should have buttons made, so that he could have park meet-ups and give out swag. Something fun that said *I met Nate from AtBLive IRL* or something.

Actually, he thought, that was *exactly* what they should say.

He hustled past the teenagers in case they wanted to tease him for being a thirty-year-old guy in a ripped Gold Rush Rapids t-shirt, alone at a theme park, but no one noticed him. Nate was incognito, which, after feeling hunted by that crazy fan of Tabby's, and that vindictive manager from the Plaza, felt like a nice change.

In his car at last, the air conditioning cranked to eleven, he snapped out a few quick replies to supporters of his tram grievance, blocked a couple of haters who found it necessary to make snide comments about his physical condition (*So rude,* Nate thought, like they had any idea if he was in shape or not) and checked his direct messages. A message from an account with no profile was not promising. He flicked it open after a moment's hesitation, hoping there wasn't something gross waiting for him.

No dick pics, just a question.

Got something big on AtB - u interested?

He frowned at the phone. Over the past few years of running AtBLive, Nate had assembled a small group of Patriots who were happy to send him tips on updates to the parks and resorts—nothing was too mundane to make his readers happy as long as they read it before the parks' official website posted it. Upcoming resort rate hikes, the possibility of serving breakfast at Big Apple Diner, a new shade structure going over the queue at Escape from Atlanta—these all meant big spikes in page traffic for his site, and new followers on his social media accounts, and together those meant better advertising banners, more clicks, and higher pay-outs.

But he rarely got anything he would characterize as "big."

How big?

There was no immediate answer. He put the phone down and backed out of his spot. By the time he'd gotten to the stoplight at the garage exit, a die-cut metal Petals encouraging him to fasten his seatbelt and pull over for any texts, the phone had lit up with the response. He picked it up again.

You're going to need more server space for this one.

The cars behind him were blowing their horns, but under the green glow of the traffic light, Nate's fingers flew across the phone's screen.

He saw her before she saw him, and got out of the car, lifting a hand in greeting. He'd parked in the farthest corner of the lot, as requested, in a space shadowed by an oak tree. Pinpricks of orange from the street-lights pressed through the spaces between the leaves and branches, but all he had to do was go behind the car and he'd be invisible, especially to anyone leaving the bright Gateway Pub with a couple of strong drinks in them. He saw her hesitate and came around the front of the car, into the light. Girls were skittish about meeting guys from the internet, he knew.

"I was in the other corner," she said in a low voice, New Jersey tugging at the edges of her vowels. "Thanks for waiting."

"You said it'd be worth my time," Nate said, feeling deliciously like a character in a noir spy movie. He wished he had a trench coat, although the hot, humid night would not exactly lend itself to such a prop.

"It is." The girl put a backpack on the hood of his Civic and unzipped it. He saw a gray binder there, no label or anything on the cover. She drew it out, flipped to the second page, pointed at the words there.

Nate's breath caught in his throat.

Mighty Missouri Revitalization: Gold Rush Rapids 2.0 and Gold Rush Ghost Town

He snatched at the binder, but the girl was quick and drew back. "Sorry," she said with a small smile. "This is the point of payment."

"What else is in there?"

"Everything. It's an executive-level presentation. Pre-stockholder." They all knew the jargon, they all knew the steps between artists' renderings and actual build-outs. They were all such nerds, really. "All it needs is the hard sell to the board. This confirms the rumors. It's all here."

"Concept art?"

She flicked through the pages and peeled one back teasingly, as if lifting a skirt to show a shapely ankle. Nate saw watercolors gleaming under the dull orange lights, bleached out colors filling in the sketched lines of a crumbling saloon with tumbleweeds in the foreground, a happy family on a raft cresting a mighty wave, a towering peak of red sandstone rising behind them. The scale was impossible, dwarfing the current Gold Rush Rapids with its tame descents and narrow final flume.

"They're really doing it," he breathed. "The full shoot-the-rapids ride. On the Mighty Missouri. *And* the Ghost

Town? All of it?" Nate shook his head in disbelief. This was a massive redo of Old Dodge City. The only thing left would be a handful of buildings on the walkway facing the river…or facing the new ride, he supposed. "I've never seen a park region get ripped up to this extent," he went on.

The young woman wasn't interested in talking it out with him. She slipped the binder back inside the bag, glancing over her shoulder. A group of guys, still wearing the bottom halves of their Big Apple costumes—knickerbockers and knee socks—came tumbling out of a car nearby and headed towards the Gateway. The first clock-outs of the closing shift were arriving. Pretty soon there'd be swarms of Patriots all over this parking lot, shouting and necking and pissing in dark corners—like this one.

"Five hundred bucks," he said desperately, his hands itching to touch the binder, flip through the pages no one outside of the company had seen.

"Two thousand," the Patriot said with a little snort, slipping the backpack over one shoulder.

"Eight hundred," Nate replied, thinking they were doing a sitcom-style negotiation, and they'd meet somewhere around twelve hundred dollars, which was the amount of money in his checking account.

"Two thousand," the Patriot repeated, taking a step backwards.

"A thousand," he sighed.

"Two. Thousand." She smiled. "You're not the only blogger, Nate."

"Fine, two thousand," he blurted. More than he wanted to pay, but she was right. He had competition for this scoop; established, older blogs with the cash to throw at a find like this. He'd make more than two grand on advertising clicks over the next week, once these pages were scanned and uploaded. But he had to move fast. An announcement from the company, a leak from another source—his chance would be over in a matter of seconds. "I don't have that on me."

"Venmo me, man." She shook her head at him like he was an idiot. "I don't take checks."

Nate didn't have two thousand dollars anywhere, but he did have a credit card attached to his Venmo. With trembling fingers, he directed the money to the email address she specified. He watched her take out her phone and wait for the email confirmation, all the while ready to spring after her if she took the money and ran. He didn't actually know what he'd do—she was small and lithe and probably ran like a gazelle startled by a lion—but fear was pulsing through his veins and he had a feeling he might catch her on sheer adrenaline.

Her phone dinged. She scrolled, nodded, looked at him with satisfaction. Then she handed over the bag. "Pleasure," she said. "You never saw me."

And she walked away through the orange-lit parking lot, leaving Nate in the shadows, his heart thudding so hard he could feel his teeth clacking together with every beat, the old backpack with its illicit cargo heavy in his hands.

CHAPTER THIRTEEN

Antonia

Martin knocked about fifteen minutes after Antonia had shut her door behind her. Oswald looked up from his bowl, startled.

"It's just Martin," she told the cat, and unlocked the door again, opening it just a crack. "What?" she asked, her tone unfriendly. She was too tired for one of Martin's emotional evenings. Sometimes, he had to be put back into his place: neighbor.

Martin smiled endearingly at her. "I have champagne," he offered, showing her the bottle in his hands.

Antonia regarded it. "That's sparkling wine," she said after a moment. "Not sure I should open my door for that."

"Do *you* have sparkling wine in *your* apartment?" Martin countered.

Antonia pursed her lips at him. "Good play," she said

finally, and opened the door wide.

Martin came in and went directly into the little kitchen, opening cabinet doors in a hunt for wine glasses. Antonia sat back down on her cracked leather couch, pulling Oswald into a fluffy ball on her lap. "What's the occasion?"

"Your first big day as a lead! You were amazing." Martin popped the cork with a dull *thunk*. The sound was too much for Oswald, who departed for Antonia's bedroom, leaving behind a two-inch scratch on her calf. She regarded the claw-mark with irritation while Martin poured the straw-colored wine and brought it, still fizzing like a freshly opened Sprite, to her outstretched hand.

"What do you think of your new job, Miss Bigshot?"

"I can't say it's what I expected."

"Some weird stuff went down today. Oh, wait!" She took a sip of wine. "You were there."

"I'll bet that kind of thing happens more often than you'd think," Martin said, although he looked slightly embarrassed. "And poor Tabby."

"Internet stalkers," she sighed. "Just what every theme park worker needs. Like we aren't under *enough* pressure."

"I can keep an eye on her, you know," Martin said.

She looked at him. "Excuse me?"

Martin missed the consternation in her tone. "Your Patriot. Tabby. You know I'm around a few days a week. I'll just keep an eye on things when I'm around, make sure that guy's not bothering her or, I don't know, hiding out on Wilderness Isle watching her with binoculars or something." He smiled at his own generosity, but Antonia could see right through it.

Good grief. Why did *everyone* fall for Tabby? Herself, included? She shook her head at him. "Martin, you came really close to getting into trouble with park security tonight. Don't do it again, okay? Leave this to us. The people on the pay-roll. You just show up and enjoy the park like you're supposed to."

Martin looked disappointed in her. He took a sip of sparkling wine and let his eyes flick around the living room, landing on the little bits of America the Beautiful ephemera decorating the shabby space—the vintage poster for the Glorious Grottoes of Promise Mountain, not really a print but an illustration taken from a calendar; the little plastic character figurines given out at Patriot training meetings for participating in the innumerable impromptu skits that were part of every curriculum; the ceramic Ophelia Owl grinning down from the bookshelf next to the television, with a few America the Beautiful souvenir hardback guidebooks from the 80s carefully stacked next to her. Antonia knew her apartment was just like ninety-nine percent of the other Patriot apartments, and just like Martin's, as well—filled with the thrift-store finds, eBay bargains and company-store cast-offs of an entertainment and leisure empire they couldn't ever shake.

Antonia thought, not for the first time, how insane they all were.

Martin drained his glass and stood up. "Well, I won't keep you up late," he began.

"Sit down, idiot." Antonia retrieved the bottle from the kitchen and refilled their glasses. "Let me just tell you something about Tabby. She's not what she seems."

Martin lifted his eyebrows.

"She's kind of an innocent," Antonia clarified. "Despite her reputation. So before you start believing everything you hear—"

"I don't hear anything," Martin interrupted. "I'm not a Patriot, remember? I'm just a passholder. I don't get your gossip."

Antonia laughed. "Oh, that's right! Oh, you little dear. You're as innocent as she is. It's just like this…she's into an idiot. And she's probably going to have to get that idiot out of her system before you can get anywhere with her."

"The blonde kid."

"Yup."

Martin swirled his glass, looking thoughtful. "Are they dating?"

She thought of the scene she'd interrupted tonight, right before she'd marched Nate to the manager's office and handed him over to Roseann for a discipline note. That hadn't been about Tabby, even if some people would probably think otherwise. The truth was, Antonia couldn't stand it when a Patriot flaunted the very basics of the stagecraft that they were taught from day one. They were entrusted with a legacy of wonder on a daily basis, and pulling out a phone in Old Dodge City was just about the worst way a Patriot could break character in front of guests. Anything she could do to hasten Nate's departure from AtB would be front and center now that she was a supervisor, and if that also hastened his departure from Tabby's life, well, she wasn't too upset about that either. But, she reminded herself, that wasn't the main reason she was going to get him disciplined right out of a job. That was just a perk.

"They're about to be," she said finally. "But it's not going to last."

Martin still looked pained.

"It's for the best," Antonia insisted. "She needs to date

an idiot or she'll never appreciate you."

"I'm sure she's dated other idiots," Martin said, attempting to smile.

Antonia bit back a pointless retort: *You calling me an idiot?* Then again, maybe he didn't know she'd dated Tabby. Might as well keep that to herself. They'd hardly been more than a few friendly dinners together, anyway.

From high on the wall next to the sliding-glass doors to the patio, Antonia's Penelope Lark clock struck the hour with a piping bird trill. She looked over. "Midnight, Martin. This was one long day." She considered the golden wine in her glass. "You know what? This is good. Thanks for bringing it over."

"You're welcome, Antonia. Thought you could use the celebration." He stood up, preparing to leave, but she pulled him back down to the couch.

"Stay, help me finish it. My grandmother always said there was no putting the spirit back in the bottle."

"That was her way of saying always drink the whole thing?"

"Yup." Antonia drank, smacked her lips, poured another. "Can't disappoint my dead grandmother's soul. She'll haunt you. And that bitch could get mean in a hurry."

So Martin settled back down, the old couch creaking beneath him, and in a cheerfully mutual decision they pulled out their phones and began scrolling through the day's weirdness, occasionally reading aloud particularly stupid or strange messages.

"Get a load of this one," Antonia chuckled. *"Patriot culture is coming to the park on your day off, but eating lunch in the underground cafeteria just like you're working because you can't afford a ten-dollar hot dog."*

"That explains the guy I saw eating a Subway sandwich while he was waiting for the parade last week. I couldn't figure out where he got it."

Antonia guffawed. "I know some guys who will get one for you with a two-dollar delivery fee, if you're ever interested. They hang out by the Gotham Ice Cream Palace."

"That's so not what I want," Martin snorted. "Trust me, my escape from reality does not include a five-dollar foot-long."

"Suit yourself, Richie Rich. They're seven bucks now, anyway."

Martin went back to scrolling. Then he stiffened and sat up. "Look at this," he said, but he made no move to show her his phone.

Antonia leaned across the couch. "Making me work for it," she grumbled. Then she gasped. "Is this for real?"

Exclusive concept art reveals plans to remake Mighty Missouri, replace waterway with family thrill ride.

"Click the link," Antonia urged. "Quick!"

The site took forever to load, and no wonder—even though it was midnight on the east coast, there were people all across the country who were still up, still scrolling Twitter, still looking for something worth looking at—and leaked concept art was a big deal. "This site's gonna crash," Martin muttered.

"Yeah, well, this is huge," Antonia said. "This is AtBLive, right? Okay, so how did that weirdo guy get ahold of it?"

"You mean, when he *wasn't* stalking Tabby?"

"Yeah, dude apparently had a full day."

Martin thumbed slowly down the page, skimming the text and reading aloud key points, pausing for long looks at the concept art. The page had only been live for three minutes and there were already thirty-two comments. Antonia leaned back against the arm of the sofa and stared at Martin, dazed.

"A new ride!" He grinned at her. "This is exciting!"

"This is *huge,*" she repeated. "And it's my land! Oh my God, no wonder they made me a lead overnight. They're playing with head-count because half the land is going to close for this to get started. They're probably shipping the senior Patriots off to other lands. This is what happened when they closed Sequoia for a six-month refurb. But *this* —" She looked at the artwork again. "This is going to take longer than six months. This is a full-scale new build."

"The whole Gold Rush end will have to close in order to add all this ghost-town stuff," Martin agreed. "And it looks like Wilderness Isle absorbs most of the infrastructure of the white-water rapids ride."

Antonia had brought up the article on her laptop and was enlarging the pictures as far as she could without pixelating them to death. "Shit, you might be right. So there goes our nice, quiet Wilderness Isle." The island in the center of the Mighty Missouri was a wooded little corner of peace in the busy theme park, with a pretty windmill squeaking away on one end and at the other, a small, Sioux-type village with fiberglass tents, horseback men with feathered braids, and crouching women in deerskin tending campfires.

Many was the time Antonia had taken a packed lunch and a can of soda over to Wilderness Isle, riding the half-empty raft that ferried guests between Old Dodge City and the island's little dock, and sat undisturbed on a bench to eat, tossing crumbs to neighborly ducks.

"I hate to see Wilderness Isle go for anything, even a new

ride," Martin sighed, echoing her thoughts. "It's a little piece of the seventies when everything else has to be digitally enhanced."

"Not to mention the last place you can go in the park where you're assured some quiet and shade."

"That, too."

"And it means this is really about filling in half the Mighty Missouri and making it into a water ride. So no more side-wheeler, no more river views…" Antonia trailed off, horrified at the loss as much as she'd been initially thrilled at the idea of a new ride.

They looked at the page until they were satisfied they couldn't glean any more info from the scanned photos, then they decamped back to their phones to look at Twitter and soak up the reactions of the collective theme park fandom —at least, the ones who were awake. The sparkling wine disappeared and was replaced by more mundane bottles of beer; pretzels were retrieved from the pantry; Oswald ventured back out and was rewarded with a spot between the friends where he could receive plenty of pats and ear scratches from both sides. For a little while, personal dramas and complicated romances could be forgotten.

There was theme park drama to indulge in, and this time, it didn't involve any of Antonia's friends.

"I wonder who was crazy enough to leak all of this," she said.

"Someone who doesn't care about their job," Martin replied. "I hope they already have something else lined up."

CHAPTER FOURTEEN

Protest

Tabby

Tabby was opening the sunglass wagon again.

She'd clocked in at ten fifty-eight with high hopes of getting on register in Sam's Sweet Shop, because on such a bright, hot day as this one, the sunglass wagon should have been open already. But no, she drew Sunglass Wagon as her first post, and so she had to trudge out across the hot concrete to the tarped and shuttered Conestoga to get it opened for the day.

One thing the Wagons had going for them was a beautiful view, and Tabby couldn't help but notice how lovely the Mighty Missouri was as it curved lazily behind the hedge separating the water from the walkway. From somewhere on the other side of Frontier Island, the side-wheeler tooted a long good morning to her. Tabby smiled at her little world as she unfastened the pegs holding down the tarps, and rolled them into place, and signed onto the cash register. Then, almost instantly, she sold a scowling mom of twins a pair of thirty-dollar sunglasses.

At first, Tabby didn't notice anything different about this day from any other summer morning. Hot sun in a glaring yellowish sky, check. Growing crowds beginning to clot the walkways, check. Stuck at an outside location most of the day, check. This was the kind of day when a passing Patriot might call, "Hey Tabby, how are you today?" and the only possible reply was a sarcastic, "Living the dream!" Meaning that yeah, maybe they'd all been sold a bill of goods about the endless joy of working at AtB, but they weren't exactly turning in their notice, either. She found a spot in partial shade and hovered there, watching the passing families, swaying gently to the music.

She'd been at work nearly twenty minutes when she noticed the chanting.

It was a distant rumble of noise, like a faraway storm not yet clearing the horizon. She looked towards Promise Mountain, where the sound seemed to originate. Nothing amplified; it wasn't part of the stage show. Maybe an impromptu parade? Tabby didn't follow sports, but maybe some championship had been decided yesterday and the team was being celebrated at the park today.

But this didn't sound like a parade, either. And anyway, it would have been advertised backstage: banners hung at the entrance to the Underground, notices in the elevators, a handwritten message on the white-board next to the clock-in computer. Patriots didn't like surprises.

The noise grew in volume. It was definitely people making all of that sound. Maybe all the Brazilian tour groups had converged at once and were chanting like they were at a World Cup match? But this wasn't musical, either.

This sounded like a swarm of angry wasps. Tabby squinted past the log cabin marking the boundary between Old Dodge City and the rest of the park, towards the towering hulk of Promise Mountain in the hazy distance, desperate for any giveaway of what was coming. A few dozen feet away, she saw the turkey leg vendor at the Patriot's Place breezeway step away from her cart, holding up her hand to block the sunlight as she looked for the source of the oncoming noise.

And then there it was.

A sea of people, shouting and waving, marched on Old Dodge City with the sort of determination that had conquered the West *for real*.

They came over the wooden bridge from Promise Promenade to Old Dodge City with loudly tramping feet, waving signs that curled at the edges from being rolled up secretively into backpacks and purses, scrolls of protest that never would have made it past security otherwise. Moving as one enormous mass of humanity, they poured past the facades of the Shootin' Arcades and Professor Cloud's and Sam's Sweet Shop and right past Tabby, who scampered out of their way and watched from the shadow of the wagon, transfixed.

She was used to doing impromptu head counts, so now she estimated the mob was about fifty or sixty people strong, mostly adult men. There were some women too, and a few older children, thankfully no small ones. She thought they must be protesting something the company had done; America the Beautiful was but a subsidiary of Taylor Enterprises and, like any large corporation, Taylor invested in things that went directly against the sweet and family-friendly image they presented to the world. This was going to be about bottled water drying up rural wells in Florida, or campaign contributions to alleged Fascists.

Then a shouting, sweating young man turned his sign in her direction, and she saw the slogan for the first time.

Landmark Gold Rush Rapids and Save the Mighty Missouri!

Tabby's hand went to her mouth.

That was what they were chanting, too. She could hear it now: "Save the Mighty Missouri!" in the burr of a dozen regional and international accents. People who lived here, she figured; the article had only come out at midnight, no one could have flown here, or driven all night, to do a protest less than twelve hours later.

Right?

She looked at their righteously outraged faces as they vehemently shouted for their theme park river to be preserved for all time, and she had to wonder.

Park guests who weren't part of the protest were shunted to either side, and Tabby soon found herself backed against her wagon as more and more strollers crammed into the dwindling space left to them. A woman looked at her with wild eyes, shrieking kids howling from their stroller. "What the hell is this?" she demanded.

Tabby could only shake her head. There was no Themed Reply for this kind of behavior.

When the protestors passed, giving her some welcome breathing room, she saw the Patriots from the shops across the walkway come out to gape after them. The families shoved aside were enjoying a kind of survivorship bonding moment; they were holding up their phones, taking video and pictures of the departing mob, laughing nervously with each other. A few of them bought some sunglasses from Tabby, who worked the register with shaking fingers.

"I hope Sonia isn't working this morning," she said out loud, handing a receipt to a bemused looking father of three.

"Me, too," he said supportively.

Sonia

Sonia was beginning to wonder if there was some problem with her training record.

When she'd signed in at eight-thirty this morning, she could have picked up any of nine positions that were part of Gold Rush Rapids' opening procedures. Positions handling the attraction queue and lining-up guests like Grouper or Load A or Load B or Dispatch. Back-of-house positions handling security, safety and ride control. It took a lot of people to run a hybrid dark ride/coaster with multiple dark scenes, water-filled flumes, animatronics figures, and a total ride time of twelve minutes, thirty-two seconds. A lot could go wrong in that amount of time, and working the critical positions was a point of pride with a lot of Patriots, Sonia included. She was damned good at Dispatch and had trained dozens of new Patriots on grouping, helping them divide parties and get the guests loaded into ride vehicles as fast as possible to keep the Dispatcher sending out vehicles at optimum time.

So on an opening shift, she usually hoped for one of those positions—getting the ride dispatch area and queue ready for guests, snapping up ropes and setting stanchions in the queues, before sending out the first arrivals. It was a great start to her day.

But no, she picked up Greeter.

Again.

"For God's sake!" She stared at the computer for so long that a queue formed behind her, growing antsier as the clock ticked towards 8:29.

"We've got to clock in, Sonia!" someone hissed. "Move it already!"

Sonia moved to one side, forgetting to log out, and the girl behind her gave an exaggerated sigh as she clicked the button for her. "What's *wrong* with you?" she demanded.

"I got Greeter again. I have literally only done Greeter for the past five shifts. Could it be broken?"

"It's just luck of the draw," the girl said pitilessly, smiling at her own assignment. Dispatch. "Maybe someone will pick it up after open and you can get a new assignment."

Sonia doubted it. The past few days, there hadn't been enough staff to get her out of Greeter before her lunch break. Rumor had it that staffing wasn't sending any new summer interns to Gold Rush Rapids this year, and they were going to have to make do with what they had. If Sonia hadn't just paid the collections agency enough to get them off her back, she'd have been rejoicing about the amount of authorized overtime available this summer. As it was, she just wanted to survive on her forty hours for a while. Anything more than that while working so many shifts at Greeter was just a slog.

She trudged out of the break room, up the ramp that led from Rapids' back-of-house operations, and through the rustic-looking gate into the sprawling concrete plaza in front of the attraction entrance. The pavement was painted a rich earthy orange and weathered with cracks and bumps and the imprints of leaves and hooves, to give it the appearance of a broad dirt clearing somewhere in the American West, a hazy term given to everything west of the Mississippi and before 1900. Real cactus and aloe vera plants adorned the hillside leading up to the Rapids' indoor queue, which was reached through a maze of switchbacks at ground level. Everything was lined with a rustic wooden fence, which was actually made of fiberglass. In the distance, the plaza dropped into the wide walkway which sloped into Old Dodge City, and the brown Mighty Missouri lazed through a green curtain of elms.

It was a beautiful sight first thing in the morning, before the endless guests began trundling their strollers up the hill, sweating and dropping water bottles, spraying sunblock everywhere, smoking as if they had no idea that in the twenty-first century, in a so-called civilized society, you couldn't just light a cigarette wherever the hell you wanted. Without humans to muck it all up, Old Dodge City was the most beautiful place in the world, and it all belonged to Sonia. She had to pause for a moment and take it all in. Sonia leaned against a fence and took a deep breath of clean, unsweaty morning air.

Her supervisor came stalking over, hands behind his back. "Sonia, grab the QwikRide sign and put it out, please, and then go check all the switchbacks to make sure they're set for a sixty-minute queue. We're prepping for a fifty-k day."

Sonia decided to ask him while she had him. "Richie, what's the deal with me getting Greeter all day, every day? Can you look at my training record and see if it's messed up?"

He pushed thin eyebrows together. "It's just luck of the draw, Sonia."

"No, this is something else," she argued. "Listen, who is the opening manager? I want to talk to them."

Richie shrugged. "It's just me this morning."

Sonia gaped at him. "We can't open an attraction without a manager!"

"Well, we are." Richie moved a stanchion, pointedly starting her work for her. "So, can you just get the entrance plaza set for an overflow queue?"

She bit her lip before she said something rude. "Fine, Richie," she grumbled, pushing off the fence.

Sonia hoisted the heavy A-frame sign for the QuikRide entrance from its hiding place behind the back-of-house gate and brought it out to the entrance plaza, setting it near the metal-ringed hole in the ground where she'd begin building the overflow queue. Fifty thousand guests was a very busy day. She began the tedious process of setting up the wooden poles in their rings, creating the switchbacks that would hold up to ninety minutes' worth of guests as they wound through the plaza.

When she was done, she was sweating and the morning opening announcement was already playing over the park's speakers. Then the usual twangy banjo music took over. A low rumble behind her announced the presence of the ride vehicles, filtering through the lift-hills and slipping down the ride's grand finale water flume. An intern who had been granted today's First Ride squealed dramatically on the plunge towards the rocks below. Sonia sighed, feeling something which registered right between contentment and resignation. Gold Rush Rapids was cycling normally, the park was open, the queue's wait-time sign read "15 minutes." It was showtime.

Sonia walked down to the Greeter position, where a thin

rope was clipped across the pathway to the plaza, and reeled it back to its nook in the bushes. Then she stood with her hands behind her back and a smile plastered on her face, as the sun picked out the ripples on the Mighty Missouri and the first guests began to appear on the streets of Old Dodge City.

Another day in paradise.

All morning Sonia spieled her spiel, her howdy pardners and her restrooms are thataways and her QuikRide is to the lefts and her stroller parking is to the rights. The morning crowds were steady, coming at her in ever more sticky waves as the heat began to ramp up, and there was a scent of perspiration mixed with coconut sunblock in the air that would only get stronger as the day wore on towards lunchtime, mingling with fried chicken and French fries and hot dogs and churros. Sonia sweated under her costume and hoped fervently her break would come early, and an indoor assignment, somewhere dark and quiet, would come her way afterwards.

Unless the computer really was broken and wasn't giving her anything but Greeter anymore. Sonia nodded mechanically at guests and wondered if Richie had quietly unchecked all of her training records. Would he do something like that to her? But why? She barely knew him.

Then, a strange hum of noise made her gaze snap from vacant to focused. She looked down the slope towards Old Dodge City and saw a large group of people walking—no, *marching*—across the bridge. They were waving signs. A mob? A protesting mob, in America the Beautiful?

Her radio crackled and she hastily popped her dangling earpiece back into her ear. She heard Richie's voice, fuzzy with static. "Greeter from Gold Rush One. Duty manager says do not allow the approaching crowd into the entry plaza."

Was he kidding? Sonia counted a good fifty people down there, making steady progress through Old Dodge City as little family groups leapt out of their way. She saw Security Patriots lurking ahead of their route, but they weren't blocking the mob…so why should she even try?

She pressed down the button on her radio. "Negative, Gold Rush One. I'm not going to be able to stop them from doing anything."

The reply was quick. "Sending assistance to Greeter. Attention all units this frequency, non-essentials report to Greeter."

Sonia watched the mob hit the base of the slope and had an idea. They could be funneled off to the gate next to Gold Rush Rapids and sent backstage—but only if the ride wasn't running. Otherwise, they'd be within striking distance of moving vehicles, a massive violation of safety protocol. "Gold Rush One," she said, "cycle down the ride and we can push the crowd through the gate."

There was a pause. She knew Richie was calculating the number of guests in the inner queue and the overflow. At least seventy-five minutes' worth of them. "Negative. That's security's call."

Of course. Richie didn't make enough money to make a hard call about cycling down a busy ride, and there was no Manager on Duty this morning to do the dirty work and close Gold Rush Rapids. This was crazy. What was going on? She squinted at the signs, and suddenly they came into focus.

Save Gold Rush Rapids!

The Mighty Missouri is an American Icon!

Sonia realized why they were here, and her heart stuttered for a moment.

She'd done this.

And they were coming here to take over Gold Rush Rapids. Or something. Who knew what a bunch of crazed park fans were capable of?

Sonia got back on the radio. "Gold Rush One, e-stop this ride and let's get these guys out back. They're coming for our attraction. Repeat, they're coming for *our* attraction."

Suddenly, Richie was at her side. His face was pale, his thin lips bloodless.

"Where the hell is the manager?" Sonia demanded, heedless of the surrounding families, all now avidly watching the protestors proceeding up the slope towards them. "You shouldn't be responsible for this."

"I'm not going to be responsible for this," Richie said. "And you won't be, either. Let them pass, let them go wherever they want. This isn't on us. It's for Security to handle." He lifted his mic to his lips and tersely said, "Dispatch, this is Gold Rush One. E-stop the attraction."

You didn't question a command to hit the Emergency Stop button. Sonia heard, "Ten-four, Gold Rush One, e-stop in progress," and then there was a shriek of screaming wheels as ride vehicles hit their braking zones and slammed to a stop. Guests began shouting; a tearful wailing went up from some startled child on the ride. Beyond the QuikRide entrance, Sonia saw the backstage gate open and a blue-shirted contingent of Security Patriots poured out.

She stepped back with Richie, pressing their backs to the fence as guests shoved their way out of the queue and the mob steadily approached, miserably aware that she was, in fact, responsible for this.

***

Nate

Nate leaned on the wooden fence alongside the sparkling little waterfall of Gold Nugget Creek and trained his telephoto lens on the crowd marching up to Gold Rush Rapids. The water in the creek spilled noisily on round rocks and polished quartz as it splashed down a green embankment on its way to join the Mighty Missouri. But no one was leaning over the wooden fence to admire the tumbling creek right now.

Everyone's eyes were on the drama taking place on the slope just ahead.

Guest were standing around in tight, nervous groups all around Old Dodge City. Some of them had been shoved aside by the mob; others had just wandered over from the Forgotten Forests or Pirate's Bayou and were surprised to find a bona fide riot taking place in front of Gold Rush Rapids. Nate listened to their chatter, waiting for someone to mention the planned destruction of this entire end of Old Dodge City, but so far, no one had any idea what was going on.

"What do they want?" a kid of ten or eleven asked.

"No idea," said his father.

"Maybe the ride is dangerous," a nearby man suggested. "Maybe someone died on it."

"We would have heard about that," the father said. "It would have been on the news."

"We didn't watch the news last night," the kid's mother said. "We were at Denny's."

"That's right," he remembered. "Maybe someone *did* die."

Nate couldn't take it anymore. Casuals! Enraging! They didn't even research this incredible place before they arrived, they didn't read his blog or any other AtB website, they didn't make plans to help them avoid long waits or eat at the best restaurants around the resort. No, they just showed up and stood in lines like cattle. And what was worse: they didn't understand the park's themes or the many backstories or why vintage dark rides and beautiful corners like Frontier Island were a precious reminder of Lawrence Taylor's legacy, his dream for the park. *They* were the reason why management thought they could just rip out Gold Rush Rapids, an opening-day attraction, and replace it with character meet-and-greets in a plastic ghost town, or turn the calm waters of the Mighty Missouri into a thrills-first flume ride. They were ruining *everything*.

"They're protesting management's plan to close Gold Rush Rapids and the Mighty Missouri and replace them," Nate said tightly, looking back at the family. The boy who'd started the conversation with his innocent question met his eyes, looking frightened. He was wearing a "Cowboy Up!" hat, Nate noticed, as he continued: "They're here to demand the park's historic attractions are given some respect."

The father tugged at the collar of his blue golf shirt. He looked amused. "Can you believe that," he said to his wife, who was wearing a fitted tee with the words "Namastay in Bed" glittering in gold sparkles across the front. She gave him a bored shrug in response.

"So what are they building instead?" the other man asked.

"A thrill ride and a character area," Nate replied, distaste dripping from every vowel. "Where there used to be three family attractions, they'll have one with a big height requirement and one that's just for little kids to get their pictures taken."

"Three?" The golf-shirt dad raised his eyebrows. "I see two. Gold Rush Rapids, and that boat." He nodded over to where the side-wheeler was laboring around the turn.

"And Wilderness Isle," Nate said.

"That's not a ride," the dad said dismissively.

Not a——! Nate saw sparks. "It's an *attraction*. An opening-day attraction. Lawrence Taylor designed it himself."

"Oh, I'm sure that's the company line, alright." Golf-Shirt Dad winked. He actually *winked!*

Nate stared at him. "Why would you say something like that?" He glanced down at the kid, who was watching the proceedings with interest. "You've got a kid here."

"Matty's no fool," Golf-Shirt Dad said comfortably. "He knows the difference between fantasy and reality. Right, Matty?"

Matty gave his dad a thumbs-up.

Nate was horrified. "You're not here for reality. You're here to enjoy wonder and fantasy come to life. The wonder of America! The dream of the Patriots! That's the whole point of being here!"

Matty's mother looked uncomfortable with the direction the conversation was taking. "John, I think we have a QuikRide time for Sequoia Expedition coming up. Maybe we should get going?" She started to move towards the transition from Old Dodge City to the Forgotten Forests, where two massive pine trees flanked a wooden sign over the pathway, proclaiming it the gateway to "The Vast Unknown Forests of the Americas".

"That's the one where you ride the bumpy Jeeps!" Matty

exclaimed. "Come on, Dad!"

Golf-Shirt Dad paused for one more look at Nate. "You're one of those fanatics, aren't you?"

Nate pulled himself up straight, sucking in his stomach as best he could. "I'm a *fan*," he proclaimed proudly.

The dad chuckled, turning to join Matty and his mother. "Idiot," he said as he left. "What do you think *fan* is short for?"

Nate was tempted to jump after him, grab his stupid golf-shirt collar, get in his stupid face, demand an apology to him and to every fan up on that hill and to the whole damn park and to Lawrence Taylor currently spinning in his grave, but he also knew he was literally within spitting distance of being trespassed from the parks, so he stood still, quivering with outrage, as the satisfied family made their way into the forest. Matty made *vroom-vroom* Jeep noises all the way.

Then he realized the other man, the loner, was still nearby and still watching him. "What?" he asked harshly, picking up his camera again. The protestors were at the entrance to the Gold Rush queue now, bewildered families watching from the switchbacks, while Security formed a solid line behind them, keeping them from re-entering lower Old Dodge City. The only way out now would be via the service gate, where Nate had no doubt they'd be escorted to waiting sheriff's deputy cars. He respected them even more so for the realization that he'd never be brave enough to protest at AtB and risk arrest, or worse, getting trespassed. He was here to document, though. That had to count for something. Nate started taking pictures, the expensive camera clicking obediently.

"I'm interested," the man said eventually, still watching

him with bemusement. "You're very passionate. Those people up there are obviously very passionate. What makes an amusement park such a big deal to you?"

"A theme park," Nate corrected. *Click. Click.*

"A theme park," the man agreed. "Sure."

"I can't speak for everyone's reasons," Nate began. *Click.* "For me, for a lot of us, it's simply that this is the place where the outside world ends and a better world begins. It's curated. It's ordered. It's clean and there's always a perfectly timed music loop playing. It's beautiful. And it's where we came when we were children, and we always wanted to understand it better, inside and out, get to know the wonder of it for ourselves, hold on to the feelings it gives us all the time, not just when we're here..." *Click-click-click.* "It's just the place where we feel most like the people we want to be," Nate finished, feeling like he'd just delivered a manifesto on his life's work.

The service gate was open now, and the protestors were being urged through by the Security team, with the Gold Rush Patriots in their prospector costumes bringing up the rear. Behind that, a few Patriots were escorting the stranded riders on the stopped attraction down the series of evacuation staircases. It took twenty minutes of safety resets to come back online after an e-stop, longer than most guests wanted to wait while sitting in the scorching sun.

Nate documented it all in beautiful, brightly colored photos that would grace his blog in a few hours. He paused for a moment to Bluetooth some of the pics to his phone and then tweet them with a few words of context—*The view from Gold Nugget Creek as protestors escorted out, full article coming soon.*

The man behind him watched for a few minutes more,

then turned on his heel and walked away, and Nate didn't think about him again.

CHAPTER FIFTEEN

Antonia

"So, today was weird," Tabby said, leaning over the cash-room counter. "Did you hear about the protest?"

Antonia, counting out change from the big safe in the corner, muttered, "Twenty-five, thirty, thirty-five, forty, forty-five, *fifty,*" in a passive-aggressive tone that she knew Tabby would not recognize, then rubber-banded the fives and added them to the stack of ones already on the counter. She wrote down the total in the Cash Out column of the daily change log, then said, "I did not hear about the protest. I've been here two minutes and you're already hassling me for change. I haven't even gone up to the manager's office to pick up the afternoon briefing. And I don't know what happens after that…I've never been a closing supervisor before, if you'll recall."

"There was a protest," Tabby said eagerly, happy to be the first to deliver the news. "A big group of guests with signs marched up to Gold Rush Rapids. I think they were all arrested."

"What were they protesting?" Antonia asked, but even as she said it, she knew.

"The new rides, the ones that were on AtBLive last night. You saw *that*, right?"

"Yeah, that one's hard to miss if you have an internet connection." *Everyone* was talking about the AtBLive post. Antonia supposed it might be possible to miss the news if you weren't a dedicated, hard-core theme park fan, but for the likes of them? It was front-page news and probably would be for a long time to come. And an actual, physical protest in the park was going to be national news for everyone. "That must have been wild," Antonia said, her interest piqued despite herself.

"Oh, it was! I had just gone out to open the sunglass wagon—" Tabby poured out the story, which Antonia found was a little more tame than she'd expected.

"So they were all just allowed to protest and then escorted out through the Gold Rush gate?"

"Yeah, supposedly there were police cars waiting to take them all to the station and everything."

Antonia suddenly hoped Martin had not decided to join them. She pulled out her phone and texted him: *where are you today*

No time for punctuation.

Tabby eyeballed her phone. "I thought Roseann said they were going to start enforcing the no-phones-in-the-cash-room rule."

Antonia glanced at the camera bubble in the cash room's corner, hovering above the safe and the counter where she'd counted out the change. "Roseann says a lot of things," she bluffed, but she stuck the phone back in her pocket. A phone infraction was the last thing she needed, especially since she'd just stuck Nick with a discipline note over his phone yesterday. "Let's get going. I have to get up to the office, so closing huddle isn't late."

In the hallway behind Professor Cloud's, Antonia's phone buzzed and she snuck a peek. Martin: *At home, why?*

She dropped the phone back into her pocket, breathing a sigh of relief, as they opened the door and stepped into the crowded shop.

Roseann was the only manager in the office when Antonia came in, tapping away at her keyboard with fingernails just short enough to be inside AtB's appearance code, but still, in Antonia's mind, too long, too showy for their wholesome family park. She paused as Antonia let the heavy door click behind her, the electronic lock snapping back into place with a *thunk*. "Are you my closer tonight?" Roseann trilled, as if she had not written Antonia's new schedule for the week.

"With Mark," Antonia confirmed. "I'm shadowing Mark, you said."

"Oh," Roseann sighed. "About that…"

Antonia's eyebrows went up.

"Mark got pulled to Forgotten Forests tonight. They were short-handed. I said you could handle it. I'll be around all night if there are any problems."

So this would make one and a half shifts as a supervisor, without any training beyond a half-shift following Roseann around on calls. *And* it was a closing shift, which meant she was responsible for yards of procedures which she hadn't even been briefed on, let alone trained on. There were specific protocol to follow for closing individual stores, for getting cash drawers back to the cash room, for counting out the money and delivering it to the central bank, for dismissing Patriots once their stores were recovered and stocked for the next day…

Antonia was still convinced something else was going on, some reason why headcount was screwed up and there weren't enough supervisors to conduct her training properly. They were just breaking way too many rules for the explanation to be innocent. And if Antonia screwed something up tonight, *her* employee record was the one that took the hit. Not Roseann's, or any other manager behind her impromptu promotion.

"Roseann, I don't know the closing procedures," Antonia pointed out, hating herself.

"There's a checklist right there." Roseann pointed a red talon at a fat binder sitting on the empty desk next to hers. "Everything you need is in there. Sit down and take a look! And your mid, Alma, is still out there until six thirty. I told her to handle afternoon huddle with the closing team. It'll be fine! All you have to do tonight is follow the directions in the binder. Cool?"

"Cool…" Antonia sat down at the desk and opened the binder, flipping through the tabs until she got to *Close — Regular*. What was an irregular close, she wondered, and skipped ahead to the next one, which was *Close — Special Event Night*. Ah, of course. On special event nights, like when a big company bought out the park for an employee party, only certain stores stayed open late, and the rest closed in tiers. It changed everything about the day. She went back to the *Regular* section and ran her eyes down the closing timeline, finally getting up to make a copy of the page, which detailed everything from when to close Professor Cloud's Register 3 to what time to have a Patriot fill the soda cooler in Sam Sweet's Candy Shop.

"I can do this," she muttered.

"That's the spirit," Roseann said absently, still typing. "What a pro."

Antonia met up with Alma, a black-haired transplant from Ponce who looked about twenty-two and was in fact in her late forties, on the porch in front of Sam's Sweet Shop. The afternoon was baking-hot, but there was a rumble of thunder in the air and everyone was on high alert for a weather advisory to come wavering through their radios. Then it would be showtime, everyone rushing to throw down the tarps and close up the outside merchandise and food vending locations as quickly as possible, while the ride operations Patriots either evacuated their attractions (if they were outside) or prepared for an onslaught of new guests to flood their queues (if they were inside).

The weather advisories were always issued at the last possible minute, in the name of inconveniencing the guests as little as possible, which made the actual moments of closing and evacuating something like the climax scenes of an action movie, with a lot of barely contained panic from everyone involved, most of all the confused guests.

"You've got a good team tonight," Alma told Antonia. "They know how to close. Not a lot of interns to slow you down. And if there's a weather advisory, they know to go."

"That's good," Antonia replied. "I printed out the procedures—"

"I told Winston to close the minute I wave my hand at him," Alma interrupted, as if Antonia hadn't spoken at all.

Her eyes were trained on the lanky Patriot across the walkway, who was selling a child a pair of heart-shaped Petals the Goose sunglasses. "The same for Minnie over at the pin wagon. I don't like all this running around like a chicken with my head cut off just because they can't decide about the weather until it's already lightning everywhere. So I warn everyone at the carts to be ready and watch me, and then I stay out here on the boardwalk where they can see me."

Antonia nodded, impressed with Alma's informal weather alert system. Much quicker than phoning each cart or rushing to them one after another, giving the instruction in person, the way the managers did a weather close.

"If you close a location and it don't reopen, don't forget to get the money out the drawer. One time, I see somebody, I don't say who, having a panic attack because the safe is short, and it turn out all that money still out in the register at the wagon."

Antonia laughed. "That would definitely be my move."

But Alma wasn't paying attention to her at all. "Hey, you know that guy?" She gestured with her radio, while carefully turning her chin in the other direction, so that the target wouldn't realize they were being pointed out.

Antonia looked to the right of the sunglass Conestoga and saw Nate standing nearby, eyeballing Winston with unnerving focus. At first, she couldn't figure out what he was doing; then she realized the blogger had his phone out in front of him. He was filming Winston—who, admittedly, was not a star Patriot. He was one of the mid-list workers who had been working here just long enough to not care about living up to the park's rigorous standards anymore, but wasn't yet bitter about the years he'd wasted running a cash register stuck inside of a fiberglass Conestoga wagon.

At the moment, Winston was lounging against the wagon's front ledge with a cheerful disregard for the iron-clad rules against leaning, his eyes on the clouds gathering overhead rather than the guests passing his wagon.

"I know him," Antonia said grimly. "We got into it last night."

"That's what I hear," Alma agreed. "You want to get into it again? I don't like to see him filming my Patriots like that."

Antonia warmed to the possessive way Alma spoke about the front-line employees. This was how she planned to manage, too. "He's not doing anything actionable yet," she said hesitantly. "Unless…I can *prove* he's filming a Patriot who isn't part of entertainment."

"Go stand in front of him, see what he does when you block his shot," Alma suggested. "Might be funny." She grinned.

"Okay," Antonia said, grinning back, and she stepped off the boardwalk, wove her way over to the wagon, and very casually stopped right in the middle of Nate's shot. Once settled in his way, she put her hands behind her back and gazed out at the passing crowds, smiling and nodding, in the manager's stance she'd seen so often.

And then Antonia had one tremendously gratifying moment.

Nothing happened—nothing anyone could see. But she had a *feeling*. She stood there with her hands behind in her back, in her slacks and shirt, with her earpiece in her ear, and her position of authority in this fantasy world, and she saw the way people looked at her. The way Alma was watching her with approval from the boardwalk. The way

Winston straightened from a slumped mess to a straight and tall, exemplary Patriot.

She was in charge, at the park she loved, at last. And now, as a supervisor, she was one jump from management, from wearing her own clothes, from never running a register or stocking shelves again—unless she was jumping in to help her Patriots, because she was a team player.

It was happening, just the way she had hoped and dreamed for so long. Ambition and hard work truly did pay off.

Antonia's heart was so full at this moment, she barely registered Nate's mounting annoyance. Nate was a side-quest, a distraction. The real game was right here, standing in her position of power, with all of Old Dodge City laid out before her.

When Nate finally dropped his phone back into his pocket and stalked away, careful to give her a wide berth as he went, Antonia finally glanced his way. He flicked a look over his shoulder and she met her eyes without a hint of recognition in her serene expression. And when he turned away again and kept on shuffling with the rest of the crowd, caught up in the surge of humanity pushing towards Gold Rush Rapids, she allowed herself a triumphant smile. She turned that smile on Winston, who thought it meant he was doing a stellar job, and he stood up straighter than ever, pulled a roll of Edgar Eagle stickers off the register, and started handing them out to passing children.

This is it, Antonia thought. *I'm leading.*

CHAPTER SIXTEEN

Tabby

"This is nice," Tabby said for the third time, feeling utterly hopeless.

"Yeah," Nick agreed, brushing back his teen-idol blonde hair. He grinned at her wolfishly, and Tabby felt a surge of confidence. She leaned forward, her elbows on the bar, and tilted her face at him. Just in case he wanted to kiss her.

"Oh my God," Nick said, looking past her. *What* was that play? Jesus, what a joke."

"A total joke," the bartender agreed, looking hard at Tabby as she put down another margarita in front of her. "It's almost like they have no idea what they're doing and are coasting on their good looks."

Tabby winced, and the bartender winked, pushing back a cloud of tight dark curls in a slow, calculating way. "Not talking about you, princess," she murmured, and shoved a sloshing beer glass at Nick before she went down to the next group of thirsty Patriots.

Tabby glanced at Nick, blushing. She wasn't sure the bartender was right to blame him for this unsuccessful first date. Things would be fine if she had any idea how to hold his attention. After all, they did well enough together at the park, when she was more interesting than the job at hand or the goings-on in the break room.

But when confronted with a bar full of televisions all tuned to a different sporting event, she simply couldn't compete. Nick couldn't seem to pay attention to her at all. One moment, he was looking over his shoulder at a motocross race; the next he was looking past her left ear, as she turned to look earnestly at him, to see a soccer match on the big screen at the end of the bar.

When Tabby agreed to meet Nick at the Gateway after work that day, she'd thought they'd have plenty to talk about. After all, they had so many of the same interests. The parks, mainly. She wanted to talk about the protest with him, and share what it had been like when the mob had gone marching past her Conestoga wagon. She wanted to discuss the leaked concept art for a new version of Old Dodge City, and get his opinion on losing Wilderness Isle and the Mighty Missouri for a new thrill ride. She'd figured they'd discuss gossip and rumors they'd both picked up throughout the course of a day working at a theme park: what scheme some crazy guest had cooked up to try to sneak into the park without paying, or which celebrity had recently been escorted around the service entrances to rides while wearing a fake mustache and wig. They could even discuss cartoons and movies related to America the Beautiful—the classics Lawrence Taylor had built his entertainment empire on.

After all, wasn't this what made a tribe out of all of them: their love for Taylor properties and characters, the cartoons and theme parks that had defined their childhoods? Their culture was an unabashed nerd culture; sports and fashion and entertainment outside the Taylor empire were only admitted to the conversation when there was absolutely no other option besides grim silence.

But Nick wasn't playing by their rules tonight, and Tabby was disappointed in him.

He slapped his hand on the bar, exclaiming about another botched play of some sort, and she sighed and slipped off her bar stool. She wandered off to the restroom, hoping she'd meet a friend along the way who might join her and offer some advice. When no one in the cavernous dining room looked more than passingly familiar, she went out to the patio and found Elena and Sonia at their usual table overlooking the lake. Both were still in their work costumes, so Tabby was surprised to see mixed drinks in front of them.

Some Patriots had costumes which could only be spotted with a discerning eye, like the ones who worked front desk at Sequoia Point Lodge and only had to shed their fringed vests to look as if they were wearing plain white shirts and particularly orange-tinted khakis. If a park guest were to wander into the Gateway and look closely at one of these off-duty Patriots, they might discern the khakis and Oxford shirts were actually made of thin polyester, worn in spots until it was shiny with distress. Some shirts even had a strip of doubled fabric over the left side of the chest, from a time before the name-tags were magnets and constant pricks from sharp pins mangled the cheap cloth.

Most Patriots, though, were stuck with period-styled

costumes that were hard to disguise as anything but theme park uniforms. Tabby's own ankle-length skirt and ruffled blouse were pretty much dead giveaways—you couldn't pair that skirt with a normal shirt without coming off as a runaway Amish woman, and the blouse likewise wouldn't go with a pair of jeans. Sonia's Gold Rush Rapids gear walked a fine line: the hiking boots, khaki shorts and chambray shirt could be played off as normal clothes—the problem was, they weren't normal clothes anyone would be wearing in a bar next to a theme park. She'd have be in an actual western mountain town to pull it off.

Elena's was even more conspicuous. The Independence Plaza girls were supposed to wear their striped skirts to mid-shin for safety reasons, but the slight bustle effect caused by the gathered waistband was surprisingly flattering when the skirt was worn floor-length, so the younger women all wore their skirts dragging behind their heels. Combined with the ruffled eggshell blouse with its little striped tie, they all looked like Gibson Girls working the dry goods counter while they hunted for a man, and there was even a certain cult of girls who piled their hair on their heads, 1910-style, to perfect the look.

Although Elena preferred to keep her black hair in a smooth bun at the nape of her neck, she was part of the long-skirt contingent, and tonight her navy-striped skirt was pooled around her black ballet slippers. She'd at least taken off her tie and undone the faux-pearl button that fastened the high neck of her blouse, but there was still no mistaking her for a Plaza girl—one drinking a Long Island Iced Tea, in blatant disregard for rules against alcohol consumption in costume.

"You guys didn't change," Tabby blurted, surprised.

There were always a few other Patriots in various states of full or half-costuming throughout the Gateway, but it was a termination-level offense to drink in costume and she'd never seen her friends do it.

"And yet, we're not even the funniest-looking couple in here tonight," Elena slurred, grinning at her.

Elena's insinuation hurt Tabby's feelings, and her face showed it immediately. Sonia reached out and grabbed her hand. "Elena is drunk," she said solemnly. "Ignore her."

"What about you?" Tabby demanded, with a fierceness uncharacteristic of her. "You couldn't even change your shirt?"

"I forgot a spare. And I had a *day.*"

"We were all there," Tabby said. "You can't use the protest as an excuse to drink in costume. If a senior manager comes in and sees you—"

"Don't preach at us," Elena snapped, her words coming more clearly now that she was annoyed. "You're over there letting that dumb-dumb watch motocross instead of paying attention to you. If you're going to date an idiot, at least keep his attention, Tabby. You're making us all look bad."

"Mean, Elena," Sonia protested. "Come on."

"*So* mean," Tabby agreed, her voice thin. "I thought we were friends."

"Kind of," Elena said thoughtfully. "We definitely know each other. There's that."

"What Elena means is, she's drunk and needs to go home," Sonia said.

"Before someone takes her picture and turns her in?" Tabby suggested.

"That'd be just like you." Elena narrowed her eyes at Tabby. "Miss Goody Two-Shoes. Miss Prairie Girl 1898."

Tabby shrugged. "What if I am? What if I like being a Patriot? That's kind of the point."

Elena muttered something that might have been *fuck you* and went back to her drink, turning her shoulder to Tabby. Sonia looked apologetic. "Working at Plaza can be a bitch sometimes. She had a rough day."

"Whatever." Tabby made to leave, pushing back from the table with one hand. Sonia put her hand on her arm, stopping her. "What?"

"Go back in there and tell Nick you're done for the night. Go out into the parking lot and see if he follows you."

"What if he doesn't?"

"Then you won't waste any more time."

Tabby knew Sonia was giving her solid advice. She *knew* it—she just hated it. She tried to keep her face from crumpling. "What happened, Sonia? We were having such a good time at work. But here, it's like we don't even know each other."

"Work's not real," Sonia said.

"You got that right," Elena snorted, rejoining them momentarily.

Work wasn't real? Work was the only thing Tabby wanted to be real. On her worst days at AtB, she was happier than she'd ever been at home, or at school. And those were the only other things she knew in life. If work wasn't real, she thought, she didn't want to know what was.

When she finally returned to the bar, Nick was looking around for her. She was gratified to see he looked a little concerned at her disappearance.

"That guy's here," he said as she slid back into her seat. "I was hoping he didn't see you."

"What guy?" Tabby put her hand on the edge of the bar and smiled when he took hold, squeezing her fingers in his. *That* was more like it. She had a feeling that if she did take Sonia's advice and went out to the parking lot now, he'd follow her. But if he was going to pay attention to her right here at the bar, there was no reason to, right? She picked up her glass, raised it to her lips.

"That blogger guy that was stalking you yesterday," Nick explained. "I saw him come into the pub."

She coughed and put down her glass, choking on rock salt and margarita mix and maybe just a little tequila, if the bartender was feeling generous. "You know about that?"

Nick looked hurt. "I had to find out from Katia in the break room. You could have told me, so I could look out for you."

"*Katia* knows about that? Who else?"

"Um, I would say everyone? It's all over the place online."

Tabby shook her head, speechless. Break room gossip was one thing; Patriots were notorious for gossip. It was one of the most interesting things about theme park work, after all, because the insanity simply *never* stopped—it was like every single day, one crazy guest was determined to out-crazy the craziest guest of the day before. So yeah, the other Patriots who had seen the confrontations between herself and Nate and poor Martin must have been talking about it.

But online, too?

The other guests, of course. They'd been in front of dozens of people both times. Someone had probably filmed it, Tabby realized. *Several* someones. So, for the second time in three days, there was a chance she'd gone viral in the theme park communities.

Oh, God. There were probably heated, imaginative discussions going on about her right now; AtB fans were probably talking about the crazy enmity between the Old Dodge City Patriot and the AtBLive blogger who had exposed her for a theme-breaking fraud. They were almost certainly saying she'd enlisted the help of nice-guy character chaser Martin to be her watchdog.

"This is the worst," Tabby said aloud. "I'm not going to feel safe at work anymore, am I? But work is all I've got."

"Hey," Nick said softly, slipping from his barstool and wrapping a lanky arm around her shoulders. Tabby could feel the ropy muscle of his bicep and felt a stirring of warmth push through her insides. "I'll watch out for you. Don't worry about those crazies. You're never alone out there."

"Thank you Nick," Tabby whispered. "That means a lot to me." She let the words dangle there, wondering if he'd take the opportunity she was placing in front of him.

Patriots were a theatrical bunch, and it wasn't like them to pass up the chance to use the perfect movie line. Nick, the vlogger and self-made star, was no different. *"You* mean a lot to *me,"* he whispered back, perfectly on cue, and dropped a soft, lingering kiss on her lips.

Finally, Tabby thought. Maybe acquiring a weirdo stalker and going viral was exactly what she needed to pique Nick's interest. If so, she'd take it.

Let no one say she was a picky girl.

CHAPTER SEVENTEEN

Nate

The craziest time of night at the Gateway was between eleven and twelve-thirty, when the opening shift who had stayed out late and the closing shift who were just getting started were all there and mingling at once. The shift worker overlap was loud and out on the covered patio, where the ceiling was low and the lights were fewer, it grew hard to recognize faces.

Nate had quietly decided to exploit his newly local status by gathering gossip at the Gateway. Not just listening, but maybe gathering some video of Patriots at play in their native habitat. With the website's visitor numbers at an all-time high and his social media follows through the roof, he still knew his business model was only as good as his next controversy. The protest had been incredibly gratifying, but now every site was carrying the leaked Old Dodge City plans. Even with his watermark on the stolen concept art, the other blogs were happy to lift the jpegs and use them to illustrate their own spin on the story. He wouldn't be able to take full credit for any other Save Gold Rush Rapids movements without actually sponsoring them himself, and Nate wasn't about to risk his annual pass that way.

Unfortunately, his filming pursuits had been rendered mostly useless by the moving shadows and occasional flickers of light as the restaurant doors opened and closed, so he had pocketed his phone and was moving around the patio with a beer in hand, always looking as if he was on the verge of joining the next group of people in conversation, while in reality listening in for whatever gossip he could glean from the cluster he was nearest.

Often the shop talk was frustratingly obscure, using industry jargon he just couldn't translate. Fleetingly, he considered getting a part-time job at AtB so that he could learn the lingo, and know what a laughing Patriot was describing when he talked about a Signal 14 causing a fault at pad twelve and dumping the entire flume. He could guess that "dumping" a ride meant evacuating everyone from it, but the faults? The pads? Who knew? He could only imagine how much better his blog would be if he could translate all this gossip into posts that his readers could understand. Talk about an insider's look at the parks!

But there was always a good reason *not* to join the AtB roles, however temporary his employment plans might be. For one thing, he'd have to hide the ownership of AtBLive, and he'd been very public about his publisher status from day one. Nate did not want to be an anonymous blogger. He wanted to be known. He wanted to be seen. He wanted to be respected.

The other reason, at the moment, was seasonal. It was

only the beginning of what promised to be a sweltering-hot summer, and he had no interest in donning a polyester costume and standing outside in all weathers. Nate might love theme parks, but he was no outdoorsman. Air conditioned queues and gift shops were there for a reason, always ready to be ducked into when the humid summer heat grew too mucky to be borne another moment. A Patriot didn't have that kind of luxury. They stood outside all day, if that was what the job required. Nate just wasn't up to that.

"Ninety-nine percent of the celebrities you see, you never recognize," a girl was saying, and he paused behind her in hopes of picking up a few tips on spotting VIPs who were trying to remain anonymous in the parks. Celebrity photos were good for clicks from everyone, not just theme park fans, and could potentially even garner valuable links from mainstream sites like TMZ. That could quadruple his web traffic for a couple of days, driving up the value of his ads within minutes.

But the girl saw him hovering at her shoulder, and she gave him a dark look until he backed away, looking over his shoulder and waving as if he'd spotted a friend.

That was when he saw Martin, leaning against a high-top table in a dim corner, gazing through the restaurant windows with a faraway look on his face.

Nate ducked in the other direction to avoid being spotted, then he took a good look inside and saw exactly what he expected: the prairie girl herself, Tabby. She was across the crowded restaurant, standing at the bar next to a blonde-haired kid—that guy who'd been at the wagon with her most of yesterday!—and as he watched, the kid put his arm around her shoulder and leaned in for a kiss.

Nate's jaw tightened, and his hand automatically gripped the phone in his pocket. He'd gotten what he'd come for tonight, even if the video didn't work out. All those pictures…he had enough on his camera roll for an excellent post about the declining sense of pride amongst Patriots, out here drinking in their costumes, taking their phones out while working in themed areas, slipping out of character or not even trying to use themed replies when giving directions or offering suggestions to park guests.

He didn't need anything else—he'd write the article, he'd post the photos of the drinking Patriots he'd taken tonight, he'd get the clicks and stir up some serious controversy that would feed the rabid online fans for days to come, maybe even weeks, if nothing else hit the news cycle about the Gold Rush refurb for a while. And in the meantime, he'd be able to come up with a new story to grab their attention.

But before he did…he was going to get a picture of Tabby and her little boyfriend. That blonde-haired skater kid she'd spent half the day talking to at the sunglass wagon while *he*, Nate, had been forced to skulk around the park like a stalker just for a chance to talk to her. And then she hadn't even wanted to hear him out, because of this…*kid!* Nate's burgeoning crush on Tabby had slipped effortlessly into the desire for revenge. *She'd* made him look like an idiot. *She'd* tried to get him into trouble, even trespassed, from the park! When all he'd wanted to do was talk to her!

He put down his empty glass on the table behind him, ignoring the protests of the occupants seated around it, and pushed through the throng of drinkers towards the restaurant doors.

Nate had almost made it when a thin, wiry figure shoved into his path and stood there, arms crossed. "Excuse me,"

Nate muttered, trying to remain inconspicuous. But when the guy just stood there, he got pissed in a hurry. "Dude, fucking *move*."

"You're not going in there and harassing her again," the guy said, and Nate realized it was the guy from the park. The one who had followed him around all day yesterday. The one who'd come after him when he'd tried to talk to Tabby, once the kid had finally left. Rage bubbled up in his chest, and he lifted his hands to shove the guy out of his way.

But the guy saw him coming and stepped neatly to one side, and Nate found himself shoving into a group of girls who were just emerging onto the porch, goldfish-bowl margaritas in their hands. There was a lot of shrieking after that, and he realized his hands were everywhere they shouldn't be: on wet shirts, on breasts, on faces, on bare arms. He tried to push himself upright again, and things only got worse. There was a lot of shrieking and then the atmosphere of the Gateway erupted, from convivial after-dinner drinking and fun to shouting chaos.

And it was almost all directed at him.

By the time Nate had made it to his car, shaking and wet from a dozen drinks thrown at him or spilled on him, his vintage Gold Rush Rapids shirt irreparably torn at the collar from a buff guy who'd made a grab at him as he'd run out the restaurant's front door, he was more mad than frightened. They'd all read his blog the night before, he knew; they'd all gotten plenty of entertainment from the hard work he was putting in for them. Who was going to tell these kids the truth about the parks, about their jobs, about work coming down the pike that was going to rearrange their entire lives? Not their bosses, that was for sure. Not the park management. No, he, Nate, was doing that *for them*—giving them the heads-up that things were changing, that jobs would be on the line, promotions would be deferred, transfers would be denied, hours would be cut, all the awful side-effects that came with the decision to close an area and refurbish it into something bigger and better. He put himself out there for *these people!*

Nate's drive home was too fast; he was driving erratically, working through his anger by taking turns too fast, ignoring stop signs, swerving around drivers in less of a hurry. But by the time he got back to his apartment, he was back to his usual cool, collected self. Or so he congratulated himself. He transferred a dozen photos to his computer, then started typing. And it was deep into the wee hours before he sat back, smiled at his handiwork, and clicked *publish.*

CHAPTER EIGHTEEN

Tabby

"This is good," Tabby said through a mouthful of cake. "So, so good. What are you doing?" Her voice tipped upwards into a shriek by the last syllable.

"You look great, baby," Nick laughed, jumping backwards but keeping his phone steady, trained on her. "Take another bite, get that peach filling."

Tabby tried to frown at him, but just ended up laughing. Some white icing fell from her lips, little sugar shards of magnolia flower. She held up the cupcake with its bite-mark to show the future audience what they were missing. "Look at that peach goodness oozing out!" And then she took a bite.

"You were born for this," Nick told her approvingly, zooming his phone in on her mouth as she tried and failed to keep all the cupcake and peach within the confines of her lips. "You're a cupcake-eating superstar."

She laughed, icing flying everywhere, but she didn't care about the mess she was making. Tabby was having a very good day.

The night before had sucked, admittedly. They'd only just started to connect and have an actual conversation when the bar had erupted into shouting and shoving, and she'd seen some heavyset guy get pushed off the porch, drinks flying after his head as he'd run for his car. A couple guys had made to follow him but didn't get further than the handicapped spaces in the lot.

"He's not coming back," one of them reported. "Let him go home and cry about it."

"Who was it?" she'd hissed to the bartender, who was looking amused, and when she'd replied it was that blogger who'd posted the video of the Patriot in the wrong costume, she'd waggled her eyebrows at Tabby suggestively.

Tabby retreated behind Nick's back.

Even after the excitement, though, there was no keeping up with Nick, who wanted to put eyewitness reports on every single social media channel known to man. She wasn't sure why anyone would care that there'd been a brawl at the Gateway, but when Nick showed her his follower counts, she had to concede that an awful lot of people all around the world wanted to know exactly how the Patriots lived their lives, in and out of the parks. She didn't tell him the guy was Nate, because that would have just blown up the original controversy again. The controversy about *her*.

Somehow, she didn't think Nick would appreciate that she was involved with all this online drama.

Not when he was the one who was supposed to be making a name for himself as an Internet personality.

But that was yesterday, and here she was today, taste-testing the Sweet Magnolia cupcake being sold outside the Escape from the Atlanta coaster at Legacy of Heroes, and everything was wonderful. She loved Escape from Atlanta anyway, so it was no hardship to ride it three times, waiting in the standby queue once, using a QuikRide next, winking at the Patriot at load on the way out and getting back-doored right back onto the attraction for the third. They'd needed three rides to get the different faces and reactions Nick wanted for his vlog; he'd mix it later for one of his high-quality ride-through videos that got him tons of views of YouTube. Eventually, he told her, he'd make money off advertising. Tabby didn't know how far in the future "eventually" might be, but it was nice to know he was investing in a business of his own—building a brand as a theme park vlogger might not be a conventional career choice, but it was a fun one and it took a lot of hard work, so no one could say Nick was just a slacker working at a theme park instead of moving up in the world.

A fresh group of park guests came whirling out of the Escape from Atlanta exit and out onto the gift shop stairs where she and Nate were standing.

"That's my favorite ride," a girl in the group said. "*Every* ride should be this ride."

Nick lifted a blonde eyebrow at Tabby, and she laughed again as the guests went clomping past and headed for the queue entrance, ready to brave the forty-five minute wait time to ride again.

The coaster itself wasn't themed to the same high standards as the attractions back across the parking lot at America the Beautiful—you could see the steel structure of this ride, for example—but there were a couple of interior show scenes, the most memorable of which being the burning warehouse which exploded with a *whuff,* a blast of heat and a lot of smoke effects, sending the coaster shooting down the final drop. If Tabby had to categorize Escape from Atlanta, she'd call it *fun*—not exactly faint praise, certainly, but not the work of art most theme park nerds would consider the original opening-day attractions within America the Beautiful.

Only someone who didn't know any better would mistake the fun of Escape from Atlanta for AtB's best ride, and she and Nick knew it.

She loved that about him, that he *got it.*

"What is *your* favorite ride?" Nick asked as they set off down the walkway, past the antebellum columns of the Escape from Atlanta's opening scene, a white plantation house where guests filed through the front door, only to find it was just a hole in a wall with more queue hidden on the other side. That was one of the attraction's great faults, in theme park circles—placeholders taking the place of elaborate, fully realized sets. It was true of most of Legacy of Heroes, which had been built on the cheap, relatively speaking.

Tabby put a finger to her chin, found it was sticky with cupcake icing, and dropped the thoughtful pose quickly. "I think it's Sequoia Expedition," she said, glancing quickly at Nick to see his reaction. Sequoia Expedition was an old, opening-day attraction, and its cracks were starting to show. The jokes were corny; the animatronic animals were audibly creaky. Those qualities alone made it a theme park nerd must-ride.

"That's a great ride," Nick agreed. "I love when your Jeep comes around that corner and you think the bear is going to swipe you, but instead you dip down and go through the center of that huge tree. It's so unexpected on such a tame ride."

"That's the genius of the old rides," Tabby replied, warming to the subject. "They can surprise you without needing a height requirement. Anyone can ride them and have fun. Not everything has to be a thrill."

Nick swiped his hand against hers. "I like a thrill *sometimes,* though," he said, grinning at her, and she grinned back, but inwardly she was wondering why she didn't feel any thrill at all.

By the time they'd ridden Betsy Bombers and taken video of themselves getting red, white and blue sugar all over themselves while eating Rocket Pop Churros, Tabby was coming to the awful conclusion that she didn't actually like Nick as much as she'd thought. She liked hanging out with him, sure—he was fun and they could talk about rides and theming for hours, which was great. But every time he made a move on her, touches that should have made her head swim giddily weren't creating a single reaction.

I like him as a friend, she thought miserably. *Why didn't I realize that before?*

So much time wasted mooning over Nick, and now that she had him, he did nothing for her. Was this because of her childhood, growing up in the grip of her mother's mean and small religion? Maybe it had ruined her somewhere inside, emotionally speaking. They hadn't used the word "love" in her family unless they were talking about Jesus and the Holy Spirit. Love was a holy thing, too divine for daily use. Consequently, Tabby didn't really know how to use the word. She walked along in Nick's buoyant wake and wondered if she'd ever understand love the way other humans did, or if it was just a lost concept for her, completely over her head.

Just before the exit turnstiles, Nick turned to look for her, his face lit by the golden afternoon sun, his blonde hair shining like a little boy's, and she thought if anyone could be blinded by those teenage dream good looks, it was definitely her, the girl with a strange, stunted childhood, who hadn't even known what she was missing until she'd gone to college and found out it was already over.

Nick didn't see any of this on her face, though; Tabby's poker face was one of her greatest skills as a Patriot. He knew the greeter Patriot who was waving to guests as they came in and out of the park, and stopped over for a quick chat. He pulled out his phone and was showing the guy some of their coaster video, but Tabby could see the Patriot was nervous, pulling his eyes away from the phone and stepping slightly back from Nick so that his body was always facing outwards, towards the front entrance and the other guests coming towards them. Something was wrong. She pulled Nick away, waving to the Patriot, and dragged him towards the landscaped walkway that led past the parking garages and towards the AtB park entrance.

"What was that about?" Nick complained, pulling his arm free. "I know Dylan from the spring education series. We took Theme Park Story together. Dude knows everything about Lawrence Taylor history. You'd like him."

No doubt, Tabby thought. *I seem to like everyone.* "He was clearly worried about getting caught ignoring actual guests," she said. "Couldn't you tell? There must be a crackdown from their managers over there. He was pulling away from us so that it didn't look like he was hanging out with friends."

Nick looked stricken. "Jeez, I hope I didn't get him in trouble."

"I'm sure it's fine. Just…you have to pay attention when you're hanging out in the parks. You can get friends in trouble really easily. Like when you winked at the Patriot at Atlanta… I saw you pull your ID out of your pocket just enough to show her we were Patriots too."

"Everyone does that."

"No, not everyone," Tabby said quietly. "I've never done that. I wait in the regular queue, the way I'm supposed to. That way, no one gets fired. Anyway, I can pick and choose when I ride, so there's no reason for me to cut ahead of someone who's on their vacation and might never come back."

Nick's apologetic look quickly changed to one of offense. "Well, aren't you wonderful."

Tabby subsided. "That's not what I meant."

Nick held out his hand. "It's fine. Let's go to AtB and get on Sequoia Expedition."

"It's two o'clock," Tabby said doubtfully, taking his hand anyway. "The line's going to be an hour long."

He flicked his gaze at her, then back on the path beneath the oak trees ahead of them. The gates of AtB loomed ahead, all bunting and white columns. "Tabby, you've got to stop letting the rules bother you so much."

But Tabby wasn't the only one sticking to the rules that afternoon.

By the time they'd gotten to the turnstiles of AtB, the cheerful ragtime music of Independence Plaza tinkling on the breeze, Tabby could see a change in the usual behavior of the Patriots there. Everyone was standing bolt upright by their turnstiles, or with their toes precisely lined up at the corners of pavement that served as markers for where greeters were supposed to stand. Everyone was smiling urgently at the guests flowing through the gates, offering assistance with nods and open-handed gestures. They were being model Patriots. All of them.

The culture of assurance. Tabby suddenly remembered the phrase from a class in customer service she'd taken early in her Patriot internship. Building body and verbal language as reassuring and welcoming as the architecture and landscaping—that was what made America the Beautiful a place where people truly left their cares behind and felt at home, like nowhere else in the world.

It was a nice idea, and on any given day, about fifty percent of the Patriots would be producing the behaviors taught in their innumerable introduction classes and mid-year updates. The others might be in various stages of slacking off, but even a slacking-off Patriot was more polite and welcoming than an average worker at any other establishment, whether it was a theme park or a restaurant or a retail store, out in reality.

Right now, everyone was doing *everything* right, and it was creeping Tabby out.

"Something happened," she hissed to Nick. "Something's going on."

He looked up and down the row of smiling Patriots, like a line-up of Stepford Wives waiting to welcome them into the park, and his footsteps faltered for a moment. "Shit," he whispered. "You're right."

CHAPTER NINETEEN

Antonia

The entire management team was waiting in the office when Antonia came in. Their heads swiveled towards her as one. It was distinctly unnerving, like walking into a room full of robots just as they plotted their overthrow of the humans. Antonia stood in the doorway for a moment, uncertain if she was welcome. She'd been hoping that tonight's shift would be nice and normal, that she'd get to shadow someone and train the way she was supposed to. Last night had been a challenge; Alma had gotten her set up for success, but it had still taken her far too long to get registers and shops closed, and everyone had ended up clocking out twenty minutes late. She'd felt terrible about it, even though Winslow had assured her he appreciated the unexpected overtime.

"Come in and have a seat," Roseann said finally, when it became clear Antonia had no idea what to do next. "We're just waiting for Rick and then we have something to go over."

Rick was the day's usual closing supervisor. Antonia settled into a chair, feeling moderately relieved…as relieved as one could feel when the management team was looking gravely at each other and she was the only hourly employee in the room, anyway. Desperate for something to do, she took out the supervisor binder from the shelf above the little cubicle allotted to her crew and flipped it open. Nothing new for the day, just the morning opening checklist, signed off by Alma. She must be out in the region somewhere, keeping watching watch on the operation while the managers were holed up in the office.

The door opened and Rick came in. He stopped short, just as Antonia had done, but instead of waiting silently for some sign, he whistled and laughed. "Is this my termination party?" He pushed back shiny black hair from where it was always falling into his dark eyes and grinned brilliantly at the somber group.

Maureen, the oldest member of the management team at nearly seventy, gestured with one hand to the open chair next to Antonia. "Upper management has asked every team to go over the basic Patriot Values before the close of business. Then, from this day forward, we're all going to be on the pavement, enforcing the Values in our Patriots, for our entire shift. Leads, there will be zero tolerance for second-time offenses tonight. You see someone breaking a Value once, you say something and expect immediate results. You see it a second time, it's discipline. There will be a member of the team here in the office all evening in case you have someone who needs written up. If they're alone at their location, send them to the management office alone and you handle the location until you can get back-up. Understood?"

She glared at Antonia over her bifocals, and Antonia got the distinct impression that Maureen didn't think she was up to the task of disciplining her fellow Patriots.

Well, Maureen clearly didn't know Antonia had already hauled Nick up here for cell phone use. Antonia met her gaze dead-on.

"Now," Maureen said, settling into her chair and picking up the battered Training Binder they'd all read from at the beginning of their careers here, "the first Patriot Value is to look approachable and friendly at all times…"

"So, this is kind of weird," Antonia muttered. She and Rick were clumping down the stairs from the manager's office to the back door of Professor Cloud's, ready to head out onto the pavement, as Maureen liked to put it, and enforce a police state presence on their Patriots.

"It's that blog post," Rick said. "That, plus everything else."

"*Which* blog post? Not the one that caused the protest, everyone behaved for that. Can't still be the video about…" She trailed off, not willing to say her name.

"Tabby? Yeah, not that one. The one that came out this morning."

Antonia's face was perplexed. Rick pulled out his phone and showed her the headline on AtBLive.

"Shit," she whispered, taking the phone from his hands.

Patriots: The Not-So-Family Friendly Truth.

Jesus, what happened to being a theme park *fan*? Nate was just trying to ruin their lives now.

She didn't read the post, just scrolled. Pictures, so many

people she knew. All hanging out in the Gateway. In full costume, in half-costume, with name tags peeping from chest pockets or hanging from backpacks. Drinking. Smoking. General carousing. All offenses punishable by termination, all laid out in paperwork they'd signed on their very first day. You *could not* drink or smoke in public, in costume.

But they did. At the Gateway, because that was *their* place. Tourists couldn't find it, wouldn't know to look for it. And bloggers? Bloggers respected their boundaries. If they came to the Gateway, it was to cozy up to Patriots in hopes of good gossip, to make friends with someone who got good discounts on tchotchkes and restaurants and resort rooms. They'd never blogged about the Gateway and what went on there. That was a safe space for all of them.

It had been, anyway. Someone had broken the contract.

Antonia knew their lives were changing because of this post. Maybe not forever, but in some ways, something had been lost last night.

And now, something would be lost in the park, with all of these management meetings, with the disciplinary notes flying, with her own instructions to get out there and crack the whip on her Patriots.

A little bit of wonder had been stolen from their world.

Antonia had no idea she could hate a job so much.

They'd been out in the park for hours, wandering up and down Old Dodge City, in and out of the shops and to each of the wagons, keeping their eyes out for managers and whispering urgently to Patriots who were leaning, or looking down at the ground as guests walked past, or forgetting to say thank you after a sale. Neither she nor

Rick had any interest in hauling the Patriots they saw up to the manager's office for discipline. Even if she could take a certain pleasure in seeing repeat offenders like Nick get busted for phone use, Antonia knew that a police-state approach to management could not work, and she wasn't going to support it willingly. Rick agreed with her.

But they were both front-line Patriots. Maybe they were one step from management, but they were also only one step from running a register or greeting guests at a doorway. In management's eyes, they were one step too close to the entry-level Patriots and the interns.

Their opinions didn't matter in a crackdown like this.

By the time the sun was disappearing behind Gold Rush Rapids, leaving the eastern sky in a frenzy of pinks and purples and blues, every Patriot in the park was standing ramrod straight next to their assigned positions, smiles fastened to their lips, *hello* and *howdy* and *welcome* and *thank you* and *my pleasure* and *enjoy your evening* echoing through the walkways and shops and attractions. Strolling out of Old Dodge City on a quick park recon with Rick, Antonia felt like she didn't know the place. Patriots were friendly; that was a point of pride—the best guest service in the world, if marketing and travel agents were to be believed. And sure, the majority of Patriots wanted to be here, welcoming their guests and making them happy, but this was something else.

Something almost sinister, when you knew the place as well as Antonia did.

Rick went on his dinner break and left her alone in her police duties, so she wandered up towards Gold Rush Rapids, where the Patriots in the ride's exit shop were usually living in their own little world, separate from the rest of the park. There were four Patriots up there tonight, three on the floor and one on break. She walked up to the photo print counter where the occasional physical copy of an on-ride photo was still printed and packaged, and Careen, the tall blonde intern behind the counter, smiled at her with skull-splitting urgency.

Behind Antonia, a flood of guests poured from the ride's exit, through the shop, and out into the evening; only a few stopped to look at t-shirts or picture frames. The digital age had left their frontier-style print shop behind for as surely as a general store in a forgotten western ghost town.

"Howdy, Antonia," Careen said in an accent verging on the maniacal. "Welcome to this here photo-graphy shop!"

"Calm down," Antonia replied, glancing behind her at the solid fifteen feet of empty space between her and the closest guest. Older Patriots said the shop used to overflow with guests waiting for their photos to print. "You're amongst friends here."

Shauna and Lucas came over from the registers, hanging back a little in case a guest did something crazy and decided to buy something.

"Tonight's slow," Shauna said unnecessarily, pushing her red-gold braid behind her shoulder. Antonia thought she looked a bit like Tabby with the prairie-girl bit, but Shauna was showier, prettier, bustier, and Antonia still wasn't over Tabby's small-town shyness. Shauna went on, "But, I guess that goes without saying. It's kind of hard to greet everyone with a smile and a welcome when they're all running through the store as quick as possible," she added, a little defensively.

"I'm not here to yell at you," Antonia said. "Are you guys doing okay?"

There was a round of shrugs. "Maureen told me I was

receiving a verbal warning earlier," Lucas grumbled. "Apparently, she didn't like the way I was standing behind my register. I'd just finished with a sale when she walked in! I can't just teleport from behind the counter to standing in front of it the second I close the drawer."

"I'm sorry," Antonia said. "I hope this blows over soon and everyone can calm down. Not that we shouldn't be exhibiting Patriot Values ninety-nine percent of the time, but I think we all know there's a one percent called reality."

"Thank you," Careen said. "That's really refreshing, after the day we've had."

"She's only been a lead for a couple of days," Shauna smirked. "Let's see how she feels after she's been hanging out with management full-time for a few months."

"I won't ever be on anyone's side but yours," Antonia vowed, and she meant it.

Shauna heard the conviction in her voice and dropped the smirk.

"Hey, guys," someone said behind her, and Antonia turned. Tabby! Alone, and looking a little lost. She'd gotten wet on the water flume at the end of the ride, water darkening the Ophelia Owl t-shirt she'd ordered from an Etsy shop. Antonia remembered when she'd bought it, how excited she'd been to find something that was such a deep cut from the company's animated past. "So, um, what's going on tonight? Everyone's being weird."

"It's that article in AtBLive. You saw it, right?" Shauna waited for Tabby's nod. "Okay, well, the managers freaked and now we're all on notice. They're marching around like the Spanish Inquisition, looking for anyone who stops smiling for two seconds."

"Oh, God," Tabby gasped. "No wonder everyone's

acting like super-happy robots. It's creepy out there, no lie. The guests are starting to talk about it, even. This is making things worse."

"I said that's what would happen," Lucas announced. "The guests aren't stupid. They act stupid most of the time, but they're not, not really."

"Are you having a good park day, anyway?" Antonia managed to ask, even though all she wanted was to wrap her arms around Tabby's skinny little frame and hug her until she felt this awful day melting away. "Where's Nick?"

"Nick?" Careen said. "I saw him down in the Chuckwagon when I was coming in, two hours ago. I just assumed he was working tonight."

"We were…out in the parks today," Tabby mumbled, looking embarrassed. "But after we came over here from Legacy, he said everyone was being weird and he was going home." She paused. "That was like, four hours ago. I just stayed because I didn't have anything else to do."

"Well, when I was on break, he was in the Chuckwagon with a whole group of people," Careen said. "He might still be there."

"That's okay," Tabby said. "I'd rather be out in the park. Even if it's like a spooky version of the park today."

Antonia peered at her. Really, Tabby didn't want to run immediately into Nick's lovely arms? Something must have gone wrong today. She tried not to feel an uplift of excitement. There was absolutely no reason to believe that once Tabby got Nick out of her system, she'd come running back to a lesbian relationship she had clearly been uncomfortable with from the beginning. Antonia sighed, trying to push her enduring interest in Tabby out with an impatient gust of breath. "A park day sounds good," she explained when the others looked at her, curious. "I haven't had one in a few weeks."

"Yeah," Tabby agreed. "It's been…good." She looked round at each of them, and her face said it was anything but. "I better go, before a manager comes up here and catches you talking to me, a fake guest."

"Bye Tabby," they chorused. "Have fun out there!"

Antonia watched her disappear into the throng of guests pushing to get out of the gift shop and back to another ride queue as quickly as possible. When she turned around again, Careen was watching her with a single arched eyebrow. As she met the blonde girl's gaze, Careen shifted her posture and her breasts lifted an inch or two above the high photo counter.

Antonia considered her for a moment longer. She considered her options. She considered Tabby, disappearing into the park in search of who-knew-what. "Whatchu doing tonight, Careen?" she asked finally, a hint of Caribbean in her voice.

Careen's lips executed a slow, curving smile. "Getting a drink with you, I think."

CHAPTER TWENTY

Sonia

Sonia was regretting her decision to stay late for a little overtime.

Things had gotten weird.

One minute, she'd been playing hopscotch with a little girl who was too short to ride Gold Rush Rapids.

The next, her lead Richie was on her case about not keeping a closer eye on the Greeter position.

"I had to give six different people directions before I could even get over here to talk to you!" he said indignantly.

"Congrats on doing your job," Sonia said dryly, watching the little girl run back to her mother. "Have you figured out why I'm not getting any position besides Greeter yet?"

"Not yet," Richie said. "We have something to go over from management, okay?"

"Richie! You need to get to the bottom of this. It's against my, um, rights." Sonia was foggy about how the union characterized things. But she *did* know she was not supposed to randomly lose her ability to work in all her trained positions. Especially the air-conditioned ones. "I could file a grievance," she threatened.

"Can you not right now? Please." Richie ran a hand through his hair.

She realized he looked very flustered. "What's going on?"

"This thing from management." He held up a sheet of paper. "I have to read it to you and you have to agree to it."

Sonia eyed the paper suspiciously. "Is this a note going in my file?"

Richie sighed. "No. Just—just listen, okay?"

And then he read her the 5 Patriot Values like she was a first-day trainee, pausing frequently so she could answer the never-ending questions of park guests flowing around them.

"Do you understand and acknowledge your responsibilities as an America the Beautiful Patriot?" Richie droned at the end.

"Yes, Richie, I promise to be the best little Patriot the world has ever seen," Sonia sighed. "Are we through here?"

"Just..." Richie looked around as if he expected paratroopers to drop from the heights of Gold Rush Mountain. "Be on your absolute best behavior until this blows over."

"Assuming it does."

"Yeah," Richie agreed. "Assuming it does."

The Chuckwagon was boiling over with loud Patriots and louder televisions. CNN and Fox News were engaged in a pitched battle from opposite sides of the room, but no one was watching either screen. As usual, the early morning custodial staff had put the news on and stashed the remotes somewhere so that the day crew couldn't find them. This, Sonia reflected, was one of the great battles of America the Beautiful. If Nate the blogger wanted insider info for his theme park fans, *this* was the real story. Not where they went drinking at night, on their own, but the crazy stuff that went on under his very feet, while he was out wandering the parks, camera slung around his neck.

The little things were always the big things.

Antonia was sitting alone in a booth by the door, her eyes downcast. Crunched for time, Sonia shouldn't have stopped, but she paused anyway. Antonia might have some advice for her.

"I wanted to tell you congrats on getting lead," she said, sliding into the booth so Antonia could hear her over the din. "I've been thinking of requesting it myself."

Antonia barely glanced up from her inspection of the table-top. "Thanks," she murmured. "I hope you get it. You'd be good at it."

"I appreciate that," Sonia said. She didn't know Antonia well, mainly as Tabby's ex and a fellow Old Dodge City Patriot, but she did know Antonia was driven and rigorous. Was she also morose at times? Possibly. She started to get up, saying as she slid out of the booth: "You'll be a manager in no time, so remember me for the future!"

Antonia put her hands out on the Formica table and spread her fingers, stretching the joints. A knuckle popped. "We have to change things," she said softly.

Sonia, interested, stopped halfway out of the booth. "Change what?"

"The way we're treated by management," Antonia said, lifting her eyes to Sonia's. "Guilty until proven innocent."

"Did something happen? Are you getting into trouble?"

"Not me," she said. "Not yet. But this whole Values crackdown. Over a *blog* post, all of us treated like we're out to destroy the parks? Turning leads and managers into police wardens? It's not right. It's not what this place is about, not what it's ever been about." Antonia's voice grew more passionate. "And I'm *not* going to do it. I'm not going to march around looking for people, for my coworkers, to drag up to the office to get a letter, maybe even get fired. I'm supposed to be looking out for them, making their jobs easier, so that they can concentrate on the guests—that's what this job is supposed to be all about!" She looked at Sonia for the first time and her eyes were wide and filled with outrage. "I'm just trying to decide what I should do next. Do I give up the lead position in protest?"

Sonia knew her few lunch minutes had nearly expired. She could almost taste that rubbery, salty hot dog, but she knew it wasn't going to happen. She laid her hand over Antonia's. "You definitely can't give up the role," she said. "Then they win."

By the time Sonia got home that night, she'd made up her mind.

Elena was crashed across the couch, her phone in the air above her face. She waved a casual hello to Sonia. "Did you have fun being a Patriot-bot tonight?"

Sonia threw her backpack on the kitchen counter. "Oh, it was super. I think I strained my neck trying not to miss a single guest as they walked past me. Because yes, I'm still stuck on Greeter. Ten glorious hours today. And they took away my hopscotch rights. Because I can't play with one kid when I might miss greeting fifty others, apparently."

"That seriously sucks. No one is even trying to fix the Greeter thing for you, are they?"

"Nope." She lined up her hiking boots next to Elena's pretty black flats and hung up her work lanyard on the hook next to the front door. "Especially now that every lead has been deputized to be some sort of Patriot Value Commando. Richie was the closing lead, and he just kept telling me he wasn't allowed to go back and use the computer unless it was some kind of safety situation."

"So, what, no one is allowed office time anymore? How will the place run?" Elena smirked. "This can't last."

"We need a regime change," Sonia announced, throwing herself down on the armchair and setting her feet on the battered coffee table.

"What do you propose? I don't think anyone at Independence Plaza has urban warfare on their resume."

"Too busy being belles," Sonia laughed. "But honestly? Antonia got that promotion to lead overnight. I don't even have a request in. What am I waiting for? I'm going to put in for an ops lead position."

"And what is that going to do?"

"Be the change I want to see in the world?"

Elena snorted.

"Seriously, if I'm lead, it gives me a chance to stand up for other Patriots!"

"So, what, you are going to be come a lead and counteract all of upper management's ridiculous ideas about how to run the parks? Why not just become CEO, honey? Really set your sights on the stars." Elena looked back at her phone. "Margie, over at Magnolia Lodge, is texting me. She says that they're not allowed to stand behind the front desk when they're not with a guest. They have to stand out on the hard marble floor and look approachable." She groaned. "I'm going to need new Dr. Scholls."

"We can't let them treat us like this."

"Go on strike," Elena said, rolling her eyes. "Do whatever you want. I'm going to wait it out. You enact change from the inside, or whatever. The result will be the same."

Sonia left her roommate to her fatalism and went into the kitchen. Late nights always made her hungry.

While a bowl of macaroni and cheese heated in the microwave, she went over her plan again. Honestly, the whole situation felt like the impetus she'd needed for a while. This, and paying off that past-due balance on her loan with a stolen binder of proprietary company information. Working at AtB was supposed to be *fun*, dammit! That was what made up for not always keeping one's head above water, financially speaking. Management might not be interested in paying them enough to stay solvent, but they sure as hell weren't going to take away their right to have fun on the job.

And who could have fun when they were being watched all the time? Sonia flicked through her phone while she ate her late-night supper.

My manager has been on my back since I clocked in, lamented @atbbabyyyyy on Twitter. *I don't break my back for Edgar Eagle for the money, u kno!!!*

What happened? asked @opheliakween. *Too tired from smiling to even eat my sammie on break.*

It was @AtBLive and I'm gonna un-alive him, @atbbabyyyyy replied.

Nate was going to have to watch his back, Sonia thought.

And if she were lead, and she saw some Patriots deliberately give the guy a hard time, she wouldn't say a thing about it. She would just look the other way.

Sonia realized she didn't have to wait. She could go on the PatriotPortal app and do it right now. While she ate a bowl full of macaroni and cheese, she could take the next step.

A few taps. A few moments squinting at the screen.

Job Role: *Operations Lead*. Area Requested: *Any*.

And just like that, her lead request was entered.

Sonia felt so good, she got up and made herself a second bowl of macaroni. She opened a beer, too. Tonight was her own private celebration.

CHAPTER TWENTY-ONE

Martin

Martin put in a solid morning's work before he went off to America the Beautiful. This was the bargain he made with himself most weekday mornings, especially in the busy summer months, when the afternoons and evenings at the parks were wildly busy. If he got up at four, logged three hours' of work, then he could take a mid-morning break to visit Miss Sallie Mae and Miss Susie Q. at AtB. Then, in the afternoon, he would take a nap before getting in three or four more hours' work and a late dinner.

There were practical applications to this schedule as well: the broadband at the apartment complex wasn't particularly good and struggled at times of peak usage, like mid-morning when the closing park crew were waking up, and early evening when the opening crew started streaming television shows. Martin's IT work required constant connections, plus a lot of work on cloud-based services, so he had become overly sensitive to the fluctuations in service speed. In the course of the past three years living at Gateway, he'd learned that between four and seven, both a.m. and p.m., the information flowed without interruption. It was a beautiful time to work.

He'd actually picked up the habit back when Amy was still working at AtB. She'd typically worked banker's hours, between nine and five—these were, apparently, the most popular hours for meeting characters at AtB. Amy had played a whole line-up of beloved characters, even Lady Liberty herself, who met in the waterfall grotto at the base of Promise Mountain, draped in a Grecian robe and blinking through long eyelashes at her wide-eyed guests.

Amy had begun to dislike playing Lady Liberty towards the end—she used to claim that as the national discourse coarsened, so did the men who came to visit her alongside the children—but Martin had always loved her in that role. Her vivid red hair would have looked ravishing spilling over the mint-green folds of her robe, but even with it netted carefully under the blonde waves and coils of the Lady Liberty wig (of course Lawrence Taylor's goddess of America would be blonde-haired and blue-eyed—that was a reality which was accepted without much discussion amongst fans) her pale skin and sweeping eyelashes did plenty to accentuate the costume.

She was easily the best-looking Lady Liberty in thirty years, all of the character-chasers agreed. Well, except for Eddie Robinson, and he had been obsessed with the snub-nosed, cherubic round face of Lucy Steele throughout her ten-year reign as Lady Liberty. Lucy still picked up some shifts as Mrs. deBussy, proprietress of Madame deBussy's Music Shop on Independence Street, but she was in her forties now and her once dimpled cheeks were starting to sag a little with stress, and gravity, and too much foundation. Eddie still loved her, though. To the point where he'd had to talk his way out of a restraining order a few years back, after agreeing he'd *never* ask Lucy to marry him again. "Ten times is enough," Lucy had told her manager, before requesting he be trespassed. "I have three children and a husband already."

Eddie was the type of character-chaser Martin didn't approve of; the ones who gave ardent fans like him a bad name. Martin was quiet, respectful, and completely open with the characters he loved: he understood he was older than the typical fan by about twenty-five years and he would always be a perfect gentleman, and then some, in the parks.

His morning work hours finished, Martin pushed through the turnstiles at AtB and under the welcoming arches, dripping with honeysuckle and buzzing with the busy wings of hummingbirds. He sighed as the vista of Independence Plaza opened up before him: the rumbling wheels of the horse-carts, the rippling tunes of the calliope set up in front of Century Circus Corner, where a juggler was currently tossing rings while balancing precariously on a high-wheeled unicycle. A little circle of toddlers were gravely watching the juggler, and if it weren't for the strings of huge Edgar Eagle balloons clasped in their fists, they'd look as if they'd just stepped out of a Norman Rockwell painting.

Martin gazed at the children for a moment, as long as propriety would allow, and felt his heart squeeze tightly against his throat, a little thumping reminder that he was still alive, that he still loved, whenever he walked through those honeysuckle arches. Maybe the outside world was too much for him, but as long as America the Beautiful persisted, he would have a comfort zone to visit.

Moving on through the Plaza, Martin spotted Eddie in a cluster of faces gazing at Mrs. deBussy as she argued lustily with the Mayor about some insider Plaza matter. It was usually some young lady who had shortened her skirts *most* indecently, but sometimes she harangued the Mayor about the rising price of sausages. Often, Martin would hang around and enjoy the show, but not today.

This morning, the scents and sounds of Independence Plaza filled Martin with a sense of purpose, even as they slowed his feet and turned his head. The cotton candy haze of the Central Candy Factory, the fantastical wheezing of the vintage organ emerging from the Original Wurlitzer Showroom, the homey fug of brewing coffee billowing from the air-conditioned doorways of the Independence Plaza Coffee and Cafe. A ragtime band was playing their hearts out from some hidden room upstairs—at least, that was the illusion the camouflaged speakers in the second-story windows wanted him to believe, and he was happy to enjoy both the truth and the lie.

Martin was one of those theme park fans who got it all, who could believe whole-heartedly in the children's tales being bleated throughout the parks and also seek out every showman's trick being used to tell the stories, from Pepper's Ghost effects to audio cues to hidden scent emitters.

As he reached the tip board at the end of Independence Plaza, Martin noted the wait for Lady Liberty's Grotto was posted at a reasonable twenty minutes, but that hadn't been his destination for years now. Instead, Martin turned down the pathway to the left and headed for the timbered gates which led to the Forgotten Forests and Old Dodge City. He wanted to have a chat with Miss Sallie Mae.

"A private audience," Martin murmured as he passed the young man standing by Miss Sallie Mae's line. "Any chance?"

"I can do you a private audience at eleven-thirty-five," the young man replied, consulting a small notepad. The cover of which, unfortunately, announced the notepad had come from Target.

It was the little things that ruined the story, Martin thought. Aloud, he replied, "I'll be here, thanks."

The Patriot notated Martin's visit into the notebook. These things were recorded, logged into databases with timestamps. Private audiences with characters were permitted as long as nothing funny happened.

He didn't have to ask for Martin's name, which was what set this audience apart.

Most people wanted them for totally innocent purposes. Amy had done private audiences as Lady Liberty, as Miss Sallie Mae, even as a costumed Petals the Goose. They were nearly always arranged for shy children, or for Emirates princes, or for celebrities traveling by back doors and hidden hallways. There were plenty of reasons a child or adult might want to speak with a character, get a hug, and have their picture taken, without having a crowd of waiting guests watching them.

But towards the end of Amy's tenure at AtB, all private audiences had been temporarily shut down. There were whispers in the community about what had happened; Martin had done his best to shut them all out. No one was fired. No one was trespassed. No names were uttered in public. The ban lasted six months, and Amy eventually took a job at a theme park in Korea.

And then Martin came out on the other side blinking, as if he hadn't been in the sun during all of that time.

Martin checked his watch; he had half an hour until he could speak to Miss Sallie Mae alone. He glanced around Old Dodge City, but nothing out of the ordinary could be seen. It was just another June day, the white cotton-ball clouds drifting unhurriedly past the windmill on Wilderness Isle. There were screams in the distance as guests were hurled over the final flume on Gold Rush Rapids, and the side-wheeler tooted her whistle as if in reply. Banjo music plucked out *Oh Suzanna*. It was, in every respect, a glorious day.

He settled down on a rocking chair outside of Professor Cloud's to watch the Patriots at their quiet work. Most guests would never notice them, but Martin found their work fascinating, especially in the mornings when the real worker bees were still finishing up their labors. Martin loved the gray-clad, quiet men and women who did the inventories in the stores, the dirt-smeared landscapers doing the planting in the barrels of blooming wildflowers, the painters putting the touch-ups on the trim of lamp-posts.

He watched Louisa, her blue sweater wrapped around her shoulders despite the heat, stroll out to the sunglass Conestoga with a clipboard. Martin had never spoken to Louisa, but over the years he'd come to admire this gray-haired, hatchet-faced old Patriot. She was, to the best of his knowledge, some sort of inventory clerk. She frequently carried her clipboard out to stores, instructed the Patriot running the register to help her, and filled a bag with items, which she then whisked away, leaving behind empty shelves for the abandoned Patriot to fill in the best he or she could.

Martin admired Louisa's ruthlessness, her single-mindedness, the way she could weave in and out of the parties of guests moving in great groups up the street without having to glance at them, get in their way or even appear on their radar. No one asked Louisa questions. No one had ever stopped her for directions or asked her to take their photo, because, as far as Martin could tell, no one ever registered she'd actually been there.

He longed to acquire this trait, to disappear into the background of America the Beautiful, to waver for a moment and then vanish altogether, part of the flowers and the fiberglass.

Louisa was looking around the corner of the Conestoga; the Patriot who should be stationed there was not by the cash register...

She was looking irritated...

Her! Martin sat forward, his rocker creaking, his heart racing. He felt a flush of color come to his cheeks and, embarrassed, he slid back in the rocker and tucked his chin into his collar. A family clumped down the boardwalk, children chattering, dragging their parents past him without glancing his way. No one saw his red cheeks. No one knew he was watching.

He shouldn't be watching her, dammit. He shoved up from the rocker, went into Professor Cloud's, pretended to admire a new set of gem-encrusted Patriot Pal statues in the locked vitrine until it was time to talk to Miss Sallie Mae.

She'd put things to rights for him.

The room set aside for private audiences was behind Sam Sweet's Candy Shop, a tiny space dominated by a claw-footed antique sofa and armchair, both draped with a few gold-fringed throws of wine-colored velvet. The quiet resemblance to a bordello room behind a frontier tavern was certainly not coincidental; Amy had once confided to him a piece of character gossip passed between all the actors over the years, that Lawrence Taylor had held a secret affection for the fancy girls of the Old West in his heart, and he'd loved to sit in this audience room and chat with his favorite characters. Hopefully not, Amy had laughed, with any hanky-panky, any hands-on-the-knees shenanigans.

"Maybe they showed him their ankles in there," Martin had suggested, and Amy had grabbed a magazine from the coffee table and held it up to her mouth like a fan to cover her mouth in ladylike horror. They'd laughed so hard after that, and he'd basked in her affectionate glow.

Well, there would be no ankle-viewing these days; the security camera in the far corner made sure everyone kept their unmentionables decently covered.

Miss Sallie Mae was already draped over the sofa, her eyes closed. They fluttered open as Martin entered and the door was shut behind him. He heard the shuffle of fabric on the other side of the thin wall and knew the Patriot attending Miss Sallie had sat down to mind the video feed of their encounter. He pushed this knowledge out of his mind as best he could. It was hard to bare one's soul when you were being watched by a college student chewing an illicit stick of gum.

"Martin," Miss Sallie Mae greeted him warmly. "Where have you been, darlin'?"

"Oh, busy with work," he replied, spreading his hands. "You know how it is."

"I sure do. A woman's work is never done," she agreed,

the western accent she affected for her role slipping into a southern drawl. Martin didn't mind at all; they all performed Miss Sallie differently, but in the end she was always the same: a beautiful young pioneer woman who had her fair share of sweethearts and a touch of worldly wisdom from her hard life on the frontier, building the American dream with her own fair hands, supporting her kindly parents, and teaching a one-room schoolhouse full of children as rowdy as wild Indians. That was her published back-story. For now, anyway—certain members of AtB character management had begun to suspect "wild Indians" needed to go.

"Well, I like to keep busy." Martin wasn't sure where to begin, how to word what he wanted to ask. This Miss Sallie hadn't known Amy. They were reaching a time when none of the young performers would know her. He wasn't sure if that made it easier, or harder. Weirder, or more normal. "But I sure could use your advice."

"Oh, honey, I'd be happy to give you advice." Miss Sallie smiled coquettishly. "Just you tell me what's on your mind. I give great advice. Everyone says so."

"Miss Sallie, if you saw someone across the room, and you felt like there was…I don't know…"

"A connection?" she asked, looking genuinely interested.

"Not really a connection, though, but just…a sense of rightness…" Martin was grasping for some way to express himself, but already, just days after it had happened, he'd lost the thread of what he'd felt when he'd first talked to Tabby, of when he'd looked at her and seen a woman he wanted to protect. A woman he felt like he'd known forever. A woman he'd barely spoken to and didn't know the first thing about.

"Oh," Miss Sallie Mae, injecting a world of fascination into that single syllable. "Honey, is this love at first sight?"

Martin had fallen in love with Amy over the course of six agonizing weeks, looking at her over the register where she was ringing up his coffee, then asking her about her day, then taking her for a walk in the park across from the cafe, then learning everything about her, then helping her audition for her first character performer role, and finally, easily, devoting his life to her without a second thought. He didn't think it had been love at first sight. It had been interest, then affection, then adoration, then obsession.

It had gone from gentle to painful so, so quickly.

"Maybe it is," Martin admitted. "I've never felt like this before."

"In love?"

"I've been in love before. But I knew the person. I had reasons."

"Oh," she said, batting her eyelashes. "I don't know if you need reasons to fall in love, honey."

Martin wondered if that was true. It would certainly make things easier.

CHAPTER TWENTY-TWO

Tabby

Tabby had been on guard all morning.

There was so much to worry about, all of a sudden. There was that stupid blogger hiding in the shadows, watching her. She hadn't seen him yet today, but that didn't mean anything. A lot could happen in an eight-hour shift.

Then there was the management. The Patriot Values crackdown that had begun yesterday wouldn't end anytime soon; she hadn't missed the drama just because she'd been off yesterday. She'd gotten the speech from a lead as soon as she'd clocked in this morning: a complete recitation of the 5 Patriot Values, and her verbal agreement that she understood they were her responsibility to uphold at all times.

Emphasis on the *all*.

And it sucked, honestly. It was so hard to play with kids or carry on a conversation with an interesting person for more than a few sentences before she had to worry she was missing out on greeting or assisting other park guests. She couldn't physically say hello to everyone in Old Dodge City, could she? It seemed like that was the request, though. The fear of being watched and written up for spending too long on one party made her rigid and stiff when she was usually loose and playful.

She wasn't alone.

All around her, Patriots were standing at attention like they were waiting for a military inspection. This kind of atmosphere wasn't why she had dropped out of college to work here, and she knew everyone else felt the same way. They'd better drop the drama, and quick, or people were going to start quitting.

Right at the start of summer, the worst possible time to lose people.

Management and the blogger weren't Tabby's only worries this morning. There was still Nick to think about— he was coming in at noon, and she knew he'd probably get assigned to work Sunglass Wagon with her. He'd texted her a few times last night, just general nonsense about having a fun day and did she have a fun day too, and she couldn't think of anything to reply, so after the third one she'd responded with a non-committal *going to sleep now goodnight!*

It had only been nine o'clock but apparently he'd taken her at her word, because he'd just replied with a sleepy-face emoji and her phone had been quiet for the rest of the evening (she went to bed at midnight as usual). Staying off social media so he wouldn't know she was up was annoying, but she'd anesthetized herself with a thick biography of Sylvia O'Grady, Lawrence Taylor's long-time secretary and the rumored secret creator of Edgar Eagle, Ophelia Owl, and several other members of the Patriot Pals. Tabby admired Sylvia O'Grady, who was strong and capable and handled Lawrence Taylor at his most gruff and patronizing with a smooth, red-lip smile. She figured Sylvia would have no trouble telling Nick that things weren't going to progress romantically.

Sadly, she wasn't Sylvia.

Tabby didn't have the *slightest* idea how she was going to handle the Nick situation. Like every other entanglement with the opposite sex, she found herself unenthused and deeply confused. Maybe she should have stuck with Antonia. But there hadn't really been a spark there, either. Not for her, anyway.

"Miss? Excuse me, miss?"

Tabby attended the guest on the far side of the wagon with a swish of her skirts, willing herself to sink into her prairie-girl character. "Yes sir, how can I help you?"

The guest was a young father, with a sweaty little toddler clinging to his side, arms flung dramatically around his neck and face buried against his shoulder. They both looked miserably hot. "I need a hat for this little guy," the father said, his words spoken with the crisp, clean, accent-free vowels of the Mid-Atlantic. Tabby, southern-born and bred, had always admired those short, even syllables. "Something to keep the sun off his face."

"Well, sure, I can help you there." Tabby plucked two toddler-sized caps off the wagon without even having to look for their labels; she was practiced enough to know which designs adorned hats for little heads. "We've got Maracas the Parrot here or Lucky, which one do you like best?" She held the caps up for the toddler to choose.

The toddler didn't lift his head, but he did turn it slowly, revealing a few tear streaks on his pink, chubby cheeks. Tabby felt a lurch of sympathy. "Poor little buddy," she cooed. "How about a Lucky hat?"

The toddler's brow closed into a ferocious frown. "No *Lucky,*" he snapped. "No *parrot.*"

"Aww," Tabby attempted. "Don't make Maracas and Lucky feel sad. They want to keep the sun off your face!"

"No *Lucky!*" The child insisted, his expression positively incensed. "*No parrot!*"

Tabby put the hats behind her back and shifted her gaze to the father. He looked back at her helplessly.

"You don't have anything else in his size?"

"Who does he like best?"

"No Lucky," the toddler grumbled, his lips pressed to his father's shoulder again.

"Definitely not Lucky," she assured him. "Anyone else?"

The toddler mumbled something she didn't catch.

"Oh, Grayson," the father said. "He's not here. Wrong park."

Tabby smiled, catching on. "Who does he want?"

"Want Goofy," Grayson said staunchly, giving her a narrow-eyed glare.

"Oh, dear. What about…" Tabby surveyed the child-sized hats. They'd be a little big, but… "What about Harry Hound? He's pretty…goofy." She held up the hat, embroidered with a slobbering basset hound wearing a red bandana and a cowboy hat.

Grayson regarded the hat with a mixture of disgust and wary interest. He held out his sticky fingers and Tabby gave it to him for inspection. The toddler turned the hat this way and that, slurping on the fingers of his free hand all the while. Tabby and the boy's father waited in quiet anticipation.

Then he handed it back to Tabby and nodded curtly.

"You want it?" she asked.

"Harry," he pronounced. "Yeth."

Tabby reached out and deftly plucked the price-tag from the hat, breaking the plastic with a flick of her wrist. "He can hang onto it," she said. "I'll ring it up for you. Did you need anything else?"

"That's all, thank you." The father gave her a relieved smile. "Thanks for finding the Harry Hound hat. It's *kinda* close to Goofy, right?"

"This happens all the time," Tabby said with a laugh. "I've also sold Lucky the Indian Pony as one of Spirit's friends. Thank goodness there are only so many cuddly animals to make into cartoon characters. That hat will be just a little big, but you can adjust it on the back."

"Fine, fine…" He waited while she went around to the register and rang up the hat. When she came back around, his wallet was out; she took his credit card and went back to run it through. When she returned the second time, with his receipt, he was all smiles, Grayson was wearing the hat, adorably bunched up around the sides from how tightly the strap had to be pulled, and he thanked her warmly for being such a great help. "Now it's off to find mom and sis at Gold Rush Rapids!" he announced, and they disappeared into the crowd.

Tabby had three other guests waiting, and she ran through their purchases quickly, her mind still on the toddler's oddly adult responses to the hats she'd shown them. *Children are so much more aware than we give them credit for,* she thought, handing off change and wishing the last guest a very beautiful day at America the Beautiful. She looked over her wagon's wares and smiled. Everyone was happy, the sun was shining, Grayson had his hat. Even if Nick showed up or Nate was lurking behind some tree watching her, there would be no problem they couldn't all sort out with a little chat.

Tabby glanced across the walkway and saw Roseann stepping briskly her way, teetering in heels, a stern look upon her face.

The sun went behind a cloud.

"A letter in your file?" Sonia was aghast, her wobbling spoonful of pudding arrested while just halfway to her mouth. "For that?"

"It's a required part of the transaction," Tabby said miserably. "You have to ask if they are an annual passholder before you give them their final total. But it confuses so many people, half the time no one does it. You can usually tell who has an annual pass or not. Trust me, the ones paying a couple grand a year for an annual pass don't usually have kids who think they're at Disney World instead of America the Beautiful."

"So it was total set-up."

"I think so." Tabby rested her chin on her palm. "A secret shopper."

"That's bullshit, Tabby."

"I know." Tabby thought of the way she'd masterminded that transaction from start to finish. She had done everything right. She had even drawn that child out of his shell! She'd found a product which was just as good as what he wanted, since what he wanted wasn't part of their line-up. She'd let him hang onto it instead of insisting she needed to take it to the register. Told his father how to fit the hat. Gotten a little smile as he'd walked away. Everything right! Except for asking if he was an annual passholder. Because what kind of annual passholder had a kid asking for Goofy hats at America the Beautiful? Context clues were important!

Oh, she'd read the guest right, she was sure of it. The problem had been in the secret shopper set-up. They'd put together a faulty guest profile.

Although it was possible they hadn't known Grayson wanted a Goofy hat. Toddlers were unknown entities when writing scripts.

Or were they? Maybe he was an actor. Maybe he had been coached to double-cross her that way.

"Well," Sonia said, "at least you weren't planning on trying for a transfer or anything anytime soon. This will fall off after a few months and not affect you." Letters technically only counted against a Patriot's mobility for six months, and then they stopped being automatic red lights…although they never disappeared completely. "If I got a letter right now, I'd freaking kill myself."

"That desperate to get out of here, huh?"

"It's just time," Sonia said. "You know? I have things I want to do."

It's just time.

The words rang in Tabby's ears as she went back through the Underground, passing the hidden dumpsters and caged-off stockrooms which lined the passage. She paused to allow three giggling Patriot Pal characters, their animal heads popped off and tucked under their arms, pass by on their way to their dressing rooms—their waggling hips and rumps were so wide, they took up the entire corridor. The girl who was garbed as a headless Maracas the Parrot waved her thanks with a feathered hand, but it just reminded Tabby of the boy at the Conestoga shrieking *"No parrot!"* at her. She didn't wave back.

It's just time. She'd been working at Old Dodge City for six months now—there was nothing stopping her from putting in another transfer request and leaving. And wasn't it time to give another region a try? Old Dodge City was not working out. In the past week alone, she'd been accosted and stalked by a theme park blogger, had her face blasted all over social media, and been set up for a failing customer service assessment during some sort of Gestapo crackdown on everyone's onstage behavior. Oh, and she'd accidentally led on *two* of her coworkers into thinking they were going to be happy romantic partners.

Did she really need all of this stress in her life?

Greener pastures were calling. Maybe she should consider Legacy of Heroes, which was by all accounts a much more laid-back place to work. Or even a resort: Magnolia Lodge, or Metropolitan Hotel? Or at Shining Seas Water Park? It was only open from April to October, though.

She climbed the concrete stairs towards Old Dodge City, her hand running up the cool metal railing, soaking up the last few moments of air conditioning she'd enjoy before she clocked out in another four hours. In other jobs, in the real world, you could stay within the confines of air conditioning for as long as your entire shift. Should she go work in the real world?

That was crazy. Of course not. She wouldn't survive a moment outside of AtB. Tabby knew her limitations; a girl who grew up as sequestered as she had wasn't ready for reality. AtB was an acceptable middle line between life back in the holler, listening to her mama pray for hours, and living in some everyday city, working some everyday job, pretending to be a functioning adult.

At least here, pretending was encouraged.

The yellowed sign on the door read: *Smile, Patriot! You make America the Beautiful beautiful!* alongside a fading cartoon Edgar Eagle grinning into a mirror. There was a plastic mirror stuck to the wall next to the door, for the purpose of arranging one's guest-ready smile into its careful folds. Tabby paused and looked at her reflection. Slanting brows and wispy braid and green eyes and those damned freckles aside…she looked pretty good.

Smile on.

She opened the door and stepped out into the America of yesteryear. A mournful fiddle rendition of *Shenandoah* was filtering through the sultry air. The reclaimed boards of a tumbledown barn from somewhere Deep South and forgotten creaked under her sensible shoes.

"A total escape from the pressures of today," Lawrence Taylor had said at America the Beautiful's dedication, "and a total immersion in the beauty and values of the past."

America the Beautiful, she thought with a pulse of emotion. *I love you.*

She took another step, and as she did, she let her eyes flutter closed for a moment to fully absorb the song, the popcorn scent on the breeze, the wheezing steam of the passing side-wheeler.

She walked straight into another person.

Her eyes flew open, made panicked contact with his as they collided in mid-step. *Martin,* she realized, as she flailed to keep upright.

"I'm so sorry!" they said at the same time, hands reaching for one another, for balance, for assistance.

Tabby was the first to break into nervous laughter. She couldn't believe the ridiculous position she was in—clutching Martin's upper arms for dear life, her right leg somehow entwined with his left one, her eyes just inches from his chin. She could see the faint stubble of a skipped morning shave on his skin. "Oh my goodness, how ridiculous of me, I'm so sorry," she burbled. "What just happened?"

"I was just walking along the boardwalk here—the door opened before I could even react—"

"There's never anyone over here in this corner!" Tabby realized she was still clutching his arms and made herself let go, take a step back. "What were you doing over here?" They were in a secluded little alcove of boardwalk, where the Shopkeepers Only door could open and close away from prying eyes of nosy guests. A few feet away, the door to the character private audience room was situated in a little corner of its own, for the same reasons.

Tabby's eyes landed on the unmarked door at the same moment as Martin's.

There was an uncomfortable silence between them.

Then Tabby shook her head. "Really, Martin?"

She was displeased to think Martin might be a character-chaser. But something Antonia had said a few days ago came back into her head: "Our guests are normal humans. Nate and Martin are the weirdos."

What a disappointment, she thought, and then she wondered why she even cared.

Martin was blushing, an unlikely girlish pink stealing into his craggy cheeks. "I—um—I'm friends with today's Miss

Sallie Mae and it was urgent…"

"Right," she said, taking a step back. "Well, I have to get back to the sunglass wagon."

"Wait," Martin burst out, and the intensity in his voice surprised her. "I don't want you to think—it's not like—I'm not involved with Miss Sallie or anything."

"Oh, definitely not," Tabby assured him. She was continuing this conversation. What was wrong with her? A character-chaser who obsessed over a Miss Sallie Mae certainly didn't have to explain himself to her, a fully grown woman who had just been so swept away by theme park immersion that she'd closed her eyes and walked straight into him, but she sure didn't want to hear the details. "You're just friends. I get it."

Why. Do. You. Care?

"I just thought, you know…you *should* know…I mean…" Martin looked pained.

"It's fine," she said, and without even thinking about what she was doing, Tabby reached out and placed a hand on Martin's forearm. He looked down at it. Suddenly she felt her own cheeks grow hot. Touching a guest was highly frowned upon.

But she didn't take her hand away.

"Tabby, do you need any help with your guest?"

She had both hands behind her back in an instant; she took a step back from Martin. Fucking *Nick!* What were the chances? She gave him a bright smile.

"No, everything's fine. You're here! Is it noon already? Wow!" The lightness in her voice sounded obscene to her, when the world around her seemed to be shaking with a heavy emotion she couldn't explain or even identify, but Nick didn't seem to notice anything was amiss.

"I picked up Assist at the sunglass wagon, so I hope it's with you today!" Nick announced. He came to her side and nodded to Martin. "Hello, sir. I hope you're having a swell day in Old Dodge City."

She watched Martin swallow, nod. "Swell," Martin said thinly, as if the word pained him.

"I'll see you at the wagon after you clock in," Nick told Tabby. "And hey—I hope you don't have plans for tonight, because I already made us some!" He dashed out into the street traffic, dodging strollers on his way to the Conestogas.

Tabby smiled weakly at Martin, whose face had taken on a rather slack-jawed appearance. Was he…upset? About Nick? "Don't mind Nick," she said confidingly. "He's kind of an idiot, but he's a nice guy to work with."

The door behind them opened again, and Winslow appeared like a hound dog from under a porch. He paused, scratched the back of his head, and gave the two of them an appraising look. "Wow. Not a nice thing to say about your boyfriend, Tabby," he told her, winked at Martin, and walked away.

Damn Winslow!

Martin looked after him wistfully. Tabby felt her gut twist at his lost expression. "Nick is not my boyfriend," she whispered urgently. "We've been…I've spent some time with him. It's not like that."

"You don't have to explain yourself," Martin said, unconsciously echoing her thoughts of just a moment before.

"I just don't want anyone to think—" Tabby trailed off. They had both fumbled to explain themselves with the same words, which left her wondering if Martin wasn't a creepy chaser after all.

He was still looking across Old Dodge City, as if the wagons and the waterfront had taken on an urgent new significance. "I'm just a guest here. Your life is your business." He started to step away from her.

Tabby caught at his sleeve, driven by some demon she couldn't, wouldn't identify. Suddenly, she knew what she wanted—to see the haunted look leave Martin's eyes, to bring him back from whatever cliff's edge he'd been balancing on for all the time she'd known him.

"Don't go like this," she said. "We're friends, aren't we?"

Slowly, Martin turned and looked down at her, at her fingers on his shirt, back at her eyes. He was taller than she was. His gaze made her blush hotly, and she slowly released her grip on his shirt. Suddenly, the park just outside their alcove seemed very loud. She wondered if anyone was watching them, from around some corner, from behind some column. What if Roseann was watching her right now? What was the next step for two infractions in one day? She'd get sent home, for sure. She wouldn't get paid. An entirely new set of implications lined up at that threat, ready to take their turns in her anxiety pool.

Meanwhile, Martin was looking at her with an expression that could only be described as desperate. He started to speak, stopped, opened his mouth again. But no words came out.

"Listen," Tabby whispered, realizing they had to cut this short and that the job was up to her. "Do you want to get a coffee later? Someplace quiet. Not the Gateway."

"Sinatra's," Martin suggested, catching her meaning instantly.

Sinatra's. The shadowy lounge at Metropolitan Hotel,

where Molly worked behind the front desk. It was a favorite tryst spot of Patriot couples who didn't want to be seen; the bartenders were discreet, and the booths were very private. Tabby had never been asked there; her handful of flings had been grossly public, on purpose.

"I get off at eight," she said. "Eight thirty?"

"I'll meet you at the bar."

Tabby felt his eyes on her as she walked to the Conestoga wagon and took up her post. She kept her distance from Nick, who was stuck at the register with a line of guests waiting to check out. She didn't know what was happening between her and Martin.

But she didn't want to ruin it before she found out.

CHAPTER TWENTY-THREE

Sonia

Sonia woke up with an uneasy feeling in her stomach.

At first she just assumed it was the nuclear combination of nachos and volcano rolls consumed at the Gateway the night before…really, just a few hours ago. She was getting old, she thought wearily. She shouldn't be downing hot sauce in that quantity after nine p.m. anymore. Somehow, she'd thought all the Coronas she'd washed it down with would cushion her digestive system. Maybe her late-night logic wasn't exactly infallible.

Fortunately, today's shift didn't start until noon—which gave her plenty of time to stumble around her empty apartment, eat a cup of yogurt, and stand in the shower for a solid fifteen minutes. She'd read something about the healing power of steam once. This seemed like as good a time as any to try it out. Going to work at Gold Rush Rapids on a summer Friday was a trial on the best of days.

Going when it felt like a bowling bowl was settled in one's stomach just sounded like torture.

By the time she was walking into the Underground entrance, dressed in her forty-niner attire and with her name-tag affixed above her heart, things hadn't gotten much better. She was forced to admit that there was something in the air, not something in last night's food. *Everyone* looked a little green around the gills.

There were little groups of people whispering furtively outside the lockers for Old Dodge City Patriots.

And there were several Patriots crying in the corner of the Chuckwagon.

One, sure, that was normal. But more than one Patriot needing a good cry at the same time?

What the hell was going on out there?

Sonia went upstairs with her nerves on edge. She walked out into the hot June sun, ducked into the dark break room under the Gold Rush queue, and found her answer.

The leads were standing near the time-clock, their faces serious. In a booth along the wall, a Gold Rush colleague was sitting with her forehead pressed against the table, not saying anything.

Sonia's stomach gurgled, reminding her that it had, in fact, been right all along.

"You can clock in first." William was one of the senior leads, an ambitious young man whose outwardly kind demeanour was a carefully crafted mask designed to make him stand out as a management prospect. "Don't want you to be late."

First? Before *what?* Sonia swallowed and logged into the computer. It acknowledged her clock-in with a little wave from a smiling Edgar Eagle. She didn't smile back like she usually did. "What's going on?"

"You can put your stuff in your locker," Staci suggested. She was older than the average ops lead, well into her late forties, and her fading hair was practically standing up from the humidity. Alongside William's youthful good looks, she seemed yellowed with age and cigarette smoke. Staci had worked at a rural Georgia roadside tavern and sold home-cooked drugs alongside cheap beer before she'd cleaned up her life and come to work at AtB. Ops workers trended younger than Retail, and her lined face stood out in the sea of college students and recent grads, although not in a particularly positive way.

Sonia moved mechanically, putting her backpack into a locker and snapping her lock shut. She was clocked in and locking up her things, she told herself, so there was no way she was fired. This wasn't about her.

This was something *big*—something apparently affecting nearly every Patriot on the Old Dodge City side of AtB, from what she'd seen on the way in—but at least she was keeping her job.

They couldn't fire *everyone*, could they?

She presented herself in front of the leads. William smiled at her. "So, did you hear on the way in?"

"No. Hear what?" Sonia stopped herself from looking over at Emily Logan, the girl with her forehead pressed to the table. "Some new rule you have to tell me about?"

Staci smiled grimly, her pursed lips sagging over stained teeth. "Big changes coming," she rasped. "Gold Rush Rapids is going to be closing down while Old Dodge City gets some changes. We're going to be sending everyone to new locations for the duration."

Sonia's jaw dropped. She looked from Staci to William, and back again. "When?" she choked out, finally. At the end of the summer, she assumed. There was no way they'd close Gold Rush Rapids during the summer vacation rush.

"Next month," William said off-handedly. "After the July rush."

"Next *month*? They're shutting down Gold Rush in August? That's insane! That makes no sense!" Sonia was dimly aware that she was shouting. "What is happening? Why are they closing it?" But she already knew the answer to that. Nate at AtBLive had made sure everyone knew why.

"There's no official word yet, so we can't say," Staci explained wearily. "We are expecting an announcement in the very near future."

"They'll announce it next week," William said. He looked supremely confident, as if he had personally seen the memo already. "And people are going to be thrilled."

"You don't know for sure," Staci chided.

Sonia rolled her eyes at that. "We *all* know, Staci. We've seen everything online. They're closing this, they're filling in the Mighty Missouri, it's common knowledge."

"Would you like to know where you're going for the duration?" William asked. "I have your reassignment right there."

"Of course I would." *Make it as a lead,* Sonia prayed, although she knew there was no chance. Still, Antonia had gotten that overnight promotion…

"You're going to Independence Plaza," William said, making a show of consulting his list. "Where you'll work parade control and the train station."

Sonia stared at him. "Are you joking?"

"Not joking."

Parade control and train station at the park entrance: this was a punishment, right? Something even worse than working Greeter all day, every day?

Parade control was notorious for its high turnover; the shift meant hours in the sun, trying to keep crowds behind ropes or walking on the correct side of the street. And the train station was painfully boring: standing at the station waiting for quarter-hour arrivals of the steam train, then loading and unloading the cars while begging, in tones of increasing desperation, for people to stay behind the yellow line and to remain seated with their hands and legs inside the train until it had come to a complete stop. There was no grouping, no dispatch, no monitor surveillance room. No air-conditioned or indoor positions. Just standing on the bricks, all day, shouting.

Sonia began to sweat. She thought her late-night supper might come back to haunt her.

"Emily Logan is going to Independence Plaza, too," William said brightly. "So you'll have a friend. Quite a few more, actually. A bunch of you are going there. They have the most room to absorb new Patriots."

That explained Emily's current catatonic state. "Where are you going?"

"I'm going to The Big Apple," William smiled with smug satisfaction. "Lead on Gangster Getaway."

Of course. "Congrats."

Staci looked at the floor. "I haven't gotten a new assignment yet."

Sonia imagined being Staci, twenty years older than most of the leads at AtB, with a natural southern drawl ballooning against their sleek college vowels, and a face full of sun exposure contrasting with their smooth, climate-controlled cheeks. Sonia thought Staci was probably trying to climb up the ladder, but sometimes it had to feel like working harder than everyone else just wasn't enough. Sometimes? Maybe it felt like that all the time. Sonia was feeling it right now. She'd spent the past few weeks trying not to complain while no one fixed her position problems, and now all she got out of it was a transfer to Independence Plaza.

Like nothing she'd done had ever mattered.

It wasn't enough to be the most dependable person on the team, or the most patient.

There was some other quality she was missing.

Or was it just luck?

"You can take a minute," William told her. "See you out there."

And while Staci and William filed out of the break room, Sonia slid into the booth next to Emily, put her forehead down on the cold Formica table, and sighed.

By the time the end of her shift rolled around, Sonia was feeling marginally better about being sent to Independence Plaza. The June heat was sending everyone into rage spirals, and in-between waving at children and clapping for first-time riders as they swaggered out of the attraction exit, red-faced and happy, she was yelled at by various people who knew better than to shout at other adults but simply couldn't be bothered to care anymore. She let their yelling happen, smiled, and sent them on their way. The yelling guests weren't an issue today.

It was the super-fans she was concerned about.

There were a few of them roaming around this morning, taking numerous photos of places she knew they'd all taken numerous photos of before. They were here to begin mourning the loss of Gold Rush Rapids and the original rocky western end of Old Dodge City. A loss which hadn't been announced and couldn't be verified yet, but which everyone seemed to know already. These were the people who had started the protest last week, disrupting who knew how many families just trying to enjoy their day, because they liked a ride so damn much.

A *ride*.

Yesterday, honestly, Sonia might have been on their team. She loved Gold Rush Rapids; she loved Old Dodge City. She didn't want to see either of them change, not even for an exciting new ride. Hell, *especially* for an exciting new ride. Gold Rush Rapids was exciting enough, and the height requirement let in the average-sized four-year-old. It was a true family ride. Why dig it up and replace it with something that would, according to the papers she'd sold Nate, have a punishing forty-eight inch height requirement? And from the artwork, it looked like there would be genuinely scary moments, like steep drops down waterfalls. That meant more parents and grandparents and anxious children on the sidelines, waiting for their adventurous children, siblings, or friends to enjoy a ride that wasn't for everyone.

That was a true bummer.

But that was *all* it really was, a bummer, when compared to the real impacts to the Patriots working here. And that got Sonia annoyed.

Some of these super-fans were just being dramatic for the clicks, posturing in front of fiberglass rocks, live-streaming their grief to their audiences, whipping up their nostalgia to jump-start the comments sections. What did they know about the true implications of closing down Gold Rush Rapids and the Mighty Missouri and Wilderness Isle? The people who were being shifted all over the park, whose lives would change with new schedules and lost seniority and delayed transfers and new leadership styles?

Maybe no one at Independence Plaza would like her, and she'd find herself getting shuffled down in the succession instead of looking like a great candidate for lead, like she was here. Maybe Emily over there, looking glum at her QuikRide ticket check position, was going to have to work such late hours that it aggravated her chronic pain disorder and she had to quit her job and she ended up losing her apartment and having to move back home with her parents, all the way up in Tennessee. A whole life and career changed in an instant.

Things like that could happen! There was a real butterfly effect inherent in the closure of a theme park ride, and it had nothing to do with the affected sorrow of middle-aged men who had ridden it as children.

And, Sonia noted, it was almost *all* men who were out here crying their crocodile tears. Strange man-children in vintage-style t-shirts from online boutiques, with their phones out, live-tweeting their public sorrow.

What was that about, anyway? Where were the female fans?

The women must all be busy holding down jobs, Sonia thought, and barely held back a snort.

William came out for a while after her lunch break and stood alongside her, watching the growing crowd of photographers and streamers.

"How do they know we've got an end date?" she asked him.

"It must be on some message board or it got out on Twitter," he grumbled. "Just like the concept art did in the first place."

"Yeah," Sonia said, keeping her gaze straight ahead. "That was weird."

"Well, if crying fan-boys is the worst we get, I'll take it," William said. "I mean, after that protest, this is nothing."

"True," Sonia agreed. Then she had to move to one side to allow a streamer, narrating into a fuzzy mic, to get a full shot of the attraction plaza behind her. "This is just annoying," she told William. "Not scary."

Eventually, another full day as Greeter came to an end. She was almost nostalgic for the position now, as if the past few weeks were already in the history books. By sunset, Sonia had sung *Happy Birthday* to six different children, participated in a Gold Rush-themed surprise proposal, and given out her secret, favorite spot to watch the fireworks to at least a dozen parties (behind the statue of Mother Goose on the path to Fairytale Courtyard). Almost none of them would actually go and watch it there because it looked like Promise Mountain blocked the best view, but Sonia liked to think that every day a few people actually took her word for it and had a great time there.

She took her clock-out slip from Willa Montana, whose name could not possibly be real, and looked back at the crowded plaza under the gas lanterns. "Take care of her for me," she said.

Willa, sixty-two and uninterested in her job beyond the free park tickets she gave her grandchildren, stared at her.

"Good news," Richie called as she went into the break room to get clocked out. "I finally found the issue with your positions. Should be fixed tomorrow."

"That's great," Sonia said, shaking her head. "Just in time to leave forever."

"Aww, don't say that," Richie said. "I'm sure we'll all be back here in a year. They're not really going to knock it down. That's just a lot of hype."

"You think?" Sonia checked her backpack for a change of clothes. Perfect. She could stay in the park and watch the fireworks tonight. "Richie, this place is going to get demolished. Say your goodbyes."

Richie sighed as she waltzed into the changing room. He'd backed the wrong horse when he'd left Legacy of Heroes. But that was life at AtB, Sonia thought. Every day, a fresh curveball.

CHAPTER TWENTY-FOUR

Nate

Nate had to hand it to himself: he was very good at his job.

And since he was his own boss, he gave himself permission to buy himself something special as a reward. Stats were booming on AtBLive. He'd had to upgrade servers, just as the Patriot who had sold him the binder had warned him. But the great thing was that after that initial surge, he'd managed to keep things going.

The blog post about Patriots and their casual flaunting of the rules of decorum which Lawrence Taylor himself had laid out when he first opened this park had been a roaring success. That post was at three hundred and sixteen thousand views as of this morning, and it was getting pirated in all kinds of languages, which was the Internet's sincerest form of flattery.

Sure, there had been some comments and intense Twitter discussions claiming that his words had reduced the parks'

Patriots to soulless automatons, terrified of losing their jobs because one childless man had bitched about seeing people in work uniforms cutting loose after work. But Nate dismissed these comments as the rants of negative trolls. Everywhere he turned, people were smiling and welcoming him: Nate! What could possibly feel wrong about that?

He'd followed that post up last night with a less inflammatory article and accompanying video about taste-testing every hot dog in the park, which was getting him a lot of commentary—some of it mean-spirited, for sure, but when the clicks kept coming, who cared? Not Nate's advertisers, that was for sure. And if they were happy, Nate was happy.

So this morning he had strolled into AtB with the pleasing conviction that not only would he gather some great content today, he'd also treat himself. He'd buy a little something to celebrate his first amazing two weeks on the job. Not something for clicks, something for *him*. Although, of course, he'd tweet some pics and get some clicks, too.

Something was up, though. He noticed it the moment he held up his annual passholder card at the turnstile. The Patriot attending the station took his card, glanced over it, then up at him.

Her smile vanished.

Nate waited for her to recover herself—she was probably just surprised to have a theme park celeb like himself at her turnstile this morning! But the Patriot, whose name tag identified her as CeCe from Dothan, Alabama, didn't smile again. She didn't even say good morning. She just glanced back at the card, scanned its code with her laser reader, and waited for the light on the display to turn green. She handed back the card.

"You're all set," she said, then looked past him towards the next guest in line.

Nate felt his lip curl. "Good morning to you, too!" he snapped, without moving.

He suspected it wasn't his tone, but his immobility, which ultimately aroused the Patriot's attention. She lifted her gaze warily to his. "My apologies, sir," she offered tonelessly. "I hope you have a very nice day at America the Beautiful."

"Well, it won't have started with you," Nate told her primly, then he left her to think about what she'd done while he marched on into the park. He briefly entertained the idea of demanding to speak to a manager, or darting into Guest Services to lodge a complaint, but then decided he was probably still on their radar after the Tabby debacle a few weeks ago. He guessed all these front-line managers gossiped about their problem guests. Until he'd given that incident some time to blow over, Nate figured he'd better give anyone wearing a neck-tie or a pair of heels a pass. Disappointing, with a huge breach in guest service like this one, that he couldn't deal with it properly.

Well, at least he could still call out the parks' problems on his site and social media—and with the way his readership was booming with every post, that would be far more effective than trying to solve AtB's issues by reporting one surly Patriot or burned-out lightbulb to management at a time.

Phone in hand, feeling fortified against all disappointment by the growth of his platform and volume of his online voice, Nate lifted his chin and strolled into America the Beautiful, ready to find and photograph every fault.

But first, he was going to buy himself something cute.

There was quite a lot of whispering going on behind the quiet cash-wraps of the shops lining Independence Plaza. Nate was used to being relatively ignored when he wandered the Plaza's main shops during the slow morning hours. At this time of day, park guests were bypassing the shops in search of rides to queue up for, and the early retail shifts were filled almost entirely by the grizzled veterans of AtB.

Most of these old-timer Patriots had lost interest in the guests and their own surroundings many years before Nate's first visit to the park as an impressionable child, and their general disdain for their workplace was nearly as celebrated in fan circles as the fanatical devotion to guest service which was generally found in the rest of the park. Members of the Independence Plaza morning crew had outlived presidents, managers, and Lawrence Taylor himself. If Nate had been granted a warm welcome by one of these crones upon entering their shop, he might have fainted on the spot.

But he enjoyed working his way through the echoing gift shops first thing in the morning precisely *because* he was left alone to inspect new merchandise, pulling out t-shirts and photo frames and plush and taking photos to tweet to his public without any hovering, smiling, bothersome Patriots to interrupt his work. His merchandise updates were some of his highest engagement posts on any given week—and numbers soared when he came across some particularly unique commemorative or retro-design items. Opening day attractions were particularly popular with collectors and super-fans, so he was always hoping for something new celebrating one of the park's older rides.

Independence Plaza's main store was really a series of

different showrooms split by stained glass and dark, hand-carved hardwood. Walking through them was like journeying through a warren of antique shops in some northeastern American city, except that instead of brass and pewter curios, the wooden shelves held toys and tees featuring the cartoon menagerie of the Patriot Pals, and the bright logos and slogans of AtB's most popular rides.

Nate paused at a Gold Rush Rapids display, pulling at the sleeves of tees to straighten the design, snap a photo, and tweet it to the theme park fandom. Most of the designs he'd seen before, and the response was tepid. Certainly nothing he'd buy for himself.

Then something stood out to him in a densely packed rack of blue shirts—a gold-colored shirt stuffed in close to the back. It was probably just something from another part of the store, but he pulled it out anyway.

Nate's jaw dropped, and he quickly looked around to make sure no one else was around.

This wasn't supposed to be here.

But he had to have it.

For a *number* of reasons.

Firstly, it was gorgeous. The graphic on the shirt was an old concept art design from early plans for the park: the sandstone peaks of Gold Rush Rapids surrounded by a mining town and a wooden stockade housing a herd of pack mules. Nate still wished this version of Gold Rush Rapids existed. As much as he loved Old Dodge City's short strip of storefronts, *this* build-out of Gold Rush Rapids would have been a completely different town, with a stockade, a saloon with a dinner show, stagecoach rides, and of course, the pack mules.

A t-shirt with unrealized concept art was an instant hit in

the fan community. But amazingly, that wasn't even the best part of this random shirt. The best part was so good, Nate feel slightly dizzy as he contemplated the shirt.

It was the phrase underneath the artwork: *Farewell to Gold Rush Rapids: August 2, 2022.*

He had a closing date for the ride. He had *the date* before there was an official announcement. And it was in just six weeks!

This was the golden goose. Or the golden egg the goose laid. Something golden, anyway. It was clicks, page-views, ad dollars. Exposure. Authority. The only time the theme park community had stopped talking about the eventual demise of Gold Rush Rapids since he'd posted the concept art was when they were talking about the Gateway Pub story he'd written. If this wasn't domination of his niche, he didn't know what was.

Nate knew he was buying this shirt, if possible. But just in case someone realized what he had and took it from him, he had to document it. So Nate started snapping pictures, sweat popping on his brow as he quietly documented the artwork and the text.

He needed to get these pics uploaded to his blog immediately. This wasn't for social media; he'd post nothing on Twitter but a salacious line: Closing date of AtB's best-love ride REVEALED. All the hits were all for him…if he hustled.

But Nate knew his news wouldn't be exclusive for long. He probably wasn't the only blogger with boots on the ground in the park today. He probably wasn't even the only one in Independence Plaza right now. A quiet weekday morning was the preferred time for the many cottage industries fueled by the hungry theme park fandom: the food vloggers checking out the newest treats for their videos, the personal shoppers seeking out the latest merch designs to sell to their subscribers, the other news and views bloggers who were on the lookout for new merchandise just like him. They'd be combing through this display soon enough. And what if this shirt wasn't the only place this design had leaked? There could be hats, pennants, commemorative glasses—

Heart thudding, trying to hold back a rising sense of panic which was not supported by Nate's general state of cardio health, he did a quick once-over of the rest of the Gold Rush display. From the mountain toy-set prominently placed atop the fixture, to the baseball caps arranged between the t-shirt racks, he could see no more hints of the renegade golden shirt, no more mentions of the final ride in any of the slogans. Nate felt pretty safe in assuming the shirt in his hand was the only one…in Independence Plaza, at least.

Next: to buy this shirt without anyone seeing it. Nate glanced furtively at the nearest cash register—it was currently manned by a severe-looking, elderly Patriot, who was rearranging the contents of the cash wrap drawers with violent energy. Ethel. She didn't like bloggers, as a general rule. Would she ring up his shirt without a word? Could he rely on her dislike of him to speed the shirt through the transaction? Or would she spot the message and realize the shirt wasn't supposed to be on the sales floor yet?

Maybe if he handed it to her folded in two, tag first, she would just scan the price tag, accept the payment, and drop the folded shirt into a bag without ever looking at the artwork and message.

He watched her slam register tape and scissors into the

drawer, muttering to herself about how no one ever put anything back where it belonged, and decided there was no way to tell. She'd either not bother to check the shirt for quality control, as AtB Patriots were expected to do, or she'd go overboard checking it, out of a vengeful desire to be as thorough and law-abiding as her fellow, messy-drawer Patriots were not.

Just to be contrary, his grandmother would have said.

Nate glanced around the shop, looking down the corridor into the next room, and his pounding heart froze mid-beat. Browsing the kitchenware in the Liberty Kitchens shop was Mike McKee, the blogger behind AtBExpress. They'd met at a few different park events over the years. A few more steps, and Mike would be in the attraction shop, and asking Nate, in a friendly way, of course, just what he had behind his back.

Nate knew he had no choice. This blog post had to go live right now, whether he bought the shirt for himself or not. He looked around again, saw the dressing room was empty, and darted inside.

It was little more than a dimly lit closet, with a small wooden bench, a mirror, and a louvered door. At least the door went all the way to the floor. Nate sat down on the bench, wadded the shirt up at his side, and opened his blog app.

Five minutes later, the deed was done. The blog was up, the tweet was sent. Nate looked at his handiwork with satisfaction. All he had to do was leave the Twitter app open and he could see his reach, his influence over this community, growing in real time. The numbers next to the likes and retweets flipped hesitantly at first, then more quickly, then to double and treble. This was breaking news.

This was trending. This was viral.

And it was Nate's.

He didn't need the shirt anymore; didn't need the hassle of dealing with Ethel or risking Mike's professional interest.

Instead, he left the shirt crumpled under the bench, hidden by the dim lighting. Later, some Patriot would scoop it up and toss it onto a pile of merchandise to be rehung. One of the other Patriots would see it should never have made it to the sales floor, and rush to hide the mistake.

But the damage had already been done.

Nate smiled and walked into the sunshine flooding down Independence Plaza.

CHAPTER TWENTY-FIVE

Antonia

Antonia was filled with regrets.

She'd gone on break at eleven, and found the Chuckwagon too full of sourpuss morning people for her comfort level, so she'd kept walking and found herself a booth up at the Independence cafeteria, where she could eat her chicken tenders in peace. Her first week as a lead, and she was wishing it had never happened.

Or, rather, that so many of the circumstances the promotion had brought with it had never happened.

It had been a quick slide down: the Values crackdown, followed by a late night with Careen that went—well, it went okay, she supposed, although Careen had gotten blind drunk in a way Antonia found distasteful—and then the next day she'd gone off on that nice Ops girl, Sonia…

It was all just a blur of messiness now.

And her decision to stand up for her Patriots? A failure.

In the past few days, she'd tried and failed to uphold her own values instead of management's whip-cracking of the Patriot Values. All she'd managed to do was alienate the people who had been her colleagues just a few days before, and arouse the management team's suspicion that she wasn't one hundred percent on their side.

"It's a no-man's-land for us," Alma told her grimly, counting change for a register till with practiced fingers. "Leads aren't managers, but they aren't front-line anymore, either. We have to act like management, but we aren't managers, and the Patriots out there? They know it. That's what makes this job so hard."

It *was* hard. It was harder than Antonia had expected, and a darn sight lonelier, too—to borrow a little Old Dodge City speak.

The worst was the morning shift. Patriots who had been working in Old Dodge City for twenty or thirty years barely respected management as it was. So they were not exactly welcoming when Antonia took on her first opening shift as a lead…and they were barely civil when she tried to remind them about the Patriot Values.

The worst moment was when Antonia walked into Professor Cloud's and found Jeanette with her hip hitched up on the back counter behind the cash-wrap, basically sitting down.

"Jeanette, you can't *sit,*" she'd blurted in dismay, surprised any Patriot, of any seniority, would *ever* think sitting while on the job was okay. Even in an empty store at nine thirty in the morning, when park guests were still rushing from ride to ride. She stared at Jeanette.

The older Patriot gazed back at her impassively. "Who the hell do you think you are, girl? Go back to school. I don't have time for little kids to be telling me how to sit or stand at my register."

"Jeanette, please don't use profanity in guest areas," Antonia said automatically. Inside, she was panicking. Was this insubordination? She couldn't actually do anything about it. Well, she could report Jeanette to a manager. Robbie was the manager on duty right now. He was a nice guy, young and understanding.

But he was still a manager, with a manager's expectations that she do her job without complaining, no matter how unprepared she was. And he would ask Antonia why she hadn't corrected the behavior, and when she said that Jeanette swore at her and refused to stand up, the manager would say, "Well, Antonia, if you can't get your team to follow you as a lead, I can't imagine how you think you'll ever do it as a manager..."

No. That couldn't happen. Antonia was on a *path* now. She had a career trajectory. Jeanette's withery old face wasn't going to get in her way. Antonia took a breath and attempted to reason with the woman. "It's really important that we uphold all of our Values while we're working. I'm just here to remind you—"

"Remind me nothing." Jeanette harrumphed and crossed her arms across her chest—another no-no move, which Antonia didn't even know how to begin correcting.

At that moment, Robbie appeared in the doorway.

Jeanette straightened, sliding her hip from the counter and rearranging her arms in a less forbidding manner.

Robbie regarded Jeanette for a long moment. Sizing her up, Antonia thought. Deciding how he was going to do it. Her approach had been all wrong. She almost wished she had a notebook, to jot down notes on how Robbie handled the older woman.

"Jeanette," he began, "are you feeling all right today?"

"Fine," Jeanette said gruffly, casting her gaze down. She seemed to know what was coming.

"Are you sure? I saw you sitting on the counter just now…is everything okay?"

"It's fine." Jeanette glanced furtively at Antonia. "I was just restin' for a minute."

"I see." Robbie crossed his ankles and tapped the fingers of one hand on the cash-wrap. He had beautifully manicured nails. Antonia longed to be in his position: a person of authority, a person wearing his own clothes to work, a person who could afford to get a mani-pedi once in a while. A person who demanded respect. "Well, when we're working for our guests, we can't be *restin'* on the counters. That's for break time. If you have any issues standing, you tell us, okay? Otherwise, we need you up and ready to assist our guests."

"I know. I'm…yes. I know."

Robbie lifted an eyebrow at Antonia. They both knew how close Jeanette had come to an apology, and how angry she'd be at that fact. Best to leave, Robbie's eyebrow said, and fight again another day. "Walk with me, Antonia?"

She joined him on the boardwalk outside the store. "I'm sorry, Robbie, I just—"

"Check her in half an hour," he said. "If she's leaning again, send her to the office. I can't risk some VP wandering in here and finding someone sitting down, for God's sake." Robbie rubbed the toe of his gleaming oxford along a seam between two boards. "I know you're new at this. The old ones are tough. But trust yourself to determine who deserves discipline and trust us to administer it, okay? I need this entire region to shine. Upper management is out wandering around and taking notes, believe me."

Antonia nodded.

"Good girl. I know you're ambitious." Robbie gave her a meaningful look. "You make us look good, we make you look good. That's the deal, alright?"

Robbie set off for the office and a cup of coffee, leaving Antonia on the boardwalk, the fiddle music playing all around her, in charge of Old Dodge City.

She sighed, rubbed her arms, and began walking the shops, trying to be friendly with the morning crew.

The next time she passed through Professor Cloud's, Jeanette wasn't leaning on the counter.

But the time after that, she was. Antonia gave her a moment to correct herself, but the woman looked away, chin jutting stubbornly.

Antonia sighed, went behind the counter, and told Jeanette she was needed in the manager's office.

When Jeanette eventually returned, the look on her face told Antonia there were dire consequences for her actions. And sure enough, after Jeanette's break, the story began spreading through Old Dodge City.

That new lead, Antonia, was nothing but a snitch.

So, that was how work was going.

Antonia looked down at her chicken tenders and sighed.

The booth rattled as a lithe-bodied girl swung into the seat across from her. Antonia looked up from her chicken and found an old acquaintance smiling at her.

"Lucille! This is…a surprise."

Not a pleasant one, although this wasn't Lucille's fault. Antonia just wanted desperately to be left alone.

Lucille tugged back her long, golden hair and pulled it effortlessly into a bun. She was dressed in a plain t-shirt and shorts, but she was still wearing her Miss Sallie Mae make-up. Her pink cheeks, dark lashes and heavy eye shadow looked garish without her full Victorian garb to back it up. "You don't say, Antonia. I never see you around Independence. What brings you up here?"

"Chuckwagon was full." She gave an unhappy poke to her lunch.

Lucille shrugged, uninterested. "So, I talked to your friend Martin today."

Antonia stopped pushing around her chicken tenders. "Oh?"

"In the private room."

"Oh, no."

"He was fine. Martin never touches."

"That's not what I—of course not. It's just that he only wants privates when he's depressed. And when he's depressed, then I have to start worrying about him. And I've had a rough week as it is."

Lucille pulled a granola bar out of the pocket of her shorts. "Oh, he's not depressed now. He's in love."

"Excuse me?" This could be worse than depression.

"In. Love. He told me that he saw someone and had an instant connection. I pushed him a little and boom…it's love. Love at first sight! It would be cute if it wasn't sad. That's why I thought I'd better tell you. Good thing you came up here to eat."

"Why's it sad?" Antonia asked, although she thought she knew.

"Well, he's just such a mess, isn't he? There's no way he fell for someone who's going to reciprocate. I mean, he was with Amy, right? That whole disaster? That *was* Martin, right?"

"That was Martin."

"She messed him up," Lucille reflected.

"Big time."

"I don't know what he's going to do. But he said he's been in love before and this is different because he doesn't really know the person. Which…ugh! Is he stalking some girl now?"

"No," Antonia said quickly. "Martin's not that type."

But she didn't know that for sure. What if he was stalking some poor girl? Oh, no. Martin. Antonia wanted to hug him and slap him at the same time.

Also, jeez! How had Martin's problems become hers so quickly?

"So," Lucille went on, ready for a new subject. "About Careen."

"I'm not talking about her. And who told you?"

Lucille smiled and ate her granola bar.

"It was one time. There won't be another one."

"Does *Careen* know that?"

"Shit." Antonia looked back at her chicken. This was a sticky situation to be in with one of her Patriots. Add another mistake to the list.

"I won't tell anyone," Lucille promised. "But I can't say the same for Careen. Couldn't you have picked someone a little more discreet to fool around with?"

"I didn't know she was going to tell everyone what we got up to! Who else knows?"

"Maybe two or three others on the west side of the park. Just people who would appreciate the news. People are on your side, Antonia. No one's turning you in."

"Turning me in? What for?"

Lucille lifted her eyebrows. "For sleeping with a subordinate?"

"That doesn't count for leads," Antonia snorted. "Just management."

"Well, get it out of your system now." Lucille put her feet up on a spare chair. "Before you make manager."

Usually, those words would have filled Antonia with a secret pride. When the people around you saw that you were going places, *that* was a special kind of happiness. It meant all the dreams you'd built up for yourself weren't just pie-in-the-sky, they were realistic ambitions, attainable and true.

But today, she just felt a curdling sense of betrayal. Not from Careen…but from AtB.

Antonia was on her way back from the Independence end of the Underground when she noticed the Professor Cloud's stock room door was ajar. She'd been taking her leisurely time returning to Old Dodge City, deep in dark thoughts about how disappointing her professional life had suddenly become, when she rounded the corner and saw the open door. It was not suspicious in and of itself…had Antonia not known there was no one assigned to Professor Cloud's floor-stock right now. She paused and poked her head inside, frowning when she saw who was inside.

"Nick? What are you doing here?"

The tow-headed troublemaker paused in mid-motion, his back to Antonia, his hands gripping two shopping bags. They were stapled shut, with delivery tags fluttering from their handles. Antonia saw the back of his neck go pink and knew she'd caught him at something. He turned around slowly, a carefully arranged smile on his face. "Hi, Antonia! Are you our lead today? That's great!"

Antonia grinned dangerously at him. Nick might be a world-class bullshitter, but he needed to remember Antonia knew about his little games. "What is in the bags, Nicholas?"

"They're just deliveries," Nick said defensively. "One had a broken key-chain, so I was getting a new one to replace it before it went out."

"There weren't any new ones in the store?"

"I was downstairs already when I noticed."

"How did you know it was broken? Why would you open up a home delivery bag after you came downstairs to log it in, Nick?"

He swallowed.

Antonia reached behind her and swung the door closed. "Let me see the bags."

Nick handed one of the bags over. She looked at the intact staples around the top, the receipt attached to the handles. Her eyebrows rose at the dollar amount. "Big spender," she observed. "So where are you stashing the bags that you steal?"

"Steal? No, no, you got me wrong—"

"Easy, buddy. There are no cameras in here. And I'm not even on the clock—I'm still technically on my lunch break." She inspected the other bag, which Nick surrendered without a peep, his defenses completely broken. There were more high-dollar items on this receipt. Together, the bags were worth over four hundred dollars. "Last week, when I was working floor-stock, Retail Delivery had me replace a missing bag for them," she said casually. "Two figurines from the collectibles case, worth two hundred bucks. There were emails to management about it. The big bags get noticed, Nick. Better scale back this week."

Nick was staring at her. Antonia sighed and put the bags down, letting them sag against her legs. "Nick, I'm not new around here. I know deliveries don't just disappear. You're hardly the first person to realize they're easy targets. And I'm not going to turn you in."

His fearful expression shifted to confusion. "Why not?"

Why not? That was a good question. Why not turn Nick in, watch him squirm and break during an investigation, enjoy his eventual escort off property alongside a security guard, rejoice in his total removal from her life?

Because this wasn't who she was.

Even though Antonia had no love for Nick, and even though stealing was clearly a separate issue from the Patriot Value crackdown upstairs, she couldn't continue to be a part of this atmosphere of fear and surveillance which had descended upon America the Beautiful. If her beloved theme park was going to turn into a police state, she simply wasn't going to play along anymore.

She wanted to strike back, make a stand for the Patriots.

She didn't say all that, though. She didn't yet know what she was going to do. She just knew that she wasn't going to turn in another Patriot, even if that Patriot was Nick, until it felt like they were being treated like humans again.

"You're not worth the trouble," Antonia said finally, trying to maintain the lofty position she'd always asserted over Nick. "Just put the bags back. I'll walk with you."

Nick looked appreciative, but he hesitated as she turned to leave. "Someone is coming to pick these up," he said. "They're not for me…I wasn't stashing them to get on my way out or anything."

Antonia's hand stilled on the door handle. "Who?" If it was Tabby, if this little idiot boy had gotten Tabby involved with his sordid doings…

"Marcelo, from Big Apple Ops," Nick said. "He's the delivery man. He makes all the pick-ups."

"The delivery man? You're talking about the Retail Delivery department."

"No," Nick insisted. "It's just…this isn't the only place… I'm not the only one pulling bags."

"Nick, are you telling me there's an organized crime situation taking place at America the Beautiful right now?"

"Yeah," Nick said. "That's it."

The premise was simple: pick up a few bags a day, spread out all over the park. Not just high-dollar receipts, but carefully selected transactions to make sure everything had resale value without tipping off Retail Delivery that there was an internal theft problem. One package might be a home delivery filled with collectible trading pins, relatively cheap on their own but still worth a tidy little mark-up value online. Another might contain a few hundred dollars' worth of apparel or even middle-grade jewelry—sterling silver, never gold.

"The key is to avoid a pattern," Nick explained to an astonished Antonia. "Marcelo keeps tabs to make sure we aren't getting too repetitive. We get a warning. But everyone is pretty careful."

Antonia's palms were sweating. She pressed them against the split-rail fence. They were standing behind the hat wagon. There'd been no way to loiter any longer in the corridor—both of them were expected to be out in guest areas, working—but the music here was blaring loud enough to drown out a quiet conversation. "So Marcelo is like—a crime boss?"

"I don't think he's at the top," Nick said. "I think he's just at the top of AtB deliveries. I don't know who he answers to, though."

The side-wheeler was surging majestically up the Mighty Missouri behind them. Antonia timed her next words to the hoot of its steam-whistle. "Are you making good money?"

Nick flashed a grin at her. "I am."

Antonia didn't leave work that night with the express intention of joining a theme park merchandise theft ring. But when she opened the mailbox at the apartment complex and pulled out a handful of thin, hateful envelopes, she thought she knew what was coming next.

Oswald was meowing when she came inside. He twined around her legs, nearly tripping her as she dropped the envelopes on the kitchen counter. "Yes, yes, I know," she said absently, looking at the printed addresses on the envelopes under the harsh fluorescent light. How often had she wanted new lights, softer, that didn't feel like the kitchen of a Wendy's? There wasn't extra money for kinder lightbulbs.

The return addresses confirmed what she already knew: debts she couldn't meet. Not with the promotion to lead, not with all the summer overtime in the world. The student loans that were supposed to be her ticket to a better life, the credit cards she'd turned to when she couldn't make the student loans. The car payment, because she needed to get to work. The electricity she needed to live a normal contemporary life.

She had the normal bills everyone else in the freaking

United States had, and she could not pay them! What was wrong with her? She worked. She worked hard. She had gotten a promotion. She was doing work she did not believe in, solely in hopes of making more money. And in the meantime, she still ate cheaply. She still scrimped.

And still, she had fallen behind.

What was wrong with her?

Antonia threw herself down on the sofa without feeding Oswald first. The cat protested noisily for a few minutes. Then, realizing something much more serious than dinner was going on, he jumped up beside her and curled up alongside her face, purring vigorously. Antonia put her hands against his soft fur and cried.

CHAPTER TWENTY-SIX

Martin

Martin was on his way over to Tabby's apartment when the news made it to his smartphone.

She only lived a few blocks away from him, but they weren't going to hang out at her apartment—that was too intimate a move for their first date. The drinks at Sinatra's that she'd suggested a few days ago hadn't actually happened; Tabby ended up staying late at work that night and had apologetically texted him to cancel. He'd understood, and fought the impulse to drive back to the park, maybe bring her some dinner. Martin had been accused of being smothering in the past. He was not going to make that mistake again.

Instead, they had agreed to take a walk around Magnolia Lodge Resort on Tabby's next day off. The grounds and hotel were easily AtB's prettiest resort property, and the azalea gardens behind the hotel were quiet even in high season, making them a favorite place for Patriots to escape for a little while.

Iced tea and a stroll around the azalea gardens were a quiet, sweet sort of first date idea which Martin had thought would suit Tabby even better than drinks at Sinatra's, and she'd certainly replied to him quickly when he'd sent her a text suggesting it. He suspected she would love a little old-fashioned romance. There was no way for him to know what sweet little Tabby, the demure runaway from Kentucky, had experienced with men before. The only mutual friend they had was Antonia, and he knew enough of their history to mind his manners and not ask her what she thought Tabby might enjoy.

But he did know Tabby was nothing like Amy, and Amy had not been fond of walks at Magnolia Lodge. Amy was not fond of any scenario in which she was hidden away from prying eyes. Amy's primary goal, in any social situation, was always to be *seen*. For some reason, she'd even wanted to be seen with him. Martin was not being particularly down on himself when he pondered on the unlikelihood of this desire, even now, years later. He was very ordinary. Amy had never been. Pick that apart and get to the core of the apple? He wouldn't even know where to start.

Anyway, he was trying to shake off the ghost of Amy, the never-ending desire to analyze all that had happened. He would not let Amy's shadow spoil his day with Tabby. He was going to be a chivalrous gentleman with Tabby, the strong and kind man she desired and needed—and in the strange aftermath of emerging from After Amy, that was what he needed, as well. He could use a shy, freckled maiden to pin his romantic hopes upon. No more stars on the make for Martin, that much was for sure.

Martin put his car in park, looked up at Tabby's building, and picked up his phone. He would check in on the fandom, using some mindless rumors to distract himself from all those leftover memories of Amy circulating in his brain. And then he would recenter, regroup, and go upstairs to get the girl.

That was the plan, anyway. But the chatter he saw on that bird app was so enthralling that he actually forgot to get out of the car, or even turn it off. Martin just sat there idling, the air conditioning blowing mightily against his cheeks, while he read the incredible news, then scrolled through all the instant debate and takes which followed it, the opinions and rumors multiplying by the second, the numbers ticking upwards while he read the tweets.

He was still sitting in the car fifteen minutes later when Tabby came downstairs, looking confused. She didn't get straight into the car, but went to the driver's side door and knocked on the windows—understandable, Martin realized, since they'd never actually been anywhere together before. Then he realized that he was ruining his first date with Tabby before it started and put down his phone with a guilty start. He hopped out of the car. "Hey! I'm so sorry."

"What are you doing down here?" Tabby asked, her little forehead creased. "I looked out the window and saw you, but when you didn't come up, I got worried."

He wanted to kiss the worry from her frowning face, but wisely refrained. "I accidentally got caught up in the news."

"Did something happen?"

"Someone figured out that Gold Rush Rapids is closing in August."

Surprise widened her eyes. "Oh! But who—"

"Nate," Martin conceded, hating to bring him up.

She scowled—an adorable expression, Martin observed. "He's probably making it up to get attention."

"He found a shirt with the date on it. There's photo evidence." Martin suddenly realized they were sweating in a hot parking lot when there was a nice cool car next to them. "Come on, we can talk about it on the way to Magnolia Lodge."

Tabby seemed distant on the short drive, looking out the car window as the apartments of Gateway gave to the wooded land behind America the Beautiful's sprawling complex. After a few minutes, the road was bordered by manicured hedges and the dark, glossy leaves of magnolia trees, and Martin turned at the elegant white sign announcing Magnolia Lodge.

The hotel was a sprawling white structure, just three stories tall and extending in wide wings from a central lobby adorned with deep verandas and dark green shutters. The second-floor verandahs overlooking the gardens were a favorite haunt of Patriots in need of quiet time away from the bustling parks, while hotel guests, intent on wringing every last drop of theme park fun from their vacations, only rarely discovered the shadowy decks with their wicker chairs and lazy ceiling fans. There was no better place to sink into a cushion, set a sweating glass of tart vodka lemonade or an innocent iced tea on a glass-topped table nearby, and let the background music softly loop its way through Prohibition-era jazz. The hotel guests appreciated the verandahs and gardens of Magnolia Lodge as expensive atmosphere, but the visiting Patriots gratefully accepted these relaxing spaces as their due.

A walk in the gardens followed by a drink on the verandah was considered an excellent first date amongst Patriots, especially in the evenings, when twinkling lights in the trees and hedges provided fireflies even when the bugs weren't in season. But it was because of the overtly romantic implications of evening at Magnolia Lodge that Martin had suggested a daylight walk in the gardens. Since he wasn't a Patriot, Martin didn't know the old AtB gossip about Tabby's supposed string of one-night stands. All he really had was impressions of her, the little ghost in Antonia's wake: she seemed shy, quiet, and porcelain-doll-like with her big-eyed gaze. So he decided to treat her with delicacy, like a kid-gloved debutante who might have stood on the wide front steps of Magnolia Lodge two hundred years ago…had Magnolia Lodge been a real manor home and not a thirty-year-old facsimile at a theme park resort.

"Do you want a drink first, or later?" he asked her as they walked between the marble columns surrounding the front doors and into the cool lobby. All around, the bustle of a hotel on a summer weekday echoed: bellmen loading carts, front desk clerks giving directions to rooms, children in a rush to get to the rides howling over the delay. The resort lobby was beautiful: an oval anteroom set all around marble columns, dark wooden reception desks and dim oil paintings hinting at pastoral landscapes, but it was definitely not relaxing. Tabby quickened her stride and led Martin down a side corridor, bypassing the lodge's high-ceilinged grand lobby with its deep sofas and tinkling piano music. He had no choice but to follow her.

"That part of the place is always too much for me," she said finally, slowing her steps and turning back to smile apologetically at Martin. "I always have to rush through it or it stresses me out."

"I'm sorry—if I'd known I wouldn't have suggested—"

"No, I love the rest of the place—and the gardens! But we can stop at the pool bar to get a drink… it's much more relaxed. And I know a special way to get there."

It was already apparent Tabby knew the hotel better than Martin. She led him through a few quiet hallways—one of which he was certain was for staff only—until they emerged through a side door onto a tiny, shade-scattered patio. A charming fountain crowned with a white stone pineapple graced the center. Beyond, an inviting path led away beneath a clutch of close-growing magnolias, their dark, glossy leaves beckoning to strollers in search of solitude.

"Wow," Martin breathed, looking around in surprise. "I know about the walks by the pool deck, but this is really hidden."

"My roommate works here," Tabby admitted. "She's shown me a few things."

Martin hoped the quiet might loosen up Tabby a bit, let go of her usual reserve. He wanted to get back to the moment they'd shared on the boardwalk just a few days ago. That moment had been breathless—astonishing—a lightning bolt of shared attraction, of mutual recognition, which Martin had never felt before…not even with Amy. With her, the attraction had been so one-sided and the pursuit so slow and painful.

Martin had to admit he was in no hurry to survive the agony that had been After Amy again, and falling in love seemed like the surest way to find that misery again. But that moment with Tabby—she'd felt it too, and the surety of that had nearly knocked him off his feet.

And yet now she walked beside him so quietly, a shy maid in a secret garden, and it seemed like she could barely stand to look at him. Where had that flash of knowledge, that astonishing moment of realization, gone? He knew he hadn't imagined it!

"Tabby," Martin ventured finally, "are you…nervous?"

Beside him, the girl swallowed. Not the *girl,* he reminded himself, the woman. Small, demure, freckle-nosed as a girl certainly—but still a woman.

"I am," Tabby replied at last, and then she laughed her melodic little laugh, which somehow held all the Kentucky accent she tried to bite back in her regular speech. "I'm sorry! I just…we've barely spoken and now I don't know what to say. I *do* want to be here, though," she added, looking up at him with an earnest expression. "Please don't get the wrong idea. I'm just—no good at small talk, I guess."

Martin smiled, feeling his whole heart was exposed upon his face and powerless to hide it. "Well, let's skip the small talk! I already know it's hot out, so the weather is covered." She laughed. Emboldened, Martin said, "Tell me more about you. Where are you from?" He knew she was from Kentucky—her name tag said as much, but there was more to a person's story than the state where she had been born.

Tabby turned back to the pathway ahead of them. Her feet scuffed fallen magnolia leaves, green on one side, brown on the other. "I'm from a very small town in the mountains. One flashing red light, the only grocers are the veggie stand and the Dollar General, that kind of place. I'm the oldest of five. I got into a college in a town about forty miles away, but I had to drive in every day. And then I came here, and I just knew I never wanted to go back."

Her voice took an edge at the end; Martin wondered what she'd left behind, or what she'd run away from. "Four siblings is a lot, huh? Must've been hard to leave."

"It was, and it wasn't. My mama—my *mom* needed help, all the time. She didn't want me to go, not even to school. But I had to get out, see what else was out there." She paused. "See who else I could be."

"And have you been many people?" Martin teased gently.

"A few," she said, smiling. "With varying degrees of success." She tossed back her pale hair, looked up at Martin. The wistfulness in her eyes made his heart turn over. Something—many things—had happened to this girl. He took her hand and squeezed, hoping she wouldn't feel trapped by his grip. He got the feeling she'd escaped cages before and would be nervously awaiting the next sign of entrapment.

"Well, I am from northern Virginia," Martin began, to take the spotlight off her, give her some breathing room. "I worked in IT right out of college. I moved here five years ago because…because I love the place, I guess." He cursed the lapse—he'd nearly admitted he'd followed a girl here. A girl who broke his heart. It wasn't the kind of thing you opened a fragile new relationship with. "I came here a lot as a kid," he said carefully. "You know, like a lot of people here say. I'm no different."

Keep saying it, and maybe it would be true.

The secret path dropped them at the entrance to the azalea garden, which stretched from the resort's pool area back to the resort's thickly wooded boundary. Somewhere beyond the tree-line was AtB's well-hidden laundry facility. Suddenly there were intrusions: other people walking the paths, the faint horns of jazz filtering from hidden speakers, splashing and childish screaming from the pool. Martin sensed the brief intimacy he'd been encouraging from Tabby would now be withdrawn. Who wanted to share their soul while families and half-dressed kids screeching about the swimming pool went scampering past?

But Tabby just grinned at the kids as they ran by, their bare feet slapping on the concrete, and her mood seemed so much brighter that he could hardly mind. "Well, of course you'd come here and stay," she said, giving his hand a startling squeeze. "What's your favorite thing about AtB? The whole place, not just the park."

Martin was so surprised by her shift in demeanor, he stumbled into an answer which wasn't at all accurate. "Walking to Promise Mountain at midday, when Rainbow Falls catches the sunlight and makes all those prisms."

A lie. That *had* been his favorite…but not After Amy. Martin shook his head. "Wait, I changed my mind. I love the view of Wilderness Isle from the top deck of the side-wheeler. It's like going back in time."

Tabby laughed. "Two things? Greedy. All right, then. I can't choose Wilderness Isle or the side-wheeler because I look at those two all day, every day. But I do love wandering around The Big Apple, especially that little alley behind Cousins Pizza. Have you ever been back there right after sunset?"

"When the whole skyline is a silhouette against the glowing sky, and the soundtrack in the upstairs windows changes from music to the sound of the big immigrant family getting ready for dinner? You bet, and you're right— it's amazing. I love it when the older kid drops the plate."

"That smashing sound!" Tabby's giggles were enchanting. "The first time I heard it, I *jumped*. I was just sitting back there eating an ice cream cone. I love the whole thing. When Mama starts yelling at little Louie to sit down and eat his spaghetti, and little Louie says, 'Mama, no—' "

Martin chimed in with her, " 'Only meatballs, Mama, only meatballs!' "

Tabby threw her head back and cackled. "Hardly anyone knows about that spot, Martin! I love that you can quote it, too!"

And just like that, it was easy. They were walking on manicured paths amidst colorful flowers, speakeasy music floating in the air, discussing the minute details of their favorite place. Martin stopped worrying about how Tabby might react to every little thing he said or did, and just relaxed into the easiest, most free-flowing conversation of his life.

The pool bar came into view, white wooden columns surrounding a little crescent of bar stools. Martin noticed there was a gate between them and the pool deck, and his strides faltered—when had they put that in? But Tabby just pulled a card out of her pocket, tapped the gate's key reader, and swung it open for him. "Our employee IDs get us in all of these gates," she said with a grin. "Another tip from the roomie."

"I'll have to thank her later."

"It's a state secret, but she won't mind that I told you. Most people think you have to work here to get through the gates, but the security system really isn't that sophisticated."

"So you can get through *any* gate at AtB?" Martin pulled out a stool for Tabby and sat next to her.

"Just the ones I might have some business working in. Not like, machine rooms or something like that. But the basic doors around the parks that say 'Shopkeepers Only' or whatever, like the ones that lead to ride towers and stuff? Yeah, I can get into those. I used to work Ops in Bayou Pirate Adventure and I can still access all the doors there."

"That seems like a real oversight on their part," Martin said seriously, the security side of his IT brain taking over.

"It does," Tabby agreed cheerfully, pulling the drinks menu over. "Oh look, a frozen daiquiri sounds so good! I always get a margarita, but I should try something new, right?"

"Anything that comes with that many strawberries on top is going to be good," Martin said.

AtB bartenders could spot Patriots on dates a mile away. The pool bar bartender wandered over, tugging at his suspenders, and asked for their order. Martin ordered himself a beer and Tabby a daiquiri. The bartender leaned in close. "You want a 151 floater?" he asked her. "On the house. Patriot special."

Tabby looked confused. "A floater of what, now?"

Martin noticed her Kentucky came out when she was flustered. "I don't think you want it, Tabby. It's just straight alcohol."

The bartender winked at Martin. "Just a little something to help you forget your day," he said. "No problem." He went whirling back to pick up their drinks.

"I don't need to forget my day," Tabby said. "I mean, some days I do, but today was fine. *This* is fine. I'm not one of those people who gets too stressed out about work, anyway."

"It's been weird lately, though, right?" Martin couldn't help but ask. "The blogs, the social media. They've been putting you guys through the wringer, from what I've seen."

"It has been," she admitted. "And I'm super worried

about this Gold Rush Rapids thing maybe closing Old Dodge City? But there's always some drama at the parks. I just don't understand why it has to involve *me.*"

Martin didn't know what to say. His first thought was *it's not personal,* but for Tabby, Nate's blog *was* personal. He had literally followed her around and ambushed her at work. "Maybe the Gold Rush thing will distract him from bothering you," he said finally. "Seems like it ought to keep him busy for a while."

"It's just going to keep him around Old Dodge City more often," she grumbled. "Why couldn't he have discovered some breaking news about Legacy? I swear, if he—oh, this looks good!"

The daiquiri was everything a daiquiri should be: towering pink and white, topped with fruit and a tiny umbrella. Tabby perked up immediately.

"You know," she said after a few long, luxurious pulls on her straw. "There is one way we could get back at Nate."

"Oh? And what's that?"

Tabby grinned. "We just give him a false story to post. A big, juicy one that gets a million clicks…and is totally fake."

CHAPTER TWENTY-SEVEN

Antonia

Antonia liked closing shifts with Miles. He was a middle-aged manager who had been at AtB since college himself and knew the ropes of moving up in the company. Whenever she worked with him, Antonia got an earful of tips, tricks, and straight-up gossip about other managers in the company—people she should talk to, people she should try to impress, people she should avoid at all costs.

"Now Philip Ransom," Miles was saying, leaning against the wall in the hallway behind Professor Cloud's, "that's a guy you want to watch closely. End up on his team and you'll probably get framed for everything that goes wrong. I remember one time, he tried to set me up for the fall when there was a massive theft ring based out of Sequoia Suppliers. He implied to every single other manager that I was giving special treatment to the Patriots who were in on it, and that it was suspicious. I even got hauled in front of investigators. Guy's a jerk, plain and simple."

"Where is he now?" Antonia had alarm bells going off in her mind. She was still thinking about Nick's little crime organization, but she hadn't committed herself to joining yet. There was a part of Antonia which wanted to act out and run away, and there was another part who wanted to play by the rules and assure herself she could still have a future here. She wasn't sure which part of her was going to win out.

"He's in The Big Apple. They moved all of us out of Forests after the investigation was over." Miles looked at his iPhone, flicked through his emails idly. "That was three years ago. I'm probably due for another change soon. They don't leave us in one place too long; stops us from making too many alliances."

"I'd hate it if you left," Antonia said, and she meant it. This was the kind of alliance he meant: companionable conversations in back hallways which turned into overly sympathetic relationships. Those were bad for upper management, who needed to be able to pit employees against one another to get results.

"Thanks," Miles said, looking up at her with a smile. He was starting to go gray at the temples, but his face was still boyish and his clothes were youthful: thin, tapered trousers and brightly colored shirts; a closely clipped beard and thick black eyebrows which he used as expressively as his tone of voice. "But hey, you won't be around here forever. I see big things in your future."

Antonia turned her face away, embarrassed, though probably not for the reason Miles would assume. "We should probably head back out there."

Miles shrugged. "It's parade time. The stores will be

empty. Want to go to the office and have a cup of coffee?"

Antonia loved watching the night-time parade, *America Illuminated!,* but she loved the idea of sitting in the manager's office, sipping generic Keurig coffee, even more. "Can't say no to that."

The office was dark and quiet, everyone else gone home for the night. The parade was late on summer nights, not starting until nine-thirty, and the park would close an hour later. It would take them another hour to finish: get the registers counted, the deposits dropped, the safe balanced, the shelves straightened. The closing shift went from frantic to peaceful, and even though Antonia had been committed to working mornings before, she appreciated the evening's logical pace.

And at night, when it was just herself and the manager on duty making conversation as the park slowly emptied out, she could feel herself growing ever closer to that next step in her career. Suddenly, stealing merchandise was the farthest thing from her mind. She must have been crazy to even consider it. Or maybe really dehydrated. She should work on that. More water during the day.

Miles settled down in his desk chair while she hovered over the coffee station, popping K-cups into the machine, dumping sugar into the mugs. He chuckled, and she looked over her shoulder at him. "What's so funny?"

"This email. Casey Walden up at Independence Plaza is noticing a trend in missing merchandise bags from the delivery bins. Thinks there might be something going on downstairs."

Antonia went cold all over.

"A trend?" She managed to ask.

"Mmhmm. I don't think I need to say anything out loud,

do I?"

There was a tradition at AtB about not saying unpleasant truths aloud, about not inviting the outside world into their hallowed halls, where nothing bad could ever happen. When absolutely necessary, clinical code words and euphemisms, like "shrink," or, "she unfortunately had to leave the company," were used to get the point across.

The phone at her hip buzzed urgently, and she unclipped it with one smooth motion. "Dodge City Retail, this is Antonia."

"Antonia? I have a guest here saying their package wasn't delivered to their hotel? They're—" the Patriot's voice dropped to a hushed whisper, "they're *super* mad."

"Tell them to please look around the store and I will be with them in a moment," Antonia instructed. She hung up and handed Miles his coffee. "Looks like I'm needed. A missing delivery."

He tilted his head at her, one eyebrow conveying his interest in what should have been a mundane situation. "You don't say? I wouldn't mind seeing what time and day it was supposed to have gone out."

Antonia suddenly wondered if there was already an investigation going on. A spreadsheet, perhaps, of time windows, dates, and items being passed around by AtB managers, tracking the missing packages, looking for the common bonds.

Nick wasn't going to get out of this with his job, she realized. *None* of the participants were.

And just like that, her decision was made. Of course, it was easier to choose a side when you knew which one already had the upper hand. But maybe she had already known this was how things would go down. She'd been at

AtB long enough to know the employees usually didn't win their little rebellions. Management always came out on top. And if there was one thing Antonia needed desperately, it was to come out on top.

She smiled at Miles. "Well, you should come on down and we'll Sherlock Holmes this thing. Plus, we'll make our guests happy and all that."

"Sure," Miles agreed, putting down his coffee. "Happy guests, happy life."

The folksy showroom of Professor Cloud's was starting to buzz by the time they slipped through the store's back door, the parade's cheerful tones fading down the walkway. Amir, the Patriot who had called for help, was standing behind the cash-wrap next to the door, his face anxious. Facing him down from the other side of the counter were two hard-eyed women, their blonde helmets tamed with mousse and streaked with showy dark roots. Were those highlights or lowlights? Antonia didn't know much about white lady hair, but she did recognize this particular style as one that seemed to signal trouble, as if there was a signature look for discontented moms on the rampage.

To her relief, Miles stepped right up and took the opening parry, asking if the guests could please explain their situation so he could get to the bottom of it? Antonia stood back alongside Amir, for once happy to be relegated to the powerless position of costumed Patriot.

"Yes," the woman on the left said, her voice lending a knife's edge to the simple syllable. She was dressed in a loose-necked beige top with the words *best day ever* in a loopy script across the chest, and her tan arms were draped in silver bangles, the charms hanging from each one rattling as she raised and then lowered her hands on the counter for some sort of emphasis. "We are missing items that were promised to us. And we paid a lot of money for them! The hotel concierge said to wait another day, but that's just not acceptable. Where are our *things?*"

"That's right," the woman on the right chimed in. *Her* inspirational slogan was *do all things with love.* The *o* in love was a little heart. Antonia had to wonder if the woman had ever taken advice from a shirt before. She had a face which seemed painted in perpetually petulant lines. This was a woman who called the manager for every imagined slight. "I have to say, the service here has gone downhill. We've been coming here for years and this year has been the most disappointing visit yet. I think we might go to Orlando next year, honestly."

"Well, I don't like to hear that we're disappointing you," Miles said blandly, his face a mask of polite kindness. "Can you show me the receipt from your purchase yesterday?"

The woman who wanted to do all things with love gave him an acidic glare. "We didn't *get* a receipt. It wouldn't print and the cashier said that wouldn't be a problem. We had reservations for dinner. We were in a hurry."

"We're in a hurry now, too," the woman having the best day ever interjected. "We have passes for Bayou Pirate Adventure and the kids want to get going."

"That's not a problem," Miles said, his smile never slipping. "Let me just get your contact info, and the items you bought and the time of day, and I can sort everything out for you. I'll get your package back to your hotel in a few hours."

The women glared at his assurances, suspicious of his charm, but in the end they folded, wrote down their information, and departed, their stiff backs disappearing into the afternoon crowds now spilling off the wooden boardwalks and into the broad walkway of Old Dodge City.

Amir breathed out. "I need a drink of water," he said to Antonia. "Do you mind?"

"Go right ahead. I'll watch your register."

He went through the back door, a flash of fluorescent light illuminating the frontier gloom of the store for a half-second, a little moment of time travel.

Antonia looked at Miles, who was studying the piece of paper he'd taken down the women's details on. "What did they buy?"

"Some collectible pins. Hopefully we have all those still. A Patriot Pals rodeo play-set they could have bought anywhere, even back at their hotel. That's easy to replace. A pillow trimmed with feathers." Miles glanced around the shop. "We have those?"

"In the back corner. They're pretty tacky."

"If only that was surprising." Miles chuckled.

"So we are just recreating the order and shipping that to them with an express courier?" Antonia could handle all of that on her own.

"Recreate the order…just to make sure we have everything in hand. But then let's do a little research. See if we can find out just where the original package went."

Antonia didn't want to make things too easy for Miles, but by the time he'd figured out that the women's purchase had been properly paid for, bagged up, walked downstairs for delivery service and then never signed off on by the delivery driver (a dour-looking elderly man who drove his golf cart with grim precision through the corridor's crowds of gossiping college students), she knew they'd end up in the Cloud's stockroom eventually. And there they'd find the hiding place for the packages Nick was taking. Hell, Antonia thought, they might even find Nick taking a nap.

Luckily (for Nick) the blonde boy wasn't curled up in a cozy corner of the stockroom for a siesta, but there *were* several bags stashed at the back of the shelving unit where Antonia had seen him hide the bag before. She managed to make the discovery seem casual, even making sure that Miles was standing right next to her when she felt behind the bins, one by one, until she pulled out the right ones and the bags were in full view. She didn't need one iota of suspicion falling on her for this. It had to look natural.

Miles looked at the delivery slips stapled to each bag. There were three of them, and they each came from a different store. "This one's from Sequoia," he said thoughtfully, "and this one's from Professor Clouds, and *this* is from The Big Apple, which...is weird."

"Does that mean it's park-wide?" Antonia asked, making her eyes round and wide. "That would be crazy!"

"It sure seems that way. There are three different areas right here." Miles frowned down at the bags. "And the merchandise in them is all really different. Pins...a ride t-shirt...three mugs and an Edgar Eagle hat? Wouldn't you think a theft ring would go for high-dollar items?"

"Did the last one?"

"Yeah, it was all one big ticket. This...is an assortment."

Antonia nodded, fixed a studious gaze on the receipts. "You know...it kind of makes sense. Every single one of these items is a park exclusive. You can't buy this stuff at a Target, or on Amazon. Even though they're just pins, they still have a resale value."

"EBay?"

"I think so."

"Holy shit." Miles looked around the stockroom, at all the gray bins lining the metal shelves. "What if there's more?"

"We can have someone check. I think we have a few extra people tonight." There wouldn't be more, she thought, unless they've recently stepped up their game. Nick had said the key to the continued success of the ring was the low volume from each supplier. Three bags seemed high, actually.

Miles was still looking over the shelving units when Antonia heard the door knob click behind her. She whirled around just in time to see the wide-eyed expression of a young woman she didn't know, dressed in the swirling scarves and knee breeches of the Bayou Pirates Adventure. An impulse Antonia didn't stop to question made her shake her head, hard, at the girl. The Patriot ducked out the doorway and closed the door, almost silently, behind her.

Miles turned. "Did someone open the door?"

"The floor stocker, but I waved her away," Antonia lied.

"We should have locked it, but I guess they all have keys. All right, well, I'm guessing there's nothing else in here. But send someone down to check when they have a minute, anyway. And I'll take these up to the office and send out some emails. I think we might be able to set up a camera, catch whoever is stashing these."

Antonia followed Miles out of the stock room, glancing around the corridor for the girl in the Pirates uniform. But in the little groups of chattering Patriots outside the Chuckwagon, filled with females dressed in Old Dodge City skirts and blouses, Patriot's Place gowns, and a few Plaza girls in their long brocade skirts, she didn't see a single Pirate. She wondered if there was another stashing spot along the corridor, a backup location, and decided there probably was. This was a well-organized set-up, after all.

For now.

CHAPTER TWENTY-EIGHT

Sonia

Sonia always found a walk around the park after a day shift made for an interesting headspace. After spending eight or ten hours alternately yelling at guests and being yelled at by them, she enjoyed the sensation of finally feeling free to ignore her fellow man.

Sonia loved to put on a cheap Patriot Pals t-shirt and get out there in the crowds, letting the tides of humanity ebb and flow around her. They were tugged not by the moon's gravity, but by parades, shows, rides with heavy-throughput dumping endless waves of giddy guests back onto the walkways, character photo-ops drawing the pausing members of the populace who couldn't quite decide if they should join the queue and pose for a photo with a furry costumed character or a dolled-up actress, or simply move on, embracing the credulousness of adulthood.

To the untrained eye, there was no way to determine

where all these people came from or where they were going next, but Sonia did not have an untrained eye. She was a theme park veteran, and she wove in and out of stalling families, bickering couples, and sunburned retirees without hesitation, without having to slow her stride.

And if she enjoyed not having to care one bit about any of them, at the same time she was curious about the people around her, a curiosity born of watching them come and go from her attraction all day while she was rooted in one spot. She got out in the park to witness her customers in their natural environment, when they weren't trying to figure out the mechanics of Gold Rush Rapids' height requirement or the fastest way back to the park entrance without waiting for the steam train. What were families like when they were just strolling, taking it all in?

The crying fanboys, she noticed, had pretty much been confined to Old Dodge City. Everyone in The Big Apple looked chipper enough, eating their hot dogs and candy apples as they took photos with the fake subway station railings and against the window of Chung Lo's Chinese Restaurant, where plastic ducks hung in the window by their long brown necks. She meandered through the princess dress racks of the stores in Fairytale Courtyard before passing the colonial town of Patriot's Place on her way back to the Forgotten Forests, where the shade from the huge pine trees planted along the walkways—marginally narrower than the rest of the parks' promenades, to complete the illusion of being lost in the forest primeval— sank the stifling summer evening temperature to an almost-bearable level.

Here, families were eating purple ice creams and sharing fruity crepes, their smiles tie-dyed with berry stains. The big wooden bear who loomed above the entrance to Forest Trading Company was unwittingly starring in some Internet kid's vlog, the adolescent girl's voice piping as she narrated her day at America the Beautiful into her phone.

Sonia considered riding Sequoia Expedition, but she didn't know the Patriot standing at the entrance and she didn't feel like waiting in a queue posted at ninety minutes. Instead, she wandered into the attraction's exit shop, Sequoia Suppliers, where a steady stream of excited guests flowed past the photo screens and the cash registers just past them. Since photos now downloaded automatically onto the America the Beautiful app, only the occasional technophobe or confused foreign tourist stopped to admire and purchase prints of their party's surprised faces as they were confronted with Ursa Major, the ferocious bear god lurking in the heart of the Great Sequoia Forest. Ursa was one of the best animatronics in the entire theme park industry, so the faces people made when it roared down on their ride vehicle *were* pretty spectacular.

The two Patriots stationed at the photo registers had given up trying to engage any of the park guests hurrying past them and were just chit-chatting, their fingers drumming with boredom on the rough wooden counter. They both looked like young college students, here on their summer internship—they probably had some decent fresh gossip, and Sonia was curious anyway about the machinations of the Retail side of things. She sidled closer, fingering a rack of bear-shaped key-chains, so that she could listen in on their conversation.

"If it wasn't official, it is now. This guy took pictures of the shirt. I think heads are rolling up at Plaza over putting it out on a rack."

"That's ridiculous. Like whoever put that shirt out had *any* idea it wasn't supposed to be on the rack yet. No one tells us anything. We clock in, we go into the stock room, we start putting out merchandise. That's literally it. There's no one standing there saying, this goes out Wednesday, this goes out next week, or whatever." The second girl was positively livid, her cheeks turning red as she vented. "That could have been me. You know how often I pick up stocking shifts in Plaza."

"Wait, it was you?"

"No, dummy, it *could* have been me. Like, that's a mistake I could have made if I'd been there. Forget it. I'm just… forget it."

"No, I get it."

Sonia wasn't sure she actually got it. But that was the thing about the college students…they were hilariously clueless. Sonia didn't remember being that bad at social cues and conversation when she'd been nineteen or twenty.

"So, is she getting fired?"

"Who?" The second girl looked up at smiled at a passing guest, in an effort to pretend she was doing her job. Sonia glanced around and saw a manager in an oxford shirt and tie walking through the store. She moved around to the other side of the key-chain rack, effectively hiding herself from the Patriots.

"Hey Tom," the first girl said, presumably to the approaching manager. "Slow in here today."

"Slow? I see nothing but guests." His voice was derisive, a little cutting.

"All of them looking at their photos on their phones. Come on, Tom, cut this position and let us go somewhere more fun." The second girl was daring, Sonia thought. She didn't mind pushing the manager to see what she could get. A bold strategy.

"I should just send you home," Tom replied. "Since you're not making me any money."

"I could stand in their way waving key-chains around," the second girl offered. "If you think that would help."

Tom laughed. "No, just look available. Nothing is going to help. I was just messing with you guys."

Not bad, Sonia thought. Didn't get her out of the store, but didn't get her in trouble, either. Tom was okay. Except for that line about not making him money. She was glad she didn't work in an area measured by its revenue. Sonia couldn't care less if she made money for her boss.

"Well, in that case, why don't you tell us what's going to happen to the Patriot who put out that Gold Rush shirt in Plaza?"

Now *that* was daring.

Tom's voice was wary. "What Patriot are you talking about?"

"The Gold Rush shirt, Tom. With the closing date. We know all about it. So what's going to happen?"

"It was an honest mistake."

"Come on, Tom. We heard Plaza Retail management all got called on the carpet."

"Who told you that?"

"The ghosts in the Underground."

He sighed. "Nothing is happening to whoever put the shirt out. The Patriot isn't at fault. There wasn't any signage or anything telling the team not to stock the shirt."

"That's good," the first Patriot said. "I'd hate to see someone get in trouble over it."

"Someone *did* get in trouble," Tom continued, lowering

his voice. Sonia stood absolutely still, willing the guests to stop shouting and laughing as they passed through the echoing passage of the shop. "Nicolette, the stockroom manager."

"Fired?"

"No, not fired. But after the way they spoke to her, I doubt she sticks around. This is going to ruin her career here. I mean, there has been way too much negative press about the ride closing already, and it hasn't even been officially announced! So no, it didn't go great for her."

There was quiet for a moment. Sonia brushed her fingers along a line of key-chains, wooden tags with names carved into them, *Sarah* and *Sara* and, weirdly, *Sarai*, a name she'd never seen before. A group of teenagers went past, rowdy, punching the air with their fists, shouting about the way they'd faced down the giant bear of the forest. She imagined an apartment somewhere near the theme parks, where a woman named Nicolette was drinking a beer and considering her options now that her career with the company she loved was coming to an unsightly end.

"I liked Nicolette," the second Patriot said finally.

"Well," Tom said, "sometimes being likable isn't enough."

Sonia had heard enough. She slid around the key-chain rack to make her escape and the Patriots, plus Tom, jumped.

"Can I help you with anything?" The first girl asked.

Tom's glance slid down Sonia's wardrobe-issued khaki shorts, and his eyes narrowed slightly.

"Just looking for my name on these key-chains," Sonia said. "But it seems like you're all out."

"What name were you looking for?"

"Sarabeth," Sonia lied quickly. "It's always kind of a long

shot."

"I don't think we've ever had that one," the girl said regretfully.

"I don't think anyone has." She smiled, and the Patriot smiled back at her. "Well, I better go meet my family." She waved and dove back into the crowd departing the building, wondering why the gossip she'd heard made her feel slightly dirty.

At the doorway, she paused and looked back. Tom had already wandered off, and the Patriots were standing alone at their cash wrap again. No—not alone. Someone had paused to buy a t-shirt and something small, something in a little box that Sonia couldn't quite see. A piece of jewelry, maybe? She waited, not sure what she was watching for, as the guest rang up the order and filled out a hotel delivery slip. The Patriot put the bag behind the desk, thanked the departing guest, and then turned to her coworker to say she'd be going downstairs.

Then she did something odd.

She winked.

Sonia knew there was a corridor entrance just outside the shop, hidden behind a cool grove of pine trees, and she darted out, slipped behind the trees, and was down the stairs into the cool damp of the Underground before the Patriot had time to go through the store's back door. She wanted to see what the girl did with the package, though she couldn't quite put her finger on why. There was just something about her—the way she'd challenged Tom and gotten away with it, the way she'd gotten him to open up about the fired manager. The wink to her colleague. This girl had a power about her that a college-age Patriot should not have. She got away with things. Forgotten Forests was at the end of its own corridor; what might she do down there, on her own?

The Patriot came down the stairs from her shop while Sonia hid behind a cluster of wide pipes feeding mysterious chemicals to the many animatronics and effects in Sequoia Expedition. There was a box at the end of the stairwell for packages, and a clipboard for logging them in. The Patriot logged in the package dutifully, then looked around, lifted it back out of the box, and strode off down the hall, the bag swinging from her hand with an admirable lack of caution.

Sonia understood the girl's casual nature at once. If anyone saw her walking with purpose down the corridor, they'd assume she was taking a bag to another location for her manager and never question what was in the bag or why she had it.

Sonia was trying to figure out how to follow her up the empty corridor without being noticed when fate sent her a little help. A large group of teens on an educational tour came galumphing down the corridor towards her hiding place, their tour guide shouting over them with facts about the Sequoia Expedition. "This attraction has the largest number of moving animatronic figures in the theme park industry!" he was saying desperately, herding them towards the queue stairwell. "Please remember you cannot touch anything, though!"

Sonia slipped through the crush of teens and went scampering up the corridor, her footsteps now covered by their shouts and the echo of their sneakers squeaking on the concrete. Ahead of her, mingling with the other Patriots in the more populated main corridor ahead, she could still see the Patriot walking confidently with her bag in one hand, swinging it nonchalantly. Then she veered into the

Old Dodge City corridor.

Sonia came around the corner a few moments later and paused, her gaze scanning the corridor ahead. There were girls in the flowered aprons of Cowboy Cal's laughing outside of the Chuckwagon, and an older man wearing Engineering grays peering into a fusebox under the vast network of tubing below the Shootin' Arcade. No one in the chocolate-colored skirt and green blouse of the Forgotten Forests.

Then she came out of a room to the left, a room Sonia had never really noticed before. No bag in her hand.

The Patriot looked at Sonia.

"Weren't you just in my store?"

Bold, Sonia thought. Not even trying to hide it.

"Yeah. I came down to grab something from the Chuckwagon. Can't afford theme park prices until payday, you know?"

The girl laughed. "Girl, you're not kidding. Not even on payday, if we're being realistic."

"Well…bye." Sonia ducked past her and went into the Chuckwagon, not bothering to turn and see if the girl had looked after her. She looked around the packed break room, her heart thudding in her ears and her hands shaking now that the moment had passed. She went into the closet where the elderly Korean woman sat on her chair, waiting to ring out the Patriots as they picked up their sad convenience-store lunches, and bought a frozen coffee. Then she went back into the corridor and leaned against the wall facing the room without a sign, the plain beige door set right across from the Chuckwagon entrance which she had never, ever considered before.

She waited and waited, but no one else went in or out.

CHAPTER TWENTY-NINE

Tabby

"Okay. I think everyone's here?" Tabby looked around the booth at her friends, a flush of excitement pinking her cheeks. She had never done anything like this before, never set herself up as *in charge* before, and she thought she liked the feeling. Usually, when a lot of people were looking at her and she wasn't spieling an attraction, she assumed it was with derision or mockery. Now, she felt like she was a person who commanded respect.

Because every person, every single one, whom she had told about planting a bad blog post, had loved the idea. Coming up with a ridiculous story for Nate to post on AtBLive as verified fact, then watching him deal with the fall-out and lose the credibility he'd built just days ago for finding out about the closure of Gold Rush Rapids? What sweet revenge it would be!

By now, Tabby wasn't the only one who had been

suffering at the hands of Nate's petty blogging. Everyone knew now that his posts on Patriots not showing proper respect for AtB policies were the reasons for the recent police-state they'd all been dealing with. There were more than a few Patriots with discussions on previously clean files who had a bone to pick with this self-styled journalist.

In other words, just about everyone working at AtB thought Nate was an asshole and it was time to take him down.

Martin sat at Tabby's right, and she appreciated his upright, quiet support. If he'd been disappointed their first date had turned into an anti-blogger plotting session while she threw back tourist-priced daiquiris, he hadn't let on. Instead, he'd helpfully borrowed a legal pad from the Magnolia Lodge front desk, then scribbled down notes while the two of them threw ideas back and forth. The date had ended more chastely than she'd expected, but in a way, she was relieved. Tabby had secretly reveled in the soft kiss, close-lipped and warm, that he'd placed on her lips at her front door. It was nice to feel like a prize to be won for once, instead of a cheap means to an end.

Sonia was wedged into the corner of the booth opposite her, tapping her hands on the table while she waited for their drinks to arrive. Sonia had arrived directly from a work shift, still wearing her khaki shorts and hiking boots, although she'd pulled on a Maracas the Parrot t-shirt over her button-down work blouse. Maracas was grinning maniacally, his namesake instruments clutched in both blue wings, evidently engaged in some enigmatic dance of his people. Tabby wondered if Sonia had known, when she'd pulled on that shirt, just what Tabby had in mind for her fake news story. Because if a coincidence, it was just too perfect.

The rest of the booth was rounded out with the usual suspects: Antonia, looking serious and powerful, as if her ascension to lead was a mantle of respectability she could not shed in her off-hours; Sonia's roommate Elena, Tabby's roommate Molly. Sitting beside Molly was Eton, a clean-cut ex-college intern from Shining Seas Water Park, who had been dating Molly off and on for the past few months. Tabby had objected to Eton's inclusion at first, but Molly had gotten a preview of her idea and had insisted having plants in as many parks and hotels as they could manage was key to the plan working. Their idea was so far-fetched, it could take multiple sources for Nate to believe it.

"So we're here tonight because we have to agree on the story," Tabby began. She took heart from the appreciative nods around her. Only Sonia looked a little surly, and that was just because she'd literally just come from work and needed a drink. The waitress appeared just then, and alcohol was doled out; Sonia brightened immediately. Tabby let everyone take their first sip as she continued, "Molly, Martin and I put this together and we think it has a great shot at getting picked up as truth *if* we all stick to it."

"Well, let's hear it," Elena said. "I'm ready to take this guy down."

Tabby took a deep breath. Just saying the words made her feel ridiculous. The story was *too* stupid—no, it had to be stupid, it had to be insane, that was the point. "This is a complete redo of Forgotten Forests. They're going to take out every single tree and turn it into an extension of the southwest theme from Gold Rush Rapids. The replacement is going to be a South of the Border-style area, like that weird rest stop in South Carolina? It's going to start out with the desert, like Mexico, and then turn tropical. The main attraction is going to be a salsa dancing show featuring Maracas the Parrot and friends. The area is going to be called," Tabby swallowed and looked down, overwhelmed by the incredulous faces staring at her, "it's going to be called Paradiso Valley."

"Paradiso Valley," Eton repeated. "With Maracas the Parrot and friends as the main attraction."

Sonia's cheeks hollowed as she sucked down her Long Island Iced Tea through a blue straw. Her eyebrows were raised.

Tabby put her hand under the table and felt clumsily for Martin's hand. He took it the moment he knew what she looking for, and squeezed tight.

Elena nodded slowly. "Paradiso Valley. Cut down the pine trees and replace them with palm trees. Take out the bears and replace them with parrots. Worst of all, take out the all-America all the time buzz AtB is known for, and give some credit to another country on the continent. The one that half our guests are terrified of." She gave Tabby an assessing look. "That's…genius."

Tabby had just been about to declare the entire idea a false alarm and request input from the table. "You think?"

"Absolutely. This will create so much controversy online, Fox News will be calling for the CEO to resign before they even bother fact-checking it. Nate will be completely discredited."

"It's just crazy enough to work," Eton agreed.

Tabby's heart was soaring, and she felt dizzy with relief. She turned to smile at Martin, who gave her a pleased grin back—then his lips slackened as his gaze focused on something just past her.

Tabby turned and saw Nick wandering over, hands in his pockets, the picture of a bored, careless school boy in search of something to break for fun.

"Guys!" Nick said cheerfully. "Am I missing the secret meeting?"

Tabby's mouth went dry.

Around the table, everyone's faces registered confusion.

"I'm only kidding, you guys." Nick laughed. "I'm just surprised to see so many faces from all over property in one place. Eton, man, how you doing?"

"Fine," Eton said warily. "Just the usual."

Nick grabbed a chair and spun it around, pushing the back against the table's edge and settling down with his legs straddled around it. "How do you even know these ladies? And this gentleman," he added, nodding to Martin.

"How do you know Eton?" Molly asked suspiciously.

Eton wiggled unhappily in his seat. "I met Nick when he was doing a vlog about the Betsy's Bombers girls. I, uh, introduced him to the Bombshell of the Month."

Nick waggled his eyebrows wolfishly. Tabby wondered if she could ever see him as anything but a cartoon villain now. "And I appreciated the introduction." Then he glanced at Tabby. "Still not as cute as you, though. What have you been up to, freckles? I haven't talked to you in days."

Days, Tabby thought. That really didn't sound like a long absence, especially while sitting next to the guy she'd kissed a few days ago.

She felt Martin's fingers slowly slipping away from hers, and it took a lot for her to not grip them tightly.

"Well, I had my regular days off, Nick," Tabby replied as steadily as she could, despite the hot rush of despair closing up her throat. Next to her, Martin was stiff, his muscles clenching as he tried to keep his thigh from touching hers. Well, it was a *booth,* Martin, they were going to touch a little! "I'm working tomorrow, though."

"I'll see you there." Nick smiled at her warmly. Despite herself, Tabby felt a flash of attraction. She'd been into him for months. It wasn't her fault that her body hadn't kept up with her brain.

Sonia had finished her drink with impressive speed and was now eyeing the Nick situation with something like disgust. Tabby wondered how long ago her lunch break had been. Was she drinking on an empty stomach? That could be dangerous.

"Nick," Sonia said, "You are a clueless little man child, did anyone ever tell you that?"

Nick smiled at Sonia, because Nick smiled at everyone. Tabby thought that Nick didn't know what it was to be unloved, uncelebrated. Nick was used to being the center of attention, and he had never had to distinguish the negative spotlight from the positive. She used to find that attractive, as if she could somehow acquire that same happy-go-lucky personality. But now she knew it meant there was nothing underneath the surface.

"You're so funny, Sonia," he said. "I love it when you're around."

Sonia sighed and pushed her empty glass across the table. "Is this meeting adjourned? Because I cannot do this without another Long Island. And some nachos."

Tabby's meeting had fallen apart, and it was all Nick's fault. She looked at the wood grain of the table. A few minutes ago, she'd been in charge and everyone had admired her. Now, things were back to normal. She was on the periphery, while someone stronger had nudged their way to center stage.

"I think we know what we're up to," Eton said carefully. "I feel pretty good about it."

"Me too," Elena agreed. "Sonia, want to go up to the bar and order some food? I'm starving."

"God, yes." And before anyone could move, Sonia had ducked under the table, pushed past their legs, and emerged next to Nick at the end of the booth. She gave him a little shove as she stood up, his chair rocking onto two legs, and cackled as she walked away, shaking her hips more than was strictly necessary.

That had all gone pretty badly, by all measurements Tabby could think of. And yet, the story was ready to go. She'd send everyone the write-up; they'd forward it to Nate as if it was an official memo they'd found mistakenly posted to a public server. And Nate wouldn't be able to resist so many copies of the same memo, identical and from different parks and resorts, flooding his inbox. He would take the bait.

So even if Martin was sitting so stiffly next to her that he might as well have been made as stone, and even if Nick was sitting at her left with a foolish grin that told her he didn't understand their dating days were already over, and even if the others were hastily scooting out of the booth to go in search of bar food, at least this one thing was going to happen. At least Tabby had set something in motion which was going to get revenge, for all of her Patriots, on the one person who had set himself up as their nemesis.

It felt bigger than her, and Tabby had never done anything that felt bigger than her besides join the team of Patriots in the first place.

Nate

Nate's post on peeling paint at attractions around AtB had netted him thirty new followers on Twitter and sixty-three new email subscribers, and he was starting to feel pretty satisfied with the direction his life had taken. Sure, putting "Theme Park Blogger" on one's LinkedIn page could look pretty strange to the guys back home, but could his old schoolmates who had gone the more traditional work route tout a following like his? People followed Nate for his opinions and connections. That *meant* something in this world.

After so many days in the parks looking for flaws, his eyes had attuned to this filter and he didn't have to work very hard to find the problems which, in his opinion, parks management was letting slide in gross deviance from Lawrence Taylor's original vision for the theme park experience. Maybe Walt Disney had done it first, but

Lawrence had done a tremendous job in following in the big man's footsteps, from clean-cut animated characters to family theme parks which espoused cleanliness and attention to detail above all else. There were never supposed to be overflowing trash cans, flecks of missing paint, or burned-out lightbulbs in the perfect toy box world of America the Beautiful. And Nate, like Lawrence Taylor himself, wouldn't stand for a single violation.

His readers wouldn't, either.

Whether that was because he had whipped them up into a frenzy with his constant nit-picking posts or because he had simply offered up a voice for thousands of people who felt the same way, well, that wasn't a question he pondered very often. What mattered were metrics, and what mattered was ad revenue, and what mattered was change at the parks. And he saw it every day, the way the Patriots stood straighter and their smiles stayed on longer and the merchandise was arranged more tidily and the attraction queues were swept more frequently. Nate and his angry fans were making a difference at AtB. And he was proud of his work.

From a wrought-iron bench outside of the ice cream parlor, Nate opened up his Twitter account and checked his mentions for the fifteenth time since his last post, an hour ago, about the sorry state of the Gangster Getaway queue. There had been dust on several of the ivory lampshades in the parlor scene, where the queue wound through Mama Carleone's house to show where Big Mike and Little Sal got their start in the Family Business. One actually had a *cobweb* hanging from it. A small cobweb, sure, that he'd had to zoom in with his camera to capture, but still! What was custodial doing, if not keeping Mama Carleone's parlor as pristine as the matriarch herself would have done?

It was a travesty, and Nate had said as much in his post, along with several other egregious violations of cleanliness and ride quality he'd noticed throughout the attraction. For one thing, the slightly garbled speaker that broadcast a direction to riders, in a cartoonish Brooklyn accent, to enter cars from the left and pull down the handrail, was definitely getting worse. It should have been replaced weeks ago. And he could barely even *see* the flashes from the gun muzzles in the big Chinatown shoot-out scene! How was this ride even open?

As usual, his Twitter replies were a mixed bag. Some fans, some haters. That was to be expected—not everyone could give up their boring lives to become career AtB reporters, building a dream life out of the enduring and timeless dreams of Lawrence Taylor, so there was going to be a jealous contingent. Nate was fine with this. Occasionally he did get annoyed and strike back at them, but generally he ignored the most trivial critics and blocked the most persistent and vitriolic ones, the guys who wrote long threads pointing out his many shortcomings as a human and as an AtB fan. (It was almost always guys.)

The fans always far outweighed the haters, though. People used social media to live vicariously. They followed stars and influencers on Instagram and Twitter because these were the people they admired, people who were able to shuck the nine-to-five and get out and *live*, and Nate was one of those people. He was a star to so many people now. He was a success story. He was a dream come true.

Nate listened to the tinkling music as it trilled prettily through this perfect, late nineteenth-century American town, and flicked through the words of support from his adoring public.

You're doing a great job keeping us updated Nate, love your work!

Can't believe that those lights are still burned out. Keep their feet to the fire!

Thank goodness for nate or the atb middle managers would never have to get out in the park and see what's wrong with it today.

God you're such an asshole.

Nate frowned and glanced over the profile of that last commenter. It was a guy—of course it was a guy—with a beard and a beer in his hand, at least, in his profile picture. His twitter handle was @AtBeersnob. Hardly as clever as he probably thought it was, Nate thought with a shake of his head. Jackass. He blocked the profile and moved on. If AtBeersnob thought he was an asshole, there was no need for him to see Nate's tweets, then, was there? He wouldn't mind being blocked at all.

He went back to his mentions, scrolling with his thumb.

Can you tell us more about the Gold Rush Rapids replacement? We need to know when it's coming! Too many rumors.

Nate hit reply.

They're not rumors, and the closing date is real! But I don't have any more info for you. Yet.

He sent the tweet, then put his phone down on his lap and considered the current state of his whisper network.

The truth was, he barely had one. While some of the other bloggers here fed off a fairly reliable current of clandestine updates from Patriots in both park and office positions, Nate hadn't been here long enough to cultivate that sort of network. Or he hadn't been friendly enough with the Patriots. It was possible that no one wanted to talk to him because he was so truthful, really showcasing everything that was wrong with the parks—not just the peeling paint, not just the burnt-out lightbulbs, but also the lack of sincerity and engagement from the Patriots.

And that wasn't his fault! Nate wasn't going to apologize for reporting on the Patriots who weren't willing to do their jobs. The Patriots made the parks, everyone knew that. All the fresh paint in the world didn't matter if the people who inhabited its spaces weren't up the legacy of Lawrence Taylor, who had valued friendly, kind, outgoing young people who were ready to tell the stories of his attractions every day in the parks.

But it would be nice if a few of the Patriots recognized the value of his hard work. He wasn't doing this to get people in trouble. He was doing this work so that they didn't lose the edge they'd had for decades, the ability to change lives and give people experiences they cherished for lifetimes. He was doing it to keep management working hard and to keep guests coming back. He was doing it for them.

He was an *ally*.

Nate looked at his phone again.

This guy thinks he's so great when he's just a nerd who can't get a real job.

He sighed. He'd had a real job. Pass.

Nate put his phone away and stood, walking into the ice cream parlor with an air of surrender. A person could only sit underneath the eaves there, with the false and delicious scent of sugar cones being blown out by the scent-distributing fans installed on either side of the shop doors, for so long before succumbing to the need to consume an ice cream cone of one's own.

All part of the whimsical joy and wonder of America the Beautiful—right down to the killer consumer instinct.

* * *

Nate was still puzzling over his informant problem half an hour later as he roamed through the Forgotten Forests, absentmindedly rubbing at a sticky ice cream stain on the hem of his shirt. He had set off with the idea of taking pictures of new merchandise in the Sequoia Suppliers shop, but the dim store was disappointingly stocked with a lot of cheap key-chains and the same old t-shirts they'd been selling for the past year. With that blog post concept a bust, he was now peering around corners and nosing through the menus of snack bars, looking for something, anything that was new and noteworthy to put on his site. It didn't have to be big: a review of a new cupcake flavor would get several thousand hits and double-digit shares on social media. But even with these low standards, he was having trouble finding anything worth reporting out to the fanbase. It was just a very quiet day.

He was starting to think he was going to have to head home and update an old post if he was going to share any content on his channels. Disappointed, Nate wandered through the passageway into the farthest end of Old Dodge City. He was near the bridge to Gold Rush Rapids, and Cowboy Cal's Good Grub, so he didn't think he'd be getting too close to the enemies he'd made in the shops farther down. He'd decided to give that bunch their space until he could be reasonably sure they'd all gotten over their little problem with him.

Unfortunate, because he'd still like to get to know that little prairie girl better. *Tabby,* that was her name. Yeah, she hated him, but wasn't there a thin line between love and hate? He'd have to try again with her. Not right now, obviously, but soon.

Nate leaned against the split-rail fence that set up a barrier between the rocky landscape of Gold Rush Rapids and the flowing crowds on the promenade and gazed out towards the Mighty Missouri. Sad, to think this river was going to be chopped up and made into a ride. A steady stream of vloggers were walking along the waterfront, making content before the refurbishment walls went up. He was watching them work when a voice startled him.

"You're Nate from AtBLive."

Nate jumped so hard, the voice might as well have belonged to a ghost of Christmas past. But when he turned, he only saw a round-faced girl in a Gold Rush Rapids costume. She had a backpack over one shoulder and the spot on her chest where her name tag should be was empty, so she was on her way in or out. Nate studied her for a moment, trying to place her face, but couldn't. She wasn't one of the ones from the Tabby incident.

"That's me," he said. "And you are?"

"A Patriot getting off work," she said. "As you can see."

Her voice was a tad more combative than Nate was ready for. "Whoa," he said, lifting his hands. "I don't want to start any trouble. I'm just taking a walk through the park."

The girl quirked one arched eyebrow. "Who said anything about trouble? You have a guilty conscience?" Then she shrugged. "That's not why I'm talking to you. Look, I work in Operations but I get around. I know where to listen. And I heard something crazy that you need to know about. I'd just forward it in an email, but I want you to know I'm serious about it."

Nate suddenly realized he *had* seen her before. In the dark parking lot of the Gateway Pub. "You're the one who got me the binder."

She looked him in the eye, her jaw hard. "That's right. I did."

Nate grinned. Now *this* was a valuable informant! He might not have many Patriots in his network, but did anyone have a contact like this crazy Gold Rush Rapids girl? She'd gotten him the scoop of the century with the binder of concept art. If she was promising him dirt that was even crazier than *that*, he was all ears. "Tell me everything you know. I promise I'll make it worth your while."

CHAPTER THIRTY-ONE

Tabby

By nine o'clock that night, the blog post was all anyone could talk about.

Tabby had worked until seven and then gone home ready for full hibernation mode, exhausted from the summer crowds. It hadn't helped that she'd been working with Nick at the Conestoga wagons all day *again*, or that she'd seen Martin from across the promenade, walking along slowly with his hands in his pockets, and that he hadn't come over to talk to her. Tabby had been so frustrated at being stuck at the wagon, she could have screamed.

Before the crackdown, she might have just told Nick she was going to help a guest who looked lost and dragged Martin off to one side to have a quick conversation. But now, with managers and leads watching their every move, she was trapped in an endless loop of "Howdy!" and "Y'all have a beautiful day!" She was forced to watch Martin disappear into the crowds without so much as a shared glance, helpless to stop him.

She just *knew* that Nick, in his endless innocence and ignorance, had fucked up this relationship for her, and she didn't have any idea how to get it back. She'd never *been* in a relationship. What did people do, when they had misunderstandings and weren't speaking to one another? How did she fix this? Tabby decided it was time to turn to sitcoms, which had been her lifeline with the outside world when she'd been trapped in the trailer back in Kentucky. Maybe Ted and Robin could give her some answers.

But all the relationships on *How I Met Your Mother* seemed to be long, drawn-out, exhausting affairs with constant misunderstandings and a lot of repeat break-ups. Tabby wasn't sure that was what she wanted. Maybe it was better to be alone?

Such was her mood, her feet on the coffee table and her spoon in her ice cream bowl, when she picked up her phone and saw that Nate had, in fact, written a solid thousand words all about her ridiculous, insane, unbelievable story. The memos had gone out late last night, and Sonia had muttered something to her in the Chuckwagon at lunch that day about talking to him in person. But she hadn't dared hope it would really work.

Here it was.

SAYONARA, SEQUOIAS? ATB'S NEW LAND IS ALL ABOUT THE AMERICAS, WITH A LATIN BEAT AND MARACAS AS YOUR HOST.

"Oh my God," she muttered, sitting up with a start. "Oh my God, we got him.."

Texts started rolling into her phone, covering up her view of the story before she could even read it. The top one was from Sonia.

HOOK LINE AND SINKER!!! I HAD THE BASTARD AT HELLO!!

She should have known, Tabby thought. She should have known Sonia would seal the deal. Telling the others probably hadn't even been necessary.

Well, she was new to subterfuge. Next time, she would be more economical.

She skimmed the other texts: Molly, Eton, Elena. All thrilled they'd played a part in the ultimate prank on AtBLive.

Tabby answered the texts from everyone in the group with the sort of quiet diligence she applied to everything— people had been nice enough to text her. She was going to be polite and text them back. But the truth was, once she'd seen Martin was not one of the senders, she'd lost interest in all of it. She just wanted more ice cream, and maybe another run at relationships with Ted and Robin.

She texted Antonia instead. *Martin isn't talking to me.*

There was a long pause, a few minutes which could feel like hours in the iMessage world. Then the phone lit up again. *I'll handle Martin.*

Tabby was considering what this could mean when Molly came in the front door, huffing under the weight of several plastic grocery bags.

"We did it!" she announced. "Are you eating ice cream? Hide it from me. I'm switching to low-carb. I had to go up a costume size at the wardrobe building today."

"Maybe it was just the skirt you checked out," Tabby suggested. "You know they don't come in very even sizes. But hey, the blog!"

"I know! I nearly drove off the road when I saw an alert

about a new post. I turned on mentions from his account. What are people saying?"

"It's pretty early yet, but..." Tabby scrolled through the AtBLive account replies. There were a lot of derisive comments about his sources and integrity, which, *true,* she thought with a little smile. But there was a decent minority of people, at least right off the bat, who believed the story and were simply freaking out about the impending loss of the Forgotten Forests. There was also a considerable amount of racism. "I'd say it's sixty-forty in favor of people thinking he's been duped."

"Is that all?" Molly came into the living room and peered at Tabby's phone. "Honestly, that's a lot fewer than I expected."

"It doesn't matter if they believe him, though," Tabby said. "I mean, the point is that he puts out something so ridiculous that he's proven wrong. Not that he puts out something no one believes."

"I guess. I must have had too much faith in people or something." Molly went back to putting her groceries away.

Her words came back to haunt Tabby the next morning.

"Molly?"

"Hmm?" Molly came out of the bathroom, toothbrush in her mouth.

Tabby was leaning against her bedroom door; she hadn't even made it into the hallway yet. "Molly, the Internet is scaring me."

"That's normal," Molly mumbled around a mouthful of foam. She went back into the bathroom, spit and rinsed, and returned. "What's up now?"

"Um...white supremacy?"

Molly shrugged a *what else is new* shrug and plucked the phone from Tabby's cold fingers. She scrolled. Her eyes widened. "Oh, no way," she whispered. Her eyes met Tabby's. "This is some dark shit, Tabby."

"I know!"

"And this came from *your* story?"

"I mean…yes? But this isn't what I meant!"

Molly ran her finger down the comments and stopped at one, reading it aloud. "*'America the Beautiful's attempt to pander to the Hispanic immigrants in this country is disgusting and goes against the spirit of the parks. Lawrence Taylor was building a monument to America by Americans, not America by Mexicans. And what about illegals!! I suppose they are welcome for free!!'* Gross, who would write this?" She scrolled up again. "Ah, the illustrious Hairy Trousers. Now that's a screen name to forget."

"Wasn't *Hairy Trousers* the name of an old Patriot Pals cartoon? Something with Lucky the Indian Pony—oh no. That was racist, too, wasn't it?"

"It wasn't considered racist at the time. But it's definitely racist now. Just like all of these commenters on this post." Molly handed Tabby back her phone. "Welp, we knew we should never underestimate the power of truly terrible people on the Internet. It was bound to get racist."

"I know, but…Molly, what if this gets back to me?" Tabby couldn't stop staring at the comments on Nate's blog. And this wasn't where it ended. Stuff was *really* ugly on AtBExpress, the old message board site. She'd gotten up in such a good mood this morning, too! Eager to hop online and see if Nate had been taken down by his own gullible hubris, she'd opened up Twitter, seen several dismaying tweets referring to a racist response on the

AtBExpress boards. It hadn't taken a search to find the post and its dozens of affirming replies—it was the top performing post on the site.

Popular and growing in popularity every minute, judging by the plus ones and replies sprouting up underneath it. Even if this guy was eventually banned by mods and the post taken down, the furor that *she* had caused would not be forgotten. People were going to talk about it for weeks. And one week equaled one decade in social media time. AtB fans were going to be labeled racists, and it was going to affect them all in some way.

Just a week ago, this guy had single-handedly made their work lives so much more difficult.

If AtB management responded to this PR mess with stronger controls on Patriots and what they could say and do in public or on the job, *she* would be responsible for it.

Molly shrugged. "You wanted to take him down. The bigger this is, the worse he'll look when it gets denied. And I imagine there will be a PR response by ten a.m. at the latest."

"I wish this hadn't happened," Tabby said hopelessly.

"So some people are going to out themselves as racist," Molly said, heading down the hall towards the kitchen. "Big deal."

But Tabby couldn't shake the conviction that this wasn't going the way she'd wanted at all. Were people going to spend any time decrying Nate and his foolishness in posting what was a patently ridiculous rumor? Or were they going to just indulge in the sweet, sweet internet drama that ensued every time someone typed the word "racist"? People might get so caught up in tearing apart the Hairy Trousers type and his ilk that they'd forget to tear apart Nate for taking a false story and posting it as a confirmed insider tip.

All the hits his site got out of this might just improve Nate's position.

Had she been fooling herself? A purveyor of click-bait couldn't be taken down with false stories. Click-bait existed for traffic, pure and simple.

This had been a mistake.

Tabby occasionally allowed herself to wallow in the fact that the world was just not fair, and this was one of those moments. She slumped back onto her bed, closed the blinds, and pulled the pillow over her head.

She didn't have to work until the afternoon, anyway.

When she got to work that afternoon, Antonia was waiting for her, leaning against the computer behind Professor Cloud's where they clocked in and out for shifts. Her earpiece was in and her sleeves were pushed up to her elbows—it was another hot day. Still two weeks until the Fourth of July weekend, but it felt like the dog days of August under the sun.

"Busy out there?" Tabby asked, the classic Patriot greeting to someone already at work.

"Oh, you bet," Antonia replied with a grimace. "Gold Rush Rapids had a three-hour wait earlier. I think it's down to ninety minutes now, but you know how that can fluctuate."

"Three hours! It's that crowded?" Tabby had a momentary desire to run away. Three-hour wait times were usually confined to Memorial Day, the Fourth of July, and *maybe* Christmas Day, if the weather was nice enough. "I know it's a Saturday, but jeez."

"Oh, it's because of Nate leaking the closing date. People

are rushing in to say their goodbyes, get in their last rides. I think every annual passholder in the southeast is here right now. Thank goodness we don't work in Ops, is all I gotta say about that."

Tabby remembered the holiday season in Operations and grimaced. Working the queues and ride systems of Pirate Bayou Adventure over the long spring break period had been like someone had pressed fast-forward on a normal day. They had moved thousands more people through the attraction on the high season days than they did on regular days, but in the same amount of time, thanks to an unending dread of the wrath of their guests should people not manage to get on all the park's marquee rides during their vacation. The longer the lines, the longer the letters written to guest services…and the better the guests' memories about the Patriots who had told them no.

"I never want to go back to Ops," she said, adjusting her name tag. "Maybe Retail isn't the promised land they made it out to be, but at least at eleven o'clock tonight we can lock our doors and everyone has to go away. Ops will still have lines to push through the attractions for at least another hour."

"Oh, about that." Antonia smiled grimly. "We're staying open until midnight tonight. Park hours extended because of the crowds."

"Ugh," Tabby said. "I guess I have to stay, too?"

"Yes, indeed. 'Tis the season for overtime. Also, Tabby—about the story."

Tabby looked around. The shabby hallway was empty. "Yeah?"

"It got uglier than I expected. I mean, it's the Internet, we should have known, but…"

Tabby tried and failed to think of something to say. She felt a weird sense of relief that Antonia was Black, not Latina, and then she experienced the discomfort of wondering if that relief was, in itself, racist, and then she simply wanted to stop thinking. "I think I better clock in and head out. Someone is probably waiting on their break."

"Tabby, hang on a sec." Antonia peered at her. "Listen, I'm not *mad* about what happened. You didn't go out and there try to start a fight about whether brown people belong in America the Beautiful. If anything, I think you proved something."

"I proved something?"

"Yeah," Antonia said, putting a hand on her shoulder. "You proved that everyone takes this place *way* too seriously…and just how much influence it could really have. This is bigger than whether or not we have a mock-up of the Missouri River. It's about what we do with it."

"Tabby!" Nick greeted her with more enthusiasm than Winslow, even though she was holding the slip for Winslow's break. *He* just took the paper from her without expression, and went sloping through the crowds into Professor Cloud's, his hound-dog face frozen in eternal depression. "Thank God you are here to save me from Winslow."

Tabby regarded Nick with skepticism. Had he not noticed that she had been avoiding him, ignoring his texts, putting his accounts on mute so that she wouldn't accidentally like or comment on something funny he'd posted before she realized who it had come from? More than a week had gone by since she'd been alone with him, on that date at Legacy of Heroes, and in that space of time she'd distanced him from her mind, and fallen into some sort of inexplicable fascination/crush with Martin, and really, that was enough for her to deal with! She didn't have time for Nick, also.

"What's it been like out here?" she asked, deliberately trying to keep things casual, work-colleague in nature. She straightened a few rows of sunglasses and walked around the Conestoga wagon, looking for gaps or messes. Nick wasn't known for his attention to detail or tidying-up abilities—which was a shame, since that was exactly what the Assist position was for.

"Fast and slow, they come in waves. Most people are heading straight for Gold Rush Rapids."

Tabby could see this just by looking over the walkway through Old Dodge City. There was a decided pattern to the ebb and flo of the park guests. A majority of them were banking right after the Conestogas, making for the turn and the slight incline to Gold Rush's entrance. A marked minority were walking with the slow abandon of the casual guest, consulting maps, peering in shop windows, and generally getting in the way of everyone who had come with the express purpose of riding Gold Rush Rapids as many times as possible before it closed forever. "Passholders," she guessed. "They don't buy a lot of sunglasses, so I guess we'll be kind of slow out here."

"Perfect," Nick said. "We can just talk."

Perfect, Tabby thought, stifling a sigh.

"When I get off in a couple hours, I'm going to wait for you to get your break," Nick said. "Something I want to show you."

Tabby didn't like the sound of that at all. "Nick, don't wait around for me. That's not necessary."

"No, I think this is something that…I think it can help you out. It's really helping *me* out. At least, until I get my YouTube follows a little higher and start making some money off ads, you know?"

She narrowed her eyes. "Are you trying to get me into a pyramid scheme? Because I have no buy-in money, I'm bad at sales pitches, and I don't have anywhere to store all the crap you'd make me buy."

"No, not at all!" Nick paused and thought. "Well, in a manner of speaking, maybe it is. But there's no buy-in. And no storage. And you don't have to get anyone else in on it unless you really want to. But I think we're almost at capacity."

"So what is it? You can't tell me right now?"

"I can't."

"Not even a hint?"

"Not even the teensiest little hint." Nick smiled at her. "But, you know what, Tabby? I think after everything AtB has been putting you through, with the rogue blogger and all that shit, you're going to like this."

"Don't swear in front of guests, Nick. Christ." Tabby straightened her skirt and went over to the register to attend to a pale-faced dad who was holding a pair of sunglasses and a baseball cap. Judging by the pink sheen on his forehead, he had waited just a little too long to buy the hat. "Well, howdy!" Tabby said, switching into her customer service voice. "Did you find everything you're looking for, sir?"

CHAPTER THIRTY-TWO

Martin

Martin had been roaming around AtB since mid-afternoon. He should have been working, but he just couldn't concentrate today. Every time he looked at a line of code, the letters and slashes just blurred together into a mishmash of nonsense.

So he'd given himself permission to take a sick day and headed out into the steamy June afternoon, stopping off to talk to his favorite characters as he looped around the park in a big counter-clockwise loop.

He'd already had a nice conversation with Miss Susie Q. in front of the Liberty Bakery, and would have talked with her for longer if she hadn't looked at her watch and announced that she needed to meet her young man on Lover's Lane, would he please excuse her? That was code for the end of her set, and Martin knew, as he watched her walk away, that before he reached the end of Independence

Plaza, she would already be in the actors' green room on the second floor above the bakery, pulling off her bonnet and wig of auburn sausage curls, sighing as she massaged the broad smile off of her aching cheeks.

But that was fine; that was part of the deal. Martin moseyed on down the street, pausing to shake hands with the Mayor, who was getting ready to preside over a ribbon-cutting at Plaza Memorial Gazebo, a daily ritual performed at eleven a.m.

He was aware that the costumed performers of America the Beautiful lived a kind of Groundhog Day existence: every day the Fourth of July, or maybe the day just before the holiday, in a summertime haze of small fluttering flags and uplifting brass bands playing their music just around the corner, just out of sight—a parade on the way or maybe on the way out—a prospect of fried chicken and lemonade and ice cream sundaes for lunch.

No, really—that was the signature lunch special at Independence Plaza's famous Corner Restaurant, and you could get it all day long, although it cost an extra six dollars once they switched to the dinner menu at four o'clock.

The real Fourth of July weekend, interestingly enough, did almost nothing to heighten the patriotic holiday fervor that pervaded Independence Plaza from January to December. They were already at peak Independence Day, all day, every day. The only way to tell a real July Fourth photo of the Plaza from an April or September photo was the sheer number of people in the July photo.

But the crowds were already here, two weeks early. Martin had noticed the extra people on this steamy Friday, the lines at the turnstiles extending into the walkways from the parking garages; the queues for big attractions pushing past two hours. AtB was bursting at the seams, and if this kept up from now until the Fourth, the park was going to be an absolute zoo on the holiday itself.

The extra crush altered Martin's experience. When he spoke to Miss Susie Q., he was keenly aware that children were pulling at their mothers' hands and young women with hungry Instagram needs were sighing loudly, anxious to get a photo with AtB's most beautiful Victorian heartbreaker if only this strange, single man would move on. When he paused to take in the stirring view of Promise Mountain's cascading waterfalls from the broad central square at the end of Independence Plaza, he was jostled rudely by several families who weren't in the mood to stand around and gawk. There was a sea of humanity flowing down the promenades and splitting around him like a rock in a flooded river—most of them, he noticed, turning left to head into Old Dodge City. But Martin was in no hurry to head out West. He turned right, into the quarter-sized skyscrapers and sparkling clean tenements of The Big Apple. He joined the ninety-minute queue for Gangster Getaway without even glancing at the alleyway running behind Gotham Ice Cream Palace.

It wasn't until late in the afternoon that he made his way into Old Dodge City, his footsteps coming more slowly and sweat stinging his eyes after a day in the sun. He rarely stayed in the park all day—the advantage of being a local was short in-and-out visits rather than all-day marathons—but Martin couldn't see the value in going home to a laptop that he didn't want to look at, and to an emptiness he didn't want to listen to. He knew what he *did* want, which was to see Tabby, to look at her freckles and her sandy-colored braids and her pale eyes. To hear her voice and feel that rushing sensation of *rightness* that she gave him.

And that was why he stopped to meet every character and rode rides he hadn't been on in months and saw shows he hadn't bothered with in years. To put it off, to put *her* off, because he was afraid of her. And he was afraid of Nick.

The Double Patriots of Patriot's Place were red-faced in their bonnets and gowns as he slowly wandered through their midst, just a few dozen feet from the wooden bridge which led into Old Dodge City. He lingered over candles in the Candlemaker's Shoppe, and briefly considered the line to meet Edgar Eagle in His Eyrie before he decided he had waited long enough. Another forty-five minute wait wasn't going to work for him now. It was nearly six o'clock, and Martin was hungry, and for once he didn't even want theme park food. He wanted to see Tabby, talk to her, find out if she wanted to see him again…and then he'd allow himself to leave, drive off-property, get some decent food. Or not, if her answer took away his appetite.

He walked across the bridge, the babbling brook beneath his feet dunking merrily into the murky Mighty Missouri at his right. The music from the hidden speakers switched from a stately colonial tune on strings to the sprightly sounds of a banjo, some ubiquitous folk song he'd somehow never known the name of. Ahead on the right were the Conestoga wagons, and he knew, down to his gut, that was where he'd find Tabby.

Martin made himself walk the last hundred feet, let himself be pushed along by the surging tide shoving its way towards Gold Rush Rapids, before he stepped out of their midst and stood before the Conestoga wagon.

Nick was talking to Tabby.

Martin ducked behind the wagon, his heart pounding and anxious, yet somehow slow and miserable all at once. Why was that blonde kid always around? Was there some sort of conspiracy to make him and Tabby hook up? Or was the kid behind the conspiracy? He forced himself to stand still, to listen.

"Come on, Tabby, the minute you get on break, go straight to the Chuckwagon and I'll show you."

"Fine," Tabby said, her tone flat. "If you promise it's worth my time."

"It's worth your time. I know you'll be into it! Once you see it."

"Don't disappoint me, Nick," she said, and there was a teasing tone to her voice now that made Martin's heart sink. So friendly! So comfortable! Nick was so young, too, her age. What had made him think he could compete with that?

"Tabby," Nick said, "when have I ever disappointed you?"

There was silence, or as near to silence as there could be when one was standing in a packed theme park, a banjo squealing from a nearby speaker shaped like a bird house.

He heard Tabby sigh. "Dummy," she muttered. "He's not going to let up on me, is he?" There was a rattle of plastic sunglasses, and Martin realized that Tabby was alone. He stepped around the corner of the wagon and saw Nick disappearing into Professor Cloud's.

"Tabby," Martin said, in a voice that wasn't his. "Hey."

She jumped, whirling around, and surveyed him with startled eyes. "Martin! You scared me."

"I didn't want to intrude on you and Nick," he said, somehow managing not to grind the boy's name between his teeth.

"There's nothing to intrude on. He just talks nonstop."

Martin's heart lifted a little from its resting place somewhere around his ankles. "So maybe I should have… rescued you?"

"That would have been nice!" Tabby laughed.

Martin suddenly felt dizzy, as if all the blood had rushed to his head and then just as quickly vacated it, leaving him empty-headed and oxygen-deprived. He put a hand on the Conestoga wagon to steady himself, hoping he didn't look as wobbly as he felt. "Next time, I will," he heard himself promise. "One knight, coming right up."

Tabby was looking at him like he was delightful, which was not helping his current skittery state, but he didn't want to the expression to go away, either. "I had been hoping you'd come by soon," she said, her lips somehow forming the very words he'd longed to hear and told himself not to expect. "I thought things were a little weird at the Gateway the other night."

"Well, we were stressed," Martin said valiantly. "With the whole…with the story and the plans. That was probably all it was."

"Tabby?" another voice said.

They both looked up, startled. It was Miles, the manager on duty. Martin had run into him before, had liked him. Antonia had nothing but good to say about Miles. Martin stepped back, ready to give up his position with her so that she wouldn't look bad in front of her manager.

The manager glanced over at him and smiled. "My apologies. I didn't mean to interrupt." Then he turned back to Tabby. "I need to send you on break a little early this evening, so if it comes up soon, can you just head out on it? I apologize, we're just a little short-handed."

"Of course, not a problem," Tabby agreed promptly, although Martin thought she sounded a little flustered. Was it just because she was talking to a manager, did she always get like this—or was it something to do with an early break?

Was it something to do with *Nick?*

Martin sent a thunderous glance towards the innocent wooden facades of Old Dodge City, but of course, Nick was long gone.

"Thank you," Miles was saying, turning to go.

"Where's Antonia?" Tabby asked suddenly.

"What's that?"

"Isn't Antonia the lead tonight? I'm just…I would have thought she would be handling breaks and stuff." Tabby's voice faded at the end of her sentence. "I mean, I know you can do it, too, I just…"

"Oh, no that's fine." Miles laughed. "I do know how to run breaks, I promise! But I needed to put Antonia on a special project tonight. That's all."

Tabby glanced back at Martin as the manager sped off into the crowds. "That's pretty unusual. Miles is one of the good ones who doesn't mess around with the leads' responsibilities."

"Yeah, and why does that matter so much?" Martin wondered, temporarily distracted. "Antonia is always going on about managers doing her job for her. What's the big deal?"

"It sets a precedent," Tabby said gravely. "Everything here is about precedent. You set a precedent, you make a business case for that precedent and it becomes common practice, and before you know it, boom, hours are cut, people are losing their apartments. It's a slippery slope."

"Jeez." Martin shook his head. "People just have no idea

what really goes on at theme parks, do they?"

"If they did, they wouldn't even come."

He knew he couldn't hang around her all evening. That would raise red flags to her managers, especially considering Tabby's history of stalkers, and anyway, he didn't want to come off as clingy.

But despite resolutely telling Tabby to have a good night, and that he'd call her tomorrow, Martin wasn't able to pull himself away from AtB, or even out of Old Dodge City quite yet. He went and inspected the wait time for Gold Rush Rapids first, noting Tabby's friend Sonia, from the anti-blogger meeting, waiting at the greeter position with a vacant expression on her face.

He decided one hundred and eighty minutes was too long to wait for a ride he'd been on dozens, perhaps hundreds of times, even if it *was* going to close forever in a matter of months, so he meandered off again, walking through the passage to the Forgotten Forests, taking a jouncy, bouncy ride on Sequoia Expedition.

He stopped to say hello to Harold Bear, who had shuffled out for a meet and greet just as Martn's Jeep returned to civilization.

The bear lifted his paws and touched the fur near his eyes, then his nose, then reached out and touched Martin's chest, shiny plastic claws tapping against his shirt.

Eye nose you. I know you.

Martin smiled, wondering which of his character friends was inside the bear suit. It was such a pleasure, knowing these people all around him. He often felt bad for the vacationers here, who didn't have close, personal connections with the humans of America the Beautiful.

Dusk had fallen by the time he rounded the curve back into Old Dodge City, and as he meandered slowly up the walkway, he saw Tabby walking away from her Conestoga, carrying a white break slip in her hand. It *was* early—she was only about an hour and a half into her shift. Still, even in walking away, he felt a lifting of spirit watching Tabby that all the character meet and greets in the world hadn't yet been able to give him.

"This is real," he whispered to himself, just to relish the solid sensation of the words on his lips and tongue and cheeks. Words so true and permanent they required muscles to lift and deliver. So this was what it meant to manifest.

"She's too young for you," a voice said at his elbow.

Charming and melodic, the trained modulations of a master character performer. But there was an edge there was a well, a serrated knife blade Martin could almost feel pressed against his throat.

"Amy," he said, and that, too, was a manifestation.

CHAPTER THIRTY-THREE

Antonia

Antonia's mood wasn't on the work before her. It was on bigger, more serious work—the things she could be doing someday, to better America, through this theme park.

If people were really going to take America the Beautiful as some sort of microscopic United States, the miniaturized representation of everything that was good about this crazy country, then it was management's *responsibility* to start using that influence for good. In the face of the racism debacle, Antonia didn't think Tabby's story was ridiculous anymore. She thought it ought to be true.

"Because America is being used as a generic term for one country when it really represents two massive continents filled with dozens of countries!" Antonia told Miles.

They were sequestered in the darkness of the manager's office. Banjo music leaked faintly through the walls, along with the occasional squeal of a child.

"Okay," Miles agreed absently, clicking through his emails. His elbows were on the desk, dangerously close to an open can of Coke, and Antonia moved it for him before it ended up all over the floor. She'd be the one to clean it up if that happened, anyway. Since Miles was doing important manager work, and she was just a Lead hiding out in the office when she was supposed to be out keeping tabs on the Patriots. "And what do you want me to do about that?"

"Nothing," she sputtered. "I just...I think there's opportunity here to change the national mood about race and immigration, over a long period of time."

"And you want a theme park to take that on."

"Not just a theme park," Antonia insisted. "AtB is an institution. It has an exhibit in the Smithsonian. AtB has directly affected the American experience."

"Well, I'm not saying you're wrong," Miles replied. "But I *can* tell you it's above our pay grade. Now, back to the deeply pressing national issue of a couple of merch bags being stolen on the daily. The camera test worked out and they're setting them up to start taping in the morning. I imagine we'll get some answers pretty quickly and start rounding up our suspects. Once they're cut loose or prosecuted, depending on what Legal wants to do, we're going to get all kinds of bitching about privacy. Remind everyone who complains about hidden cameras that they signed off on being filmed when they took the job, and that they're on security cameras around the corridors and in the parks constantly, anyway. This is no different."

"Except this is a set-up." Antonia pointed out.

"For people who are *stealing*," Miles amended. "Pretty sure there's no moral ambiguity about who is in the right here."

"No, I know." Antonia pushed out of her chair and pulled down the closing checklist binder, feeling a need to do something with her hands. Something about the camera set-up, the ease with which the company could step in, observe, and fire people, made her feel itchy. It wasn't that she supported Nick or any other Patriot in their decisions to steal from the company. It was that she got *why* people were doing it. She had those bills on her counter in her apartment right this minute, absolutely killing her.

And there was an added, sinister level to the way they were going about this: it worried Antonia that something so carefully crafted, so jealously guarded, as this elaborate and delicate theft ring could be outed and ended in a matter of minutes—merely by Miles, a low-level manager, sending a couple of emails to the right people.

The whole thing really illustrated the absolute power of the corporation, to define the parameters of every single interaction the employees had—how many hours they were allowed, how much money they received for them, what benefits they were entitled to, how they were surveilled on company property, even what they were allowed to do off the clock.

Antonia wondered if she was becoming a socialist.

Miles tapped away for a few more minutes while Antonia studied the binder. After a couple of weeks on the job, she thought she had the routine down pat. It was the wild card moments that threw her. Like the Patriot Values debacle, which, thankfully, was winding down now. Things were just about back to normal, if you ignored all the drama on social media. And the huge line backed up at Gold Rush Rapids. And she'd heard a couple of reports over the radio that the Forbidden Forests were getting more busy than usual, but that was due to Nate's blog.

Everything else seemed pretty normal. They were just going to set up a sting on some of her coworkers and fire them. No big deal.

Miles's phone dinged, and he glanced at the message waiting. "They're ready to start taping. Can you stay up here and monitor the feed?"

"What?"

"It would be better if we caught the person in the act instead of going back to the tape and confronting them later. That's what Security is saying, anyway. And this is decentralized, so the feed isn't going to their monitor room. Your assignment for tonight is to sit up here, watch the monitor, and call me the second something looks suspicious."

Antonia's mouth opened, but no words came out. She was going to sit here and watch a security camera feed of a stock room—her entire shift! "Wouldn't my time be better spent out on the floor? We could have a Patriot come up here and do it."

"No, needs to be a lead. Can't have just anyone watching security footage." Miles stood up and stretched. "Call me and let me know the minute you see something, okay?"

He picked up a radio, connected it to his bluetooth, and left the office.

Antonia stared at the closed door, then at the monitor, and sighed.

She finally felt comfortable as the closing lead, and she ended up as the resident narc.

Not much traffic went in and out of Professor Cloud's in mid-evening. The floor stockers did their big pulls of merchandise in early afternoon, when they arrived, and in late evening, after the night parade drew guests out to the streets to find their spots for fireworks. In the hours in between they put out the merchandise they'd brought up from the stockroom in a big plastic tub on wheels called "the whale," straightened items on shelves, and took their hour-long breaks up in the main dining room, slouching in booths with bottles of soda and gossiping about everyone back in Old Dodge City.

Consequently, Antonia's first few hours on stockroom-watch were mind-numbingly boring, and she finally gave up on constant vigilance and took out her phone to thumb through some games. But even the best matching games and word hunts were boring after a while, and she was growing increasingly paranoid about missing something, imagining movement on the screen every time the screen seemed to flicker or waver even slightly.

Six o'clock, her appointed dinner hour, came and went without a sign of back-up from the other Lead or from Miles, and Antonia's stomach began to growl. She walked backwards to the coffeemaker, her eyes on the screen, letting her gaze dart away just long enough to make sure she was grabbing the right K-Cup, and had the cup under the spigot. She reached into the cabinet beneath the coffeemaker and blindly pawed around the managers' snacks until she came out with a granola bar, then she took that and her coffee back to her desk chair. Someone would come for her eventually, or she'd call Miles and ask who her relief was, but this would get her through until things got ridiculous.

Antonia had just bitten into the granola bar when the screen changed. She sat at attention, the crumbling granola tumbling down her blouse, and watched as the door opened inward. The camera, set just to the right of the door against the ceiling, showed her the head of the person entering first. That was all she needed to see: that thick mop of blonde hair could only belong to Nick.

Antonia picked up her radio and was about to call Miles when Nick turned back to the doorway, reaching his hand out. There was somebody else? He was taking someone in? She leaned forward, wondering if a second member of the theft ring was about to be revealed.

Then she let out the breath she'd been holding with a long, sad sigh. "Oh god, honey, what are you doing?" she whispered. Of all the people she had expected to see following Nick into a life of crime, Tabby had been at the bottom of the list.

CHAPTER THIRTY-FOUR

Tabby

Tabby saw Nick leaning on the beige concrete wall outside the Chuckwagon, just as he'd said he would be, and she cursed Miles once again. If he'd just left her break on schedule, she wouldn't have come down here for another two hours, and surely Nick would have gotten bored and left by then. Waiting around for hours wasn't something Nick's restless, fun-loving brain could commit to. He would have shrugged her off and gone in search of good times and good content before many more minutes had passed.

But here he was, looking at his phone, and Tabby's step faltered just a little, not really ready to continue dealing with him. But then she remembered Martin back there in the park, and Tabby straightened her narrow shoulders. She had to be tough and put an end to all of this. Nick had to understand there was nothing romantic left between them. That attraction, fierce and bright, had burned out. He had to know that.

If only to put Martin's mind at ease.

Nick looked up from his phone and smiled. For a moment, his TV-star good looks tested Tabby's resolve. Nick was still the blonde-locked dream boy, the cutie of Old Dodge City, if not all America the Beautiful, and he'd been ready to date *her!* But that was a silly argument, Tabby chided herself. Because she knew now that he had nothing but his pretty face to offer her.

Tabby walked right up to this smiling face with her chin jutting and her lips pressed tightly together. "Nick, before you say anything—"

"*Super* quick," he interrupted, grabbing her by the hand. Before she could react, Nick was pulling her across the corridor. Some passing Cowboy Cal's girls giggled, looking back over their shoulders at what they clearly considered to be a positive development for Tabby. He stopped right outside the blank metal door to the Professor Cloud's stockroom.

"Nick, what on earth—"

"Shh…wait. It's worth it. I promise." Nick looked up and down the corridors, as if whatever he was up to required absolute privacy. Shaken into surprised acquiescence, Tabby looked around too—and when the corridor momentarily cleared of approaching traffic, she turned back to Nick expectantly.

He had already pushed open the door. Smiling, Nick drew her into the stockroom and closed the door.

"Nick," Tabby whispered. "Don't."

"Don't want?" He dropped her hands and turned away from her, walking down one of the stockroom's narrow aisles. Pausing next to a shelf he seemed to pick at random,

Nick knelt down and began to pull out a gray plastic bin, its interior stuffed with fake gemstones that kids could buy as souvenirs—just $12.99 to fill a bag, bag must fully close.

Tabby watched him in confusion. She was suddenly aware of her break ticking by. Why was she wasting her time on this nonsense when she could be sitting on her ass for a much-needed thirty-minute break, eating something salty from the Chuckwagon and drinking a Coke? "Nick, I need to go eat."

"It's not here," Nick said, and she could hear the new stress in his voice. He leaned in further, tugging, and the bin fell to the floor. Gems scattered across the concrete, purple and green and red and blue. "Where did they go?"

"Oh, *damn,* Nick, look at this mess!" Tabby rubbed her face in her hands and then knelt, picking up the gems closest to her feet. "Help me clean this up, you dummy."

But Nick suddenly shoved back from the shelving unit and looked at her wildly. "They know about the bag drop," he said. "Oh, shit, Tabby, they found it."

Tabby stopped moving and looked up at him. A sudden understanding was curdling in her chest, like a curl of spoiled milk rising to the top of a coffee cup. "Nick, what did you do?"

He looked at the floor, at the plastic jewels surrounding his feet. He was still wearing his black work shoes, and they were starting to pull apart around the soles. He needed new shoes. They all needed new shoes, all the time. For maybe three weeks out of a year, their shoes were new enough to not desperately need replacing. If there were presentable black shoes which could survive the miles of wear-and-tear of just one week at America the Beautiful, they were too expensive to be on the feet of lowly Patriots.

"Nick," Tabby hissed urgently. *"What. Did. You. Do."*

"It was just a way to get ahead of the ad costs," he said, still looking at the ground, still not moving to pick up the merchandise he'd scattered over the floor. Someone was going to have to clean it up, Tabby thought. Neither of them were on the clock, but she was still on a shift, so it was probably going to fall to her. That was some shit. That was what she got for letting Nick drag her around. That was what she got for talking to him at all.

She should have known better.

She should have cut Nick off weeks ago. Even before their stupid dates, when she was just mooning after him and trying to get his attention, when she'd been dazzled by his pretty face and sunshine hair, she should have known then that Nick was going to be bad news—now and forever, because some people were simply too selfish and too foolish to comprehend the damage they could wreak on other people's lives.

But how could she have known that? Everything she'd done since she'd come to America the Beautiful had been a lesson. Hard lesson after hard lesson. She had come here with nothing, with an upbringing which had prepped her for little besides a teenage pregnancy, an abusive marriage, and a collapsing mobile home somewhere in a Kentucky holler. She had escaped through college and through AtB, but it wasn't like her luck in escaping had come with a ready-made education in the wiles of the world downloaded directly into her brain.

She still had to make these mistakes, over and over again. She still had to learn everything for herself.

Tabby straightened, dropping the jewels she had picked up, and put her hand on the door handle behind her.

"The ad costs," Nick repeated. "You have to pay to promote posts, that's the only way to build an audience. I was investing…"

"I have to go."

"Don't go, Tabby," Nick said pleadingly. "Please don't leave me with this."

That was when she decided she hated him.

"You want me to go down with you? When I've done nothing? Thanks, Nick. Thanks for letting me know exactly how important I am to you. Nothing but someone to keep you from feeling alone." Tabby felt a sneer twist her lips. "I should have known you'd end up getting me into trouble if I gave you your way. Good luck, Nick."

She opened the door handle and turned to leave.

But the way out was blocked—by Miles, looking triumphant, and by a security guard, looking winded—and behind them both, Antonia, looking horrified.

CHAPTER THIRTY-FIVE

Nate

The best thing about the blog post? It had to be that it hadn't mattered how wrong he'd been.

Nate had gotten a call from AtB's press office bright and early the morning after the post went live. He'd looked at the number in astonishment before answering his phone—the exchange gave it away as an official AtB number. He'd answered as professionally as possible: "This is Nate from AtBLive. How can I help you?"

As if he had a fleet of staffers and anyone could have answered the phone.

The woman who had called him was straightforward, her voice brooking no nonsense. She shared her bullet points in clipped sentences. There was no such plan in place to change the Forgotten Forests. All the company's creative efforts were focused on developing a family-friendly experience at the all-new Gold Rush Rapids and Old

Dodge City expansion, details of which were forthcoming later this summer. "And which you already shared word of with your readers," she added, somewhat acidly, "so you're well aware it's coming."

Nate felt slightly sheepish that he'd printed so much confidential information about the Old Dodge City changes and made this woman's life more difficult. She sounded pretty hot, actually. It was a shame she'd never give him the time of day.

He waited for her to say goodbye and hang up, already mentally composing the retraction he'd add to the post. Crazy, though. The girl from Gold Rush had seemed so sure. And he'd gotten the memo from several other sources

—

"We'd like to offer you a spot on our next blog publisher briefing," the PR rep went on, not sounding as if she'd particularly like to offer him anything besides a kick in the balls. "We haven't narrowed down a date yet, but it should be in late August and will include tours, some presentations, and some ways that the press office can work with you to provide the best and most timely information to your readers."

Nate's jaw had dropped. All of this, and he was being *rewarded*. He was being added to the list of approved bloggers, invited to press events! He'd made it!

"I'd like that," he told her. "Thank you very much."

Celebrating the good news with an evening at AtB was an easy decision. He noticed, but chose not to publicize, some random sign-wavers near the AtB parking entrance who were protesting the replacing the Forbidden Forests with of Mexicans. But he was happy to live-tweet some of the insanity going down around the long queues for Gold Rush

Rapids.

Besides, if he waited here long enough, the girl who had sold him the binder might show up.

He'd been standing near the entrance plaza for about an hour and the sun was setting behind the mountain when she appeared to take over for the current Greeter.

"Greeter again?" the current Patriot said, smirking. "You always get Greeter!"

"It's fixed now, this is just luck of the draw."

"Well, thanks for the break, Sonia." The Patriot took a slip from her and headed towards Old Dodge City.

Sonia, Nate thought. He'd been planning on confronting her, but now he lost his nerve. He started to slink away.

"Hey you!" Sonia called. "Nate, you racist asshole, get over here."

The Patriot on her way to break turned around. "Did you just say that *in front of guests?*"

Sonia rolled her eyes. "Get over it, Kenisha. Look around you. No one even noticed me saying it."

It was true, Nate realized in surprise. The absence of swear words was supposed to make America the Beautiful an enchanted land free from profanity…but swearing had become such a normal part of modern vocabulary that apart from one or two aggrieved glances in Sonia's direction, there was no reaction at all. No one died. No children lost their innocence. Lawrence Taylor didn't rise up from the grave to smite the transgressor down.

Interesting, Nate thought. Not that it made swearing onstage okay, but…interesting. Something to think about. Maybe something to write about?

The moment he spent considering the lack of outrage was a moment lost for him. Sonia took the opportunity to cross the rock-studded concrete in front of Gold Rush and stand before him, hands on her hips. She glared at him, saying nothing, until he couldn't stand it.

"What?" he asked, for lack of any other coherent thought. She just looked so damn angry and terrifying.

"I know you wrote that story to try to get the racists up and going," Sonia snarled. "I read it. You put your own twist on things. You made it as divisive as possible, and you did it to get clicks without ever considering what effect that would have on people. The point of the story wasn't to be racist. The point was to rumor the closing of a beloved attraction. You're an *asshole*. A *racist asshole*. And I want to be sure you know it. So when you're out there enjoying your blogger fame, you still know that you're a racist asshole."

"You fed me a false story!" Nate protested. "The press office called me and told me none of it was true! I should be yelling at you!"

"Did you pay me for it?" Sonia asked.

"What? No."

"Well then, I gave you free publicity," she said, shrugging. "I don't see what you're mad about. The only people who should be mad are the ones who care about AtB as a place where people can live and grow, not the ones who want to lock it up in some precious little whitewashed version of America's past."

"You fed me a fake story to try to collapse my blog," Nate retorted indignantly. "Don't think I didn't figure that out the second the press office called me. You weren't just mistaken, and all those memos—those were from friends of yours, right? Who cooked it up?"

"So what if they were? Did it work? Who is the failure here? You didn't confirm the story. You didn't do the bare minimum of journalism work, Nate. How is that on me?"

Nate tried and failed to come up with a response to this. Sonia seemed, against all odds, to be absolutely correct. Or maybe she really was just smarter than he was.

Either way, he still came out ahead.

"I'm not a racist," he said finally.

Kenisha was at Sonia's elbow. "I know this is really important to you as like, a weird personal vendetta, but I'd really like to go on my break, and I can't until I know you're going to take over my position."

Sonia shrugged the other Patriot off. "Fine, I'm taking it over. Go to break." She gave Nate one more poisonous glare. "Nate, please remember you're a racist asshole. Every time you are gloating over how you came out ahead on this one, just keep in mind the racist asshole part. Can you do that for me? Thanks."

She turned on her heel, leaving an astonished Nate in her wake.

Several other guests, all of them lone men, had paused to eavesdrop on the argument. One of them held out a hand. "Are you Nate from AtBLive?"

"I sure am," Nate said, feeling a little dizzy.

"Great to meet you! I'm a fan!"

"That's great," Nate replied absently. "I appreciate it."

"Come on, man, I've got a QuikRide pass for Gold Rush Rapids. We'll take you with us."

There was a chorus of *yeahs* from the other guys.

"I don't have a pass," Nate explained. "I have to wait in the standby queue."

"Nah," the fan said. "We'll just bug the greeter until she lets you ride with us."

Nate glanced over at Sonia. She was watching him with

beady eyes.

"I think I have to be somewhere," he said evasively. "But thanks! Enjoy the ride!"

Nate scurried away, leaving his fans in his wake.

Nate had found his way into Professor Cloud's and was browsing around a new collection of gem-studded Patriot Pal statuettes when he heard a commotion by the store's back door—the one he knew led to a hallway and the stairs to the corridors.

Now, Nate knew that he'd been granted a reprieve from the press office, even if he had started an international online incident that was apparently outing many well-known theme park fans as white supremacists, at least at the hobbyist level. He knew that he'd posted confidential information once, and total bullshit information immediately afterwards, and that the preferred reaction from the higher-ups at AtB was probably something closer to a tar-and-feathers treatment rather than welcoming him into the fold. But he knew they couldn't discount things like clicks and engagement, and AtBLive had both.

And they trusted that *Nate* knew that once he was invited into the official blog family, he would be expected to keep things on the up-and-up. No more stolen binders of concept art. No more articles with a twist guaranteed to flare up controversy—because Sonia was right, of course. He *had* seen the potential for conflict when he'd written the post, and even if he hadn't meant for it to be overtly racist, he'd definitely written it to try to get people emotional over changing America the Beautiful from a strictly USA-park to an international "Americas" park. He'd written it knowing he was going to drive a wedge between political extremists on both sides. He'd written it as *any* savvy blogger who wanted hits at any cost would have written it. He'd done a good job, actually, even if the racists had been way louder than he would have preferred.

But he knew he was expected to put all of that behind him now, and find other ways to titillate readers.

He knew all of that and still he was drawn towards the sound of a kerfuffle the moment it presented itself, because that was just who he was.

An incurably nosey man, with an ear for drama and a taste for gossip.

Nate found an interesting case of collectible trading pins to browse right next to the manager, who was on his phone.

"Tell the security guard to meet me at the Professor Cloud's stockroom. Right now, that's when! Yeah, we have it on tape, but I'd rather catch him in the act. Them. There's two of them. Yeah, across from the Chuckwagon. Thank you. Yes, *now!* Thank you. Okay." The manager ended the call and glanced at the Patriot next to him. "Winslow, hold down the fort while I'm gone."

The Patriot looked non-committal, but the manager ducked through the door without waiting for an answer.

Nate looked at the door yearningly, the white light from the fluorescent bulbs in that utilitarian hallway slipping under the wood and casting a modern glow on the old-fashioned surroundings. He was dying to know what was going on beyond that door. What he wouldn't give for a Patriot ID badge right about now! He could give chase to the manager, slip down the stairwells he knew were back there—he'd seen the photos posted on backdoor blogs and insider forums—and hide behind steel columns when necessary, racing like a spy through the network of corridors until he found whatever it was that required a security guard. Right across from the Chuckwagon. And where would that be?

He knew better than to open doors. He knew he couldn't go wandering around in Patriot-only areas. He'd be caught. He'd be trespassed.

Nate forced himself to walk around the store slowly. He took in the merchandise on the walls, he nodded at the Patriots standing by their tills. He walked back to the counter near the door, resolute that he'd walk right past it, and out the front door into the park, and get over it.

The Patriot left to mind the shop, Winslow, had walked away from the till. He was standing in the front door, looking out at the promenade, at the people filing past in the gas-lit darkness.

And he'd left his ID lanyard laying next to the till.

Nate looked up, just to confirm something he'd already known: Professor Cloud's was an old store and didn't have security cameras aimed down at each register the way more recently opened stores had. Smooth, blank ceiling stared back at him. No sneaky lenses.

There was nothing to stop him. No one was looking.

With one smooth movement, the ID went into Nate's pocket, and he ducked out of the other shop door. Winslow would notice if he went through the back door, but there weren't many corners of AtB that Nate hadn't inspected thoroughly, and he knew about the door in the alcove just a little ways down the boardwalk.

Nate dropped the ID over his head and felt it bounce against his stomach, and the sheer boldness of his plan made him feel invincible again. He was going to find out what was happening across from the Chuckwagon…and who knows what else he might find down there, in the forbidden corridors.

What a day, he thought, pushing open the door and looking down at the beige-painted staircase. What an amazing *fucking* day he was having.

CHAPTER THIRTY-SIX

Sonia

Kenisha finally went on her break with a warning look for Sonia, tossed over her shoulder like a grenade, and Sonia smirked at her in response. If Kenisha still wanted to impress Richie, well, he was the lead on that night and she would have the opportunity to turn Sonia in for shouting at a guest and whatever she'd overheard…if anyone would believe her story.

That was what led Sonia to do it in the first place: the realization that no one would ever believe it of her. She had an excellent track record. Her lead request had been approved for consideration by other regions looking to fill positions. She had behaved herself through the whole Greeter-only debacle, not filing a grievance even though she'd been well with in her rights to do it. Sonia was a Patriot with a good reputation, and, crucially, Kenisha was not.

"Welcome to Gold Rush Rapids!" Sonia announced to an approaching family, her smile as big and broad as a Western sunset. Two adults, male and female, dragging two little children, twisting and complaining in their parents' grip. Both adults looked exhausted and determined, which was a common expression for parents who had made it to the evening hours after a full day at a theme park. "Can we just measure the heights of your little whippersnappers there?"

The mother pulled up short, toddler boy keening and yowling at her side. She shook her wrist at him, jostling his entire arm. "They're tall enough," the woman said in a voice jagged with exhaustion. "They *love* this ride."

The little girl pulling her father's hand in the opposite direction seemed to indicate otherwise.

Sonia decided to go directly to the source. Sometimes that was the easiest way to deal with reluctant parents. "All right, young 'uns, who here wants to be first on the old measuring stick?" She touched the crossbar of the height indicator. "You must be this tall to ride!"

The little girl, sensing an out, broke free and jumped under the crossbar. She smirked at the scant inch between the top of her frizzy blonde hair and the wooden bar. "Not tall enough!" she crowed. "Too short!"

The father's lips tightened. "Now Jaycee," he began tensely, "We know you've been on this ride before—"

"I'm really sorry, sir," Sonia interrupted, indicating to little Jaycee that it was time to scoot off and make way for her brother, "but if she did ride this before, it was against our safety regulations and she shouldn't have been allowed. I'm really sorry for any inconvenience. Can I suggest some of our other more height-appropriate rides?" She dropped the western act for this spiel; the occasion now called for more professional customer-service speak, filled with rounded vowels and helpful upward lilts at the end of questions.

"Now you listen here," the father hissed, leaning in. "We have ridden this ride before and we are riding it tonight. All of us."

Sonia looked from side to side as significantly as possible, to indicate that all the whispering in the world couldn't hide that this tall male guest was being disrespectful to this small female Patriot. Several passersby noticed her gesture and paused, glancing first at her and then at the parent with a combination of interest and alarm. Adding on more guests to the situation was usually Sonia's preferred way of de-escalating potential guest incidents. Shame was a powerful tool.

"I'm really sorry, sir," Sonia repeated, her voice more firm this time, a touch louder, for the benefit of the onlookers. "I can't work around any safety regulations, and you saw that her head didn't reach the height requirement. This is for the safety of your children and your fellow guests. But we do have a lot of rides with no height—"

"WE HAVE RIDDEN THIS BEFORE AND WE ARE RIDING IT NOW!" the father roared, squeezing his daughter's hand so tightly that she howled in protest.

Beside him, the mother was looking at the ground, sighing, and the toddler son was still wailing and winding his hand around in her grip, trying half-heartedly to escape, as if he knew that getting loose wouldn't get him what he wanted.

"Let me get you my manager, sir," Sonia said stiffly, annoyed they had reached the shouting stage over such a clear-cut case of Too-Short-Kid. For some Patriots, Sonia included, not escalating at situation to management was a point of pride. How was she going to be considered for lead if she was always calling for back-up instead of handling situations for herself? But here this asshole was, clearly lying about riding Gold Rush Rapids before, making her mess up her excellent track record. *Jerk.*

She hit the talk button on her radio. "Gold Rush Greeter to Gold Rush Ops One," she said into the mic. "Assistance at Gold Rush Greeter required."

"Ten-four, on my way," the manager replied. Tonight it was Gavin; Sonia liked him. She repressed a smile and assured the father, who was looking at her with blood in his eye, that the manager was en route.

"I'm going to tell him how discourteous you have been," the man growled at her.

Sonia just nodded and stepped to one side, still blocking them from entering the queue, but making sure they understood she was back to greeting every other guest arriving, and that they were no longer her concern. Had they been nice to her and simply asked if they could speak to a manager about their height requirements, she would have made friendly conversation with them until Gavin arrived. But these weren't the sort of people you made nice with. These were the sort of people you made simmer in whatever limited capacity you could.

By the time Gavin arrived, looking dapper in a blue shirt with the sleeves rolled up and freshly pressed khakis, his dark gray hair slicked back with gel, the father was fairly bursting with anger. The toddlers were still just trying to get back to their strollers, or their hotel, or maybe back home —anywhere but here. The mother had lost interest, but she stood by her man, a weary look on her face.

Gavin drew them off to one side, let them rant, nodded his head a lot, spread his hands in apology. Sonia watched with open interest as she continued doing her job: greeting guests, measuring children (some of whom were not tall enough but who bore the disappointment with grace—she handed them all front-of-the-line cards for when they were finally tall enough to ride).

When Sonia got her clock-out slip, they were still standing there, still making Gavin look slightly crazed, their children having given up on the prospect of ever returning to their stroller and sitting tiredly on the concrete. At least the sun had sunk behind the looming orange edifice of Gold Rush Rapids and given the kids a little respite from the blazing heat.

Just like the respite she was about to get, Sonia thought happily, as she headed down into the Underground. She pocketed the slip, waved goodbye to her replacement, and went back to the break room to get her bag and clock out.

By the computer, Richie was standing on his own, looking at his phone. Sonia was clutched by a sudden hunger for the truth. "Richie," she said. "Tell me why I only got Greeter for weeks. Who did that, and what was the point?"

Richie looked up from his phone, looking confused. "What do you mean?"

"Richie, come on. Someone took my work permissions out on the portal, and they're back, which is great, but…I just want to know *why.*"

Richie ran his hands through his hair and looked around. The break room was empty. "Fine," he said, lowering his voice to a near-whisper. "It was Bobby's idea."

"Bobby?" The friendly management intern, the guy who

was supposed to take their side on everything, the guy who had promised he was here to be a Patriot defender, who would lower the transfer rate so that everyone would want to stay here and be a big happy team forever and ever? Bobby was like a big, friendly hound dog. He was the last person who would do this to her. "No. That can't be right."

"It wasn't…*malicious*. If that's the word I'm looking for. It wasn't a punishment. The way it was explained to me, he wanted to see how long a person would put up with it before they demanded someone fix it. I guess he tried it out on Jasmine first and she had it fixed within a single shift. So you were the second experiment, and…you let it go for a month." Richie shrugged. "He was impressed."

"I didn't let it go, though! I asked you why it was happening before and you said there was nothing going on!"

"You didn't do anything but ask to get it fixed. You didn't threaten to quit, and you didn't go to the union. And those were the parameters. Bobby was really clear on that. Curiosity was not the same as demanding it be changed."

"Oh my God," Sonia said. "So, Bobby's insane, right?"

"I mean, he's trying to prove a point to someone, somewhere. That's all I know."

"You know what, Richie? Sometimes, I honestly think this place is going to drive me insane." Sonia ran a hand through her hair. "I mean, I love it here, but shit's crazy. And it rubs off."

"I think that's obvious, looking at the thirty-year Patriots."

Sonia shook her head.

"Please don't tell anyone about this," Richie said. "It ruins the experiment if you tell, so Bobby will be mad at me. And he's promised to help me get into management once he has a full-time position."

Sonia just sighed and walked out, not ready to promise anything. Maybe Bobby was trying to prove something about their resilience in difficult positions, or maybe he was just being a jerk. With managers, it was hard to tell.

Gavin, she noticed, was still with the family from hell—and he'd called in back-up from Guest Services. *Jeez,* she thought. All for a ride.

Sonia was ambling through the corridor under Old Dodge City when she saw the security guards following a retail manager at a pretty decent clip up ahead of her. Antonia was right on their heels, walking stiffly.

Sonia sighed. She hoped they'd turn right at the end of the corridor ahead, not left towards the bus stop. She didn't want to deal with some security drama after clocking out. She just wanted to get the hell home.

But of course they stopped just before the turn, at that blank door across from the Chuckwagon. Sonia's steps slowed. It was the door she'd tailed the Sequoia Patriot to. The room where the girl had obviously stowed that merch bag that was meant for a delivery.

You don't want to know, Sonia told herself. *Go home.*

Still, she ambled as she approached the corner. The security guards were waiting for the manager to open the door; Antonia was standing behind them, her hands to her mouth. In a few minutes, she'd be past them.

One Security Patriot said something to another. Sonia strained to hear them, but all she could hear was the husky voice of the evening radio hostess on the overhead speakers, assuring her caller that she would play the singularly inappropriate *I Will Always Love You* for the woman's six-year-old daughter, Brooklyn.

"Brook Lynn," the mother corrected tearfully. "Two words. And thank you."

"What a beautiful name," the hostess crooned. "I'm sure she has a beautiful soul."

Sonia wished they left the corridors in silence. Anything was better than this drivel.

Then, when she was almost past them, the manager opened the door.

Sonia heard a shriek from inside the room that made her jump—and turn back. Had that been... *Tabby?*

She ducked behind a concrete pillar at the corner of the Chuckwagon and peered around, but she couldn't see past the bulk of the security guards blocking the entrance. Heart pounding, she willed one of them to move. She heard voices—a boy and a girl—and instantly realized she was hearing a tearful, panicking Nick.

Why would Tabby be in that unmarked room with *Nick?* What was he doing to her? Did Nick have it in him to assault a woman? Sonia couldn't really see it happening, but her mother used to say that still ponds hid dangerous depths, which she had always taken to mean that anything was possible—even perfectly nice people doing terrible things. And Tabby did have that history, made up or not, which had kept not-nice guys panting over her all last year. If Nick had heard she was easy and had just been taking a break from guys for a while, he might have decided it was time to she got back to work. With him.

She heard him saying something, but she could barely make out the words under Whitney Houston's throaty roar. Was he apologizing? Was he saying he didn't do it? Sonia was about to leap out from behind the pillar and demand to know what was happening when she realized someone else was with her. She turned, and their eyes locked.

For a single shocked moment, Sonia couldn't move. Couldn't think. Couldn't believe what she was seeing. Then she managed to get control of her lips, her tongue, her brain.

"What the *fuck* are you doing here, you racist asshole?"

CHAPTER THIRTY-SEVEN

Antonia

Antonia knew her job was to stay by the screen, make sure everything was on the up and up during the raid or the arrest or whatever the hell it was they were going to do down there, but she couldn't sit by and wait while Tabby got hauled out of the stockroom alongside that little rat Nick. She, Antonia, was the one who had sounded the alarm. She had put her job in front of Tabby, and she felt heartsick over it. Not just heartsick—*sick*, sick. Antonia felt like she was going to throw up all over Miles's desk, and maybe that wouldn't be such a bad thing.

But as soon as she put down the phone, she knew she had to try. Had to see if she could stop this thing from happening—at least from happening to Tabby. There were no cameras trained on the outside door, so she could haul open the door, tell Tabby to run, and slam it shut on Nick's surprised face without ever being spotted by the camera, without ever having to take the blame for ruining the raid she had called in herself—assuming, of course, that Nick didn't tell on her. And why wouldn't he, really?

So maybe it wasn't the best plan, but it was the only way she could redeem herself. Redeem herself *and* keep her job, which was non-negotiable. The same things which had led her to consider joining Nick's stupid crime ring were the same things which would keep her from martyring herself to save her friend. Whether Tabby went down or not, Antonia would still have student loan payments. She would still have rent. She would still have her car. She would still need to eat. And while yes, Tabby could lay claim to all of those needs as well, there was one crucial difference between Antonia and Tabby right now.

Antonia hadn't gone into that stockroom with Nick tonight.

But there was no way Tabby had known what was waiting for in there.

Either way, Antonia thought, slamming back the office door and charging down the metal staircase to the corridor, Tabby didn't have to lose her job over this. Tabby was not involved. Tabby was a sweet, innocent, dumb little thing, but she was no idiot. If that made sense.

Antonia ran down the corridor, but as soon as she rounded the turn that would give her a view of the Chuckwagon and the stockroom door across from it, she knew she was too late. The security guards were almost there, Miles just ahead of them. He was ready to throw open the door and catch two idiots red-handed, stashing merch bags to be picked up by Marcelo's crew member on the third shift.

Well, to catch just one idiot, and one Tabby, who had

walked into the firing line with as much self-awareness as a fawn wandering into a hunting range.

Antonia stopped running then, because it would just make her look suspicious anyway, and she walked, catching her breath with an effort, past the old metal lockers with their peeling stickers and past the collections of cardboard recycling all bound up and waiting for removal and past the extra pallets of retail bags and bottled water and flats of potato chip packages, all the things that a theme park could never have too much of. She walked down the middle of the corridor, unlike the other Patriots passing by, who walked as far to the opposite side of the action as they could, never willing to get involved in anything which required security, especially if they were off the clock. She walked alone, her heart heavy, right up to the security guards, even though she knew she was supposed to be back in the office and right now, and right now, and right *now* she could still turn back, make it back up to her post, and never be caught shirking her responsibilities.

She stood behind the closest security guard, uncertain of what to do next. She saw Tabby and her hands went to her mouth to stop a squeak of dismay. Even if she'd said anything or made a noise, they wouldn't have turned; they were too intent on the goings-on inside the stock room. She heard Miles speak: "Look, we have everything we need to prosecute you. But I'm sure there are others involved with this, so if you're willing to talk, we can make this whole thing go away."

It was like he'd learned his lines from a crime television show. Would a cop ever say, "make this whole thing go away"? Would a lawyer? Was that even a promise they could make?

Antonia was on the verge of opening her mouth, announcing her presence, when a flash of movement to the left caught her eye. She turned her head and saw a man being pushed from behind a pillar by a pair of small hands.

"Nate?" she gasped.

The security guards turned. "Can we help you, ma'am?" one of them asked her, his voice heavy with boredom.

"Yeah," Antonia snapped, suddenly back in control. "You can arrest that guy for trespassing." And she pointed at Nate, who was staring at them with a look of dismay on his face, no longer pushing back at the little hands pummeling his chest.

"He stole an ID," Sonia shouted, coming around the pillar, her face flushed. "This guy's a blogger. He's looking for material to publish!"

One of the security guards, a mild-looking fellow whose name tag read "Blake", stepped forward. "Sir, you want to show me that ID, please?"

"It looks nothing like him," Sonia scoffed. "And his name is Nate, not Winslow."

Antonia stared at Nate and strongly considered screaming. Was everyone around her just absolutely insane? Had everyone lost any sense of what was right and safe and practical around this place? The blogger was in the Underground now? The most sacred place to Patriots, the *one damn place* where they couldn't be followed?

Nate looked at Blake, standing ten feet away from him with a patient expression on his bland face. He looked at Sonia, the banshee next to him who was still fixing her gaze on him with obviously violent intent. And then he looked at Antonia, and she would swear that at the sight of her, a woman who had threatened him many times, his face crumpled.

Nate turned and ran.

Blake was after him after a moment of shocked hesitation, and no wonder—chases weren't a common element of theme park security. Most people understood that they were surrounded by berms, and gates, and throngs of humanity. There was literally no escaping a theme park unless the people inside wanted you to. There would always be someone waiting for you at the turnstile, with a smug smile and a sheriff's deputy on hand.

But Nate did the unthinkable, just like he had done so many times in the past few weeks. And Antonia had to give the jerk credit: he was bold. He had built himself up into the resort's premier reporter and critic in a less than a month because he wasn't afraid to take chances. No one, to her knowledge, had ever snuck into the Underground to get a story.

And no one ever would again, after they saw what happened to Nate.

Antonia wondered if he really thought he'd get away, or if this was just the last-ditch effort of a man who realized he had just lost everything he had worked for.

Everything he cared about.

In that moment, Antonia actually felt bad for Nate. His whole life was America the Beautiful, and he was about to get trespassed from the parks for the rest of that life. What the hell would he do then?

Probably move to Orlando and terrorize the Cast Members at Disney World, she thought wryly. And with that, Antonia banished Nate and his sad fate from her head.

She had actual problems, with actual friends.

Miles was looking out of the stockroom now, and he

caught her eye. "Antonia? What's going on?"

"That blogger," she said. "The one we've been having trouble with."

"Oh, no kidding. In the corridor?"

"Yup."

"Bold."

"Yeah, that's exactly what I thought." Antonia was impatient with the small talk. "Miles, what's going on in there?"

"I'm just talking to them. I gave them a minute to talk amongst themselves. Make up their minds."

"You know that Tabby wasn't involved in this."

"Do I?"

"She told you she wasn't, didn't she?"

"She hasn't told me anything," Miles said, shrugging. "She's backed up against the wall, looking like I'm about to murder her in here, and I sent Nick back to talk some sense into her."

Antonia felt an old tugging misery, the same way she'd felt when she'd first fallen for Tabby months ago, the same way she'd felt when she'd kissed Tabby and known the girl would not be hers for long. The feeling that Tabby was an innocent who couldn't cope with the big, larger-than-life feelings that surrounded her. That America the Beautiful in its most pure, guest-friendly form was always going to be the walled city she preferred to live in, apart from the sadness of her childhood and yet still apart from the frightening freedom of the outside world. And when things like this, real world things, intruded on the safety of her theme park life, Tabby would always just shut down rather than learn to confront them.

Things like this, like Antonia's affection, that were too

frightening to confront.

She suddenly wondered where Martin was.

"Tabby doesn't have theft in her," Sonia said, and Antonia jumped, not realizing the Ops girl was standing next to her. She was looking at Miles. "You must know that. You're her manager. You've been around her enough."

"How do you know it's theft?" Miles asked, his eyebrows raising.

Sonia rolled her eyes, brash in a way Antonia couldn't help but admire. "If you have your eyes open, you see everything going on around here. I was in a store a few days ago, heard some Patriots talking about it. I saw one of them stash her bag in here. Easy to figure out. It's not the first time."

"No," Miles said thoughtfully. "It's not. Where did you hear the talk before?"

"I don't have to tell you that."

"You do, actually."

"I'm off the clock," Sonia pointed out.

Miles considered this, as if he wasn't fully sure if this was a good reason for Sonia's non-compliance or not. "You're in the corridor, though," he said eventually. A weak point, Antonia thought. "On property."

"I don't have to be. I could leave at any moment."

"She doesn't have to tell you," one of the remaining security guards said. "It's reasonable suspicion or doubt or something, I forget which. And we have to go. Blake is radioing for back-up."

"Fine, I'll deal with these two," Miles said. "Thanks for being here."

"Where is Blake at?" Antonia asked as the men started to move away.

"The Big Apple back stairwell," one of them said. "He let the guy get out into the park, I guess."

"Shit."

Antonia stared at their departing backs. So, Nate had made it out of the corridors. That, in itself, was a triumph. She wondered if he'd make it out of the park.

Then what? He grew a huge mustache? Changed his name? Got plastic surgery? She wouldn't put it past him.

"He won't get away," Sonia said, guessing her thoughts. "He's going down. And he deserves to."

"Aren't you afraid he'll take you down with him?" Antonia asked, just to see what she'd do.

But Sonia didn't back down from her appraising glance. "I made sure he can't pin it on me," she said. "His word against mine, and my evidence against his." She winked at Antonia.

And Antonia decided she wanted to know more about Sonia, after all. More about what evidence she had that somehow exonerated her from things she had most certainly done, and more about the rest of her as well: where she came from, where she wanted to be, what made her laugh. Those kinds of things.

But first, Tabby.

Antonia joined Miles inside the stockroom. Nick was, indeed, standing at the back, talking earnestly to Tabby, but she was clearly not listening to him. Or looking at him. She had her face to the wall, her shoulders heaving.

"You have to let her go," Antonia told Miles.

He shook his head at her. "I need to know how she's involved. If no one's talking, no one's leaving. And Nick is being pretty tight-lipped, too."

"That son of a *bitch,*" Antonia swore.

Miles actually jumped. "Antonia! What's your deal with Nick?"

"He needs to be honest right now and tell you he just dragged Tabby in here to show you what a criminal mastermind he is. And we both know that's not even the case. Nick's just an errand boy, just like the rest of them."

As soon as Antonia said it, she knew what she had to do.

Miles dragged a fascinated gaze over her face. "What do you know?"

"I know it's all Nick, and not Tabby."

"Antonia, you're a lead. If you know something about organized theft, you have to tell me. That Ops girl out there, well, that area's fuzzy. But you…come on. You know you have to tell me. Or I won't be able to trust you. The entire management team won't. That'll be it for lead. And your lead position…you only got it at all because they threw extra headcount at us to help deal with the Gold Rush crowds they knew were coming. You were qualified, of course, but that's how you got it overnight. And that's how you can lose it overnight."

She knew. But she was determined. "You let Tabby go, and I'll tell you."

"You *swear* Tabby's innocent?"

"I swear."

"And then you'll be honest with me?"

"I'm always honest with you." Antonia met his gaze and sighed. "But yes. I'll tell you everything I know."

Tabby

Tabby's brain had shut down, and she didn't know what to do about it, wasn't particularly pleased about it, was actually quite embarrassed about it, but there was nothing for it but to wait things out.

So she stood in the back of the stockroom, forehead against the cool concrete wall, and did just that.

Nick was whispering in her ear frantically; she didn't really hear the words, just knew that he was standing there, too close to her. Finally, she got enough control of her hands to shove him away from her. He protested, then went away from her. Back to the front of the stockroom, she supposed, back where Miles and those security guards had burst through the door and accused them both of being thieves.

In that moment, Tabby had seen a terrifying glimpse of her future: of courtrooms and plea deals and probation, of a lost job and a lost apartment and a lost car, of a bus ticket back to Kentucky and the excruciating moment she walked through the half-broken screen door of her mother's trailer, disheveled and miserable after a twelve-hour journey, somehow in the exact same position she would have been if she'd never defied her parents and Jesus and gone off to college and escaped to the sinful delights of America the Beautiful in the first place.

The idea that none of this had ever mattered, that all of this would fade behind her like a beautiful dream which ended in a screaming night terror, that she had simply deferred her fate by a few years, was the single most heart-breaking thing Tabby had ever faced.

And Tabby had seen quite a lot of horror in her life, although she never really thought about her childhood of drunken shouting and hidden meth labs and sinning pastors and bullets through beer cans in that way.

But wait—somehow, she was escaping the room, with her heart in her throat, her fingers tracing Antonia's arm as she squirmed past Miles in the doorway. They were letting her go, but she'd never be able to trust him again. She'd have to transfer out of Old Dodge City as soon as possible —assuming she *did* keep her job—or thinking about this moment every time she saw him would drive her to tears, right there in front of guests and God and everyone.

She wondered if he'd fire Antonia. She'd heard Antonia, when she couldn't be bothered to hear Nick, telling him that she knew what was happening, that she'd already known before…whatever this was. This bizarre set-up, somehow entrapping her along with Nick. She'd heard Antonia ask for her safety in exchange for information. Antonia might be giving up her job for Tabby to keep hers.

It was horrifying. It was too much.

Tabby ran.

She was wearing her Old Dodge City costume, still a prairie girl, still the theme park version of Laura Ingalls before she was Wilder, printed calico skirt and ruffle-fronted blouse with genuine imitation pearl buttons at the little collar. Slip-on black shoes and nude knee-highs. Pigtails and no make-up, just sandy eyelashes and freckles on her tan face. Name-tag pinned neatly in the little rectangle of doubled-over fabric made especially for that purpose. She didn't have a change of clothes, didn't have a jacket, didn't stop to think about any of this. She just ran up the corridor, the weight of her water bottle slapping at her hip until it popped free and went rolling away in her wake. Patriots stared, a few passing managers shouted. But Tabby didn't stop running.

When she saw the security guards, obvious and bright in their shiny blue jackets, step into the intersection of two corridors just ahead, Tabby's step faltered just a little. She could turn off to go towards the bus back to the parking lot, or keep running straight to head into the corridor beneath The Big Apple. But maybe they were going to stop her from running, and maybe, she didn't know, maybe Miles' word was enough to protect her, or maybe he didn't mean it and she was going to be arrested, anyway. Tabby's eyes darted left and right, looking for a way out. There were just the smooth concrete walls, the pallets of extra bags and merchandise, the wide eyes of the Patriots she was passing.

And then there was a stairwell. An EXIT sign.

She darted into the stairwell and raced up the metal stairs, the clanging beneath her feet a reassurance that something real was happening, this wasn't all inside her head, she wasn't still back inside that room waiting to be interrogated or led away to jail or put on a bus back home. She knew where she was, where these stairs led: they would let her out just behind Promise Mountain, into a little fenced off area where extra rental strollers were kept and rented out in the Primrose Meadow shop, part of the lovely terraced gardens behind Promise Mountain.

She burst out into a sparkling theme park version of a summer evening; the lanterns lit the gardens like big golden fireflies under the dark blue dome of late twilight. This was always the most quiet section of the park, and Tabby didn't expect to find many people milling around at this time of night.

But she hadn't counted on Nate.

Nate was in the center of the statue garden, standing beneath a marble sculpture of a woman clad in a Grecian robe and cradling a lamb—she was supposed to represent the farms of the Midwest or something like that, although Tabby was pretty sure sheep were not big business in the Midwest. He wasn't moving much, but she could see from the heaving of his chest that he'd been doing some running not typical of his daily routine. Tabby stood still for a moment, arrested by the sight of four security guards advancing towards him through the maze of low hedges containing the statue garden—there was something beyond comical about their twists and turns, when their quarry was in plain sight just a few dozen feet away, but she supposed even security wasn't allowed to trample the carefully tended hedges, lest they not be ready for the next day's laughing hordes.

After all, someone like Nate was sure to visit, take a picture, and put it online as evidence of how poorly

America the Beautiful's lovely hedge mazes were being maintained in this philistine age of record profits and minimum investments.

"Excuse me, miss?"

Tabby nearly jumped out of her skin. A young father was standing right next to her, as if he'd crept up as close as he could get in hopes that she'd turn around. Some guests never liked to say anything until they absolutely were forced into it. His gaze flicked to her chest, and Tabby realized she was wearing her name-tag.

"Oh good," he said. "You *do* work here. I'm sorry, can we get a replacement stroller? Our rental seems to have disappeared, and the claim ticket said we could get another one in Primrose Gardens?"

Tabby put her hand on her name tag, biting back a sob. She was in costume in the wrong area. *Again.* And this time, no one had told her to do it for work. Plus, with Nate over there, clinging to the Spirit of the Midwest in hopes of being rescued by divine intervention from the threat of total trespassing, someone was bound to start taking pictures of the scene. She needed to get out of here.

But first, she supposed, she had better get this guy his stroller.

"Sure," Tabby said in her clear, confident customer service voice. "Can I just see your receipt?"

CHAPTER THIRTY-NINE

Nate

Nate could see Tabby, her lantern-lit face glowing golden above that damned prairie-girl outfit, and he nearly abandoned the refuge of his Grecian shepherdess.

She'd come up here to watch him go down, to taunt him with her pretty face and her little-girl shyness, to wave goodbye as he was dragged off, kicking and fighting, to the security offices above Independence Plaza. Oh, Nate knew all about the Independence Plaza security offices! The place everyone meant when they joked about "AtB Jail."

Only, Nate knew it was no joke—there were rooms up there filled with monitors, filming every corner of the park, and little offices where a person who had broken the rules so egregiously they could never be allowed to return was sat until he signed his trespass order and was escorted off the property by a county sheriff's deputy.

He *knew* and yet here he was, clinging to the bare elbow

of this Midwestern goddess of sheep (there really was no clear backstory on the statues in this garden, something he would have loved to have written about on his blog, if he wasn't about to lose all privilege to visit here). He knew and he felt an overwhelming urge to take Tabby down with him. Look at her, in the wrong costume, again! It was like she did it on purpose, like the rules meant nothing to her!

"HEY!" Nate shouted, startling the security guards still picking their way through the maze towards him, startling the three or four guests who were left in the gardens despite being asked to leave by a few grim-faced managers. "NICE COSTUME, OLD DODGE CITY!"

That should do it, he thought with satisfaction. They would see her and evidence of her crime right in front of him.

But no one looked at her. They kept looking at *him*. She walked away, a man in shorts and t-shirt trailing in her wake. She was going to get away with it. She was simply going to act like she worked here and get away with all of it.

Nate howled in frustration. A real, live, werewolf howl, which stopped everyone in their tracks. Tabby paused, then kept walking, her thin shoulders high and resolute. The security guards stared at him. The one nearest, now just about six feet away (though possibly several minutes away, depending on how good he was at mazes) actually took a step back.

"Sir?" He called. "Are you…is everything…"

He was trying not to say *okay* because he knew it wasn't, but at the same time, what else could you say? Nate knew the feeling. He wrote things every day that should have been throwaway, ephemeral, nothingness—but thousands of people took everything he said at face value, and they either loved him or loathed him for it. The truth was, he thought, word choice wasn't even a choice most of the time. It was just the way that sentences were *existed*, the way they had always been constructed, since the beginning of language. *Are you okay?* No, of course he fucking wasn't! But what else could a person say at a time like this?

Are you sane?

Are you deranged?

Are you making plans to move back home and get a job at Wendy's?

Nate took a deep breath, because he didn't think being a crazy person was going to help his case at all. "I want to talk to someone," he said. "I have things to say which I think will make you feel differently about what I did."

The security guard cocked his head. "Is that right? How about you let go of that shepherdess lady and we talk it out."

AtB Jail wasn't like jail. Nate knew this from his relentless internet searches for images of the forbidden areas of the theme parks. Instead of bars and cots, it was a few beige-painted rooms off a beige-painted hallway, with walls so thin you could hear the tin-pan jangle of the piano music playing outside in Independence Plaza. The room filled with monitors showing every corner of the park existed, but he only got a tantalizing glimpse of it before he was herded into a small office with an old faux-wood grain desk and a faded, framed photo of Promise Mountain, circa 1985, hanging on the flimsy-looking wall. A balding security guard, his hat hanging on a hook on the door, was settled behind the desk. He gestured to Nate to sit in the leather-cushioned chair across from him.

"Nathan Potter," the security guard said. He had a Northeastern accent—Long Island, maybe, or Brooklyn. "I'm Rick."

It was a simple, eighties name, Rick. It fit the room.

"Hi, Rick," Nate said. "You can call me Nate. If you want. If that's appropriate."

"Nate is fine. You want to tell me what happened today?"

"A misunderstanding," Nate attempted.

"I don't misunderstand that you were found in a Patriots-only area with a stolen ID?" Rick held up Winslow's ID lanyard.

"No, sir. But there were—circumstances."

"What could possibly lead you to steal an ID and go down those stairs, Nate?" Rick leaned back, his voice taking on a folksy tone. An Andy Griffith fan, Nate thought. "What kind of circumstances could those be?"

Nate tried to think of any reason for him to have behaved as he had done. Anything outside of sheer, raging curiosity. Outside of a feeling that if something was going down at AtB, he had to know about it. Had to be a part of it. Had to be on the inside, no matter what. He knew this was the insanity which had led him to this chair, to this moment, but he also knew it wasn't going to get him out of a trespass.

He was about to lose the place he loved.

And then, he knew what to say.

"I'm in love," Nate said, with the air of a helpless addict. "I'm in love and the girl I love was in danger."

"In danger?" An eyebrow went up.

Too far. "Of losing her job. Of getting framed. I couldn't —I didn't know what to do. I overheard the conversation, and I panicked and grabbed the ID and ran. AtB means the world to her. I didn't want to see her get fired."

As soon as he said this, he realized his mistake. He had essentially tried to get Tabby fired the day he'd posted about her crossing the Plaza in her costume. If this guy knew *anything* about him—

"Well," Rick said, shifting in his chair. "That's real interesting. Does this girl—are you two dating?"

He doesn't know. "We aren't," Nate admitted. "She… doesn't feel that way about me. But I just want her to be happy. I thought if I saved her job, she might feel differently about me…in the future. You know?" He tilted his voice up, asking Rick to commiserate with him.

"Oh, boy, I know," Rick agreed.

Nate began to relax ever so slightly. His fingers uncurled themselves from their death grip on the armrests. "I wish everyone was as dedicated to her job as she is," he went on. "Now that other girl that was there, Sonia? She has no loyalty at all."

"What's that, now?"

It was a dangerous play and Nate knew it. "Look, you know I run a website, right? I have published some insider info before it was available to the public. That's behind me now. I've been invited to join the official blog community. The press office has made the offer and I've accepted. I'm on the straight and narrow now. But some of the things I've published before—this girl Sonia is the one who gave me the info."

Rick leaned forward. "You're saying she gave you confidential info?"

"Yes, sir."

"You want to show me proof?"

"Can I take out my phone?"

"Of course you can. This ain't no county jail. I'm not planning on shooting you the minute you put your hand in your pocket." Rick laughed.

It was all in his email: the Venmo account, the email address she'd used to accept the money. He just had to do a quick search. He typed *Sonia* into the search bar.

Nothing came up.

Fine, no problem. He typed *Venmo* into the search bar. Dozens of returns came back. He flicked down a few weeks and found the right date. But no name that looked like Sonia. He opened a few until he found the twelve-hundred dollar payment, and looked at the email address.

kcidynit@yahoo.com

It was a fake email. She'd used a fake email and, he realized, looking more closely, she'd been pretty damn insulting when she'd come up with it, too. Well, that was unnecessary.

"You got it or not?" Rick asked.

"I—I guess I don't. It looks like she used a fake email."

"Well, of course she would have used a fake email," Rick said, exasperated. "Who would give away their real email address when they're selling company information?"

Nate felt like an idiot.

"Look, buddy, if you don't have anything for me, then I think the way forward is pretty clear."

"No—no! There has to be a way. You can't—this is my whole life."

Rick looked uncomfortable. "I know this is your job, son, but—"

"*No,*" Nate said fiercely, determined to just be out with it. "*America the Beautiful is my whole life.* I moved here because it was so important to me. I built this blog because it's so important to me. I can't imagine doing anything else with my life. This is all I've got. This is *all I am.*"

He sat back in his chair, spent with emotion and misery, hot tears pricking at the backs of his eyes and tightening the muscles of his throat.

Maybe he hadn't realized it was quite that serious, but those words had come from some place deep inside. They were the truth.

AtB was all he was.

"I'll do anything," he said, his voice rasping. "Anything."

Rick eyed him for a long moment. The air around them was static, electricity hanging around their shoulders, waiting for someone to make a move, to determine the course of Nate's life. If he didn't have this, he didn't have anything. And they both knew it.

"Six months," Rick said eventually. "I'll give you a six-month ban. After that—lifted. You're free and clear. Another strike, though, and you're out permanently."

Nate gave a small sob, half-relieved and half-horrified. It wasn't life, but, God, six months! What the hell was he going to do with himself for six whole months?

"Take it?"

"I'll take it," Nate gasped. Then he put his head down on Rick's desk and let the tears flow.

CHAPTER FORTY

Martin

Martin sat down in a dark corner of Cowboy Cal's Good Grub and waited while Amy went to the counter and winked her way into a couple of Coke floats. He watched her hips sway as she walked back, the drinks balanced high in her hands, little caps of whipped cream swirling above the star-spangled paper cups. She had always loved the Coke floats here. But he hadn't ever thought he'd drink another one with her, at this little two-seat table hidden away behind the saddle displays, a half-wall draped with bright silk flowers giving them the illusion of privacy in this crowded dining hall.

"Some things don't change," Amy said with a smile, putting down the drinks and settling onto her stool.

Some things don't, Martin thought miserably, *like the way your hair shines under the lanterns, or the way your smile is always making fun of me just a little.* Amy had never loved him the way he deserved. He knew that now. She had given in to him because he was a lovesick fool who wanted to give her everything, and then she had kept him that way, at just enough arm's length to keep him hungering for more, to keep him convinced he didn't have the right to love her. He'd been wrong to see her that way, and she'd been wrong to let him.

At least they'd both been wrong.

"Drink up, Martin," Amy said, putting the striped straw between her cupid's bow lips. She was still milking the fifties look she'd always been so good at, blonde curls tied up in a paisley kerchief, eyelashes painted black and at least a mile long, red lips and creamy skin. But she'd picked up some lines in Japan; Martin could see little creases around her eyes when she smiled at him, and some deeper ones on either side of her nose. Amy wasn't a beautiful doll anymore.

She was a beautiful woman, perhaps a hundred times more dangerous.

He pushed away his cup. "Did they end your contract?"

Her eyes narrowed. "I decided to come home."

It wasn't an answer, but he let it go. "Will you be working here again?"

"I have an interview or two lined up," she said deftly, flicking at the whipped cream on her drink. "I think everything will fall into place. I have a lot of friends here." Her expression turned coy again. "I've heard a few things, Martin!"

He leaned back, letting the shadows cross his face. He wasn't going to give in to her. Not after all these years. "I've been living my life, Amy. You've been living yours. We split up."

"Martin, you're such a dog." Amy laughed. "Chasing around every new girl that comes into the internships, crushing on all the new leading ladies…"

"I have done no such thing. I've made friends with them, certainly."

"Lucille says you're in love."

Lucille. Giving him away like that. Martin was a fool to trust a woman just because she wore a Miss Sallie Mae get-up. It didn't matter. "I am in love," Martin said brashly.

"With that little freckle-face Patriot from retail." Her lip curled.

He didn't answer. He thought he managed to look scornful.

Amy certainly did. "You've always spent every spare minute hanging around the *talent*, Martin, so what made you settle for someone in Retail? If you're desperate for an Old West fantasy, any one of the girls could bring home something ruffled and corseted and put on a show for you —"

"That's not what this is about," he snapped.

"Oh," Amy said lightly, leaning back. "Well, then, I guess times *have* changed."

And against his will, Martin remembered Amy's costume changes, the voluminous skirts and low-cut blouses she'd bring home from Wardrobe, the feathers and fringes, the leather and lace. She'd always said she had to sneak them out, that there were strict rules about taking home costumes, but Amy had a way with everyone. She got what she wanted, strict rules or not.

Martin wondered suddenly if he'd ever gotten what he wanted, perhaps by accident, because he'd certainly never known what it was. He'd never asked Amy to come home and play dress-up for him, but he hadn't been about to tell her no, either. Even if she hadn't been so beautiful, flashing her bloomers and nodding her plumes, he wouldn't ever have told Amy no. That wasn't how their relationship had worked.

Apparently, he thought with a sudden burst of anger, that wasn't how her relationships had worked with anyone else, either.

"Was I just a sounding board for how far you could take your private audiences?" he asked suddenly. It was a long-held suspicion, something he'd nursed along for years, a private grievance, a shadowy hurt he'd never thought he would tell anyone else about. "You practiced your moves on me, so that you'd be prepared when rich men came knocking. I never asked you to come home and put on shows for me. That was all you. I was your rehearsal partner. I was the *understudy.*"

Amy's mouth opened in silent dismay, and Martin knew he'd been right. The suspicion he'd held since those first hurt, silent days after the incident on Promise Mountain, when she'd come home with her lovely face tragic and tear-stained, announcing she'd been placed on leave. And then she'd disappeared the moment the suspension of all private audiences was announced, her bags gone from his closet, her clothes vanished from his dresser. She'd gone to Japan to play enchanted princesses for other children, other families, other *men*, and left him just a note.

Sorry it had to be this way. Love, Amy.

He wished he'd kept the note, so he could throw it at her now. But he'd burned it a few days after she'd gone, in a candle scented like honeysuckle, the frail scraps of paper settling around the horseshoe candlestick she'd bought to commemorate her three-month stint as Miss Sallie Mae. After that, she'd gone to the Glorious Grottoes below Promise Mountain, to play Lady Liberty.

And that was when it had all gone wrong.

"That isn't how it happened," Amy said finally. "I'm sorry you remember it that way. But you weren't just practice to me."

"This reunion was a mistake," Martin told her, standing up. "I'll see you around, Amy."

She reached out quickly, clutching at his arm. "Don't go."

Martin looked down at her, wishing he could peel her fingers from his skin. "Why, Amy? What do you want from me now? Because I can't see how I could possibly owe you anything."

"I'm sorry, Martin. Truly." Amy's face fell into contrite lines. "Please believe me. I'll do anything. I just…I made such a mistake in leaving you like that. I was so confused and I had just lost my job and everything was so horrible, and people online were saying such terrible things about me —"

"I remember all of that," Martin interrupted her. "You don't have to remind me what it was like when you left. I was here. I was the one you left."

"And then I come back hoping to pick up the pieces and *everyone* I know is chattering about how you're in love with this little girl in pigtails and I just…I just had to see you. I couldn't wait to do it properly." Amy wrinkled her nose in what had always been considered a charming, girlish fashion. She was too old for it now. "Can we just talk? Can we just catch up? Maybe not here, maybe someplace a little more private?"

Martin wanted to walk away. He did. But her hands were

on his arm and her fingers were so tiny and perfect and strong, so *familiar.* He could remember her clutching his arm in one of her one-woman skits, the way she'd bat her eyelashes and plead with him: *Please, mister, don't leave a girl all alone in the world!* She was always in need of saving, strong and bold and beautiful Amy. Her fantasy life was a morass of despair, danger, and deviant gentlemen.

He should have known their relationship was a rehearsal. It was all so obvious.

He started to pull back, feeling her grip tighten on his skin, and then suddenly there was another person in their little alcove, turning their couple into a trio. Amy looked up. "Lucille?"

He didn't want to see her like this. Martin tried to keep his eyes down, but curiosity drove him to look the other woman in the face. His current Miss Sallie Mae, the woman he had been using, gently and courteously he hoped, to help him emerge from the fog of After Amy.

She'd cheated him, too. But whose fault was that? He was too trusting.

Lucille wasn't wearing any make-up, and that made it hard to picture her as the heavily painted Miss Sallie Mae. But her face was the same as the woman who had listened to him pour out his stupid, confused heart. Martin sighed, embarrassed. She let her gaze flick over him, interested and frank, before dipping back to Amy. "Listen," she said, "I talked to the girls, and there's room for you for a few days if you want to stay. But when Mara gets back, we'll be out of space. So it's just for like, three nights. Is that okay?"

Amy shook her head. "Lucille, let's not talk about this right now." Martin saw her tip her head towards him, trying to indicate that he wasn't part of this conversation.

"Sorry, I have to run. I just wanted to tell you in case you didn't—in case this didn't—"

Martin watched Lucille take in the situation and wondered how someone who could behave so perceptively in costume and wig could be so obtuse in real life.

"I'm sorry," Lucille said, blushing. "I'll talk to you later."

Amy looked back at Martin. "This isn't about a place to stay," she said. "I want to make things up to you."

"No," Martin said, thinking of Tabby. "You can't."

He pulled away from her, letting her fingernails drag little white marks across his tan arm, and pushed through the crowds into the darkening Old Dodge City evening.

"She's not what you think!" Amy shouted after him. "She's not an innocent!"

"Leave her alone, Amy," he called, not looking back. "This isn't for you to ruin."

"Ask anyone, Martin. She's as good an actress as anyone else in a dress and wig around here!"

Martin was already at the front gates when Amy caught his arm again. He sighed. If he hadn't paused to watch several security guards and a uniformed deputy walking at such a fast clip towards Promise Mountain that their gait verged on the edge of running, he'd have gotten away from her.

"Not *now*, Amy," he insisted, trying to wrench away from her. A few other guests turned, curious, eager to see a domestic disturbance play out while they were stuck on the tedious business of holding down their fireworks spot.

"Then when?" Amy expertly maneuvered the two of them out of the crowded sidewalk and into the shadow of the staircase leading to the train station. She had learned to move people as an entertainer here. She had learned to manipulate with a smile on her face and a song in her voice. She could use that against him all day long. She always had. Martin knew that now.

"Not ever," he amended, but his back was against the wall, literally, and she was looking up at him with those alluring, helpless, kiss-me-I'm-your-princess eyes. "We don't have anything now. It's been *three years.*"

"You know I had to go," Amy insisted. "They were going to press charges."

"What kind of charges? No, don't answer that."

"I didn't do those things." But her grip lessened on his arm, and the lines around her eyes deepened.

The headlines had been so cruel. *Patriotic Playgirl Pussyfoots Into Prince's Palace* had been a masterpiece of alliteration, sure, but tabloids weren't known for their strict adherence to facts, and Martin had always given Amy the benefit of the doubt, even before she packed up and left. He hadn't ever truly believed she'd been turning tricks in her Lady Liberty costume, employing the Patriots who set up her Private Audiences into unwitting pimps, but as the months went by, he became more and more convinced she'd been up to *something*. Something related to those elaborate shows she'd once put on for him. He'd accidentally looked over her shoulder once when she was paying a bill and saw that Amy had more money in her bank account than her paycheck could possibly have accounted for.

After that, the facts all fell into place.

Anyway, the prince and his family had refused interviews and moved on with their lives, and Martin figured it was well for some. Amy gave some rich guy with oil well billions a happy ending to his AtB fairy tale, she got a wad of cash and moved to Tokyo, and he stayed home alone, growing older and sadder every day. All's fair in love and war, right? Unless you were the one who lost everything.

There was a fanfare of trumpets from the loudspeaker system along Independence Plaza, and a bold female voice boomed out over the triumphant brass instruments. "Ladies and gentleman, boys and girls! Tonight's showing of America the Beautiful's world-renowned nighttime fireworks celebration, *America: A Salute in the Skies,* will begin in the skies above Promise Mountain in just fifteen minutes."

"This place is about to get insane," Martin muttered. "I would really like to leave."

"Let me just tell you something," Amy said urgently. "I need you to know that I never stopped loving you, not for a minute. And when I saw you looking at that little Retail girl…I just couldn't take it, okay? I love you, Martin. I've loved you all this time. I was in Tokyo because I had no choice. I couldn't work here, you know that! But I came back because I felt that way about us, too. Like I had no choice."

She pressed her lips against his, hard, and Martin's head thumped back against the stone wall behind him. There was a smattering of applause from some teen girls sitting nearby. He wondered how much they'd heard even as he tried to stop push Amy away from him (gently, lest Security get alerted) and even as he tried to stop his body from reacting to the kiss.

But it seemed like only his brain had ever felt betrayed, not his skin or his lips or any other part of him…

And Martin had nearly given up fighting her off when Amy finally slackened her grip on him, her lips leaving his, her eyes fluttering open as she came up for air. He looked at her, but that was too intense to bear, so he looked past her and into the crowds thronging the lamplit expanse of Independence Plaza—and he saw Nate walking next to a manager. The man turned his head. For a moment, his gaze locked onto Martin's.

He looked defeated.

That's what you look like, a voice whispered in Martin's ear. *Finished.*

He stiffened the muscles in his arms and managed to push Amy off of him.

Amy stumbled backwards, exaggerating the movement. "Hey, what the hell?" she snapped, rubbing at her arms as if he'd shoved her. The teens on the curb watched with shocked expressions. Someone lifted a phone to take video.

"You can't just go around kissing strangers, lady," Martin snapped loudly. "Get drunk in another theme park. This is America the Beautiful, and your behavior is shameful."

The manager walking alongside Nate looked over, his step slowing. "Folks, is everything all right over here?" His gaze played over Amy's outfit: her exposed bellybutton, a diamond glinting beneath the hem of her cropped tee. Maybe she looked all-American; maybe she looked like a hussy. In the humid flats of South Georgia, sometimes the people in charge drew the line one way, sometimes another.

"Just had too much to drink," Martin said scornfully. "She needs to call someone to come pick her up."

Amy's expression, when she looked back at him, was one of disbelief. And he knew why: those words hadn't even sounded like his when they'd left his mouth. But she didn't know him anymore. And she was never going to get to know him.

"Can't *you* take me home?" she asked him, and her voice

was full of hurt.

The manager was looking between them, his gaze sizing them up. Beside him, Nate stood with a contrite air, but Martin knew he was dying to interfere. It wasn't in the blogger's nature to stand by and let controversy unfold without being able to stick a poker in the flames and stir the logs around a little, build up the blaze. The manager rocked back on his toes at last. "Do you two know each other?"

Martin sighed. "A long time ago," he admitted. "We just ran into each other tonight."

"Ladies and gentlemen! Boys and girls! In just five minutes, we will be celebrating the spirit of America together with America the Beautiful's famous nighttime fireworks presentation, America: A Salute in the Skies. Ideal viewing locations can be found all around America the Beautiful. Please find your spot now, because America: A Salute in the Skies, begins in just five minutes!"

All of them waited out the fireworks announcement with the same expression of aggrieved patience; all of them were theme park veterans and knew the spiel by heart. It was an unexpected measure of togetherness that Martin found rather heartening.

"If you can take her home," the manager said, once the echoes had died away, "you'd be doing me a favor. I've got my hands full tonight."

Martin realized the manager must recognize him as a park regular. Hell, he had a ten-year pin on his name tag. He might even recognize Amy.

"That's fine," Martin said. "I can do that for you."

The manager walked away, Nate obediently by his side— but the blogger couldn't help throwing a curious glance over his shoulder as they went on up Independence Plaza.

Amy looked at him for a long moment. "Are you going

to drive me home?"

"I told him I would."

"I'm staying with Lucille," she said challengingly. "Lucille had a *lot* to say to me about you and your behavior."

"Unlike me," Martin said wearily. "Who has nothing to say about *your* behavior."

"She said that little girl—what's her name? Kitty? She said when she got here, she slept with every international intern in sight. They thought maybe she was looking for someone to take her back to South America or Europe with them, like maybe she was just trying to get out of the U.S."

"I don't care," Martin sighed.

"Martin, think about what we could have together. Let's put all of this behind us." For a person who almost definitely hated him, Amy certainly had the pleading face down. "Tell me you'll think about it."

"I'll think about it if you'll just come on."

The music began to swell around them, a big blithe reimagining of the militaristic marches of Sousa and his ilk. The lights dimmed and people began to murmur in anticipation. This was the perfect time to leave. Martin turned on his heel and walked out of the train station at the very moment the first red, white, and blue clusters of fireworks exploded above Promise Mountain, staining the concrete at his feet in the colors of America, and nearly every other country he could name off the top of his head, as well.

"I'm not coming with you," she called. "I'm not going to sponge off you."

The music and explosions nearly drowned out her words, but Martin still heard them.

"I want to do things right with you, Martin."

CHAPTER FORTY-ONE

Sonia

When she was pretty sure she'd been forgotten, Sonia ran up the nearest stairwell, just to get away from all the drama as quickly as possible. She found herself still in Old Dodge City, which was a good thing since she was wearing her costume, and ran down to the restrooms to change her work shirt out for the t-shirt she kept in her backpack. Then she set off at the fastest clip she could manage with all the families milling around, hoping to find Tabby, or Nate, or both of them—although hopefully not in the same place.

The security guards standing near the back entrance to Primrose Gardens were the first good indicator that she'd figured out where one of the runaways had gotten. They were redirecting everyone who tried to get into the Gardens, sending them back into Fairytale Courtyard or The Big Apple, or down into the Glorious Grottoes around

Promise Mountain. Sonia blessed her non-slip work shoes as she turned off the path, ducked through a small door near the Gotham Ice Cream Parlor, and made her way through a series of Patriot-only service hallways connecting the different eateries in this section of the park. Because Promise Mountain's waterfalls needed such complicated piping and pump systems, there wasn't much corridor access right here, which meant the back-of-the-house ops for restaurants were shared aboveground instead of below. It was perfect for Sonia's needs.

Skidding across the film of grease coating the concrete behind Cousins Pizza, where a dumpster, a grease trap and a large garden hose shared a space roughly the size of a large walk-in closet, Sonia took a right and headed up a short flight of stairs that would take her to the stroller rental's storage area behind the Gardens. From there, she'd be able to peek through the wooden fencing to see just what the security guards were hiding in the Gardens.

"Tabby!"

Sonia stopped short and the grease on the soles of her work shoes nearly sent her into a row of strollers, all lined up as if ready to march into battle. Tabby was at the top of the row, her hands on the handle of a stroller, her eyes big and startled. "Sonia? What on earth are you doing here?"

"What are *you* doing here?"

"I'm—getting these guests a stroller."

"You couldn't tell them the store is closed?"

Tabby looked around her. "You know what? I hadn't noticed. That's weird. Why is it closed?"

Sonia shook her head, momentarily just as confused. Then she remembered. "Oh shit, Tabby. Because the fireworks are happening soon."

Tabby frowned.

"The fireworks show closes the Gardens because they launch some of them right behind it, remember? To make it look like they're launching off Promise Mountain?"

"Oh, that's right." Tabby pulled the stroller out. "Well, then I better get this to this guest and send him out of here. I guess the security guards missed him somehow."

Sonia watched Tabby with astonishment. Did the girl have some sort of disassociation disorder? Didn't she understand that she shouldn't be here anyway, in her Old Dodge City skirt and fresh off running away from an investigation? She wheeled the stroller over to the gap in the fence, nodded and smiled as she handed it off to the guest waiting on the other side, and then gently pushed the door closed. Sonia huffed impatiently as she made her way back over.

"We have to *go,*" Sonia said.

"I don't know where to go," Tabby said. "This honestly might be the best place for me. Do you think all this will blow over if I wait it out?"

"Ordinarily I'd say no, but with Nate running away like that, maybe? He's a bigger target than you, since he was trespassing on the Underground. And they have Nick, anyway."

"He's guilty of something bad, right?" Tabby frowned. "Because I honestly don't know what's going on down there. Nick started pulling down bins, he said everything was gone, he said they were on to him, and then the door opened and I panicked. And I don't *want* to know," she added, seeing Sonia's expression. "If Miles is going to talk to me again, I need to be able to tell him truthfully that I have no idea what's going on."

"That's fair," Sonia said, nodding. "But we still can't stay here. And there are security guards at the Underground entrances. So, unless you have a change of clothes…"

"This is the perfect place to wait," Tabby said. "No one's coming back until after the fireworks."

"Well," Sonia said, looking around at the dark little yard. A small concrete overhang offered some cover from sunlight and rain for some supplies and towel bins. "I guess we could wait it out in the shelter there."

"Is that safe?" Tabby asked.

Sonia shrugged. "What's the worst that could happen?"

"It's *singed,*" Tabby announced, once the house lights had come back up and the ash had finally settled. She was looking at the little irregular burns in her skirt with dismay. "Burnt right through. They're going to notice this the next time I turn in my costumes."

"I'd just throw that one away and eat the expense." Sonia was giving herself a once-over. As the pyro hit its highest notes over their heads, Sonia had really thought she'd made a grave error in suggesting they stay hidden behind the stroller shop. The fireworks bursting all around Promise Mountain and above Primrose Gardens had been nonstop, and with the constant explosions leaving sulfurous fumes in the air, neither of them could properly breathe, or see, or hear. Cardboard casings from the exploded shells came tumbling down everywhere, along with a glowing rainfall of hot orange embers. Sonia hadn't liked to think someone might actually be in mortal danger during something a theme park fireworks show, but the America the Beautiful operation was clearly in a league of its own.

Still, they'd survived, and now they had to figure out

where to go next. Custodial Patriots would be arriving soon with large roaring vacuums to suck up all the fireworks debris and get this part of the park back open to guests. They might even reopen the stroller shop.

"Okay. With you in costume, we've got nowhere to go but back downstairs," Sonia said resignedly. "But they've got to be done looking for Nate by now. They probably caught him while we were in here. So I'm sure they're not watching the stairwells anymore."

"But they're going to see two people who are covered in ash." Tabby brushed at her arms. "God, look at this—it leaves yellow marks on your skin."

Sonia rubbed at the yellow dots on her own arms and sighed heavily. Tabby was right. Anyone who saw the two of them was going to ask questions. And hiding in a fireworks fallout zone during the show was absolutely a terminable offense.

Sonia tried to think of any way to get out of the park without being seen and came up dry every time. "It's impossible," she said. "We're just going to have to risk it…"

And then she heard the steam train's high-pitched whistle.

"We can't just jump onto the back of a moving train," Tabby argued, but she didn't stop moving. She slipped on a slick patch of sidewalk, where the sprinklers which poured water on the rooftops during fireworks shows had left behind dark pools. Custodial crews would push the water into drains with their long squeegees…and they'd be here any minute. Sonia grabbed Tabby's arm to help her hold her balance. They didn't have any time to waste.

"The train goes at about twelve miles an hour," Sonia

told her matter-of-factly. She'd been on the tour. "And it will be going even less than that when it moves onto the switch to get it out of the park. It will be *crawling*. And there won't be anyone riding in the caboose. I am telling you, we won't be spotted."

America the Beautiful's genuinely historic, gleamingly beautiful, narrow-gauge steam train was one of the park's few true antiques. Sonia had learned all about it during a Patriots-only tour—the kind of event where the guides gave out more information than they would ever tell the general public.

Things like the standard safety equipment this antique train wasn't equipped with. Theme park attractions were built to keep guests in their seats and to shut down if anyone tried to get out. But the steam train and its accompanying excursion cars didn't have anything like that. No pressure mats, no cameras, no intrusion alarms. There was just the elegant blue and red engine, huffing along slowly as it pulled four open-sided sightseeing coaches, and the little red caboose in back, an American flag fluttering from its tiny platform. It was the most low-tech thing in the park.

And, even better for Sonia's purposes, the train's roundhouse wasn't even inside the park. Every night, a Patriot hopped down from the engine's cab, unlocked the gates crossing the train tracks, and flung them open. Then the Patriot clambered back up and slowly drove the train through the gates, before walking back and closing them again.

For about ten minutes a night, there was a hole in the park's tight security.

That ten minutes was all Sonia and Tabby needed.

Once through the gates, there would be nothing standing between Sonia and Tabby's freedom. Just darkness, the road to the Patriot parking lot, and the promise of escape back to their apartments.

And showers, Sonia thought, brushing at the itchy ash still clinging to the back of her neck. She would do anything for a shower at this point. Hitching a ride on the back of a theme park train was the *least* of what she'd do.

Tabby came to the hedge marking the back perimeter of Primrose Gardens. On the other side, a little grass lawn ran down to the railroad tracks. She looked around. "Are we going to go down to the station? No, there are lights on over there. What's the plan?"

Sonia sighed. Tabby was totally out of it tonight. Maybe the fireworks had rattled her brain. "Just follow me down to the tracks. We'll be right by the switch over here. We can wait in the shadows until the train pulls up and then we'll have time to climb onboard while the engineer gets out to move the switch. We'll just crouch down on the caboose's little porch thing and wait until we're outside the gate. Then we'll hide in the bushes until he drives to the roundhouse. Got it?"

"You make it sound so simple."

"It's *going* to be simple," Sonia insisted.

But first, the train had to finish carrying guests for the night. Sonia and Tabby settled into a shadowed hiding spot beneath the hedge and listened to Primrose Gardens reopen. The custodians came and went, then the tinkle of park music filled the night as the speakers were turned back on, and finally the chatter of guests and the rumble of stroller wheels returned. On such a warm night, after such a crowded day, the park would stay busy until closing.

The two of them shrank back into the bushes every time the train came around, lit up like a pleasure boat, with dozens of guests on board. The second time, though, the train was nearly empty. "Next time will be our run," Sonia whispered after it passed, the caboose lantern swinging in the darkness. "I guarantee it."

Tabby just nodded. "Another twenty minutes until it gets back here, though."

"At least."

Tabby sighed. "Sonia, tonight was a combination of so many weird things in my life, I don't even know how to compute it all."

"I figured," Sonia said. "Since you're being so quiet. You usually have stuff to say."

"So far, it's just been a weird, weird summer."

"Yeah," Sonia agreed, thinking of the psychological test of the Greeter position, of the impending closure of Gold Rush Rapids and her transfer to Independence Plaza, of the protests and the blog posts and the Values crackdown. And now the theft sting, and all the wild events that had led to their hiding in the bushes behind Primrose Gardens in sulfur-stained clothes. "There must be something in the water," she said idly.

"For real!" Tabby's whisper took on more strength. "I mean, I had that blogger come after me, and that led to this. I started dating Nick, and that just collapsed immediately. And then there's Martin…" Tabby's voice trailed off.

"What *is* going on with Martin? Are you two a thing?"

"I think we are," Tabby said softly. "I mean, I'd like for us to be. It's been kind of complicated. Nick's always there…and Martin's older than me…"

"Nick is no longer going to be a problem," Sonia predicted wryly. "And most men don't worry about age differences, so if you're fine with it, I guarantee you he is, too."

"I guess I just don't know how to be a girlfriend," Tabby said. "Like, what that even means. I wasn't allowed out much back at home. I messed around with a few people when I got here and, boy, that backfired."

"I didn't realize," Sonia said vaguely, not sure how much Tabby knew about her reputation from her first few months at AtB. Those rumors had basically faded, though. With fresh interns every few months, it was hard to hold on to notoriety very long around this place.

"I know what people think of me," Tabby blurted. "I know you did, too. You don't have to pretend."

Sonia put up her hands. "Hey listen, I'm a no-judgment zone. You got no problems here."

"The things they said…" Tabby's voice trailed off wistfully. "I didn't think it would be like that. I was so new, you know? I'd never been anywhere. Even the college I went to was like a small town. I barely felt like I'd left my mama's trailer."

Sonia felt an equal desire to know more about Tabby and to never, ever learn anything else about Tabby. She suspected there were multitudes beneath that freckled face and those clear blue eyes, and all of them were sad. "Well," she said eventually, "I think that's behind you now. Martin's certainly not the kind to go around listening to gossip from a bunch of Patriots. He's—well, he's…"

"An adult," Tabby supplied. "A grown-up man with grown-up problems. And we're a bunch of late-bloomers, I guess. We can't face the real world, can't get real jobs, I couldn't even stay to finish college. Even if he didn't believe the rumors, even if he heard them, he's going to get tired of me either way. I'm not like him."

Sonia considered Tabby, her face downcast in the shadows. "You know what's funny? I don't know Martin super-well, but I'd say you guys are an awful lot alike."

Tabby looked up, a question hovering on her lips, and then they both jumped as the train whistle sounded up the tracks.

"Get back in the bushes," Sonia whispered, as if the train was already upon them. "We have to hide until the engineer flips the switch and gets back on board. We'll only have a few seconds to get onto the caboose, okay?"

Slowly, laboriously, the train huffed past them, steam hissing from its belly, the steel wheels rumbling on the rails. The engineer was looking down at his controls, but even if he'd looked out the cab's side window, all he would have seen was darkness and shrubbery. Sonia huddled close to Tabby, their sweaty hands clutched together. The enormity of the moment, of both the potential pay-off and the potential for being caught, were so heavy she thought she wouldn't even be able to push herself off the ground when the time came to leap for the caboose.

The train went all the way past them before it came to a slow, grudging stop.

"Did it go too far?" Tabby whispered. "It went past the other track."

Sonia shook her head. "It'll make sense in a minute."

Then, a conductor hopped down to jam the switch in the other direction. Sonia hadn't expected a second person on the train. She felt Tabby's hand clutch at her elbow. Sonia took a deep breath and watched him take hold of the switch handle. This didn't change anything.

It would all work out.

The conductor was a young guy, fresh off his own college internship, and sweating under his smart black vest. The little watch chain hanging across the vest's front pocket glinted in the light from the lantern hanging from the train caboose. Sonia had always thought guys looked cute in this costume, and tonight's conductor, though unwelcome, was no exception. She'd seen him in the break room a few times and thought, *mmhmm.*

He wasn't great with the switch, yanking at the tall steel handle ineffectually for a few moments before the engineer shouted something unintelligible, which caused the conductor to turn around and start yanking in the other direction. The handle slowly shifted, and there was a creaking as the rails directly in front of them followed suit, creating a curve.

Now the train could back onto the siding that led to the roundhouse.

Back onto the siding? Sonia shook her head, one hand going to her mouth. That was why the train had pulled so far forward. They weren't going to turn in engine-first. They were going to back all the way to the roundhouse.

Tabby's breath was coming faster and faster. "Sonia, the caboose is going in *first.*"

"I guess I never paid that much attention to the way the trains go," Sonia hissed as the train began to creak noisily backwards, the conductor vanishing from view as the caboose moved past them. "Where do you think he's going to go? Is he going to walk along the track to make sure it's clear? Because if he does, um..."

They'd be seen no matter what they did.

"Oh, you know what? He's going to get in the cab with the engineer," Tabby whispered. "It's not protocol, but that's how they do it, because they're tired, and there isn't anyone out here at night for them to hit."

"How do you know that?"

"One of Nick's vlogs," Tabby said. "I just remembered. This idiot conductor spilled everything. I'm surprised he didn't get fired."

"You never know what will get you fired," Sonia remarked resignedly. "So, ready to stowaway on this train?"

"I'm ready."

They waited until they could see the conductor's feet walking away on the other side, heading up to the engine. The engine, and the engineer inside, were still on the main track. The caboose and the last passenger car were already on the switch track, turned towards the roundhouse. This was their shot—once they crossed the no-man's-land of grass and rock between the hedge and the rails.

"Will they see us?" Tabby looked at the twelve feet between them and the safety of the train cars.

"I feel like they're not paying any attention. It's so late."

"Well, here's hoping."

They looked at each other, and then, at once, they both scampered across the grass. Sonia waited, her tongue between her teeth, for someone to shout at them.

Then they were alongside the passenger car on the siding, and she knew they were hidden. They'd made it.

"Easy," she warned Tabby as they ran up to the caboose's little ladder. "I know it's just inching along, but if you fall under it…"

"It's fine," she said, grabbing the ladder and hoisting herself up. "Believe or not, this isn't the first time I've climbed onto a moving train."

Sonia didn't know what to say to that. *Later,* she promised herself, as they settled down on the caboose's rear platform. She'd get the whole story out of Tabby once they were safe.

The dark woods inched up on either side and claimed them. Sonia watched as the chain-link fence, topped with very unwelcoming barbed wire, slipped away on either side. The open gates hung from their hinges, a huge chain and padlock dangling from one side. And then that was that.

"We're out," she whispered. "We're on the other side of the fence."

"He's got to jump out and close the gates as soon as the engine clears," Tabby reminded her. "Then he'll get back on the engine. *Then* we can run for it."

By now they'd been hiding and on the run for so long that Sonia could barely remember why. Was it really for something so simple as staying in a fireworks exclusion zone during a show? Or were there more reasons than that, heaped up over the months and years they'd been working here, all the drama that had somehow blazed up into a bonfire since this summer began?

"Would we really have gotten fired for watching the fireworks from the stroller shed?" she wondered aloud, trying to simplify it all. "Let's say that's all we were doing."

"Yes," Tabby replied. "So even if that's not really why we're here right now, that's enough."

Sonia was pretty sure it was the only reason *she* was here right now. But she didn't regret chasing after Tabby. This girl was strange, and fawn-like, and maybe prone to attracting stalkers she didn't need…but in her own way, she was strong and nimble, and Sonia really did like her.

The gates clicked closed, the clink of the metal audible even over the low hiss of the engine, four cars away. The engineer called out: "That's a wrap!" and the conductor laughed as he jumped back onto the engine, his feet heavy on the metal.

Tabby hazarded a look around the edge; Sonia watched the back of her head as she inched her face along the caboose's back wall, barely daring to breathe. If she was spotted now...

How fast could they run?

"They're not looking," Tabby hissed. "Let's go. Together. Right next to each other, so there's less time for them to see us."

The train was creaking towards the roundhouse; they would run out of brush to hide in if they waited another minute.

On the other side of the trees, a bus went by, taking Patriots back to the parking lot in a more orthodox fashion.

Sonia waited until the bus was gone. Then she grabbed Tabby's free hand, and they pushed off the caboose together, hit the ground running, and shoved into the underbrush. Sticks cracked beneath their feet.

"What was that?" the conductor called. Sonia stilled, yanking Tabby back. They were under the low-hanging oak trees now. They should be invisible. *Should be.*

"Deer," the engineer said. "Shitloads of deer around this place."

Sonia squeezed Tabby's hand, and Tabby squeezed back, so hard it hurt.

They didn't move again until the train was in the roundhouse.

CHAPTER FORTY-TWO

Antonia

Oswald was meowing dolefully when Antonia walked in the door.

"Have you been doing that the whole damn time?" she asked the cat. "Or is this just something you do the minute you hear my key in the door?"

Oswald yowled at her, showing the ridges of his pink throat. Antonia tossed her bag and keys on the kitchen counter and opened the fridge door. "Fine, just wait, just *wait...*"

She had put salmon feast dinner in his dish and was just handing it over to the climbing, complaining cat when she heard Martin's light tap at the door. Past midnight and Martin was coming over. Super. She opened the door and turned back to the kitchen without waiting for him to come in, rooting around for something to snack on while Oswald licked his chops over his salmon.

He was leaning on the counter when she turned around, hummus in hand. One look at his face and she knew her night's troubles weren't over. "Jesus, Martin, who died?"

Never say that, her mother would scold her. *For all you know, someone did die.*

"I mean, what's wrong?" she amended. "And do you want some hummus?"

"I'm good," Martin said.

"Far from good. Why don't you tell me what's up?"

"Amy came back."

Antonia put the hummus down on the counter between them. She regarded it for a moment, as if trying to decide if she still wanted it.

"I'm sorry," Martin said, straightening. "It's late, today was a holiday. You must have been really busy. I'm not going to do this to you."

"Martin," Antonia said, "do you have any idea what happened to me tonight?"

He looked startled.

"And to Tabby, and to Sonia, and to Nick, and to Nate, for that matter?"

"Nate the *blogger?*"

"Yessir."

"And Tabby—what the hell happened?"

"Oh, lord, Martin. Where do I even begin." Antonia got crackers out of the pantry and popped open the hummus. "I'll go first. Just because mine has so many moving parts. And then you tell me yours. I need to know everything about what happened with Amy."

"Well, we've finished this bottle." Antonia shook the last few drops of wine into Martin's tumbler. "I guess that's a new land-speed record for me and a Pinot."

Martin grimaced as he took the cup from her. "Sorry about that."

"No, it was bound to happen." She glanced at the clock. "Two a.m. Have you decided if you're going to call her yet?"

"I can't call her at this time of night."

"Martin, if she doesn't want to answer the phone, it'll be on do not disturb. It's not like you're going to make it ring or something. This isn't the nineties. And if she's up, she's going to be happy you called her."

"She's not going to be happy about why."

Antonia leaned back and took a sip of her wine. To be fair, at this hour, it was more like a swig. They'd covered a lot of ground tonight. Relationships. Rumors. Witness statements and trespasses and terminations. Antonia felt like the first half of June had been at least a month long, possibly two. Summers at America the Beautiful were always hard, but this one was simply ridiculous. And now her eyes were getting heavy. If Martin would just make the call, she could send him home with a clear conscience and go to bed happy. And *end* this day already.

She picked up her phone and handed it to him. "Call her."

Martin took it from her and walked across the room, as if he'd find some privacy by putting six feet of space between them. Antonia rolled her eyes and put her feet up on the coffee table. *"Nasty,"* her mother would have said about such behavior, but one of the great joys of living on one's own was doing whatever one wanted, no matter how hard one's mother tried to instill a sense of decorum. Coffee tables were the new ottomans. Because who could afford an ottoman?

"Amy? It's Martin."

Maybe she should give him more privacy, she thought. Maybe she should go into the bathroom and turn on the fan.

"I gave what you said some thought."

Antonia considered her bare feet. Maybe she should at least put on socks when she put her feet up on the table where she ate her meals. Maybe she could go that far.

"And it doesn't change the facts. I'm attracted to someone else. I'm *seeing* someone else."

Antonia thought about Tabby, the freckle-faced innocent she'd crushed so hard on, and how perfect her sweet little chatter would be with Martin's quiet, interested manner. They would be adorable together, their heads pushed close together over small tables at theme park restaurants, surrounded by a teeming world that was too much for both of them—but which would probably be manageable if they kept one another nearby for support.

"I'm sorry," Martin said stiffly.

Antonia turned her head and shook it, hard. He saw her and waved his hand at her: *go away!* She frowned at him.

"I'm sorry this is the way things happened," he said. And then he ended the call and dropped the phone from his ear. He looked at Antonia with exhaustion in every groove of his face.

"You need to go to bed," Antonia told him. "We both do."

"I have to talk to Tabby."

"Not tonight. She's in bed."

"You *just said*—"

"Oh, you're right." Antonia got up. "I'll give you privacy

for this one. But don't mess it up."

Antonia's bedroom was a small haven of fat gray pillows and thick white blankets. She'd seen the color scheme in a decorating blog once and fallen for it, the way the monochromatic tones seemed to evoke a rainy day, the pleasure of snuggling under the covers and refusing to get up, and the way the white bed furnishings made the bare bedroom walls feel like a choice, instead of a cheap apartment paint job.

Oswald was already curled up in a nest of pillows when Antonia came in. At the sight of her, he stretched without bothering to get up, a black-and-white Rorschach in her little cloud of a bed. She slipped onto the duvet next to him, kicking her feet up, and flicked through the contents of her phone idly. She didn't have to work until four o'clock the next day. There was no rush to go to bed or hustle Martin out of here, and she was still in a decent haze from all of that wine.

Oswald poked one white foot against her arm, tucking long silvery claws into her arm. "Brat," she said affectionately. "I can't send him home yet. We'll go to bed when he works everything out with Tabby."

Come to think of it, she could hear him now—Martin must have been pacing around the room and then stopped close to her door, the silly man. He had apparently gotten through to Tabby despite the hour.

"Jesus, Tabby, you should have—and then you *what*—wait, you're kidding me. This is all a joke. Right? Please tell me you're kidding."

Antonia began to feel concerned. Her own night had been hellacious enough, what with having to give Miles full permission to interrogate her back in the manager's office, while a union rep looked on, making notes in his little black notebook. She'd explained the full extent of the theft ring, and then sat silent, unable to answer, when Miles asked why on earth she hadn't turned Nick in immediately.

The shop steward had cleared his throat.

Antonia looked at him. He was an older guy from the engineering department, not someone she'd ever spoken to before. He just happened to be on second-shift and available when Miles had called out, asking for one to be present at an investigation. "Do I have a leg to stand on here?" she asked hopefully.

"What's that? Oh, no, I wasn't—" He smiled at her with something like regret. "I just had a tickle in my throat."

That had been the end of Antonia's hope in the union's ability to keep her out of trouble. So she'd decided to put her faith in Miles, and the friendship they'd nurtured over the years. Not to tell *all* the truth, certainly, but at least to show that she had the company's best interests at heart. She was hardly going to admit that she hadn't told because she'd considered *joining* the theft ring.

"Antonia?" Miles asked gently, and his tone gave her the courage she needed. He didn't want to fire her. He was on her team. This was exactly why upper management moved park managers around so much, she thought, before carefully arranging what she wanted to say.

"I didn't think what Nick had shown me was *official* evidence," she began. "Because if he moved the hiding place, anything I told you would be more like hearsay. Just a petty rumor. So when you got involved, I knew that the investigation would be more official...it wouldn't just be me tattling on a fellow Patriot. I really just didn't want to ruin the chance of an official investigation from finding out *everyone* involved in the theft ring."

It was a good response, she could see that right away. Miles looked suitably impressed. He made a few notes, then said, "I have to tell you, Antonia, that was pretty solid thinking. We've seen little personal conflicts get escalated into he-said she-said accusations before, and I'd hate to have lost the chance to shut this entire thing down just because you have a history with Nick…"

"Wait," Antonia had said, astonished. *'I* have a history with Nick?"

"And Tabby," Miles amended.

"I don't think that—how do you even know about that?"

"Antonia," Miles had smiled. "Everyone knows everything here. This is a very small town."

Antonia had subsided, but she wasn't thrilled at the notion that everyone had always been aware of everything: her failed romance with Tabby, her subsequent targeting of Nick—*not* that she'd actually had to target him for discipline, Nick was a terrible Patriot on his own, he didn't need any help getting into trouble.

But still. Ugh. Maybe it was time for her to move on from Old Dodge City, too. Start fresh as a lead where no one knew her backstory.

"Tell you what," Miles said, closing his notebook. "I think we have enough here. I appreciate your honesty. Come in tomorrow as usual and we'll take it from there."

"Take it—what else are we going to do?" She'd assumed the matter would be closed.

"Antonia, you must know we're going to have to transfer you," Miles told her gently. "You're far too involved in the Patriots you're supposed to be leading. But there's so much movement going on right now, no one will notice one more transfer out of Old Dodge City. We'll look at it tomorrow."

The shop steward had made one more note, closed his notebook, and made his way over the coffee machine to fix one for the road.

And that had been that.

There was a tap at her door. "Come in, Martin."

He pushed into her room. Oswald looked at him, then Antonia, thoroughly fed up.

"I have to go see Tabby."

"At two o'clock in the morning? You two are disgusting. Go to bed, Martin."

"She's off tomorrow."

"I know she is." Antonia sighed. "She's not in trouble, by the way. I got her clear of everything."

"That's good. She and Sonia sat through the fireworks in Primrose Gardens and then stowed away on the train to get out of the park without being seen."

"They did *what?*"

"I just need to see her with my own eyes after...after everything."

Antonia almost felt that she did, too.

"One thing, Antonia—did she for sure keep her job?"

"Yes," Antonia said. "I saw that in writing. She isn't in trouble. I handled everything."

"And Nick?"

"Escorted out. Like Nate was, I assume."

Although Nate had an obnoxious ability to land on his feet, so she wasn't as positive as she ought to have been, considering the enormity of his crime.

Martin leaned heavily against her dresser, despite his vow to rush over to see Tabby right away. He ran a hand over his face and rubbed hard.

"Antonia, if you were in charge of America the Beautiful, would it be like this?"

"What do you mean?"

"Just…all of these crazy people. Me. Nate. The nuts on the outside, who can never stop looking in. And the people on the inside, like Nick and Sonia and Tabby and *you,* always in a constant war between fantasy and reality, chased around by people like us who just want to keep the dream going a little bit longer…" He brushed a hand across his face. "Sometimes I don't know who I am. I don't know why I'm like this. I don't know why I need to live in this dream world."

Antonia got up, pushing aside the thick duvet, and went to Martin. She wrapped his tall, gangly frame in her arms, feeling the distinction in her own power, her own substance. She reveled in it. If *she* were in charge…well, maybe one day she would be in charge. "Martin, we can't help the things that broke us, and we can't help the things that help fix us."

He was hugging her back, sad and lonely and hurting Martin, her neighbor who had always needed saving, who had finally found a girl who needed just as much saving as he did. They were on their way to a happy ending, Antonia could feel it. They *all* were. Ties had been broken tonight, and other ones had been forged.

"Go see your girl," Antonia said finally, stepping back from the embrace. "Go chase your fairy tale."

The official announcement came down from AtB's PR department internally first, then externally a few hours later. By then, though, the world already knew.

At least, the buzzing, seething, frothing online fandom already knew.

AMERICA THE BEAUTIFUL ANNOUNCES EXCITING EXPANSION TO OLD DODGE CITY. On August 6th, 2023, America the Beautiful's premier family-friendly Old West-themed attraction, Gold Rush Rapids, will temporarily close to enable the construction of Ghost Town, a lively and exciting area where guests of all ages can immerse themselves in a western town full of fun spooks and thrilling excursions! Whether ordering a sarsaparilla from a ghostly bartender in the haunted saloon or taking spooktacular family photos in the spirited photography parlor, guests will be delighted with all the changes coming to one of our most popular regions of America the Beautiful. During the closure, which is expected to last eighteen months, Gold Rush Rapids will receive cosmetic and technological updates, enhancing the well-deserved popularity of this opening-day America the Beautiful attraction.

* * *

"I can't believe we're keeping the Mighty Missouri," Tabby said for the millionth time. She was sitting on a split-rail fence overlooking the water, on one of the quiet paths that zig-zagged around Wilderness Isle's wooded acres. Across the river, Old Dodge City heaved with summertime crowds. "You know what, Martin? I love this old river. I was heartbroken about losing it."

"Even the side-wheeler?" Martin asked, grinning as the whistle blew somewhere on the other side of Wilderness Isle.

"I could probably live without that whistle," Tabby admitted. "Although…something tells me I'd miss it if it were gone. I don't really want anything to change here. I'm excited for Ghost Town, but also, I don't care that much and I would be furious every time I saw it if we really did lose Gold Rush Rapids for it. So I guess I'm just a stick-in-the-mud like the rest of you crazy theme park fans." She laughed.

"You'd get over it. That's part of being a fan…you accept the misery of losing the old stuff, then you slowly get into the new stuff. Sandwich?" He held out a PB&J from the little cooler they'd brought along for their day in the park. The Fourth of July was not the day to wait in line for anything popular—food, included. So they'd brought their own supplies and were spending the afternoon in quiet places where the crowds rarely thought to go.

So far, Wilderness Isle was the winner of the day.

"Thank you," Tabby said, taking the sandwich. "I think we should just stay here until they close the ferry. It's so quiet here, we could take naps if we wanted."

"Except for the steam whistle, probably," Martin agreed.

He sat on a flat stone at Tabby's feet and bit into his own sandwich. "But it's a good spot and I can always run to the ice cream cart by the ferry for fresh supplies. We can survive here."

"We'd make amazing pioneers," Tabby laughed. "All my training in Old Dodge City is finally paying off."

"Do you think you'll stay through the ride closure?"

Tabby shrugged. "They're moving a lot of people out. Management says that when the street is a dead end with a construction wall, people won't even come to the stores. But they're going to wait and see how bad it gets before they make decisions about closing any stores. So I think I'm good for a while. And if they transfer me, that's okay, too." She remembered how disappointed she'd been when her Retail transfer had been for Old Dodge City. Now she was so grateful. If she hadn't come to Old Dodge City, she wouldn't have met Antonia.

And if she hadn't met Antonia, she wouldn't have met Martin.

They'd been dating for three weeks now. It wasn't a long time. But it felt like they'd been together forever. She thought about him first thing in the morning and last thing at night. They texted each other constantly. They wandered resorts on her days off, and he brought her supper when she had closing shifts. He liked to wander through Old Dodge City during her shifts, not hovering or watching her, just waving as he walked by, letting her know he was around if she needed him.

He'd stopped character chasing.

Tabby knew Martin had never been one of the really serious character chasers, the ones who took constant photos with costumed characters and built up massive social media followings full of gossip about the talent. But it was still nice to know he'd given up his quiet obsessions with Miss Sallie Mae and Miss Susie Q. Tabby was sure the women playing those characters were very nice people, but if she was going to be this man's girlfriend, she wanted to know he was interested in the real thing.

In this particular scenario, real was better than fantasy.

"Hey, you two." Antonia came down the path, a giant frozen lemonade dripping down one hand. "I had a feeling you'd be hiding back here."

"Antonia! You don't have to work today? And I thought I was lucky to get the day off."

"Oh, I have to close at Legacy," she said. "But that's not for hours yet. We close at two o'clock in the morning, so I don't start until five forty-five."

"Jeez." Martin looked pained. "Why is that park open so late? Everyone's here for the fireworks."

"They're going to try to keep folks out late, buying booze," Antonia explained. "It's a different world over there."

"But you like it, right?" Tabby had been missing Antonia sorely since she was transferred to a lead position at Legacy's main entrance shopping complex. "You don't miss it here?"

"I like it," Antonia confirmed, smiling at her warmly. "I'm learning a lot and they're a lot quicker about putting leads into management training, so it was a good move. But I want to come back here someday. Just…wearing my own clothes."

Tabby laughed. "I get it."

"So how is Old Dodge City? You talk to anyone since the news came out?"

"No, I haven't been over there today," Tabby said. "I mean, look how busy it is. But I'm guessing everyone's pretty thrilled, like we are."

"I was kinda looking forward to that white-water rapids ride," Antonia admitted, looking over the calm river. "But I can see why people prefer this."

"There was a huge letter-writing campaign," Tabby said. "And you saw that scheme to temporarily tank the company stock, right?" Antonia nodded; it had dominated the news cycle, both theme park and real-world, for twenty-four hours last week. "Seriously, if Nate hadn't leaked the concept art, none of that would have happened. They would have gone forward with the rapids ride and closed all of this."

Antonia ate a spoonful of frozen lemonade and looked pensive. "I can't believe we have to give Nate any credit. What a messed-up world we live in."

"Well…" Tabby gave Martin a sidelong glance. He nodded at her and she went on. "You should probably also know that Martin's been working on a little project because of Nate, too. And he found out yesterday that it's moving forward."

Antonia looked between them. "Well? What is it?"

"Martin, you tell her."

Martin brushed his hair out of his eyes and looked at the ground. "I'm going to produce the site for a new inclusivity project AtB's launching next year. They're still working it out in committees, but eventually, they're going to start fixing their little racism problem in the parks and the fandom."

"They're going to try, anyway," Tabby added. "Which is better than doing nothing."

Antonia nodded slowly. "Well, that *is* true. I guess Nate isn't the worst thing to have ever happened to this planet, after all."

"Wait, what now?" Sonia was suddenly in their midst, clutching a bottle of water. "We're celebrating the racist asshole now?"

"He outed the other racist assholes," Tabby explained. "And now AtB actually has to do something about quietly encouraging a racist fandom. So, I guess celebrating is a strong word, but…"

"Jeez," Sonia said, perturbed. "You show up late for one conversation, and the whole world changes on you."

Sonia had worked that morning, so she was off for the evening and not leaving the park in case it reached capacity and the entrance was closed to new arrivals. Tabby was happy to add her to their little party on Wilderness Isle; after their escape by train a few weeks ago, she and Sonia had a special kind of bond. Partners in crime, literally.

Once the sandwiches were gone and the side-wheeler had passed, promising them twenty minutes without an ear-splitting whistle, the little group found themselves falling asleep. Tabby tucked the light hoodie she'd brought along under her head and lay gazing up at the treetops, their leafy fingers waving against the blue sky overhead. A lazy fiddle serenaded them from a distant speaker, and as the water of the Mighty Missouri lapped its concrete banks and the Fourth of July crowds flowed back and forth on the distant shore, Tabby closed her eyes, sighed with contentment, and drifted off to sleep.

Acknowledgments

America the Beautiful has been an incredible place to design and build over the past six years. I know I'll never stop wanting to visit this park, and I appreciate all the early readers who have been fans from the first draft. You'd be instant annual passholders, and you'd probably abuse your privileges. I love that for all of us.

I couldn't have written a book about theme park culture without having lived it, and as everyone connected to the daily life of parks knows, that means making big sacrifices in terms of paychecks and family life. After all the weekends and late nights I spent entertaining other people's kids, I am both appreciative and apologetic to my own family. I hope we had enough fun on all those Disneyland vacations and theme park days out to make up for my absences. I think we did!

To the theme park employees who bear the incredible burden and privilege of making lifelong memories for their guests and who, in many cases, are charged with a special and almost cult-like task of holding up the original vision of their parks' founder, thank you for all that you do. It's never easy, often miserable, and occasionally deeply rewarding work. We are all grateful to you for doing it so well.

About the Author

N.K. Reinert is a novelist with a passion for vintage theme park lore. Reinert writes an occasional newsletter about theme park culture called Imaginary Memories, available at ImaginaryMemories.substack.com. But these days, Reinert prefers building out the virtual America the Beautiful theme park to visiting real ones! You can learn more about America the Beautiful and find bonus content at atblifestyler.com.